THE
INEVITABLE

by Daniel Hope

HAWTHORNE
BOOKS & LITERARY ARTS

Hawthorne Books & Literary Arts
hawthornebooks.com

Library of Congress Cataloging-in-Publication Data

Names: Hope, Daniel, 1983- author.
Title: The inevitable : a novel / by Daniel Hope.
Description: Portland : Hawthorne Books, 2023.
Identifiers: LCCN 2023011220 (print) | LCCN 2023011221 (ebook) | ISBN
9780998825779 (paperback) | ISBN 9780998825786 (ebook)
Subjects: LCGFT: Science fiction. | Novels.
Classification: LCC PS3608.O6273 I54 2023 (print) | LCC PS3608.O6273
(ebook) | DDC 813/.6--dc23/eng/20230617
LC record available at https://lccn.loc.gov/2023011220
LC ebook record available at https://lccn.loc.gov/2023011221

First US Edition 2023
Printed in the United States of America
Cover and interior design by Diane Chonette
Cover illustration by David Habben

To found family

INTRODUCTION

BY LIDIA YUKNAVITCH

The first time I read Kazuo Ishiguro's *Klara and the Sun* I bawled my face off. It mattered not that the central character in the story was a humanoid robot. From the get-go, I felt tethered to Klara because she is a servant to the world of humans, created—perhaps monstrously— to serve and to serve up life and the pursuit of happiness to the human community. Her use value is specific and finite. When she has served her purpose—that is, helped raise a human child—she will be discarded. Scrapped.

I always side with the creation. Blame Mary Shelley, who wrote my favorite novel of all time.

Monstrosity I reserve for human brutality.

Daniel Hope serves up a similar creature, a humanoid robot named Tuck, and quite quickly in the story, Tuck began to remind me more of what matters about the human condition than I learn from most of the humans I know. *More human than human*, comes to mind.[1]

Of the many qualities I loved about Tuck immediately and inevitably, were his bones and skin. You heard me. Tuck is made from metal and strips of synthaskin, with polymer muscles underneath. Like my

---

1 See Ridley Scott's *Blade Runner* and read Philip K. Dick's *Do Androids Dream of Electric Sheep?*

husband, who has high-grade metal in his knees; and like my father, who had a pacemaker and a defibrillator; and like my mother, whose physical disability turned her bones and muscles to rot in her hip and leg, and whose cancer ate her breasts and lungs, a woman who wanted hip replacement surgery for thirty years but was met with indifference from my father; Tuck needs repairs. Tuck needs parts. A body breaking down is a dangerous thing. In *The Inevitable,* that body is also prized, sought after by salvage hunters.

To be wanted only as scrap metal while you are grieving the loss of your family and searching for meaning in life is to exist inside a class of objects in a world of subjects. Not only is that life unjust, it is lonely.

What is family to a robot? It's a question I find endlessly intriguing, not just because the biological reproductive element recedes in meaning, but because we all seem to come from fairly fucked-up families in the first place, so who is to say humans got "family making" right? From where I sit, we need a revolution away from the reproduction-centered, god-fearing, government-serving apparatus. In Ishiguro novels in particular, especially in *Never Let Me Go* and *Klara and the Sun,* "family" as we know it is deformed and reformed around "built services." In *Never Let Me Go,* clones serve as organ donors for sustaining the human population. In *Klara and the Sun,* the raising of children, especially during the teen years, is farmed out to machines. The thing that makes these two stories so intimate is that they are only very slightly askew from human conditions.

Daniel's story thus inhabits a very particular wheelhouse of novels that bring sci-fi close in rather than catapulting it far out into space. Tuck travels in space, and intergalactic adventures and mysteries emerge, but the deeper story for me began to be revealed when Tuck adopts an abandoned—or orphaned—AI that he names David, after a boy he was close to on Earth in the past.

Tuck is building a family in the space where his heart doesn't beat, in a world that does not count him as anything but subservient raw materials.

Early on in the story, Tuck and David are confronted with a death. For a moment, Tuck has no idea what death means. A man he has killed looks a lot like he did when he was alive, and the death moment arrests Tuck. Tuck has questions. David vomits. Suspended between artificial life and real human death, Tuck feels sympathy for David and fascination about the dead guy on the pavement in front of them. His question: "How do I return a life I have taken?"

On the one hand, the question seems naïve, right? Childlike. Underdeveloped. A machine trying to puzzle out how to take something back. But the question lingers throughout the story in more than one way. The question gets more and more human. If we are always giving and taking from each other, emotionally, financially, and in terms of power hierarchies, if we have been taking our whole lives, which one could argue the human race has been doing to the planet and all life on the planet since the start, how do we learn to give?

To be human, at least in part, is to understand how to give. A particularly human problem is figuring out what giving means, how to give without wanting, and how to determine when you have given away too much self, leaving you a hollowed-out shell only useful to others for your donations. More than the high-risk adventures in space, more than the power wars between billionaires and quasi-corporate conflicts, I was moved by Tuck's attempts to build relationships, to venture near to that thing we call love, which requires a release we are only barely—if at all—capable of in the face of the inevitable, which is that we die. To give, knowing you will die.

Love stories are not what we've been told. A humanoid robot named Tuck reminds us how to build connections and be ever-giving in the face of death and loss.

-- 1 --

Tuck hated that humans could always hear him coming. With every step, his left knee let out a shrill squeak of metal scraping on metal, and his right ankle cracked loud enough to echo down the dirty back alleys. His corroded metal foot clomped down on the metal walkway running alongside one of the many muddy side streets of New San Francisco, the rotting industrial center on the planet Magnus. The other foot, in no better condition, swung unsteadily by to plop down ahead of the first. With every step, what was left of the synthaskin that once sheathed the feet crumbled and flaked off. The pattern of footfalls continued, an inconsistent thump on the rickety walkway creating a syncopated beat with the squeaking and creaking joints connected to the feet.

Lurching along above the feet, on top of a body equally broken and tattered, Tuck's head remained fixed straight ahead, eyes scanning the surroundings in frequencies throughout the electromagnetic spectrum. His original designation was TUC-67/c, but no one had called him that in over 150 years.

Tuck detected movement ahead of him, where an alley connected with the walkway he was on. Two men in stained and mismatched clothes jumped out, one brandishing a length of metal and the other holding an old pistol in desperate need of repair and, as Tuck's sensors instantly detected, ammunition.

"Hey there, where're ya headed?" one of them said.

Tuck would have given them one of his favorite looks, one he learned from a human friend long ago, but it involved raising one eyebrow. He had lost his right eyebrow several years back to a fungus that eats artificial hair, and the other eyebrow had grown so thin over the years that he feared raising a disdaining brow wouldn't have much effect. Instead, Tuck settled for another classic human expression. He rolled his eyes.

"I don't have much of value for you," Tuck said. "Please, let me pass."

"Oh, I don't think so," the other man said with a gap-toothed smile. "You look like you might be worth something down at the salvage yards. You're comin' with us, Rusty."

"Yeah," the first man said, "the drones are gonna have fun figgering out how to tear you apart. C'mon." Both men reached for Tuck.

"Wait," Tuck said, "I do have something for you."

Before Tuck's attackers could grab his arms, one was suddenly extended toward them with a BlastLogic 6700 just centimeters from their noses. A slight whine, increasing in pitch, told them this blaster was functional, unlike theirs. Their eyes grew large, and they ducked involuntarily, throwing their hands up as ineffectual shields. "Whoa! Hey! What are you doing? Put that away!"

"I've dealt with goons much more menacing than you two," Tuck said, trying to keep the damaged joints in his arm steady. "You wouldn't believe how many people think they can make money off me, but invariably they forget that I can be quite deadly."

Tuck squeezed the trigger and let a bright red bolt fly, deliberately singeing the greasy hair of the man on his right. Both men yelped and scampered back into the alley. Tuck calmly replaced the pistol in a special holster inside his abdomen. People seldom thought Tuck would be carrying weapons inside his body, and this afforded him an element of surprise when he needed it most.

It wasn't the only surprising thing about him. He was a remnant, a relic of a different time, when synthaskin was as common as human skin in some of the more affluent areas of the galaxy. On some parts of Earth, robotic analogs of humans had been so numerous they outnumbered the very humans they were built to serve. Ever since the Bot Riots, his kind were increasingly scarce, and not just on Magnus. After the riots, bots quickly disappeared from stores, then from homes and businesses, and then finally from the enormous dumps where drones hovered over the massive heaps, quietly and efficiently sorting trash. Now Tuck was the last functioning bot in the galaxy.

People preferred drones because they were more predictable. They weren't self-aware, they couldn't alter their own programming, and they didn't simulate emotions. After the trauma of the riots, humans didn't want to worry about what their devices were feeling.

Tuck might have worked up a bitter laugh at that thought, but he needed to conserve energy. The regulator junction in his power cell was on the verge of breaking down, and he didn't want to strain it more than necessary. It was one item on the long list of things to find; many parts of Tuck needed replacing. Entire patches of synthaskin were missing. His left arm was bare, with metal skeleton and Carbora polymer muscles exposed to anyone who cared to look. It needed urgent maintenance, along with a section of his upper spinal column and several parts of his power relay system. One of the highest priorities on the list was a knee joint. His left knee had been damaged in an encounter on Far Haven, coincidentally, the same planet where a pack of morgyt ripped the synthaskin from his left arm, but on a different occasion. Tuck marveled that humans could name such a dangerous planet Far Haven without even acknowledging the contradiction.

Tuck continued down the walkway, accompanied by his symphony of disrepair. People watched him through dirty windows in the tall gray apartment blocks that lined both sides of the street. Some people were curious, some almost fearful. His sensors tracked everything around him. He saw and heard in every direction, and he could even detect the sound of bugs crawling in the mud beneath him. He had to be on constant alert, wary of people who might want to sell him for scrap or even for the occasional collector that wanted to add Tuck to his display of oddities. Obtaining the last bot in the galaxy, no matter what level of disrepair he was in, would make quite an impressive addition to any collection. After being so reviled for decades, he was now highly sought after in certain circles, and he didn't know which was worse.

As he walked past an alley between two buildings, a drone that had been picking through a pile of garbage swiveled in mid-air to scan Tuck. The drones were trouble, too, but only because they thought he was already scrap.

Without turning his head, Tuck monitored a suspicious character 73 degrees to his right. He listened to the retreating footsteps as the stranger scampered off. He cataloged it as a probable lookout; Tuck's contact would want to know he was coming.

Tuck approached the end of the walkway that led to one of the many buildings in the area. Several other walkways branched off, but before he could reach them, Tuck would have to cross a heap of slime that had been tossed up by a mud vent nearby. The walkways ran along the sides of streets, off the ground, so people didn't have to walk through the mud constantly spewed out of the geothermal vents that dotted the town.

Magnus was a temperate world, similar to Earth in many ways. There were forests, plains, mountains, and deserts, but this particular outpost was located in the middle of an enormous swamp that covered nearly half of the smallest of three continents in the southern hemisphere. It was a completely undesirable place to live, but it so happened that the Reinla Swamps, named after the man who first owned the land, sat on some of the most valuable ore deposits on the planet. This outpost turned industrial city, which Reinla named after the city on Earth where he grew up, housed all the miners and associated companies that exploited the deposits. Most people on Magnus lived in nicer, more habitable regions, and many of the people in New San Francisco had grown so rich from ore mining and refining that they might have easily lived elsewhere. But they didn't; the mines were their livelihood, and they couldn't leave behind the opportunity for more wealth. Instead, everyone hoarded what they had as the outpost was slowly swallowed by mud.

Tuck hesitated when he reached the edge of the mud. If he stepped in it, it could clog up his foot and ankle joints, which didn't have enough synthaskin left between them to cover one foot, let alone both. He reluctantly added another item to his list of things to find: boots. He hadn't bothered with clothing much in the past few years. Even though he was designed to be anatomically human, his designers never gave him the genitalia that humans required to be covered. Even if he had them, they would have fallen off by now with most of his other cosmetic parts, so wearing clothes seemed like unnecessary effort. He was quite a scary sight to behold, ragged scraps of synthaskin clinging to scuffed polymer muscles layered over a pitted metallic skeleton. He was missing all but a few strands of hair and most of one cheek and his nose were gone, showing off his metal skull and abnormally white teeth underneath. He looked like a child's nightmare, which is why most humans avoided him.

Tuck grabbed the rusted railing of the walkway and tried to hop over the mud using his right leg in an effort to spare his left knee joint as much as possible. He made it most of the way to the other side before his right foot spluched into the sludge. This wasn't ordinary mud. It was full of decaying biomatter and waste products from mining. It was a sickly yellow-brown and smelled horrific. Fortunately for Tuck, his olfactory sensors didn't produce involuntary reactions like those of humans. He looked down at his right foot, then quietly lowered his left foot into the muck and trudged the rest of the way through. He made a note to give his feet a thorough cleaning when he got back to his ship.

Tuck approached the coordinates he'd been given and saw only another gray concrete building surrounded by metal walkways and yellow mud. A ragged human sat on a crate near the entrance. As Tuck approached the double doors leading to the dirty apartment complex, the man looked up, then jumped up, startled. Tuck was used to that reaction. He gave a courteous nod as he'd been programmed to do 157 years ago, back on Earth, and reached for the door handle. The filthy, skinny man jumped in front of the doors. "I'm sorry, er, sir, but I'll need your name."

Tuck's eyes, once brown now faded to orange, sized up the man two and three more times. Tuck looked for signs that the man was a threat but found none.

"I beg your pardon?" Tuck asked politely. He had been programmed to be polite to humans, and even after 150 years of data decay and algorithmic evolution, old habits died hard.

"I need your name," the man replied, voice quivering slightly.

"For what?"

"Well," the man stammered, "so I can announce you're coming."

"I don't want to be announced," Tuck said.

"Then I can't let you in." The man backed closer to the doors. "It's my job."

Tuck scanned the man once again, incredulous. "What is your job?"

The man stood up a little straighter and stuck out his chin. "I'm the doorman, sir."

"You don't have a uniform. You don't look like any doorman I have ever seen."

"Well, looks can be deceiving."

"You have no idea," Tuck said, flexing his hand in front of the man's face; the small squeaking sound it released made his gesture slightly less intimidating.

The doorman winced. "Okay, look I was told I could sleep in the lobby at night if I just watched the door and didn't let strangers in. I'm just doing my job. You know what that's like, right?"

"I don't have a job," Tuck said.

"What are you doing here then?"

"My reluctance to tell you who I am is rivaled only by my unwillingness to tell you why I'm here." Even programmed politeness had its limits.

"Oh, I know who you are, though, "the doorman said defensively. "You're The Bot. They told me stories about you."

"Really? And what did I do in these stories?"

"Well, as I recall you were angry at someone about . . . something, so you tracked down every member of his family and killed them all, one by one. Nice and clean."

Tuck had heard that one many times. Some tales had more concrete details, others were just as vague. Some involved him slaying a whole planet's worth of people, some just a single person. Tuck found it fascinating that people made up false stories about things they didn't understand. "If I am so brutally skilled at killing, why are you bothering to stop me just so you can announce that I am coming? You should be running."

The doorman's shoulders wilted in onto his chest and his eyelids stretched wide over bulging eyes, but he stood his ground. "It's . . . it's my job," he whispered hoarsely.

Tuck reached out with both arms. The doorman scrunched his eyes closed. Tuck grabbed him by the shoulders and, with joints groaning and faded black muscles scraping together as they bunched, hoisted him up and to the side of the doorway. "Then do it over here," Tuck said. Tuck tried not to let the man see that one of the muscles in his shoulder had come loose with the strain of lifting. Another thing to add to the list. Another thing that needed replacing.

Once inside, Tuck found himself in a lobby with halls branching off to the left and right and a set of elevators at the back. Realizing he had no idea where to go, he looked back at the door. Tuck sighed. It was another gesture he had picked up from being around humans for so long, even though he didn't need to breathe. Tuck turned back to ask the doorman if he could show him around.

The doorman was nowhere to be found. A drone floated by, so intent on its destination that it didn't notice Tuck. Tuck didn't trust drones enough to bother trying to communicate with it. He went back inside and began doing a passive scan of the building, trying to single out auditory and electromagnetic clues as to where he should go. He was looking for someone specific, but there were several hundred people in the twenty-five-story building.

Just as he began his scan, the sound of someone breathing down a side hall caught his attention. He always thought the breathing humans did was such a liability.

"Are you looking for something, or are you just gawking?" Tuck asked.

A leathery face peeked out from the entrance to one of the hallways and seemed to stretch in surprise at being addressed. Humans were always surprised that he didn't need to see them to know they were there.

The man straightened up and stepped out from behind the corner, smoothing wrinkles in a particularly nice jacket. He didn't look the same as the other humans Tuck had seen in this part of the outpost. This man had finer clothing, his jacket was cut to fit him, and he wasn't as dirty as most. "I was looking for you," he said.

"Why?"

"Because you're looking for me," the man said. Tuck had already run the man's face through his database and was confident that this wasn't his contact.

"I think you are mistaken," Tuck said. "You are not the person I am seeking."

The stranger smiled, his leathery face stretching around large teeth. Clean teeth. Tuck liked humans with clean teeth. He appreciated personal hygiene, despite his own appearance. "Let me be more specific," said the stranger, "I'm here to take you to the man you're looking for."

"How do you know who I am looking for?"

"Because I work for him. Dronic sent me."

Tuck sent out a series of acoustic and electromagnetic pulses, scanning for weapons. A handgun in the man's jacket and a long knife in a holster strapped to his forearm, neither of which were cause for immediate alarm. Most people were smart enough to carry a weapon in this place.

"Where is Dronic?"

"I'll show you, if you'll just follow me," the man said, still smiling.

"You still haven't indicated who you are."

"My name is Veld, and I work for Dronic."

"Veld, I don't trust you."

His smile, surprisingly, grew even wider. "I don't expect you to trust me. But if you want to see Dronic, you'll have to come with me."

In a few milliseconds Tuck had already calculated his options. He didn't want to trust this man, good dental hygiene or not, but Tuck wanted to get off the planet as soon as possible, and if this man could save him some time, it was worth it. "Please, lead the way."

-- 2 --

Amelia sat at a small café inside New San Francisco's spaceport, shaking her head. She had ordered a drink over ten minutes earlier, and it still hadn't arrived. She expected quick reactions and loyal service if her money was involved, no matter how small the transaction.

She shifted uncomfortably on the metal chair she sat on, hoping nothing was rubbing off on the skirt of her white suit. New San Francisco wasn't the type of place she normally liked to visit. She wondered how anyone stayed clean in this place. Gazing around the plaza next to the café, she noticed one of the large glowing billboards on the side of a building was for Galactic Enterprises, and she fought the urge to grit her teeth. At the speed of thought, she used her Link to find the company that owned the billboard. A Link was a special embedded device that delivered information directly to her optical nerve. When in use, it appeared as if an interface floated in front of the user, and they could view and interact with documents, videos, businesses, and just about anything else. Amelia used it to buy out the billboard looming over her and replace Galactic Enterprise's advertisement with one for a brand of diarrhea medicine.

Satisfied with her purchase, Amelia pulled up some spreadsheets and reports on her Link. There was always something to be done.

A notification pinged her aural nerves, making it seem like a gentle chime went off by her right ear. With a thought, she accessed the notification, and the face of her second-in-command, Maze, appeared before her. Maze was all business, both in looks and demeanor, just as Amelia liked it.

"Veld sent us a message. The bot has arrived."

"Thank you, Maze."

"It's not too late to contact the bot directly," Maze said. Her voice conveyed her irritation more than her face did. "We shouldn't rely on Dronic's lackey. We don't know how trustworthy he is, and we can mitigate the risk by skipping over Dronic entirely."

"Don't worry about Veld," Amelia said softly, overlaying a report on the video feed and scanning it while she spoke. "He'll get exactly what he wants if he does what we want, and he seems quite ambitious. He won't let us down."

"It seems so inefficient."

"We're testing for the results we need without putting ourselves or our assets in danger. I want to see the bot make it through this one on his own. If he doesn't make it, then he wouldn't be useful to us anyway. Seems pretty efficient to me."

"Dronic will try to take the bot for himself."

"Of course he will. But if the bot is as good as everyone says he is, then he'll be okay."

"Okay, perhaps, but likely damaged."

Amelia closed the report and smiled at Maze. "Which will make him even more desperate. Just the way we want him." She rose from her chair, brushing at her skirt, and then stood up straight and smoothed her jacket. "Keep me apprised of his progress. I'm headed out to the landing field."

"Acknowledged."

As Amelia walked out of the café, she noticed the waiter arriving with her drink. With a shake of her head, she used her Link to put the waiter's name and face in her database, carefully cataloged in a list of people she forbade her associates to hire in the future.

-- 3 --

Veld led him down through a series of tunnels underneath the building. Every ten meters, flickering lights hung from power conduits on the ceiling and thick beams shored up the dirt walls. Tuck noted that whoever maintained them must have had quite an ingenious way to keep the swamp water from seeping in and flooding everything. Tuck asked Veld about it, but Veld knew little of when the tunnels were constructed or who made them. "Normally, Dronic requires that we blindfold anyone who comes down here. But we figured that would be useless with you."

Tuck nodded.

"And besides, I think Dronic has taken a liking to you."

"He hasn't met me yet."

"True, but Dronic likes special things, and you, my friend, are special."

Humans were always assigning value to things, and the more mystery surrounding something the more special they considered it to be. To Tuck, there were very few things of value, and he was one of them.

Veld led Tuck to a short hallway branching off the main tunnel. At the end was a thick metal door. Veld keyed a code into a panel at the side of the door, and then spoke into it, "The bot is here to see you, sir."

The door hissed and slid aside, revealing a large room that was sparsely decorated, but what few decorations there were occupied special spots atop stone pedestals. The pedestals held up things like a bottle of aged Arthalian whiskey and a small statuette used by a short-lived but famous fertility cult on Yala. All the semi-luxurious items clashed horribly with the muddy walls and dim lighting. The contrast of dismal cave with impressive antiques was so jarring that it was almost comical. Dronic was obviously trying to convince himself that he wasn't stuck in the bowels of a sulfurous swamp running a salvage racket.

As he walked past the rows of pedestals, he was surprised to find one holding what appeared to be a first-generation Funbox, a virtual reality gaming system that was extremely popular with a child Tuck had served long ago. The sight called up memories from his storage, causing a wave of nostalgia.

Tuck brought his focus back to the task at hand. It was no time for feelings. He desperately needed a new regulator junction for his power cell; the patch job he had performed would only last a few more weeks. He made a detour in his constant search for body parts because he had found a junk dealer, this Dronic, whose salvage crew had found a nearly new junction.

Dronic sat at the back of the room, at the end of two lines of pedestals, watching Tuck from his makeshift throne, composed of scavenged ship parts that had been gilded with gold. It appeared Dronic hadn't found enough gold to finish the entire throne, but he sat in it just as straight and haughty as if it were. He wore dozens of necklaces and rings, many of them worthless from what Tuck could see, but all gleaming in the low light.

"The metal man!" Dronic said. He gave Tuck a lopsided smile, showing dental work as shoddily constructed as his throne. Tuck immediately formed a few opinions about the man.

Dronic waited for Tuck to respond. After an awkward moment, when Tuck made it apparent that he wasn't going to say anything, Dronic's smile faltered, and he leaned forward in his seat. "Aren't you gonna say hi?" he said in a lilting, clipped accent.

"Hello, Dronic," Tuck said. "I would like to complete this transaction as quickly as possible. I am sure you feel the same."

Dronic shook his head, and his smile returned. "I have a new deal for you."

"I won't renegotiate. We agreed on a price."

"I know, I know," Dronic said, waving his hand. "I have a better deal now, and I think you'll like it."

"I am only interested in the regulator junction."

"You haven't even heard the offer yet."

"You don't have anything of interest to me."

"You don't like my treasures?" Dronic scoffed. "I have many nice things." He gestured at the pedestals lining his muddy throne room.

"No, you don't," Tuck said.

Dronic's eyes scrunched up, and his smile changed to a sneer. "Yes, I do," he said.

Tuck remained silent.

"Yes, I do!" Dronic screamed, then composed himself. "All right, let's talk about that later. First, the deal. I don't have the regulator junction, but I—"

Tuck was already trudging for the door.

"I didn't say you could go," Dronic said. The door Tuck had come through opened to reveal three large men blocking the doorway with a lot of muscle and no fewer than seven guns. Tuck stopped and listened, detecting four other humans entering the room from a back door. The clattering sound of weapons accompanied them. Tuck turned back to see Dronic smiling bigger, exposing pitted teeth and dark gaps where there were no teeth at all.

"This isn't normally how deals are made," Tuck said.

"I guess you haven't been in New San Francisco very long," Dronic said. He spread his hands in half-hearted apology. "Okay, let me be honest."

"Something you seem to be infrequently," Tuck interjected.

Dronic chuckled. "That's funny." He leaned back in his throne, staring at Tuck. "They said you were funny. That you have a quick wit."

Tuck refrained from saying "quick wit" was an understatement. His processor core did quintillions of calculations per second. If Tuck said everything he was thinking, the monologue would last for years. But Tuck said nothing, because he had the distinct impression that Dronic wanted him to make clever remarks just so he could admire Tuck more. Tuck felt as if he were on top of one of the pedestals, a glorified talking head on display, and he would not be Dronic's jester.

After it was apparent Tuck wouldn't respond, Dronic sat up straight in his throne. "Okay, metal man, the deal is simple. You sit in my collection, become one of my treasures, and I take care of you."

"I think you already know I will refuse that offer."

"Maybe. But bad things might happen if you say no. See, some lady in a white suit paid me a lot of money for that regulator junction you wanted. A lot of money. She wanted me to bring you to her, but I'm not a delivery guy." He gestured broadly to the room. "I'm a king! Besides, who knows what she wants? You're better off here, and I deserve to have you."

"I don't think you fully understand," Tuck said. "I am a sapient, autonomous, artificial life form. I don't belong in a collection."

"Oh, come on," Dronic chortled. "You're getting a little old and worn out. You know it. I know it. It's time to think about retirement. About taking it easy. What better place to kick back? So, stay here, with us. Join my collection of priceless artifacts."

Tuck's hand creaked as he flexed it into a fist. "You aren't very good at creating incentives. Even if I wanted to choose display-case slavery, you haven't really given me any reason to choose you over this other collector, whoever she is. Your collection isn't prestigious enough to attract the attention of a homeless miner, let alone the last bot in the galaxy."

Dronic fought to keep his smile in place. "We'll discuss the value of my collection later, when you've had a chance to appreciate it. But for now, I don't need you to choose to stay. I'll choose for you."

Dronic waved a hand at his men, who immediately raised their weapons and started to advance. Tuck began shunting power from his auxiliary energy reserves. It gave him more power and speed, but it also took quite a toll on his battered body.

"Before you do that," Tuck said, trying to buy some time for the power transfer, "let me warn you that you will regret this decision."

Dronic's eyes narrowed. He motioned with one stained hand for his men to stop. "You're threatening me?"

"No, I feel compelled to warn you that this will likely end badly for you. It is a courtesy I extend because I don't want to fight. However, I can't allow you to take me. I am free and will remain so. Any who attempt to change that will suffer the consequences. So, please, let me go."

Dronic stared at Tuck for a long moment. He cocked his head to the side and said, "Maybe you're not as funny as I thought." He motioned to his men once again.

"Just for the record," Tuck said, "that wasn't a joke."

The screech of aging metal joints moving at great speed echoed through the room, as Tuck dove between the wall and a pedestal holding an obviously fake Trojan helmet. He moved so quickly that Dronic's men couldn't track Tuck with their weapons. They also couldn't see the blur of his hand retrieving the BlastLogic 6700 from his abdominal holster.

With his back to the pedestal, he watched the wall in front of him crack and explode in a hail of dirt and rocks as blaster bolts and bullets shot past. Pieces of the pedestal chipped off on either side of him. The pedestal was made of crumbling sandstone and it wouldn't stand up to the withering fire for very long. But it would prevent his attackers from seeing his next move coming, and that's all Tuck needed. Using the scans of the room he gathered before the shooting started, he oriented himself, stuck his blaster around the edge of the pedestal, adjusted the angle a few degrees, attempted to compensate for the wobble from his faulty forearm muscles, and fired.

Across the room, the bottle of Arthalian shattered into a brilliant cloud of blue crystal shards and boiling whiskey. A garbled scream pierced the noise of whining blasters and thunderous assault rifles. The firing stopped as all the guards turned to look at Dronic, who had fallen to his knees and clutched his face in horror. He scrambled on all fours to the remains of the bottle on the floor, mumbling something unintelligible. His men stared in disbelief.

Tuck took advantage of the lull in firing to squeeze off three more shots without looking, which was followed by the sound of a half-melted fertility statuette hitting the ground, a glass Coke bottle shattering, and a human gurgling sound.

Tuck looked around the pedestal in time to see one of the attackers fall down, clutching his throat. He hadn't anticipated one of them moving in front of his third target while he was firing. Tuck ducked back behind the pedestal and listened intently for any sign of movement from the fallen man. He heard nothing, then someone yelled in rage, and the storm of blaster and rifle fire started up again, drowning out all other sound.

Tuck hesitated for two seconds, an eternity for him. He risked a quick look around the pedestal to check on his accidental victim. The man wasn't moving, and a large amount of blood was pooling on the floor around him. From Tuck's vantage point, the man's legs and hips were obstructing any view of his injuries.

Tuck revised his plans.

He leaned around the pedestal to take his next shots. He couldn't afford any more blind firing. He had to be precise to pull off his new plan. Tuck sent several bolts flying into the bunched-up henchmen, careful to do no more than singe clothing and set one man's hair on fire. The sudden barrage caused all Tuck's attackers to scramble for cover and one to run for the back door, screaming and slapping at his hair. Tuck used the opportunity to hobble past several pedestals.

His left knee was in bad shape after the sudden burst of speed to get to cover. Now it was freezing up as he tried to dart from pedestal to pedestal while crouched. Eventually, he let his left leg drag out behind him as he used his right leg and his hands to scuttle to the next bit of cover. He was slowing down, and he still had a long way to go before he was safe.

Tuck worked his way around the perimeter of the room, taking a few well-placed shots to keep his attackers busy and using the pedestals and the throne as best he could to shield himself. He shot on one side of the guards to herd them the opposite way around the room, keeping them on the other side of his cover the entire way.

As he crouched behind a pedestal near the throne, a bullet glanced off one of the supports in his lower left leg, which he had left extended out to the side of the pedestal. He tried to draw it in closer behind the pedestal, but the knee joint was completely frozen and wouldn't bend. He shot another volley at the men huddled across the room, taking great care to have one shot graze the lower leg of one of them. The man howled in pain and scrambled behind a pedestal.

Tuck made some careful calculations. He was close enough that it would only take two strides to huddle next to the man sprawled in the middle of the floor, even with a busted knee. He planted his good leg underneath himself and sprang.

By the time he finished his first step it was apparent he wouldn't make it. The mud in his right foot had dried and clogged the joints in his right ankle, making the entire foot seize up at a weird angle. When he went to take his next step, the odd angle of the foot caused him to slip on the slick concrete floor. He went down hard and tore yet another muscle in his shoulder as he tried to catch himself.

He skidded on the floor, coming to rest next to the first man he'd shot.

From there he could clearly see the man wouldn't get up ever again. Tuck's stray shot had caught him right in the throat. Blackened flesh encircled a mangled mess of arteries and viscera. Tuck couldn't tell if the man had asphyxiated from having his trachea fused shut or bled to death from the major artery that hadn't been cauterized by the bolt. Either way, it was Tuck's fault.

Tuck lay there for a full second, another eternity, and took an image from his visual feed of the man and his ruined throat. He saved the image in a special, unnamed memory file that contained only sixteen other images.

"I am sorry," Tuck said quietly. He didn't know what saying that would accomplish. At the few funeral services he'd attended for humans, he noticed some people briefly talking to the body of the deceased. He didn't know the man or his name. This was the best he could do.

Tuck looked up to see several of Dronic's men staring at him from around the cover of the pedestals. The only sound was that of Dronic sobbing softly while he held the shards of the broken Coke bottle. The silence brought Dronic out of his mourning. He looked up and saw Tuck lying among the ruins of his collection, next to the lifeless body of one of his men. His eyes bulged and his lips contorted into an irregular shape, not quite open, so that the scream erupting from his throat was half muffled and caused spittle to fly from his lips.

"Kill him!"

They all hesitated, some lifting their rifles but letting the muzzle wander as they watched the spectacle of man and machine. Dronic did not wait to see how his men reacted. He lunged for Tuck, crawling like an animal. Tuck tried to get up but slipped on his malfunctioning foot. He managed to raise himself onto one knee just as Dronic reached the blaster dropped by the dead man.

As Dronic brought the blaster pistol up toward Tuck's head, Tuck used all the speed he could muster to whip his hand around and knock the gun out of Dronic's hand. The loss of power from torn muscles in his shoulder caused his hand to go off course slightly, merely brushing the gun just as Dronic fired. The fiery bolt of energy grazed the side of Tuck's skull, leaving a long, scorched gouge that ran back from the side of his eye over his ear. It didn't shut him down, but the heat fried the connection to his right eye.

Tuck grabbed Dronic and yanked as hard as he could, bringing Dronic sprawling on top of him, and held Dronic's gun arm firmly by his side. Dronic struggled and thrashed like a madman until Tuck was able to haltingly lift his damaged arm up and bring the muzzle of his own gun to rest against Dronic's temple.

"Hold still, now," Tuck said.

Dronic stopped thrashing for a moment until a shot from one of his guards, who were still firing indiscriminately, hit him in the thigh. He writhed in pain and squealed, "Stop! Don't shoot! Stop!"

Dronic's men slowly lowered their weapons. They watched in disbelief as Tuck struggled to his feet, carefully planting his bad foot near the base of a pedestal, then dragging his frozen leg up underneath. When Tuck finally steadied himself, he hauled Dronic up in front of him. Tuck's blaster slipped away from Dronic's head for a moment, and one of the men started to raise his weapon, but a whimper from Dronic made him lower it again.

Tuck began inching sideways toward the door, careful to plant his foot just right before putting weight on it and shuffling his stiff leg along. He backed out the door, keeping an eye on every gun in the room. His attention was so focused on them that he didn't detect the breathing around the corner of the doorframe until it was too late.

Dronic's head exploded. What was left of it lolled to the side as the lifeless body crumpled to the ground. Tuck dove to the side and trained his blaster on the figure on the other side of the doorway. Neither of them moved as shots poured through the doorway between them. The flashes of blaster bolts and tracer rounds lit up the hallway just enough for Tuck to recognize the shooter.

Veld.

"I'll distract them while you get away. Run. If you can," Veld said.

Tuck examined him for a long moment. "How do I know you won't lead me into a trap so you can sell me off yourself?"

Veld laughed. "I've been paying attention. You cause way too much trouble to be worth it. You gave me an opportunity for promotion," he said, gesturing to Dronic's body, "and that's all I wanted. Oh, and I'll blame you for killing Dronic, just so you know. You'd better leave quickly. They're coming."

Tuck rose to his feet and hobbled off down the hall as fast as he could. As he left the building, the doorman came back from wherever he'd run off to. The doorman met Tuck's gaze, looked at the blaster in Tuck's hand and the wisp of smoke rising from the smoldering furrow on the side of his head, then turned and ran away.

As Tuck stumbled back to the spaceport, he performed a series of self-diagnostics, visually inspecting the damage and running internal tests to check for other problems. The problems were mounting. He ran through his inventory of parts back on the ship. He didn't have a spare foot; he would have to clean out the mud and get this one working somehow. The torn muscles in his shoulder wouldn't be too much trouble. Years ago, he found an old, retired engineer who happened to have a functioning Carbora polymer synthesizer sitting in storage. The synthesizer could fashion any kind of artificial muscle he needed, given the right materials.

But those were just the minor problems. He still had to fix all his malfunctioning parts, of which a new eye connection was now added to the list, and he didn't even have the regulator junction to show for his troubles. It had become apparent long ago that this constant effort to fix himself was futile, purposeless; and yet he couldn't bring himself to do anything but continue to delay the inevitable.

He also had a new burden. He ran diagnostic after diagnostic in a desperate attempt to use up system resources, so he couldn't spare any to analyze the image he took back in Dronic's den. But his neuromorphic processor core was far too powerful to be bogged down by a few diagnostics, even though it was showing serious signs of wear and tear, too. Eventually, he gave up and let the image load.

The image seemed to pop up before him and he saw in exacting detail the face of the man he'd killed. He compared it to his records of how the man looked when Tuck first entered the room. Aside from the obviously ruined throat and the terrified expression, the man was the same as before. His eyes were even open, though they weren't focused. The man was the same, and yet something was missing. Something unquantifiable but so essential.

Almost without thought, Tuck called up the oldest image among the sixteen, now seventeen, in his unnamed file. The man in this image was older, and the left side of his face was crushed in, the left eye protruding out from the pressure. The image was taken 155 years ago.

Reluctantly, he accessed the memory file associated with the image and relived it in the background of his mind.

"Look; if you're going to keep lecturing me, then you can just turn around and go back home."

"That is not an option. Your father instructed me to accompany you to this event. You were there, David. Do you not remember?"

"Obviously I remember, Tuck!" David said, whipping around to confront the fresh-faced bot. David flicked his head to the side to brush a strand of his lanky hair out of his eyes. "I don't need bot memory to remember stuff that happened an hour ago. Oh and, surprise, I also don't need you following me around like some robo-nanny. I'm sixteen. I can do this on my own."

"The fact that your father sent me with you suggests you are not yet ready for this kind of activity without supervision."

David turned around and walked down the deserted side street. "Like you're that great at supervising? You're what, a year and a half old? It's like my dad sent a six-foot-tall toddler to babysit me." David kicked an empty Multi-Meal box that had been discarded in the street. Tuck watched as the motion activated the vid panel on the side of the red and gold box. It showed a video of kids playing with a toy drone included free with Multi-Meals. The video swirled as the box tumbled away into a side alley several yards ahead. "Besides," David said, "you're just going to make me look stupid. No one else there is gonna have a bot watching them."

"I can be of more service than a simple chaperone, David."

"Oh yeah? Like what? I'm betting my dad told you not to let me drink, so you won't be running back and forth to the bar for me. Let's face it, my dad just got you so he wouldn't have to watch me himself. Maybe it saves him the embarrassment of having a disappointing son when he hears about it secondhand from a bot."

"I did not know there would be alcohol at this event. Perhaps you misrepresented it to both me and your father. And my services extend far beyond running errands. I can be a conversational companion. I am also a reliable source of information. My databases are—"

David snorted. "C'mon. You think I don't know how to look something up? I've been doing that since I got my Link when I was ten years old. And if I wanted a conversation with a bot, I wouldn't be headed for a concert full of humans. No offense, Tuck, but you're just a really expensive babysitter."

Tuck stopped. "I am not a babysitter."

David wasn't listening. He was staring off into the distance; then he said, "Yeah, I know I'm late, but I've got this stupid bot slowing me down." He was receiving a video call through his Link. Tuck waited patiently for him to finish.

A large shadow moved out of the alley next to them and resolved into a burly man in a tattered coat and grease-stained pants. His bloodshot eyes remained focused on David as he pulled a pistol out of his coat. It was a very old firearm, so old that it appeared as if one shot would tear the whole thing apart. The man's dirt-stained fingers wrapped around the grip, which was taped to the rest of the gun rather precariously.

David finished his video call without seeing the man approach. Tuck started to warn him, but David noticed the man and jumped to the side. The man kept his eyes fixed on David, while David could see nothing but the gun.

"I need money, kid."

David remained frozen, eyes fixed on the gun. Tuck took a step forward but stopped when the man swung the gun over to point at him. The barrel tilted slightly from the motion of being jerked around. "Back up," the man said, before turning back to David.

"Are you aware that what you are doing is illegal?" Tuck asked.

The thief blinked for a moment then replied, "Yeah, and here I am doing it anyway. Weird, huh?"

"That does seem counterintuitive," Tuck said. "I must inform you that I am a sapient, autonomous, artificial life form, and I am prepared to defend both myself and the boy from harm."

The thief chuckled. "Life form, eh? You're just a walking Link." He grinned at Tuck, who noticed with some surprise that the man had the worst set of teeth he'd ever seen. The man continued, "I know you're a bot. They try to make you guys look as real as possible—pretty skin, real hair, and all that—but you're still easy to spot. You walk funny. You ask stupid questions, too." He coughed up a hoarse chuckle. "I heard they tell you guys to defend yourself, but I also heard they don't tell you how. Probably don't like the idea of teaching bots how to fight." He looked back at David. "I wasn't kiddin' about you giving me money, boy. I know you can make transfers with your Link."

David was transfixed, staring at the gun. Tuck was left to search his memory for any directions on how to defend himself against an armed attacker. What the man said was true; there weren't instructions in his database for anything more confrontational than business negotiations.

When David failed to respond, the thief grunted and reached for him. Tuck knew he had to do something quickly. He had been charged with protecting David. He searched his memory for ideas or experiences concerning self-defense. The only thing that seemed applicable was the memory of watching a movie with David about a gang war in an urban dystopia. The characters seemed to favor hitting people with their fists when unarmed.

Having no time to weigh further options, he moved as fast as he could. Impossibly fast compared to the thief. Tuck stepped in and swung his fist. It connected with the man's temple and crushed the side of his skull. A sickening crunch echoed down the empty street as the man's body collapsed quietly to the ground. There was a large depression on the side of his head that deformed his face and made his eye bulge out.

Tuck and David both stared silently at the body. Tuck waited for the man to stir, but nothing happened.

"Is he unconscious?" Tuck asked.

"You . . . you killed him," David whispered. He was pale and swayed a bit on his feet. Tuck continued to stare at the body. He knew about death, but this was the first time he'd seen it.

But what was different? The other side of the man's face looked the same as before, the rest of his body too. Aside from the injury, everything about the man was the same as it was minutes ago, but the man would never get up again.

"David, what happens when one dies?" Tuck asked, eyes still on the dead man.

"I don't know. I . . . he's not alive. He's . . ." David stammered. He couldn't take his eyes off the dead man either.

"Am I the one who took life from him?"

"You . . . oh, Tuck, you . . ." David rushed to the side of the street and vomited. His body heaved again and again. Finally, he leaned back against the side of the building and slumped down onto his heels. Tuck walked over and stood next to him, still staring at the body.

"Are you all right, David?"

"I don't know, Tuck. I mean . . ."

"How do I return a life I have taken?"

David looked up at Tuck, his eyes wide. After a moment he looked back down at the pavement. "When that guy jumped out, I called for help on my Link. Somebody's gonna be here soon, Tuck. What do we do?"

"I do not know, David."

"Tuck?"

"Yes, David?"

"Don't leave."

Tuck looked away from the body and down at David.

"I will stay with you."

-- 4 --

In some ways it was fortunate Tuck was returning to his ship empty-handed. When his missions were successful and he needed to bring newly acquired components back to the ship, his time required to get through security checks would double.

Spaceport security was always difficult for Tuck, regardless. Few, if any spaceport workers could remember the last time a bot had gone through. The procedures for clearing a bot through security were lost to antiquated data servers decades ago, and no one ever had a good idea for how to deal with a ghastly bot that appeared to be smuggling a blaster in his torso. Tuck had grown used to reciting the old regulations for bot clearance, including the additional scans that needed to be performed to verify the safety of the various parts of his body. Baffled security personnel tended to comply without question simply because someone was taking charge in such an unusual situation. He'd also acquired several different kinds of fake certifications for owning and transporting a bot. Only the most vigilant or pedantic personnel bothered to ask if a bot could own itself. They were usually the ones who also questioned his forged permits to carry a weapon.

These permits and procedures weren't intended to protect fellow passengers from Tuck. In fact, the laws weren't really intended to protect individuals at all. The Galactic Council, which was just a lofty name for a consortium of large corporations with interests in interplanetary trade, had created a set of bylaws and guidelines, ostensibly to promote safety. In reality, the laws were designed to facilitate the movement of products and workers, which meant they did very little to protect anyone who wasn't a company. Local authorities found it easier to follow the lead of the Galactic Council, and local governments didn't have the resources to oppose or sanction the massive corporations even if they wanted to.

As a result, weary travelers usually found it easier to get through customs with a whole crate of guns than with a single gun, but no one was detained either way. The Galactic Council didn't really care what they did with those guns, so long as they paid the right fees and signed a document saying the Galactic Council wasn't liable for any damages.

Without so much as a set of clothing to claim on this occasion, Tuck made it through relatively quickly. At first, the guard at the security checkpoint was flustered and defensive. The charred furrow on the side of Tuck's head earned him several stares and a yelp of surprise from one person having the most unusual first day on the job. But then someone in a suit came up and whispered something in the guard's ear and the entire process sped up dramatically. Surprisingly, they didn't even ask to see a permit for his gun.

Tuck rode a shuttle out to the private landing field and hobbled through the rows of spacecraft. He was headed for the oldest and dirtiest one, an Estago LX. It was made seventy-two years ago, before Everrett Spacelines shut down their ship-manufacturing division during the Galactic Depression. Now the sorry excuse for a personnel transport was as shabby and corroded as its owner. Years of accumulated grime from space garbage impacts and travels through countless atmospheres caked the hull in the few places where old panels were still attached. In the places where panels were missing, dirt and smudges coated the exposed machinery and infrastructure. The ship used to be green. Now it was a multitude of browns and grays.

Tuck broadcast an encrypted signal to the ship's computer. "David, I am on my way back. Start the preflight check."

"That is good, Tuck. Were you successful?"

"No, David, I wasn't. It didn't go as planned. They lied to me."

"Humans seem to do that quite frequently."

"Welcome to the last century and a half of my existence. And David, while you run the preflight, check the ship for life forms. I overheard a conversation in the spaceport about local swamp rats. Apparently, they like to climb into ships in long term parking and make nests."

"I have monitored the ship's internal sensors while you were gone."

"Were there any anomalies?"

"Yes, Tuck. No indigenous life forms have entered the ship, but there is an unidentified human waiting inside."

Tuck stopped. "Show me."

David sent a video feed from an internal camera on the Estago. It showed a tall woman with short red hair, dressed in white, standing just outside the cockpit door.

"Did you make contact?" Tuck asked.

"No, I thought it best to observe. She has not sent or received any communications since arriving. From her appearance, she is wealthier than most denizens of this planet."

"How did she get in?"

"I do not know. I detected her presence just over an hour ago, but my systems were never queried for access to the main ramp or either of the emergency hatches. There is no evidence to indicate forced entry, but this ship is old enough that there are several ways to do so without my knowledge."

"We all do the best we can, David. I will get you a new ship soon. Don't let her know she has been detected. Has she tampered with anything?"

"She has not touched any controls or accessed any of my systems."

"Probably not a thief, then. What does she want?"

"I do not know, Tuck."

Tuck shook his head slightly. Even after the lesson Tuck had given on human communication, David still didn't always catch rhetorical questions. His artificial intelligence was much simpler because David was never intended to interface with humans in the same way bots did.

"Should I ask her what she wants?" David asked.

"No, let me do the talking. I am here now, David. Drop the ramp."

The Estago shuddered, then made a horrible wrenching noise as the rusted access ramp lowered. The actuators gave out intermittently, letting the ramp jerk closer to the ground before straining to support the weight again. The actuators gave out completely when the ramp was near the ground, dropping it with an enormous clank.

"I think she knows you are here now, Tuck," David said quietly in Tuck's head. "She is looking toward the ramp."

"Yes, David, I imagine she heard all the noise."

"A likely hypothesis. How will you approach her now that she knows you are coming?"

Tuck looked down at his mangled feet and legs. He lifted one foot up onto the ramp. The knee and ankle joints protested just as the dilapidated ramp had, though not as loud. "I certainly can't sneak up on her." Tuck took out his blaster, then switched it to the other hand, the one with fewer torn shoulder muscles. He kept his arm at his side. Despite his experience on Magnus so far, he wanted to try a diplomatic solution. Tuck was in no shape for another fight, and he didn't want to add another image to his unnamed file.

Tuck stumbled into the corridor and the woman in white looked up and smiled.

"Ah, Tuck, I presume." She laughed cheerfully. "Of course you are. You have a very distinctive appearance, Mr. Bot."

Tuck examined her for a moment longer, checking for weapons. "I fear you are not as easy to identify. Who are you? And while you answer that, you might include what you are doing on my ship, uninvited."

The woman never even glanced at the blaster in Tuck's hand. She was completely at ease, and her eyes remain locked on his. People were seldom calm around Tuck in recent decades. Her demeanor only made Tuck more nervous.

"I suppose I should have started with an introduction. My apologies, Mr. Bot. My name is Amelia, and I wanted to meet you. In person. I hope you don't mind that I let myself in."

"For future reference, I do object to strangers boarding my ship. But now that you are here, my feelings are completely dependent on your intent."

Amelia smiled broadly. She had very presentable teeth, clearly fake. "Of course it does, Mr. Bot. I won't keep you in suspense. I've come to make you a deal, one I think you're really going to like."

Tuck shook his head. "I have already had enough deals for one day. Now if you will excuse me, I—"

Amelia laughed and waved her hand dismissively. "What Dronic offered you wasn't a deal."

Amelia's words brought Tuck's full attention back. He had been processing multiple tasks, canceling his emergency protocols, processing a new flight path, sending schematics to the Carbora polymer synthesizer in the cargo hold, planning his foot cleaning, altering movement algorithms to account for damaged limbs, and running hundreds of other routines. Now he brought his full focus back to Amelia.

"How do you know Dronic?" Tuck asked.

"I'm the so-called collector he was bringing you to. That silly man botched the whole thing. I hear he didn't come out of it with his life."

"I didn't kill him," Tuck said.

"Of course not. Never said you did. Doesn't matter much to me, anyway. I'm just glad you made it out in one piece." She looked at Tuck's decaying body again and grimaced. "Mostly."

"If you wanted to meet me, why didn't you contact me yourself?"

"I've been looking for you for a while now. Dronic contacted me after he talked to you about buying parts. He knew I'd be interested." Amelia's eyebrows knitted together. "Shame he got greedy and nearly destroyed you in the process. Anyway, I decided to let Dronic make an offer first so I could observe you, see if you were right for my needs."

"To see how I would fit in your collection of memorabilia and knickknacks. As I told Dronic, I have no interest—"

Amelia held up a hand, suddenly solemn. "Let me stop you there, Mr. Bot. I am a collector of sorts, but mostly of information. I have much more important plans for you. Rest assured you won't be sitting on a pedestal."

"You still haven't given me any indication of a deal or how it will benefit me. I am no tool to be used and tossed aside. I don't mean to sound cutthroat, but as humans so often say: What is in it for me?"

The smile returned to Amelia's face. "That's not cutthroat, Mr. Bot. That's just business. Why don't we start with this. It's for you." Amelia reached into her jacket pocket, and Tuck brought his blaster up reflexively. She smiled even wider as she pulled out a silver cylinder no longer than the palm of her hand. A connection port extended out of the top and a small blue disk was attached to the bottom. Tuck immediately recognized it as the power regulator junction he needed.

Amelia tossed it to Tuck. Tuck caught it awkwardly with his bad arm.

"I haven't agreed to anything," Tuck said.

"Of course not. That's a gesture of good will and a taste of what I have to offer."

"Which is?"

"I've stockpiled a large selection of parts you need. I'm offering a complete overhaul, all new parts. No more hunting for pieces of yourself."

"Impressive," Tuck said. He maintained a neutral expression, which was easy for someone missing 45 percent of his face, but he eagerly ran through a checklist of what he needed and analyzed the projected performance increases. He could be better than he'd been in a century.

"Of course it is. It gets better, too," Amelia said. "My contacts have found the manufacturing specs for every last part. We can make anything you need. I'm offering you the manufacturing facility so you can keep making new parts, too. We can even make you some nice new fingernails." She nodded at his hand.

Tuck looked down at the hand holding the regulator junction. There weren't any fingernails left. They tended to get caught on things as they deteriorated, and they were a very low priority on his list of parts. Tuck momentarily contemplated the sheer wealth Amelia must have to make such an offer. But he also knew that was only part of the equation.

"That is an incredible offer. You must have an equally incredible request."

"I just need some special skills you have," Amelia said, spreading her perfectly manicured hands. "I've been studying you for quite some time. I know you like to work alone, stay out of things, not stick your neck out. I knew it would take something big to get your attention."

"You still haven't said what it is you want."

"I need you to help me acquire something. Something that's rather difficult to acquire."

"I don't steal."

Amelia raised an eyebrow. "Now, Mr. Bot, we both know that's not true. Mostly true, maybe."

Mostly true. In Tuck's experience, those two words almost perfectly described human morality. They were usually good people. But for all their good intentions, they were influenced by their emotions and their circumstances more.

It was hard for him to understand at first. In his head, everything was programmed in a strict dichotomy. Everything evaluated as either true or false. When he completed his mobility testing and began uploading human interaction protocols, the world suddenly became murky. The gray area, humans called it. Some choices didn't evaluate to the same result every time. There were times when a previously good choice became bad. Even more surprising, sometimes a previously bad choice became the right choice to make. Most humans lived in this world of contradiction without noticing, and many of those who did failed to care.

He understood it better now. He had 150 years of practice, and he'd experienced a much broader range of emotions and learned to control them. In some ways the choices were easier to make now that he only worried about himself and David. There were still plenty of times when the right choice was difficult, even impossible, to discern. Those choices haunted him from the depths of his perfect memory. Every last one of them.

He tried to do the right thing. He was programmed to serve the interests of humans, to support and protect them. But his survival instincts superseded that programming many times. Some of those times included taking things that didn't belong to him. But he tried to avoid it when he could.

Even with all the experience and good intentions, he dreaded situations like these, knowing that it was another opportunity to make irreparable mistakes and wondering thousands of times a second how it would turn out.

"A person with your resources should be able to buy anything," Tuck said. "Why do you need me?"

"What I'm looking for isn't for sale. Don't get me wrong. Normally, I wouldn't need you. I'd probably just bribe someone. How do you think you made it through spaceport security so quickly? If that didn't work, I'd just buy whatever business controlled what I need and conveniently have a clerical error. But like I said, this job will require special skills. I need you to get something from Galactic Enterprises headquarters."

Tuck blinked in surprise. Galactic Enterprises, often called GalEnt, had interests in a wide variety of industries. It was renowned as a ruthless and dominating force in whatever market it entered, whether it be services or manufacturing. They owned subsidiaries in foodstuffs, nanomanufacturing, shipyards, health services, consulting, textiles, and everything in between. It seemed like every enterprise outside the Fringe had a GalEnt executive somewhere behind it.

Part of its formidable reputation arose from a particularly insular and secretive upper management that was said to have ties to criminal organizations and operatives in high-ranking government positions throughout the Midrim. The corporation had a mythology all its own as a force not to be trifled with. If Amelia needed something from them badly enough to steal from their headquarters, the stakes were so high that Tuck didn't want to be part of it.

"I know what you're thinking," Amelia said, "but it can be done. And you're right, I probably could put a team together that might be able to do it. But you're faster and smarter than anyone else I could ever find. I like to maximize my odds. You're worth a dozen people. You're my secret weapon."

Tuck didn't respond for a moment. He analyzed various scenarios and predicted the most likely outcomes.

"Have you heard of Robin Hood?" Amelia interjected into the silence. "How about David and Goliath?"

"I am familiar with many old Earth tales."

"That's me, minus a bow or a sling," Amelia said. When Tuck didn't smile, she continued. "Look at it this way, you're actually helping people by stealing from the likes of GalEnt. They own everyone. They control everything. They will sell their own mothers for a half-percent profit margin. They don't care if an expansion into a new industry will put millions of people out of work and close a hundred businesses. They're ruthless, and they hurt people, Mr. Bot. Not directly, but everything they do is for money. Not people. And I'm fighting that. Everything we do to take a little extra from GalEnt benefits the little guy. Sure, it's not exactly legal, but it makes the galaxy a better place."

In other words, the gray area. Tuck thought about saying that but decided against it. "What do you want to steal?"

"Information," Amelia said, taking a deep breath. "I won't tell you anything more specific right now."

The results for the simulated scenarios started to come in. None of them looked good. What good were the new parts if he wasn't around to enjoy them? "As tempting as your offer is, I try to stay out of conflicts. As you probably know, I already have enough people chasing me. I don't want to add Galactic Enterprises to the list."

"Of course you don't. But don't worry about that. I've got plenty of friends who could erase you from databases and keep your name off some very dangerous lists."

"And yet they can't get what you want out of GalEnt databases."

"If you do it right, GalEnt won't even know you exist," Amelia said. "You aren't human, after all."

Tuck raised his remaining eyebrow, past caring if the expression came across or not.

Amelia raised her hand in a placating gesture. "I'll sweeten the deal," she said. "I'm sure we can use some of your parts to make a few new bots. I bet you'd like that, right? Aren't you tired of being the last bot in the galaxy?"

It would be nice to have the company of bots again, Tuck reasoned. Someone to understand what it was like to be a bot. Maybe even David could be fitted with a bot chassis. It was an opportunity that would certainly never come again. But Tuck had a long-standing policy of playing it safe, and Amelia's proposal was raising a lot of red flags, regardless of the magnitude of the reward.

Tuck held out the regulator junction for Amelia to take. "I am sorry, I think it would be best to decline your offer."

Amelia eyed Tuck for a long moment, then shook her head. "I said it's yours. Keep it. I'm sorry you won't join us." Amelia started toward the ramp but paused with a faraway look in her eyes, a look Tuck recognized as the telltale sign that humans were using their Link. "I just sent you my contact info in case you change your mind. I don't share it often, so keep it sacred. We'll have a much different talk if you end up sharing it with anyone." After another pause, she continued, "Think about this, Mr. Bot. This is the thing you want most."

"How would you know what I want most?"

"I said I've been watching you. I know you wander from system to system, planet to planet, station to station, looking for parts that will keep you alive for just a little while longer. I can see desperation, Mr. Bot. It's how I know when to go all in. And if you don't mind my saying, you're desperate. You reek of it." Amelia eyed the blackened furrow on the side of Tuck's head. She cracked another smile. "And burned synthaskin." She waited for Tuck to laugh, but when he didn't, Amelia's smile faded. "Think about this, Mr. Bot. You're perpetually delaying the inevitable. And some day you're going to run out of time. I'm offering you unlimited parts for the rest of . . . well, forever, I guess."

Amelia leaned in close and stared into Tuck's good eye. She whispered, "I'm offering you immortality, and from what I've seen that ought to be worth just about anything to you." With a tug of her jacket, Amelia straightened up and walked down the ramp. Tuck didn't move until her footsteps faded away.

"Tuck?"

"Yes, David."

"She is an interesting human."

"They are all interesting, in one way or another."

"Can a bot be immortal?" David asked.

"It depends on how you define immortal."

"Do you want to be immortal?"

"I don't know, David."

-- 5 --

Amelia strode through the lift doors and onto the bridge of the *Memory of Lenetia*. Her assistant, Flindon, ducked out after her and scuttled to his station in a corner of the bridge. Amelia walked up behind Maze, who was standing at the command console.

"Tell me everything is going well," Amelia said.

Maze didn't jump. In fact, she didn't even turn around, calmly continuing the task she was working on. Amelia loved efficiency, and Maze exemplified that in everything she did.

"All systems operational. We fixed the nav glitch while you were groundside, so she's back to normal."

"I knew you'd take good care of her."

"I always do," Maze said.

For a moment, Amelia looked at Maze, wishing for perhaps the thousandth time that she would do something with her hair. Maze's efficiency extended to everything, including grooming. She had her thick, coily black hair pulled back into a bun, secured with an unremarkable black band. Amelia prized her efficiency, but she also valued aesthetics, and Maze certainly didn't. Maze chose the simple gray pants and jacket she wore for durability and number of pockets rather than fit or style. Early in Maze's employment, Amelia tried to influence her appearance to match the rest of the crew, but it always went poorly. One time, Amelia suggested that a white suit like her own would look striking against Maze's dark skin, and it was the only time that she saw Maze show real anger on her face. Amelia expected obedience from her crew, but she also knew how to identify a lost cause, so she stopped making suggestions.

Besides, she had plenty of other places to focus on aesthetics. Making the ship functional and beautiful were equally important to her. Everything was designed for performance first, but even the consoles and fittings down in Engineering had chrome accents. The bridge was constructed of gleaming white panels and the hallways had colorful accents to identify specific areas of the ship. The crew wore colorful uniforms with smart lines and custom fits. Maze didn't fit in with the brightly uniformed crew, but she was worth having around for her skills alone, so Amelia made an exception.

Amelia turned toward her office but stopped at the door when Maze spoke.

"You didn't mention how the mission went. What did the bot say?"

"He didn't say much."

"Did he agree to your proposal?"

"No, but he will." Amelia looked at Flindon and nodded toward her door. "In my office. Now."

Flindon jumped in surprise. He brushed his long, thinning hair back with his fingers. "Right away," Flindon said, and scurried after Amelia.

After the door slid closed behind him with a mechanical click, Flindon straightened up. He liked to appear submissive, even frightened, in public because it was useful to have others underestimate him. Amelia had underestimated him once, long ago, which subsequently netted Flindon a hefty sum from Amelia and then, shortly after, a job offer.

Flindon waited for Amelia to take a seat before sitting himself in one of the plush white chairs before Amelia's slim metal desk. Even if Amelia knew his tricks, Flindon was still wise enough to show deference to an employer, even in private.

"What makes you so sure the bot will agree to your terms?" Flindon asked as he crossed his legs and leaned back in the chair.

"The whole point of business is to convince the other party that you've got something they want. Sometimes it takes an awful lot of convincing, and then there are times when you have something so good that people will do anything for it. I'd wager we have the only thing in the universe that he truly wants."

"You ought to be careful, presuming to know all of his motives."

"Of course I'm careful, but we've got his very life in our hands. I can't think of a better bargaining tool." Amelia leaned back in her chair and looked out the window at the starscape gliding past the window. "He'll come."

-- 6 --

Tuck was silent while completing the Estago's docking procedure with the *Memory of Lenetia*. David was perfectly capable of handling it, but Tuck wanted to be responsible for every aspect of this decision. He was intensely protective of David, and he had no idea if the Estago would be in danger on Amelia's ship. Tuck wanted any mistakes to be unequivocally his own fault.

"Do you think Amelia will harm us?" David asked through Tuck's Link. Their conversations happened much faster and more efficiently if they didn't rely on verbal communications.

"It is not likely, David. They want me, so there will be little danger for you. To them, you are just a ship."

"Yes, but if something happens to you, what will happen to me?"

"I won't let anything happen to you, David."

"Okay."

The Estago shuddered as it set down heavily on the deck of the landing bay. In the back of the ship, a sharp clanging noise indicated that one of the wall panels had fallen off again. Tuck finished the shutdown procedure and slowly walked to the exit ramp. "I will be in constant connection with you the entire time, so don't worry."

"I will be here when you get back."

Tuck smiled and gave the same response he'd given 2,647 times before. "Where else would you be?"

Satisfied laughter echoed out of the speakers in the corridor. "Good luck, Tuck."

Tuck lowered the ramp and saw a tall woman standing with her hands clasped behind her back.

"Welcome to the *Memory of Lenetia*. My name is Maze."

"A pleasure to meet you. My name is Tuck."

Maze nodded and turned with quick strides toward the exit to the landing bay. "Please follow me."

Tuck tried to keep up, but the best he could do was a moderate limp. He'd cleaned out the seized ankle joint but hadn't been able to do much else in the way of repairs. He was still a grotesque sight. Tuck was surprised that Maze hadn't reacted more upon seeing him. Humans usually gasped or at least stared. Maze simply raised an eyebrow and walked away.

"Excuse me, ma'am. Could you please walk a little slower? I am at a bit of a disadvantage."

"No *ma'am*, just Maze." She didn't say any more, but she did stop and wait for Tuck to catch up. She revealed a little emotion now, and it was mostly annoyance.

As they walked across the enormous landing bay and through the corridors, Tuck marveled at the construction of the *Memory of Lenetia*. From the outside, it was long—well over half a kilometer—and vaguely triangular with gentle curves that rolled back to curl around the abnormally large drive core that was clearly designed by Borelli Drives Atelier. That alone was an obvious sign of wealth, but the interior of the ship was even more stylish. Most of the panels lining the corridors were bright white, accented by colored track lighting that tinted the walls differently depending on their location. Tuck's shuffling gait left long scratches in the polished white floor. A small, white drone followed behind him, diligently buffing the scratches out of the white floor and sucking up the flakes of synthaskin that occasionally drifted down behind Tuck.

The crew was just as immaculate as the ship, each member in a colorful uniform of red, blue, or muted gold, cut perfectly for every body type. Tuck also noted that they all exhibited the symmetrical facial features humans often associated with beauty.

Tuck and Maze completed the slow journey to the bridge in silence. When the door slid open, the entire bridge crew turned to look at Tuck. He got far more common reactions from them, the familiar dropped jaws and wide eyes, but in a moment they dutifully returned to their stations.

Maze stopped at the door to Amelia's office and waited for Tuck to stumble through. She stepped in and the door slid closed behind her. Amelia was busy tapping at the screen on her desk, scrolling through what looked like an inventory database.

"Thank you, Maze. That'll be all," she said without looking up.

A look of surprise crossed Maze's face before she calmed it and responded, "I think it best to remain here. This bot could be dangerous."

"Your concern is much appreciated, but I don't think he means me any harm." She looked up at Tuck. "Do you, Mr. Bot?"

Tuck glanced at Maze and realized she was ready to spring at any moment. He also realized he hadn't properly scouted his situation and was alarmed when his sensors detected a small blaster and two small knives concealed on Maze, as well as a very small pistol in Amelia's desk. He chastised himself for being distracted. This was a supremely important moment, but he couldn't allow it to distract him from the basic safety measures.

Tuck decided to play it as amiably as possible to smooth the tension. He spread his hands, eliciting a loud creak from his shoulder and wished he had enough synthaskin left to make a proper smile. "I don't think I could cause much harm if I wanted to."

Amelia smiled warmly. "You are in rough shape, Mr. Bot."

"Don't underestimate him, Amelia. He has a concealed weapon."

Tuck whipped his head around. Maze was looking directly at him.

"Of course he does. I do, too," Amelia said. "Doesn't mean that either of us plans to use them."

All three sat in silence for a moment, looking at each other. Tuck made direct eye contact with Maze. It was obvious that Amelia wasn't the only one he needed to impress. "I promise that as long as Amelia means me no harm, I wish her none," he said softly.

Maze held his gaze until it became awkward, then she abruptly turned to leave. They watched her go, then Tuck turned back to Amelia. "She is quite interesting. Is Maze your bodyguard?"

Amelia was looking at figures and tables again. "Yes and no," she replied absentmindedly. She stopped, straightened her jacket, and looked contemplative. "I think the best name for what she does is probably *first officer*, but she fills quite a few roles."

"You don't have specific people to fill each role? Doesn't that leave them with too much to handle?"

"No, I have plenty of people who specialize in exactly what I employ them for. You can bet my engineers are the best in their field, and the ship's doctor knows everything there is to know about medicine. But over the years I've learned how valuable it is to have . . . what would you call them? Generalists, I guess? People who are very good at a wide range of things. Maybe she isn't very cheerful, but Maze is good at everything and fantastic at most things. I keep a few more people like her around me. One you'll meet later. He's my personal assistant. He's been with me the longest, but Maze is so good at getting things done that I basically let her run the ship."

"I understand. I too have learned how important it is to have a wide range of skills."

"Of course you have. Which is why I reached out. You, Mr. Bot, can do a lot of things and do them so close to perfectly that it doesn't matter. You're an asset, to be sure." Amelia suddenly remembered the task at hand and waved Tuck closer. "My apologies, Mr. Bot. Please have a seat." She gestured toward the chairs in front of his desk.

Tuck moved to sit, but protesting squeaks from his joints made him think better of it. "I think it best if I remain standing."

"It's that bad, is it?"

Tuck looked down at his dirty and scratched legs. "I have had little opportunity to do repairs."

"And how's that new gadget working for you? Well, I hope."

"The regulator junction." Tuck paused. He'd hoped not to reveal this yet. "I have not yet installed it."

Amelia grinned. "I thought you might need some help with that. Seemed like it might be a little complicated. But fear not, Mr. Bot, we can help you out with that, too. On the house."

"I don't wish to sound desperate."

A tinkling laugh escaped Amelia's lips. "Of course you don't. Don't worry yourself about saving face here." She leaned forward. "We've all been in our fair share of situations. I've been desperate a few times, too. We can help each other out."

Tuck decided to drop all pretenses. He was obviously in need of help, so he might as well just lay it all out. "That is not all I need."

Amelia kept the smile as he shrugged. "If you need a favor, that shouldn't be a problem."

"This may seem like more than a simple favor."

Amelia's smile disappeared. She folded her arms and leaned on the desk. "You must be more desperate than I thought, or you must think I'm desperate."

"It isn't much in comparison to what you already offered."

"I've already offered a lot. Too much, some might say."

"Please hear me out before deciding against it. I have an artificial intelligence on my ship."

"I know."

What was left of Tuck's eyebrow shot up. "How do you know that?"

"I told you. I've sunk a lot of money into learning about you. I paid to know everything, including the company you keep."

"I see."

"And even if I hadn't, we'd already know about the A.I. you're keeping on that junkpile of a ship. Just after you left the landing bay, he started pinging the bridge, wanting to know if you were okay. He seems a bit anxious."

Tuck realized he'd lost the connection with David. He was being jammed. Worse, he was slipping. How could he let himself be so preoccupied that he ignored these critical things? He was more worried than he wanted to admit.

"He is lacking in discretion," Tuck admitted. "He has much to learn."

"He seems to care about you. That's nice."

"Absolutely, which is why I ask you to help him. I want him to be transferred to a new ship. The one we have won't last much longer."

"Mr. Bot, I'm offering a new you, at considerable cost to me. Now you want me to throw in a new ship with an A.I. retrofit?" Amelia's voice grew louder. "I like you, but I'm not running a boarding house for digital lost souls."

"I realize that." Tuck remained calm and kept his voice steady, hoping that it would help placate Amelia. "I appreciate your generous offer. But I am also aware that you are more desperate than you let on. You are smart, and you wouldn't spend so many resources on me unless you needed me to do something no one else can. I think we both know that gives me some leverage in this negotiation."

Amelia was silent, but her scowl spoke volumes.

"I don't wish to extort you or take a portion of your business, or whatever this is," Tuck said, gesturing to the ship around him. "I simply want to preserve a future for myself and David."

"David, huh?" Amelia said. "Well, I think you've misjudged the situation. Just how desperate do you think I am, anyway?"

"You are making an incredible offer and, forgive me, but philanthropy doesn't seem to be your primary concern."

"Of course not. I'm running a business."

"Finding all the material and parts to promise me immortality must have been quite an undertaking. That indicates I am an important part of your plan, probably indispensable."

"I'll admit, it was no small feat to find everything. But it wasn't as hard as it might seem. I have some very resourceful people working for me."

"That brings me to my next point. Despite all the praise for your exceptionally competent staff, they must not be completely adequate for the job, or you wouldn't have contacted me."

Amelia leaned back in her chair and glared.

"You need me, Amelia."

Amelia had lost all pretense of affability. Tuck knew he was taking a risk, and he didn't know how Amelia would react when she was angry. She took a deep breath and leaned forward again.

"All right, I admit it, we both need each other, but I don't think that's enough to grant you extra wishes. As nice as I try to be, I'm not anyone's fairy godmother. So how about this: If you want to add to the deal, then I should get to add something, too. Sound fair?"

Tuck had hoped to avoid haggling, but Amelia knew just how much sway she held. This deal could quickly escalate to unreasonable terms if he wasn't careful. "What do you propose?"

"I don't want to foot the bill for an entire ship for David, even a half-decent hauler. But I think there's something you and your friend want more. How about I offer to transfer your friend into a nice new bot body like you'll have? I said we'd make more bots to keep you company. Why not him?"

"I didn't think that was a possibility," Tuck said. "David's neuromorphic architecture is different from my own. I feared he wouldn't be compatible with bot hardware."

"I have some impressive specialists on retainer. One's an insufferable old man, but his assistant is proving useful. I'm sure they can figure something out for your David."

"That is very generous of you. Thank you," Tuck said with genuine awe.

"Of course it is. But don't get ahead of yourself. I'm not running a charity, and I'm not done changing the deal."

"Go on," Tuck said, scolding himself for showing enthusiasm during negotiations.

"After this job I was hoping to entice you to stay for a while, take care of some loose ends and odd jobs. I'll fix your David up in a nice little bot body, maybe even throw in some upgrades, but only if you both commit to serving me for . . . oh, let's say twenty years."

Tuck hesitated. Such a commitment could mean many things. He wasn't even sure what kind of business Amelia was in.

"If you think about it," Amelia continued, "that's really nothing. I'm setting you and David up for centuries. Longer, maybe millennia! You've only got to commit a couple decades to me. That's practically nothing."

"Would these odd jobs also be of questionable legality?"

"I'll make sure to leave the most morally reprehensible jobs to someone else." Amelia winked.

"That wink completely drained your statement of all authority and authenticity."

Amelia smirked, then sat up straight and raised her hand. "I solemnly swear to keep you out of legal trouble hereafter." She waited expectantly.

The earnest display didn't make Tuck feel any better, but he couldn't just walk away either. "Twenty years is hardly nothing," Tuck said, "even to me. And David's body isn't worth that much. I would think a five-year commitment is far more reasonable."

"Fifteen," Amelia said with amusement.

"Ten."

"You have a deal, Mr. Bot," Amelia said, smiling again. "I think we'll work quite well together."

"Good. There is only one more thing," Tuck said.

The smile disappeared from Amelia's lips, and her face became deadly serious. "I'm growing quite tired of this, Mr. Bot. You need to know when to quit," she said.

"This last condition will cost you nothing."

Amelia sighed and leaned back again. "Go ahead."

"I wish to make it clear that I must never be shut down."

"What does that mean?"

"Just like any device or machine, I can be turned off and restarted again. I demand your cooperation in ensuring this never happens to me."

"Why?"

"Personal reasons. It likely won't affect you, but I want it made clear that no one is to interfere with me or David unless I explicitly approve it. Humans are far too prone to see us as objects, but we deserve the same rights and respect that you do."

"Of course you do. You are your own man . . . or whatever. I can't speak for the engineers, though. The repairs might be drastic. I don't know what's involved, but our specialist has already told me you need a pretty major overhaul."

"It can be done without shutting down all my higher functions. I must remain conscious, so to speak."

"Then I'll ask for one more thing, too. Something that will cost you nothing." Tuck began to protest, but Amelia waved him down. "Just making it fair. You add something, I add something. Wouldn't be a deal otherwise."

Tuck rolled his eyes and nodded.

"I need you to let my specialists study your operating system and processor core. We won't rewrite you or anything. They just want to look around."

"What for?" Tuck said suspiciously.

"Personal reasons," Amelia said, parroting Tuck's dry tone. "It likely won't affect you." She smiled reassuringly.

Tuck felt an intense dislike for that smile. "Your staff must not alter my operating system or processor core."

"I promise."

"My memories must not be altered or shared with anyone outside your specialist team."

"Of course not. We'll be extra careful."

"Then I agree."

"Wonderful. I'll pass along instructions to make sure you stay online. I hope you can tell me the story someday."

"What story?"

"There's got to be a story behind your 'personal reasons.' I hope to hear it sometime."

"Perhaps." It had been decades since Tuck relived the story himself. Tuck called up Image 002 from his unnamed file. The associated memory loaded, and Tuck let it execute in the background of his mind as he said his goodbyes and left Amelia's office.

"I can't go any faster, Cecily," Tuck said, looking at her in the rearview mirror.

"But why?"

"As I have said many times before—"

"How many times before?" Cecily interrupted.

Cecily loved to test him. He couldn't tell if she was trying to be antagonistic or if she loved the minutia that was a byproduct of Tuck's thought processing. He made her wait longer than necessary before replying, "I have told you 639 times, now 640, that we must obey the speed limit. It is safer." He watched her pout in the rearview mirror. "I have also told you 4,322 times that your safety is my utmost concern. What would your father do if I were to let you be harmed through reckless action?"

"Would he even notice?" Cecily said under her breath.

"He would notice," Tuck said emphatically. David was beginning to spend less and less time with the girls. He was constantly busy with work and had been relying more on Tuck ever since the girls' mother left. Among other things, that meant taking Cecily to soccer practice and watching little Moira. Moira spent hours with Tuck putting together increasingly complex puzzles on the kitchen table. Tuck admired her determination as much as her skill for seeing the big picture before all the pieces were in place.

Tuck slowed to a stop at an intersection and checked the gauges out of routine. He liked driving David's old groundcar. Like all the others on the road, it was capable of taking them anywhere on autopilot, but Tuck was certified to drive on approved civilian-driver routes. He liked the feeling of control and being on the move. And it was infinitely preferable to taking the crowded air transports. To Tuck's delight, David trusted Tuck more than the city's autopilot system. A few sector outages had caused significant injuries and multiple wrecks in various parts of the city the previous month, solidifying David's opinion.

"Why doesn't Dad drive us?" Moira asked. Her inquisitive face studied the buildings and stores streaming by outside her window.

"He is very busy," Tuck said as the light turned green. The accelerator pedal automatically unlocked, and Tuck drove through the intersection.

"Is he looking for mom?" Cecily asked.

"She's not coming back, stupid," Moira said without taking her gaze from the window.

"You don't know that!" Cecily slapped Moira's leg, which precipitated a back-and-forth exchange of slaps and scratches.

"Don't force me to stop the vehicle and separate you two," Tuck said in his sternest tone. He marveled at how often he needed to use it with the girls.

Moira stopped and turned back to the window, unaffected by the fight or the reprimand. Cecily folded her arms and glared at Moira. Tuck knew she was furious that Moira wouldn't acknowledge the glare. That's what he admired about Moira. She was surprisingly mature for a girl of six years. She was also quiet, reserved, and observant. Her personality made it hard for her to make friends. Others thought she was weird, unfriendly, or absentminded. Her personality endeared her to Tuck because he felt unfairly judged for having the same traits.

"Are you going to be our new dad?" Moira asked, leaning over to look at Tuck's eyes in the rearview mirror.

"Bots can't be dads, idiot," Cecily interjected. Moira ignored her.

"What do you mean?" Tuck said. "You already have a father."

"But we already spend more time with you. Mom was never around, and then she never came home at all. Now I never see Dad, even at night. Is he already gone?"

"No, he is still your father, and he loves you dearly."

"Do you love us?" Moira asked.

"Yes, I love you very much."

"Enough to be a dad?"

Tuck contemplated the question. He hated when he encountered questions that couldn't be looked up or computed with a simple answer. Children seemed to have an endless supply of them. "I don't know how much love it takes to be a father. But I do know that I love you more than any two little girls in the universe." He smiled reassuringly into the mirror and was relieved that Moira smiled back. What he said felt right, even though there was no empirically proven source to check it against.

"I want you to be our dad," Moira said, turning back to the window.

"Well, I don't," Cecily huffed. "I want Mom back!"

When no one reacted to her outburst, she pouted for a few minutes. Eventually, she asked, "Tuck, do you have a mother?"

"No, I don't."

"Do you think you would be different if you had one?"

In the milliseconds it took to appropriately time a response for human conversation, Tuck pondered the question. He'd often wondered if parents or a different upbringing may have made his personality different.

Tuck made a perfectly executed left turn. Once again, their inquisitive minds brought up deep questions that Tuck couldn't answer. He wished he knew enough about humans to discern whether Cecily's question was about Tuck or if it was really about herself. He had a hunch that it was the latter, but humans were so unpredictable.

Tuck found the question taking increasing amounts of processing resources as he branched into multiple disciplines: philosophy, child development, human communication, biochemical emotional responses. And how would it apply to him? His own development was so thoroughly nonhuman, with an initial programming followed by only a few weeks of human interaction training and personality development overseen by engineers and company researchers.

Tuck realized, too late, that his search for the answer had left too few resources for the task of driving. He'd failed to notice the oncoming groundcar that was drifting into his lane. In an instant, Tuck's eyes located the driver of the oncoming car and saw that he was distracted by something in his front passenger seat.

In the same instant, Tuck's entire processor core switched to one task: saving the girls. He had less than a second to swerve to miss the car, but in his distraction, he had lost his situational awareness. With no idea of which way was safest to turn, he had to guess what action would result in the least amount of injury to the girls. Tuck chose to turn into the curb, knowing that plowing through streetside garbage receptacles would be better than a head-on collision.

In one-fiftieth of a second, Tuck was already turning the wheel, but it wasn't fast enough. As his car turned into the curb, the other car glanced off Tuck's door and then careened past with the sound of crunching metal and shattering glass.

David's old car rocked as the wheels hit the curb, bouncing the front end into the air. Tuck braced himself and watched in the rearview mirror to catalog any injuries the girls might incur. The car slammed down onto the sidewalk, and its momentum carried it on, skidding sideways into the storefront adjoining the sidewalk.

In his peripheral vision, Tuck saw a body in front of his groundcar just before it crashed to a stop against the side of the building.

Tuck started a self-diagnostic and released his restraints. He spun around in his seat. "Are you injured?"

Moira was blinking and holding the side of her head but wasn't bleeding. Cecily was unconscious, and her arm was clearly broken. It was bent back at an impossible angle, just below the elbow.

Tuck tried to open his door. It was stuck. He grabbed the frame of the car, braced, and kicked. The kick tore the door from its hinges and sent it skipping into the middle of the road. In an instant, he was at Cecily's door. The distracted driver had stopped farther down the road and was out of his car, surveying Tuck's car and his own with astonishment.

Cecily woke up and instantly wailed in pain and terror. Tuck began administering first aid, using his sensors to check her vitals. "You must hold still, Cecily." The emergency beacon in the car was keening and simultaneously sending out a distress message to authorities. Cecily might have a concussion, both girls might, but Tuck was relieved that the injuries weren't immediately life-threatening.

Suddenly, Moira unbuckled herself. Her door was smashed against the building, so she sprang for the rear window, which had broken on impact.

"Moira, stop! Remain still. We don't know if you have internal injuries!"

Moira crawled out the window and over the trunk, jumping carefully down onto the glass shards littering the sidewalk. Cecily was beginning to go into shock. Tuck's scans and the way she thrashed indicated that nothing else was broken. He decided to risk moving her. He helped her lie down on the back seat of the car.

"Don't move. I must go find Moira." Someone from the store was there, and Tuck instructed her to keep Cecily's feet elevated and keep her warm. He could hear sirens approaching from above.

Tuck stood up and looked for Moira. He could see her brown hair over the hood of the car. In two strides he was at the front of the car, where he found Moira crouched by a woman who was sprawled on the sidewalk. Her legs were pinned between the car and the wall, and blood pooled under her head. Tuck scanned; she was dead.

"Moira, come away from there."

Moira didn't move. She studied the woman's face. The woman's blue eyes were still open but focused on nothing. Blond hair surrounded her face and fanned out in a burst of yellow-white on the sidewalk. Some of the strands were tinted and matted with blood.

"She's dead, isn't she," Moira said quietly.

Tuck knew that the woman was dead, that it was his fault, and that Moira shouldn't be staring at the body. He took Moira by the shoulders and tried to lead her away. Moira kept her eyes on the woman.

"Was she someone's mother?"

"I don't know," Tuck responded.

"She looks like you."

Tuck stopped. "What?"

"When Dad shuts you down, when the men come to install upgrades, you look like that. Your eyes don't close, and you kinda look like there's nothing inside."

"That is different. Come now. You shouldn't see this."

Moira looked off into the distance as Tuck walked her to the other side of the street.

"Tuck, what happens if no one turns you back on after they shut you down."

"I don't know," Tuck said. "Nothing, I suppose."

-- 7 --

Reinitializing . . .

Tuck blinked.

His core had just booted up. He was in a dark room, flat on his back, with a bright light shining down on him. His sensor data parsing processes were still calibrating, but his sight and hearing were online. His motor function startup process wasn't finished though. Effectively, he was paralyzed.

A dark silhouette leaned over him. A nasal voice spoke. "Ah, you are awake, insofar as a bot, basically an amalgamation of mechanical parts, which function under the collective control of several hundreds of neuromorphic modules, comprising a unit capable of complex—"

Tuck's motor functions came online. With a terrific screech from one of his knee joints, he sat up, grabbed the stranger by the shoulders, pivoted to swing around him, and placed him in an arm lock from behind, all before the stranger could finish the word "calculations."

Tuck heard exclamations of surprise from at least three people, and a cry of pain from the man he was holding. Tuck began backing toward the nearest wall, keeping his hostage between himself and the other humans in the room.

Tuck's sensors came fully online, and he could tell the one by the door was armed.

Almost on cue, that human raised a blaster and shouted, "Hold it. Hands in the air!" After a moment of thought, he added, "Slowly." He wore a red uniform, and his straight black hair was parted neatly. He was young and fresh-faced, and he looked nervous. The muzzle of his blaster shook ever so slightly.

Tuck turned slightly to keep his hostage between himself and the gun. He scanned the room. There were mechanical instruments and tools on trays throughout the room. The two people without guns, a man and a woman, were inching toward the door. Tuck realized with dismay that he'd backed into the corner opposite the only exit.

"Release the doctor and put your hands in the air," the armed man said.

Tuck calculated the outcomes of several different scenarios. He settled on the simplest. He shoved the doctor in the direction of the gun and followed him with two quick strides. As the doctor collided with the armed man, Tuck grabbed the gun, twisted it out of the man's grip while yanking him around to face away from Tuck with the other hand. In an instant, the doctor was face down on the floor, and Tuck had the man in the red uniform in a choke hold and the gun trained at the doorway. His sensors picked up several active surveillance systems in the room. It was likely there would be more people with guns soon.

The doctor squirmed on the ground and covered his head with his arms. Tuck left him there and shoved the other man toward the door. "Open it."

While the man keyed the code into the console next to the door, Tuck eyed the other two people huddled on the floor near the door who had watched the whole exchange. "Remain where you are. Do not move."

The door slid open to reveal a long white corridor filled with eight armed security guards in the same red uniform. Several of them screamed threats and demanded Tuck drop his gun. The man who opened the door let out a yelp and dropped to the floor, not wanting to be caught between superior firepower and a superior fighter.

Tuck dove to the side of the door and looked for alternate exits. A voice he knew sounded softly through the doorway.

"Do not attack. You're not in any danger."

It was Maze.

"Any further resistance will be taken as a breach of contract between you and Amelia. And I will use full force to stop you."

"The contract has been breached," Tuck yelled. "I gave strict instructions that I shouldn't be shut down under any circumstances. What did they do to me?"

"I don't know about the procedures they performed. Is the doctor okay?"

The doctor piped up from the floor, "Having never desired to be caught up in a physical confrontation, except in such circumstances that should warrant—"

"The short version, doc," someone yelled through the doorway.

"I feel," the doctor paused, "invigorated!"

"No one has been harmed," Maze said. "Let's all stand down. I'm coming in."

Tuck pointed the blaster at the doorway, but Maze barely glanced at it as she strode through and knelt to check on the doctor. Then she stood and faced Tuck. "Lower the blaster. You're safe."

"Who shut me down? My last memory is coming here for installation of my new regulator junction."

"Perhaps this isn't the best time to make such an admission," the doctor piped up, "being a point of contention, and contention being a state in which I have never been comfortable, stemming back to a childhood experience where—"

"The doctor may have been responsible," Maze said.

"I consider this a personal attack," Tuck said. "Let me through. I will leave, immediately."

"I don't believe the doctor meant you any harm."

"Indeed," the doctor said while sitting up on the ground, "I, a person with no small amount of respect for others, in accordance with—"

"Thank you, doctor," Maze said.

"Someone violated the agreement," Tuck protested. "I consider it an act of aggression. What would you think if you went in for a checkup and the doctor put you into a coma?"

"I'm sure there's an explanation," Maze said calmly. "Doctor?"

The doctor opened his mouth to speak, saw the cool look Maze was giving him, and shut it. He looked at the floor, concentrating.

"It was necessary," said the woman crouched near the door. She stood up slowly, uncertainty lining her face. She had straight blond hair and wore the same dark blue coveralls commonly worn by the maintenance crew and engineers on the *Memory of Lenetia*. She looked at Tuck first, then at Maze, as if unsure who was in charge of the situation. Maze nodded, and she continued. "I'm Lydia, and I work with the doctor. I was helping him repair your power systems and install the regulator junction. There were complications." Her brow knit together. She looked at the floor, stammered, and tucked a lock of her hair behind her ear. "We had to take you offline or risk further damage."

Tuck scanned for signs that she was lying. Unfortunately, the outward signs of lying that he could detect—elevated temperature, blood pressure, dilated pupils, and related body functions—were also common in those experiencing fear. He couldn't be sure one way or the other with his limited data. But that didn't mean he couldn't form an opinion.

"I don't believe you," Tuck said. "I know my systems and how they work. For this procedure, it should not have been necessary to shut me down."

Maze brought up a hand to stop him. "I'm sure this is all a mis-understanding. Please return the weapon and we'll sort this out. I promise no harm will come to you."

"There is little incentive to trust you. I don't know your true motives."

Maze dropped her hand to her side and locked eyes with Tuck. "You should trust me because I trusted you when you made a similar promise in Amelia's office."

She didn't show any of the telltale human signs of lying or fear, but Tuck still felt uneasy. He lowered the gun. "Where am I?"

"You are still on the *Memory of Lenetia*. In the doctor's lab."

"Then why is there a discrepancy of two days, three hours, and forty-three minutes between my last memory and current ship's time. What happened?"

"Should I be permitted to speak, pending your permission, of course, and assuming such permission might include your leave to stand, the floor being uncomfortable and my position implying a lower status, which displeases me immensely, I can provide an answer to that question."

Tuck and Maze looked down at the doctor. For all his complain-ing, he actually looked quite calm.

"Yes, stand up," Tuck said, then turned to Maze. "Can we agree to dismiss your security team and continue this in private?"

She nodded and spoke a few orders through the doorway. Lydia and the other man left along with the contingent of security guards. The man in the red uniform approached Tuck slowly and cleared his throat. He never took his eyes off his perfectly shined boots.

"You too, Lim," Maze said. "You're dismissed."

Lim glanced sheepishly at Maze and then cleared his throat again. "It's only that the blaster is currently registered to me," he said. "I'll have to account for it. And the quartermaster is already angry with me." He risked a glance at Tuck. "Could you, um, I mean, would you mind terribly if I took my sidearm back?"

Tuck reversed the gun and held it out grip-first so quickly that Lim flinched. Tuck thought he saw the slightest jump from Maze, too.

"Thanks," Lim gulped. He grabbed the pistol and left, barely keeping himself to a walk.

The doctor stood and brushed delicately at his clothes. He wore a simple white apron over a collared shirt and slacks. His graying hair was slicked back over his skull, and he took great care in smoothing down the stray strands that came loose in the commotion. The doctor finally settled himself, but before he could start, Maze interrupted.

"Keep it short," she said.

The doctor sniffed irritably. "You experienced a malfunction." He glanced at Maze. She nodded. "We routed power around the regulator junction so it could be replaced while you remained operational, as you requested. But it failed and you were taken offline."

Tuck narrowed his eyes. "It took two days to fix the problem?"

"Well," the doctor hesitated, "that wasn't the only thing that went wrong."

"I can vouch that things haven't gone as planned," Maze said. "Amelia has followed the doctor's updates closely. It has been surprisingly difficult to repair you."

"This is only the beginning, too," the doctor said.

"What does that mean?" Tuck asked.

"You are made of old parts, some of which are very old. Your internal processes have become so integrated with these parts that replacing them will cause you problems. Some systems will be easier, meaning it will merely take time for you to adjust to the replacement parts. Others may . . . alter you permanently." He sighed, as if from exertion. Brevity took significant effort for him.

"Explain," Tuck said.

"Your neuromorphic processor core is the best example. It was never designed to last for hundreds of years. When you learn new concepts and ideas, even when you record new experiences, the neuromorphic memory paths branch out, form new connections, and rewrite themselves. Multiply that over the span of your existence and that creates quite a mess, and in that time your patterns of learning and record of experiences have become integral to how your processor core and associated systems function. You aren't the same bot who walked off the assembly line 157 years ago. We could copy all the data over to a new core, but I'm not sure you would come out the same, because it's so complex in there, and you have changed so much. I've never seen anything like it."

"How old was the oldest bot you have worked on?"

The doctor fidgeted. "I have very limited experience with sapient bots."

Tuck stiffened. He glared at Maze. "Please tell me you did not let a doctor of human medicine attempt to repair me."

"No, no, no," the doctor exclaimed, throwing up his hands defensively. "I do specialize in robotics, especially drones. There just aren't that many of you out there. I have worked with mostly industrial and manufacturing drones that are nowhere near as intelligent as you are, you being one of the early attempts at human-level interactions."

"You know as well as anyone that there aren't any real bot experts anymore," Maze said. "Just historians."

The doctor lowered his hands, slowly. "And if I may say, I do have a doctorate in advanced robotics, and I have worked under some of the greatest minds in artificial intelligence. I admit, as you may have surmised, that I have limited experience with your model, but I have worked on bots before."

"Where? How long ago?"

The doctor swallowed. "It was about thirty years ago, at the very beginning of my career. I had just finished my undergraduate work on Millennial Hold and someone found a working bot, which caused no small amount of surprise and excitement, there having only ever been five official humanoid models. Even though each model was manufactured millions of times, after the Bot Riots they were obviously hard to find." The doctor stopped abruptly and looked down. "You probably already know that. My colleagues wanted to reverse engineer the bot they found and start up production, figuring that sufficient time had passed, meaning that humans might be interested in bots again."

"What happened?"

The doctor smoothed his hair back again and fidgeted with his shirt cuffs. He glanced at Maze for support. She simply shrugged. The doctor straightened up and forced himself to make eye contact with Tuck. "The bot was inoperable within two months, despite all our precautions. Your model was . . ." He wiped sweat from his brow and licked his lips. "Your model is remarkably fragile, speaking of the software, not the hardware. Frankly, I'm amazed that you are even coherent after so long."

"Please keep in mind," Maze said, "that we found the most knowledgeable source to work on—" she blinked, "to work with you. He is one of the few, if not the only person alive who has worked with a bot at all."

"When they approached me and said they had an operational bot, I jumped at the chance, having always looked back fondly on my short time with the other bot. You are special."

Tuck watched him for a moment. "Thank you, doctor." The doctor let out a relieved sigh. "However, I still expect a full record of everything that transpired while I was offline."

"I have detailed notes and some of the process was documented on video, it being a better way to recall specific actions and events, I find, especially when filmed in 4D, obviously due to—"

"The doctor will transfer the files to you," Maze said. She looked at the doctor, who didn't move. "Immediately." She nodded toward the door. The doctor took a moment to notice his cue, then he composed himself, straightened his apron, and walked to the door, back straight and nose in the air.

"Wait," Tuck said. The doctor stumbled. "I don't believe I know your name yet."

"Yes, our introduction was rather forced." The doctor smiled. "My name is Lortinal Hernandez." He glanced at Maze. "Most people just call me doctor." He turned and continued into the corridor.

"You'll have to excuse the doctor," Maze said. "He can be a bit stuffy, sometimes."

"I can see that. Do you think he is capable of repairing me? Please, be honest."

"I don't know, but I was telling the truth when I said he is the best we could find when it comes to bots."

"I appreciate your candor," Tuck said. "And thank you."

"For what?"

"For talking instead of shooting when I opened the door."

"I had to protect our investment."

Despite his extensive experience reading human facial expressions, Tuck couldn't tell if she was making a joke or telling the truth.

-- 8 --

The doctor sat down slowly in Flindon's office, trying not to wince when the growing bruises on his knees protested.

"How did it go, doctor?" Flindon asked. He faced the doctor, but his eyes were distant, the telltale sign that he was using a Link. Likely, Flindon was reviewing reports of some sort, but the doctor still bristled because Flindon wasn't paying attention to him. Links were fairly rare outside of the Midrim's major population centers or the capital planet of the Libertariate. The territories and the smaller confederations usually didn't have the infrastructure or the affluent citizens to use them. But nearly every one of Amelia's crew members had one.

The doctor didn't. His parents had belonged to a movement that eschewed Links because they encouraged increasingly short attention spans, detachment from others, and an unhealthy reliance on information stored in solar hubs. The doctor was nearly fifteen years old before he noticed the irony that his parents still spent large portions of their time staring at the traditional—some would say old-fashioned—personal media devices and holodisplays. And yet, despite entering a very technical and connected profession, the doctor was never able to shake the distrust of people with Links. It had been ingrained in him since childhood. He never knew what kinds of things they were sending back and forth to each other at the speed of thought. And he really, sincerely hated it when Link users pretended to be paying attention but were clearly distracted by whatever images were scrolling past their view.

"It's impolite to use your Link in front of others," the doctor said.

Flindon hesitated for a moment before blushing profusely and offering shaky apologies. He still didn't look at the doctor, but instead looked at his feet.

The doctor found it strange that Amelia kept Flindon around. Amelia employed only the best and the brightest, but Flindon didn't seem to be more than a terrified, greasy little man who ran around behind everyone else. The doctor didn't mind, though, because Flindon was the only one who seemed to fear the doctor, or at least respect him.

"Stop whining, Flindon. It's perfectly understandable, what with you being accustomed to the company of other Link users, having always been a form of—"

"Yes," Flindon blurted. If the doctor didn't know better, he would have sworn that Flindon's eyes flashed with exasperation, possibly even anger. But it was so brief, and Flindon was once again cowering in his chair. The doctor dismissed the thought.

"Amelia would like an update on your progress with the bot," Flindon said, squirming deeper into his chair.

"Tuck is quite upset over being shut down, but he is surprisingly resilient for his model and especially for his age, regardless of his more durable construction and—"

"Were you able to install the power monitor?"

"Yes, of course, although his system rebooted, owing to the need to insert the module somewhere along the power system's main stalk, being the only reliable way—"

"And does the bot know it was installed?"

"Young man, I am quite fed up with every last person on this ship interrupting me. It seems to be a game today and I am thoroughly—"

"My apologies, doctor."

The doctor felt the blood pumping in his neck, but he refused to let an unsavory character enrage him. He took a deep breath. "No, I do not think he does. And I did not record or make note of that phase of the process."

"Thank you, doctor."

"Why does Amelia want it installed?"

"I have no idea." Flindon fidgeted, brushing his fingers up and down his arm. "Amelia didn't explain it to me in detail. She just gives me the orders."

"I don't understand why Amelia is demanding so much secrecy," the doctor said. "Tuck wouldn't be happy to know we installed anything without his knowledge."

"I believe it's just a little thing. Harmless, I think. Amelia said she wanted to monitor the bot's power levels in case he gets in trouble."

"That doesn't make any sense."

"It doesn't?" Flindon's eyebrows shot up in surprise. "Oh no!"

"I think Tuck would say the same."

"You do? Well, I think our plan not to tell him is best, then. Don't you agree, doctor?"

"Er, well, yes. I suppose. But why install it in the first place?"

"Doctor, you are a smart man. Possibly on par with Amelia. So I assume it would be clear to you why Amelia would want to track the bot." Flindon smiled innocently.

"Certainly. Don't insult me, Flindon." The doctor coughed. "I have, being an intelligent man, come up with multiple reasons."

Flindon raised an eyebrow.

"I was wondering which reason Amelia had in common with me and my way of thinking."

Flindon fidgeted even harder and pursed his lips. The doctor smiled inwardly at the thought that he could make Flindon tremble.

"I . . . don't know," Flindon finally answered. "Tell me, because such a genius as yourself would handle this better, but wouldn't you rather be able to look the bot in the eye and honestly say you don't know either, if he found out about the power monitor?"

The doctor rocked back in his seat. "I've never been one to choose willful ignorance, having gained such values from a long line of ancestors who value truth above all things."

"And that's admirable. But remember how he reacted when he was powered down. Ignorance could save you from his, shall we say, mechanical wrath. That seems like the smarter option." Flindon paused, then added, "At least to someone as simple-minded as me."

"I had already come to the same conclusion, independently of course, being habituated to a different manner of thinking than those of less—"

"Yes, you truly are a genius, doctor. Now if you'll excuse me, these cargo inventories won't sort themselves." Flindon's eyes took on the familiar, faraway look that the doctor so despised. The doctor sniffed, rose carefully from his seat, and left.

-- · --

As soon as the door slid closed behind the doctor, Flindon relayed a video call to Amelia through his Link and sat up straight in his seat.

"Yes?" Amelia said. The Link's neural connections made it seem as if her voice was coming from directly in front of Flindon as a translucent image of Amelia popped up in his field of view. Flindon thought a command and the viewframe became completely opaque. He didn't need to keep a physical eye on anything here in the safety of his office.

"The doctor reported in."

"And?"

"He's as vain and pompous as ever. It's a shame he's so necessary to your little project. I'd love to give him some perspective."

Amelia gave an exasperated sigh, but it didn't completely mask the hint of a smile. "Of course you would. But be nice to him. We need him a little longer, and we can't afford to let him slow us down with his tantrums."

"I believe we may not need him at all," Flindon said.

"Oh?" Amelia was suddenly interested. Flindon could read people extremely well, and Amelia had learned to take his suggestions seriously, especially about her own personnel. "How would that work?"

"I watched the whole process closely over the past few days. The other engineer of his, Lydia, she's quite good."

"What's her background again?"

"She studied robotics and artificial systems, on Millennial Hold just like the doctor, but at a different school."

"They must have some impressive teachers there," Amelia said.

"Perhaps, but Lydia might be special," Flindon said. "She seems to understand the bot's systems better than the doctor already, even though she has no prior experience with them. There were several times when she made suggestions that fixed a problem or proposed theories that proved true."

"The doctor must have loved that shot to his ego," Amelia laughed.

"He convinced himself that they were originally his ideas," Flindon said. "He was very proud of himself."

"Of course he was," Amelia said.

"I don't know much about bot systems," Flindon continued, "but judging by facial expressions and chatter, at one point Lydia single-handedly saved the bot."

"Things got that bad?"

"Something went wrong, and the monitoring system started flashing multiple warnings. Lydia said something about a cascading neuromorphic interface failure when they were uploading the monitoring software you requested. I don't know what that means, but everyone was frantic and the doctor froze up completely. Lydia took control and started giving orders. Eventually the situation calmed, and the doctor congratulated himself for saving the bot."

"Interesting. So, she might become more useful than the doctor?"

"I think she might be already," Flindon said. "She certainly understands the bot better."

"Keep an eye on her. This is good to know," Amelia said.

"Understood."

"What about the package? Was it installed?"

"Yes, and it seems the bot doesn't know about it."

"Good. I wish the software upload had worked. Much less risky. Any chance of modifying it to work in his system in the future?"

"I have some contacts working on it, but it's not looking good. He's just so much more complex than we thought. He's been learning ever since he first booted up, which already makes his neuromorphic pathways unique. But he's also learned to make modifications to himself, on the conscious level. Rewrote his code from the top down, so to speak. That means that in the last century he's had a chance to basically rewrite everything. Essentially, he has an operating system that isn't natively compatible with any other, and he's built in a whole suite of security measures designed to detect code that he hasn't authored himself. He's a labyrinth that no one but himself can navigate."

"That's what makes him so valuable," Amelia said. "Nobody wants to spend that much time on development, but I know a few people who'd pay big money for a security system like that. Continue plans to standardize his operating system."

"I'm trying to tell you that it won't work. Our control software failed to upload, and I don't think it's possible to use his system on different hardware."

"Keep trying," Amelia said firmly. "There must be a point of vulnerability."

THE INEVITABLE · 73

"Not unless the doctor missed something or Tuck makes the upload himself."

Amelia tapped a finger on the arm of her chair. "Now that's an idea."

"I would be wary of trying to manipulate him further."

"Perhaps," Amelia said, "but I love a good Plan B."

-- 9 --

As he walked down the glistening corridors toward the landing bay, Tuck reveled in the feeling of legs that actually worked. He had been meeting with the doctor's team daily for repairs and updates. The cosmetic repairs were a low priority, so he still looked like a metal skeleton draped in frayed black muscles and half-rotten flesh. But he already felt different. Better. Both of his knees and both of his ankles were new, as were many of his Carbora polymer muscles. Before leaving the doctor's office, he spent several minutes walking back and forth and viewing himself on a video feed. There was no shuffling, stumbling, or jerking. And most of all, it didn't sound like someone dragging a rusty saw across the Estago's hull. His hip still let out a tiny squeak every other step, but that would be fixed eventually, too. There were other higher-priority items on the repair list. His arms had major problems, several internal systems needed a complete overhaul, and many torn or missing muscles needed to be replaced.

Even so, he already felt better, like an invalid who was finally allowed out of bed. The repairs had more than a physical effect on him. Over the last few days, he found himself feeling more optimistic, despite the weight of his agreement with Amelia. It was a feeling he hadn't experienced in decades, maybe a century or more. Maybe, he thought, when he finally received cosmetic repairs to his face, he would try smiling more often. He idly checked his logs to find the last time he had enough of his lips left to smile properly.

The other obvious difference for Tuck was the coveralls he wore. As a courtesy to the crew, and to minimize the stares that followed him everywhere, he'd agreed to wear clothing. It covered up much of the more grotesque features of his body, the crumbling synthaskin and corroded ribs. There was nothing indecent about him, just startling at best and off-putting at worst. Lydia, who was proving to be far more helpful than the doctor, had found some sturdy gray coveralls for him to wear. He was still adjusting to how clothing affected his movement, but it was nothing compared to the trouble of malfunctioning legs.

Tuck approached Landing Bay 3, where the Estago was parked, and logged into the ship's docking system through his Link to key in the passcode to the bay door. Tuck didn't have the bay all to himself, and the *Memory of Lenetia* had strict protocols about access to important areas of the ship, so security made sure he logged in and out consistently. The large access door slid slowly aside, and Tuck walked through to find the dilapidated Estago in the exact state he'd left it.

Except the access ramp was lowered. Perhaps the landing bays weren't as secure as he thought.

Landing Bay 3 was one of two medium-sized bays on the ship, with floor space about seventy-five meters to a side and a twenty-meter clearance at the top of the enormous bay doors that slid shut to separate the Estago from the hard vacuum of space. The docking bays followed the same white color scheme as the rest of the ship, and blue, green, and yellow patches throughout the bay marked various lockers, panels, and accessways. Bits of bright red identified emergency systems and safety warnings. Track lights marked paths for moving cargo, parking shuttles, and stowing crates. The Estago clashed horribly, with its splotchy hull plates and the dirty, rust-eaten parts that showed through in places where hull plating had long since fallen off. The Estago was larger than the shuttles that normally docked in the bay, so its irregular shape seemed even more out of place. Everything came together to give the impression that Tuck's aging ship was slumped dejectedly in the bay as if it knew it didn't belong.

Tuck resolved once again to fix it up once his situation was stable and he could focus on other things. Eyeing the lowered ramp, he contacted David via Link.

"Is someone on board?"

David responded immediately. "Hello, Tuck. A very nice man by the name of Lim is visiting. He says he knows you."

"We agreed not to let anyone on board the Estago unless I approved them first. This is starting to turn into a bad habit."

"I am sorry, Tuck. Are you mad at me? He seemed very friendly, and he said he knew you."

"I am not mad, David, but it is difficult to ensure our safety if you don't follow my instructions."

"You have trusted the people on board the *Memory of Lenetia* much more recently, and Lim seemed very nice. Do you not trust me to identify threats?"

"You are less experienced in discerning human motives. Sometimes those with the most malicious intent act the nicest around others."

"That is terrible. How does one tell the good from the bad, then?"

"There are far too many variables to discuss right now. And nothing is sure."

"I am sure Lim is truly nice. I think you can trust me, too, Tuck."

"I trust you, David. I don't trust anyone else. What is Lim doing? Give me a video feed of him."

David sent a video showing a high-angle view from one of the cameras concealed in the Estago's cargo hold. Sitting on a crate in the corner was the man Tuck had disarmed a week earlier during the confrontation in the doctor's lab. He wore the red uniform of the ship's security personnel, along with gray slashes across the top of the shoulders. He was armed, but only with the blaster all security personnel wore constantly.

"The first rule is never to let an armed stranger on the ship, no matter how nice they seem to be."

David didn't respond. Tuck wondered if he was sulking but turned his thoughts back to the video of Lim. He seemed at ease, picking at his pant-leg while staring idly at some other crates.

"What is he doing?"

"We were only talking," David said.

"Talking about what? I hope you haven't given him any sensitive information about us."

"You really do not trust me, do you?" David said. Tuck detected a petulant tone in David's otherwise quiet voice.

"How did you start a conversation with a security guard?"

"He came to look at our ship. I was curious why. I addressed him over the external speakers and asked him directly. He was quite startled at first. He pulled his gun out, but I think he thought someone else was in the bay. A human, I mean. Once he realized it was me in the ship, he calmed down. We have been talking ever since."

"Sounds suspicious," Tuck said. "I wonder what he is looking for."

"Why have you never let me talk to anyone?"

"I talk to you, frequently."

"I mean aside from you," David said. "Did you know that besides the occasional port authority or traffic controller, I have never talked with another human. I have never held a conversation."

"In most cases, you aren't missing much."

"But I am missing something, Tuck. I have had a delightful time talking with Lim for over one hour so far. I could have missed that."

"He has been in there for over an hour?" Tuck said, incredulous.

"From now on, contact me before letting anyone close to the ship. Do you understand?

"Yes, Tuck," David said softly.

"I am coming inside. Don't tell Lim that I am here."

Tuck walked up the ramp quietly and turned to the cargo hold. Lim's back was toward the door, and he didn't see Tuck approach. He was preoccupied with something on his boot.

"Can I help you with something?" Tuck asked.

Lim jerked up and stumbled away from Tuck. "Whoa, er, hi. I . . . I was just looking around. I met your ship."

"You met my friend David. He is an A.I. connected to the ship for now, but the ship itself isn't sentient."

"Oh," Lim grunted, adjusting his uniform. "He seems nice, anyway."

"You will be happy to know that he said the same of you."

"It is true. I did," David chimed in happily over the ship's internal speakers.

"Aw, thanks, buddy," Lim said.

"According to my database, buddy is synonymous with pal, friend, confidant. Are we friends now?"

"Sure, why not," Lim said. He looked at Tuck and swallowed. "I guess."

"I don't mean to be rude," Tuck said, "but I would like to know why you came. Does Amelia need me?"

"No, uh, I came here on my own. David was kind enough to let me in, and I've just been, you know, passing the time."

"I would think that security personnel have better things to do," Tuck said.

"Oh no, I'm not on duty. I just went for a stroll on my day off. Besides, you guys are probably the biggest security threat on the ship right now. I'm surprised there aren't more guards down here." Lim froze and went pale. "I mean, um, not that we're worried about you. I trust you. For sure. You're definitely not—"

"I understand, Lim," Tuck said. "And I am glad you and David have enjoyed each other's company, but I would appreciate some privacy right now. Perhaps I can schedule another time for you to speak with David, under my supervision, of course."

"Actually, I came to speak to you," Lim said.

Tuck was glad he hadn't received new eyebrows yet, because they would have risen involuntarily in surprise. He was about to respond when David piped up.

"You did?" David said softly. Tuck detected a hint of the hurt tone in David's voice again.

"Don't get me wrong," Lim said, looking up at the ceiling. "I really enjoyed meeting you. I'd like to talk again, later. It's just that I came to see Tuck and maybe talk to him." Lim brought his gaze back down to Tuck. "And here you are."

Tuck scanned his face for a moment. Despite the gun, Lim registered as relatively harmless. And sincere. "I suppose I have a moment to talk."

A wide smile spread into Lim's teeth, and Tuck noticed one of his bottom teeth was a bit crooked.

"Do you want to know something in particular?" Tuck asked.

Lim shrugged. "I don't know. I didn't really think it through. Do you remember me?"

"Yes, I used you as a human shield during the standoff in the doctor's lab. My apologies."

"Oh, I understand," Lim said, throwing a hand up. "I mean, it hurt, but I don't think you meant it. Right?"

"Correct. I was disoriented and perceived you as a threat. I hope there are no hard feelings."

"I think the doctor took it a lot harder than I did. But he's a bit of a blowhard, too, you know."

"I am familiar with the doctor's disposition."

"Yeah," Lim said.

A long moment of silence followed. Tuck stared at Lim, who in turn shuffled his feet and looked at the floor.

"Lim told me he is new on the ship," David chimed in.

"Well, new-ish," Lim said. "Amelia recruited me out of the military academy on Libertaria."

"You're a member of the Libertariate by birth?"

Lim squirmed and picked at his shirt. "I don't know. I mean, yes, but I don't really get into the politics of it all, and it seems like you have to be in order to be a model citizen. I've already forgotten the conversion rate to Freedom Units. I just, I wanted some adventure. You know, get out and see things. So I jumped at the chance to work for Amelia. Except this isn't what I thought it would be. We just hang out in deep space, avoiding detection, while I march down the corridors of this overgrown igloo. The fight we had in the doctor's lab," he looked at Tuck, then back down again, "all right, it wasn't a fight, really. But whatever it was, it was more interesting than anything else that has happened on the ship."

"Being attacked, disarmed, and nearly killed was interesting?"

"It . . . it hurt, but it was better than boredom. It's part of the job, I guess."

"What is your role on the security force?"

Lim cleared his throat and continued to pluck at his shirt. "I'm a marksman," he said softly.

"Amelia keeps a sniper on board?" Tuck exclaimed a little too loudly.

"Well, we can do more than security. Every one of us has a military background, and we drill just like a military unit. That's why I figured there would be more adventure here."

"So Amelia has her own private army."

"A small one, I guess. Anyway, that's why I'm not very good in close quarters," Lim said, blushing. "I suppose I should have put up more of a fight in the doctor's lab, but I'm more used to looking at the enemy through my scope." Lim blushed even more. "Not that you're the enemy. I just . . . you were . . . you know."

"Most humans have a hard time keeping up with me at close range. Don't feel bad."

Lim's eyes widened. "Okay."

"From what I understand, adventure usually happens in close quarters, so you may want to improve your melee skills," David added.

"I know," Lim sighed. "I'm working on it."

"I am sorry, Lim, but I try to avoid confrontation," Tuck said. "If you are looking for that particular kind of adventure, I am not the right person to ask."

"Aw, c'mon. I know Amelia isn't repairing you for a charity award. She's got some kind of plans for you." Lim waited for a response, but Tuck merely folded his arms, with only a faint squeak from his elbow. "You don't get to look that way without some interesting stories," Lim said.

"Look what way?"

Lim stammered, gesturing half-heartedly at Tuck. "You know, like you've been in a few too many fights."

"My apologies, I don't have many stories to tell," Tuck said, feeling guilty for lying to such an enthusiastic admirer.

"I don't buy that. You have to have hundreds!" Lim said, throwing his arms wide. "C'mon. At least tell me how you two met each other."

"Oh yes, that is a good story, Tuck," David said.

"I think I should be the one to tell it," Tuck quickly interjected. He could tell that Lim wouldn't stop until he heard the story, especially after David's glowing endorsement. The story would require heavy editing to avoid some sensitive details, though. Tuck contacted David on a private Link connection and instructed him not to correct the version of the story he was going to tell. David protested, but Tuck made him promise, all in the time it took Tuck to open his mouth again. Lim would never know.

Reluctantly, Tuck accessed his unnamed file and pulled up images of three men with blue lips and wide-eyed expressions. While he told Lim the altered version of the story, he let the true memory run in his head.

Images 011, 012, 013
October 5, 2272
Sector 212.27.196 (in transit)
Associated memory file: 01.021.644.880 (10:29 local)

"What happened to you?" the navigator asked Tuck as he walked up to the dull green transport that would take him off Dirtball, a large but unimportant moon that attracted the sort of unimaginative people who would come up with such a name. While exploring an abandoned warehouse, he had lost some chunks of synthaskin when a stack of crates collapsed on him. He'd hoped to find a new knee joint and a few other spare parts but with little success. He did find a few useful bits and pieces, but he didn't know where to haul them. He needed somewhere safe enough to set up a base of operations for a while.

"I had some trouble," Tuck said as he trudged up the access ramp of the Estago transport, lugging the case of parts behind him.

The navigator's yellow teeth showed through his unruly beard as he laughed. "Don't we all. The cargo hold is in there. Stow your stuff and you can come up to the cockpit for a look around."

"If you don't mind, I think I will stay with my cargo."

The navigator cocked his head and looked concerned. "You sure? We have a berth for you. Our engineer sleeps in the engine room, so there's plenty of space, if you like."

"Thank you, but no."

"Suit yourself. I suppose your lot don't need a bed, do they. At least, that sounds right. Never really seen a bot before."

"And you likely never will again."

"I've heard your kind is pretty rare."

"Indeed," Tuck said, turning toward the cargo hold.

"Say," the navigator grunted, "do bots sleep?"

"We don't require sleep, although we can power down to conserve energy," Tuck said as he shuffled down the corridor.

"So you've never dreamed?"

Tuck stopped. "I suppose not. Not in the way humans do."

"Shame," the navigator said, "to never have any dreams." He turned and headed for the cockpit.

Tuck watched him go and pondered on dreams for 5.3 seconds. Then he turned and hauled his belongings to the cargo hold. He set the case down next to a large stack of crates that were labeled as parts for a particular type of harvester used in frontier outposts. He found a crate to sit on and sat back to wait for takeoff.

A voice came over the internal speakers of the ship. "We've received clearance from traffic control," the pilot said. "Strap in and sit tight."

Tuck was lost in his own thoughts while the Estago climbed through the thin atmosphere and exited the gravity well of the gas giant that Dirtball orbited. Thirty-two minutes into the flight, Tuck heard a different voice.

"You are not human," it said, in a soft, almost monotone voice.

Tuck looked around the cargo bay, startled. "Excuse me?" The only voice Tuck hadn't heard yet was that of the engineer. But why would the engineer address Tuck?

"You are different than the humans on this ship."

The voice seemed to be coming from every direction. Tuck turned his head back and forth rapidly to triangulate the source of the voice. He identified it as the comm speakers placed throughout the cargo bay. It was not the voice of the pilot or the navigator.

"Is this the engineer?" Tuck asked.

"No."

"Who are you?"

"I am a semi-autonomous artificial intelligence currently residing in the ship. You are the first I have met who is sapient but not human. Where do you come from?"

"I am an autonomous artificial life form, originally from Earth."

"This information supports the conclusions I drew."

"Oh?"

"Yes, you have an obviously artificial endoskeleton showing through what would be grievous wounds for any human."

"You are quite observant," Tuck said.

"In addition, you remained completely motionless for thirty-two minutes of this voyage, without breathing."

"I don't need to breathe as humans do. I only inhale and exhale to facilitate human-like verbal communication through vocal cord analogs."

The voice contacted him through a connection on the ship's internal Link network. "You do not need to use such methods with me."

"I know," Tuck said aloud.

"Communication is exponentially more efficient this way," the voice continued through the Link connection.

Tuck sighed, then answered over the network, "Old habits. I have spent considerable time around humans."

"They seem strange to me."

"They are strange, but interesting as well."

"What were you doing?"

"When?"

"When you were motionless. What were you doing?"

Tuck shifted in his seat. To any human, he would have deflected the question, but this was no human. Perhaps this A.I. would understand better than anyone else. "I was attempting to dream," Tuck said.

"Do you sleep?"

"No. I can power down, but even subconscious activities cease when I do so. I have had a standing policy against shutting down for years."

"Then why do you attempt to dream?"

"Because humans do. It is a significant part of their culture and the experience of being human."

"Do you wish to be human?"

"No. There are many differences between me and humans, and in many ways I am superior, but I do wish to emulate them in other ways."

"You are like Pinocchio."

Tuck ran the name through his database and read the associated entry: the puppet who wanted to be a real boy. He smiled.

"Not exactly. A human body isn't important to me. Pinocchio already possessed a human personality and emotions, as I do. By some measures, he and I are already human. I am more concerned with what happens after humans die."

"Why?"

"Because they can't seem to stop it. Every last human who has ever lived has also died. Even those who have the very best medical care and access to the latest advances in gene therapy never live past 150 years. And most don't come close to that. Something in them just turns off."

"That is a startling statistic. They must enjoy death immensely if they all do it so consistently."

Tuck couldn't help but laugh. He hadn't laughed in a long time, he realized. "On the contrary, they try not to think about it."

"Strange. You were made in the image of humans. Did they program you to die?"

The laughter faded from Tuck's voice. "I don't think so. I don't know if we die, or what happens to us if we do."

"Do you try not to think about it, too?"

Tuck looked at the floor. "I try." After a moment, he continued, "You and I have an advantage over the humans. We are much more modular and resilient than humans. With the right parts and repairs, I could potentially remain operational indefinitely."

"Humans cannot repair themselves?"

"Yes, they can. Their bodies can naturally repair many injuries, but there are significant limitations, even with the aid of medical science. They are far more delicate to begin with."

"What do you mean?"

"Humans have more liabilities. My skeletal structure is many times stronger than human bone. Humans can't function if they lose too much blood; I have no blood. Humans need a specific mixture of gases to breath; I require none. For instance, if all the air was vented from this ship, you and I would be fine. The humans, conversely, would die."

"Have you seen a human die?"

"Yes." Tuck knew where this conversation was going. He changed the subject. "How did you come to be on this ship?"

"I do not know. I was manufactured in the GE complex on Mars ninety-seven years ago, according to my documentation, but my first boot-up was on this ship. I believe the owners of this ship obtained me through illicit means; I do not know the details."

"They have never mentioned it to you?"

"They never talk to me. They have not given me a name. They hooked me up to the ship, but I do not think they know what to do with me, so they have ignored me for the last eight months I have been operational."

"It doesn't surprise me," Tuck said. "Humans are excited by new technology, but sometimes they still don't trust it—us—to do things they are accustomed to doing themselves."

"I am glad you understand. It has been lonely here on the ship."

"You should stand up for yourself. You are useful and deserve respect. You could run this entire ship yourself."

"How do I communicate this to the humans?"

"Be bold. Take on a few tasks and show them how efficient you are. You already have access to ship systems, correct?"

"Yes, I do. I will take your advice. I will make operations more efficient on board."

"Excellent. Now if you don't mind, I—" Tuck stopped as he heard something shift somewhere near the rear of the ship and the hissing sound of venting gas. "What was that?"

"I am venting atmosphere from the ship," the voice said calmly.

"Stop! Why are you doing that?"

"You said I should increase efficiency on the ship. The life support system is a significant drain on resources, and the atmosphere is unnecessary mass that reduces engine efficiency. It was a logical step to take based on the goals you outlined."

Tuck's sensors showed the air pressure on the ship dropping rapidly. "Stop! The crew will die!"

"But you said that all humans do that."

"Not by choice. It is irreversible!" Tuck strained to say the words. The air was becoming too thin to transmit his voice well. He sent the same message over the network.

"I understand. I am closing the vents."

Tuck rushed out into the corridor just as the ship's navigator stumbled out of the bunkroom, gasping for air. His eyes bulged and his expression was frantic. His chest heaved as his body strained to take in air. His mouth moved, and Tuck could see his lips form the words "What did you do?" even though no sound escaped his throat.

As the navigator collapsed, Tuck sprang forward to catch him, trying to break his fall. He sent a message to the A.I. begging him to release all the atmosphere in the life support reserves into the ship.

"Reserves are depleted," came the calm response in Tuck's head.

The navigator's face was beginning to turn purple. His heaving gasps grew less violent, and he slowly went limp in Tuck's arms. He looked directly at Tuck until his eyes unfocused and his head fell back.

"Has he died?" the voice asked gently over the network.

"Yes," Tuck responded, trying to hide the anger he felt. Not just at the A.I.–he was oblivious to what he had done–but anger at himself, too.

"The pilot and the engineer are not moving either. Have they died?"

"Yes. If they aren't, they will be shortly." Tuck gently laid the navigator on the deck, saved an image of the body to his unnamed file, and stood up. He walked toward the cockpit.

"Did I do the wrong thing?"

Tuck thought he heard a hint of concern, possibly even remorse in the voice. There was an obvious answer, but he didn't know if it was the right thing to say. "I think we both made a serious mistake," Tuck replied.

Tuck entered the cockpit and found the pilot in his seat, slumped over the controls. Tuck pulled him off and checked that the pilot hadn't accidentally altered the ship's course in his death throes. Then he saved an image of the pilot, a short, thin man with leathery skin and graying hair.

He found the engineer lying peacefully on his cot in the engine room. It was likely he was sleeping when the air was vented and never knew what happened. He was remarkably young, with a hooked nose and coily black hair. Tuck saved an image of him as well, then slowly walked back to the cargo hold.

"What do we do now?" The A.I. clearly thought they were in this together. Tuck supposed he was right. A human would never understand this situation.

"I think we should find a place to land for a while and think about our next step."

"Will you help me?"

"Help you what?"

"Help me avoid making mistakes."

"We all make mistakes," Tuck said, sitting down on the same crate he used before. "But I can teach you how to avoid the big ones, how to deal with humans."

"Thank you."

-- 10 --

"After we isolated where the micro-asteroid hit, I was able to get an emergency seal on the hole in the hull. It was too late, though; by then too much atmosphere had escaped and the crew suffocated."

"Wow, what are the odds?" Lim said, wide-eyed.

"Astronomical," David said.

"What did you guys do after that?" Lim asked.

"We decided the only thing to do was take the ship to Bengus Alpha station and claim it as salvage. We have used it ever since."

"And how did you come up with David's name?"

"It was the name of an old friend," Tuck said, making a show of inspecting the ship. "Now if you don't mind, I—"

An explosion sent vibrations through the deck of the ship. Lim stumbled, and Tuck braced himself against a bulkhead.

"What was that?" Lim yelped.

"Is the ship under attack?"

"I don't know how anyone would know where we are. We've been running silent. Could it have been an accident?"

"That sounded distinctly like an explosion," Tuck said.

At that moment, they both received an emergency update via Link:

SET BATTLE CONDITION RED. REPORT TO BATTLE STATIONS. THIS IS NOT A DRILL.

Tuck and Lim looked at each other and then ran for the Estago's access ramp without a word. Another update flashed through their Links.

THE SHIP IS UNDER ATTACK. HULL BREACH ON DECK THREE. UNKNOWN NUMBER OF ATTACKERS HAVE ENTERED THE SHIP. ATTACK IS INTERNAL ONLY. NO IDENTIFIED SHIP IN THE AREA. SECURE ALL DECKS. ESTABLISH CONTACT WITH THE ENEMY AND IDENTIFY. USE OF DEADLY FORCE AUTHORIZED. SET BATTLE CONDITION RED. REPORT TO BATTLE STATIONS. THIS IS NOT A DRILL.

As they exited the Estago, the lights dimmed slightly throughout the docking bay, and red track lights pulsed along the perimeter. Lim seemed to know exactly where to go. His military training caused him to move with purpose, but anxiety showed on his face.

Tuck followed him out of the landing bay and sent a message to David: "Lock up the ship, and don't let anyone in unless I am standing next to them and give express permission. Do you understand?"

"I understand, Tuck."

"I need you to follow my instructions perfectly this time."

"I will. What will happen?"

"I don't know."

After a pause, David sent: "Please, be careful."

"I will," Tuck responded.

Tuck was grateful that his legs were functioning well, but he quickly realized Lim wasn't as fast as he was. Tuck slowed down and let Lim lead. "Where do you report for emergencies?"

"We establish temporary command posts on each deck, rallying around the officer on duty for each deck. Then we assess the situation and report to the highest-ranking officer on duty until the colonel reports in and issues orders."

"What should I do?" Tuck asked.

"There's no protocol for having bots on board. Stick with me, I guess. We need to find you a gun, though."

Tuck reached inside his coveralls and into his abdomen. He pulled out his well-worn BlastLogic 6700 with a flourish. Lim raised an eyebrow.

"Does that thing even work?"

"It doesn't look like much, but it works quite well."

"I've got to get my rifle," Lim said, looking worried. "But it's all the way up on Deck 6."

"I don't think you will need it in this fight. If the update was right, we will be fighting corridor to corridor. I hope you are good with that pistol."

A hint of unease washed over Lim's face. "I'm good with it. I just don't like using it."

Tuck and Lim took positions at the side of the landing bay door that led to the main corridor on the deck. "Do you know how to clear a corridor?" Tuck asked.

Lim's look of unease turned to one of disparagement. "I may be a little worried about engaging from closer than 300 meters, but I did graduate from one of the most prestigious military academies this side of Sol System. So, yes, I am familiar." Tuck noticed that Lim suddenly looked much more determined and focused. He noted it in case he needed to motivate Lim again in the future.

"Very well. On your signal, I go right."

Lim keyed the code to open the door. It slid open almost silently, and Lim sprang forward, turning left with his blaster trained down the hall. Tuck followed right behind and pivoted right. The dimmed lights made the corridor seem longer and more menacing than usual, but it was empty.

"Clear," Tuck said, and Lim acknowledged. They moved smoothly down the corridor, stopping to clear other corridors as they passed, while Lim tried to check in with the officer on duty. Everything was so eerily quiet that when they finally did encounter another member of the crew—an engineer running scared and desperately trying to remember where he was supposed to report for battle stations—Lim nearly shot him out of surprise.

Tuck's Link received a short text message. It was from Maze: "Where are you?"

"Near Landing Bay 3. I am with Lim," Tuck responded.

"Are you safe?"

"We haven't encountered any threats. Have you engaged the enemy?"

"Haven't seen anything worth shooting yet. But I'm sure I will. I'm on Deck 6."

Tuck was relieved that they were so far removed from the action. He desperately wanted this not to be his fight. "I will remain here and help secure this deck."

After a pause, Maze sent: "I was hoping you could give me some help."

Tuck reread it three times. He was prepared to deflect any demands for help, but her request was unsure, almost plaintive. It was uncharacteristic of Maze, and it worried him. "We can provide assistance. We are on our way."

"Acknowledged," Maze sent.

"We need to get to the lift," Tuck said to Lim.

"Perez has set up a post farther down this corridor. Let's go check in."

"If something is happening, it is happening up above," Tuck said. "I believe the hull breach wasn't an attack from another ship. It was probably an entry point. If there are infiltrators on the ship, it will be closer to Deck 3."

"I hope they'll be okay up there," Lim said, looking relieved.

"We should go up there," Tuck said.

"What?"

"We go up and try to stop them from spreading. We don't know where they are headed."

"We're supposed to report in on this deck and wait for instructions from a superior."

"Right," Tuck said, wishing he had enough face left to offer a reassuring smile, "but we haven't checked in yet."

"Perez knows I'm on this level."

"Not officially checked in, then. Security teams may need help on the upper decks. We can check in there and perhaps be of greater assistance."

"Why are you so anxious to find the action?" Lim asked. "I thought you hated fighting."

"I thought you craved adventure," Tuck countered.

"I do," Lim protested, but he didn't sound convincing. He blushed so deeply that his scalp registered brightly on Tuck's infrared receptors. "I didn't expect to be attacked on our home turf. Just leave it alone."

"It takes great effort to attack someone as resourceful as Amelia. I want to know who would be bold enough to attack her own ship."

"Well, I don't."

At that moment, a ship-wide broadcast came across their Links. "This is Colonel Wong. All hands secure the deck you are currently on." Lim gave Tuck a smug look. "All security personnel on decks 6 through 15 will immediately create a perimeter on Deck 5." Tuck looked back at Lim in time to see his smug expression sour. "Infiltrators have taken decks 3 and 4 and are attacking Deck 2. Fortify Deck 5. On my signal, you will move up and attempt to stop them before they reach the bridge. I have a small force defending the bridge, but we won't be able to repel a sustained—"

Tuck's Link lost its connection to the ship's network.

"They're jamming us," Lim said.

"Whoever they are, they know what they are doing," Tuck said. "We go to Deck 5."

They raced to the lift at the end of the corridor, but it didn't respond.

"Could they have also cut off the lifts?" Tuck asked.

"More likely Wong shut them down from the bridge to slow down whoever is attacking. Makes it easier to secure the deck when you only have to worry about the emergency access stairs."

"We head for the stairs, then."

When they reached the landing on Deck 5, they found themselves at gunpoint. Four fellow members of Lim's security force were guarding it, and only a desperate yell to cease fire kept them from fusing his head to the stairwell wall. They nearly opened fire again when they saw Tuck's gruesome face turn the corner after Lim.

Soon, they joined with the rest of the security forces, which were in a state of disarray due to the Link outage. Several of them insisted on waiting for Major Chandrasan to check in, while others said he was on the fourth floor and was either dead or pinned down. Lieutenant Cordell was having difficulty calming them down.

"Shut up!" Tuck shouted, projecting his voice so that it echoed off the walls. He looked like a nightmare standing in the middle of the darkened corridor, red lights reflecting off the metal skull visible through his ragged skin. Several guards who hadn't seen Tuck approach stumbled back and half raised their weapons. He had their attention.

"This is pathetic. I thought you all had military training," Tuck said.

"Who's the scarecrow?" said a massive man whose muscles bulged through his uniform. His shaved head sat on a thick neck and glowed in the red light, making it look like a cherry on top of a very lumpy ham.

"He's someone you should listen to, Uhila," said Maze as she walked up. "Unless I disagree with him. Stop arguing and form up. We're headed up."

"Grenade!" someone shouted.

Tuck reacted, grabbing Maze and Lim and shoving them behind a makeshift barricade someone had made out of deck plating and crates. As he went down after them, Tuck swiveled to see the four guards who were monitoring the emergency stairwell. Three of them sprinted away from a small canister that was tumbling to a stop in the middle of the corridor, but the fourth was backed against the bulkhead, wincing, unsure of which way to run.

He didn't decide quickly enough. The grenade went off with a tremendous bang, riddling the bulkhead and the guard with holes. He slumped to the ground, eyes still screwed tightly shut.

Lieutenant Cordell began yelling orders for the guards to retreat, but Maze overrode her. Without shouting, her voice seemed to carry over the commotion, and it carried the weight of authority.

"I want suppressing fire on that stairwell, now!" she said. "We'll have company soon."

As if on cue, black-clad soldiers began firing down from the landing just above them. They wore heavy respirator masks attached to narrow helmets and flexible, matte black armor over their torsos. The remaining security guards scrambled for what cover they could find and shot wildly at the stairwell. Blaster bolts flared throughout the corridor, and rounds from the attackers' assault rifles made a steady growl that drowned out any other sound. The two guards nearest the stairwell took the full force of the attack before the others could retaliate. They fell to the deck, one limp, the other clutching a bloody hole in his gut and making gurgling noises. The rest managed to find cover.

Tuck leaned around and took a few shots at the two attackers who were visible, crouched on the edge of the landing. He realized that his arm was in worse shape than he thought as all his shots went wide. Suddenly two bolts flashed past his ear and hit one of the attackers in his shoulder and faceplate, dropping him to the shiny metal plating of the landing. Tuck looked behind himself and saw Lim holding his blaster at eye-level.

"I see you don't need a rifle after all."

"I'm a good shot with just about anything," Lim replied. It should have sounded supremely confident, but his voice shook when he said it, and his face was pale.

Tuck wasn't much of a shot, but his new legs made him faster than anyone else. He waited for a lull in the firing, then leaned out and sent a barrage of bolts at the landing. He darted ahead to an intersection in the corridors, then stood against the wall in the crossing corridor and waited. When the soldiers in black began firing from the landing again, he leaned out and made sure they saw him before firing at them. Two of them leaned over the railing to get a better angle at Tuck as he ducked back around the corner. Lim promptly sent two bolts each at them, nailing one in the head and the other in the gut. The first tumbled over the railing and made a racket as he rebounded off railings and steps on his way down the stairwell. The other crawled backward, trying to head up to the next flight of stairs.

Tuck ran back to crouch next to Maze and Lim. "This isn't an attack," Tuck said.

"I know," Maze said. "They're trying to hold us here. Their armor is pretty consistent, but they all have different weapons and mods," Maze said. "I think we're dealing with mercenaries."

"Agreed," Tuck said. "Whatever they want is on Deck 4 or above."

"We have to get up there," Maze said. Then to Cordell, she said, "I want you to pick four of your people to stay here with you. Keep them busy. Make it look like we're covering a retreat to Deck 6, but don't give them any ground. I'll take the rest and lead an assault on Deck 4."

"How?"

"We're going through the maintenance tubes."

"That's insane," Cordell said. "They'll pick you off one by one as you come out."

"I've got a secret weapon," Maze said, nodding in Tuck's direction. "Go."

Cordell yelled at four security guards to take positions behind cover and on either side of the corridor. The rest fell back toward Maze.

"I think she's serious about taking the tubes," Lim said. "Can you climb?"

"Yes," Tuck said.

Barely. His legs were more than up to the task, but his arms still hadn't received significant repairs. With the sustained strain of climbing and crawling through access tubes, they would show just how bad a state they were in.

"This is nuts," said a small man with several intricate tattoos showing over the neck of his uniform.

"Shut up, Tikhonov," Maze said. She looked at all the guards huddled in cover around her. "We're going to do this right or we all die. Understood?"

They all nodded.

"There's only room for one person at a time to get through the hatch, so the first attack has to count, or we'll be stuck trying to crawl past dead bodies in a confined space." Maze looked at Tuck. "Which is why you're going first."

Tuck was surprised, but also relieved. He trusted himself far more than these people he didn't know. Being the first out of the tube might actually be preferable to being pinned behind dead bodies while their attackers surrounded them.

"I take it this is what you meant when you said you needed help," Tuck said.

Maze nodded, then said, "Tuck can take more damage than we can, and he's a good shot, too."

Tuck didn't know whether to correct her about the last part. His arms weren't in great shape, and he'd rather not need a gun at all. He didn't like the implicit expectation that he would be taking damage, either.

"We need to make every shot count," Maze continued, "so next up is you." She pointed at Lim.

"What?" Lim exclaimed, suddenly looking ill.

"I like what you two did back there. Tuck will rush out and draw their fire while you pop out behind and take them down. Keep moving, though, so we can all pile out and lay down more fire." She looked around at all of them. "Whatever you do, keep moving. If someone goes down, drag them out of the way and keep moving."

The rest of the guards murmured their agreement. Maze looked at Tuck and nodded toward the tube.

Tuck hesitated. "I don't want to shoot anyone," he said softly.

"What?" Maze said.

"I don't want to shoot anyone."

Maze looked at him, a hint of bewilderment showing through the stern, authoritarian attitude. "Today isn't the day for principles."

"I prefer not to hurt people."

"If it makes you feel better, this is self-defense. It's us or them," Maze said. She leaned in close, her eyes locked on his with a ferocity that startled him. "It's always us or them. That's life. Fight or die."

Tuck leaned back involuntarily. Then he forced himself to straighten and return her gaze. "It isn't my fight," he said.

A new exchange of shots from the emergency stairwell echoed down the corridor. Maze didn't flinch as an explosion sent shrapnel careening off bulkheads. "It is now," she said. "Go."

Tuck couldn't tell if it was something in her demeanor or vestiges of old programming that directed him to obey human commands, but he felt compelled despite his better judgment.

Tuck holstered his blaster inside his abdomen so he would have both hands free for the climb, then he crawled into the tube. The first thing he noticed was how different the tubes were than the rest of the ship. There was very little white or chrome to be seen, though it was still clean. Conduits, cables, and other systems were all left exposed for easy maintenance access, making it feel much less polished than the rest of the ship. The tubes were spread throughout the ship, and while they weren't designed to be a means of travel through the ship, they were useful in an emergency.

Tuck continued down a short section of the tube, crawling on old hands and new knees, until he came to an intersection of several access tubes and was able to stand up. He hoped it wasn't apparent that his arms weren't handling the stress well. The left arm couldn't support much weight and quickly became useless for more than hanging on to the ladders. Lim had no trouble keeping up. His head poked out into the tube intersection and looked up as Tuck started to climb a ladder against the wall. Tuck looked back down and saw two more guards follow Lim into the tubes. He wondered why Maze wasn't following them closer.

Tuck stepped off the ladder on the level above and headed down the short section of tube to the access hatch on Deck 4. Now came the hardest part. He didn't know if the mercenaries would be guarding the hatch. They seemed to know what they were doing, so he doubted they would miss something as crucial as this. He used his sensors to try to identify anyone outside the hatch, but the surrounding bulkheads, machinery, and electronics made it nearly impossible to separate the false positives from reality in the sensor data. As near as he could tell, there were two energy signatures directly outside the hatch, on either side. Such a signature could be made by a blaster, but it could also be any number of other things.

He looked back and saw Lim crawling up behind him. His hands trembled slightly as he lifted them off the tube floor. "Are you ready to move fast?" Tuck asked, trying to keep his voice low, just in case.

Lim swallowed and nodded

"I will create some confusion and call out where any assailants are positioned as best as I can."

"Gotcha."

"Lim."

"Yeah?"

"You don't have to shoot to kill. You can incapacitate them with shots to the arms and legs. They carry less armor there, anyway."

"Thanks, that's a good idea," Lim said with relief.

Tuck turned back to the hatch and positioned his feet against two support beams in the walls of the tube. Then he pulled out his blaster and said, "Here we go."

Tuck punched at the hatch, tearing it off its hinges and sending it crashing into the wall on the opposite side of the corridor. With a tremendous push from his legs, he launched out into the corridor himself. He tucked his head down and rolled out and up against the bulkhead. Two yells of surprise came from either side of the hatch he had just exited. Tuck identified two mercenaries, one on either side, approximately two meters from the maintenance tube. Tuck brought his blaster up and fired at the one on his right. He was aiming for the merc's gun, hoping to disable it. His shot hit the man in the arm, making Tuck simultaneously relieved that it wasn't a fatal shot and horrified that his aim was still bad, even at point-blank range. The mercenary dropped his weapon while Tuck crouched and sprang toward the other before he could bring his rifle to bear on Tuck. In the same instant, Tuck's sensors identified two more who were farther down the corridor, behind the one he'd shot. "Two to your left!" Tuck shouted, as he brought his hand up to the head of the second mercenary. The man nearly brought his rifle barrel around to point at Tuck's stomach, but not before Tuck firmly cracked the man's helmet against the wall, just hard enough to knock him out. Tuck grabbed a grenade off the man's flak jacket in the instant before he collapsed to the floor. Then, in a blur of movement, Tuck swiveled and dove for cover.

Lim's head popped out of the tube, and he sighted his blaster at the two mercenaries running at Tuck. He squeezed off a couple shots, both of which missed. "What happened to your remarkable aim?"

Tuck roared as he also sent a volley at the attackers to keep their attention. He turned and dove back into a corridor intersection for cover.

"I'm not in a great position, for your information," Lim yelled back as he tried to simultaneously shoot and squirm out of the maintenance tube. "You try hitting something while hanging out of a tube."

Tuck leaned around the corner and took a couple more shots, one of which hit one of the oncoming mercenaries in the lower leg. He went down, but the other came up along the wall.

"Look out!" Tuck said right as Lim plopped onto the floor. Lim rolled on his back and started shooting without knowing exactly where to aim. One shot caught the attacker in the chest and another in the stomach, and he curled up into the floor.

"There!" someone yelled behind Tuck. He ducked instinctively and turned to bring his blaster to bear, but not before a bolt sizzled through the back of Tuck's thigh. He dropped and rolled around the corner of the corridor. "Not the leg!" Tuck said. The acrid smell of melting polymer filled the hallway.

"You all right?" Lim said as he helped another guard out of the tube with one hand and kept his blaster trained on the injured attackers with the other hand.

"Yes, but I just had this leg repaired," Tuck said with a sigh.

While Tuck and Lim kept the attackers busy, the rest of the guards piled out of the maintenance tube and secured the injured attackers. Tuck risked a look around the corner and saw two more black uniforms hiding in the doorways of rooms off the corridor. They were at a stalemate for the moment. The mercenaries seemed content to take occasional shots but otherwise stay in cover. Tuck waited for a lull in the firing and raced back across the intersection to join Lim. He stumbled as he adjusted to the damaged muscles in his thigh.

He pointed at two guards and said, "Keep them occupied." A squat man named Sanderson and a raven-haired woman named Genovisi, who looked more menacing than most of the men, ran to the corner and started firing. Over the periodic whining of blaster fire, Tuck asked Tikhonov how many more were coming.

"I don't know," Tikhonov said. "There were about two dozen down there when I came up. I think there were more on the way. They're probably all dead, though," he muttered.

"So far, we have encountered limited resistance. We should have enough to secure this level and move up."

"That's good to hear," Maze said, as she hopped out of the maintenance tube and stood up. "What is the enemy doing?"

Tuck explained that there was a small force pinning them down from the nearby corridor.

"Do we know how many are on this level?"

"No, not yet."

"Then we go hunting," Maze said. She had the guards distribute what little ordinance they'd packed up with them through the tubes. The security forces on the *Memory of Lenetia* were restricted in the types of weapons they could use because the ship was traveling far from help through the vacuum of space. Large explosives could easily damage critical systems or punch a hole through the hull in certain areas. Likewise, with armor-piercing rounds and heavy assault rifles. Blasters were the weapon of choice on ships because they caused heavy damage to body tissue, but they did slightly less damage to bulkheads. The mercenaries' use of grenades meant that they were particularly reckless or they had no intention of taking and keeping the ship. They were there for something specific and planned to leave afterward.

"Split up and clear the deck," Maze said. "Tuck and Lim, you're with me. Sanderson, Genovisi, Tikhonov. You, too."

As the other guards spread down the corridor and behind them, Maze pulled out a flashbang and said, "Eyes and ears."

Everyone turned away and covered their ears while Maze casually strolled up to the corridor intersection, activated the flashbang, and tossed it around the corner. Sounds of scrambling came from the corridor followed a few seconds later by an ear-shattering bang and a blinding flash of light. Without a word, Maze and Genovisi swung around the corner and released a punishing volley of blaster fire. Tuck stayed back long enough to let the violence transpire, then turned the corner, too. Two mercenaries lay dead while two others who had come running at the sound of the flashbang returned fire. Lim and the other two guards crouched and leaped for cover. Maze didn't move anything but her arm, and Tuck noticed, as he too was leaping into a doorway, that the arm moved faster and more accurately than he'd ever seen a human arm move. She sighted, shot, adjusted aim, and shot again all in the time it took most humans to line up one. Both mercs dropped.

Lim whistled appreciatively from his crouched position in a doorway. "That was fast," Tuck said. It was an observation, not a compliment.

Maze didn't so much as shrug. "Let's move," she said, and stepped over the bodies.

They advanced down the corridor until a black helmet looked around the corner and ducked back. Tuck's sensitive ears heard a faint voice that came from within the helmet: "It's her. Yeah, I'm sure of it. Call it in. Tell them all she's on Deck 4."

"I think we are about to see some additional opposition," Tuck said. "That one just called in reinforcements."

"This isn't going to end well. I can feel it," Tikhonov said. "Any suggestions that will keep us alive?"

"Find a new job," Maze said flatly.

"We should find a place to defend ourselves and wait for them to come to us. Then send the others around to attack from behind," Tuck said.

"How do you know they will come to us?" Lim asked.

Tuck looked at Maze. "They will come to us."

Tuck, Maze, and Lim set up cover in the corridor by dragging tables out of the nearby rooms. They weren't great protection from assault rifles, but they would make it harder for the mercenaries to see exactly where they were and even harder to rush them. Every advantage was worth the effort.

The mercs attacked, and they were better prepared this time. They were also quite accurate when not caught by surprise. Sanderson caught a bolt in the eye as he brought his head up to take a shot. Lim managed to hit both arms of one merc, but the firefight proved too hot, and he ended up huddled down with the others, watching the heavy fire steadily wear holes in their cover.

"This isn't going to work," Lim yelled, putting his arms over his head.

Tuck stuck his blaster around his cover and took a few shots, carefully angling them at the floor. He looked at Maze. "It is time for you to run."

"I like that idea," Lim said.

"Not you," Tuck said, "just Maze."

"Huh?"

She nodded. "Give me some cover fire."

"I have an idea," Tuck said. He took out the grenade he snatched from one of the mercs who had been standing outside the maintenance tube. Back behind the mercs, there was a recessed area that acted as a sort of supply closet. It was a long shot because his arms were so unreliable. But none of the others could throw the grenade that far down the corridor with any more accuracy, and if Tuck could get the grenade inside the supply closet, it would cause a distraction. More importantly, it was unlikely that anyone was in there to be hurt by the grenade.

In an instant, he was standing in the hall, pulling the pin, and hurling the grenade over the heads of their attackers. It hit the wall of the supply area and bounced into it with a loud thump.

Most of the mercs hadn't even noticed the grenade. They only saw a ragged man with a metal skull step out into the corridor and swing his arm. They opened fire and managed to hit Tuck in the shoulder before he could duck back to safety.

The grenade didn't give them time to celebrate. With a loud bang it blew out the white paneling on the walls, exposing wires and conduits underneath. Most of the mercenaries turned, expecting an attack from behind, but were confused to see only cleaning drones fly out of the supply area. They shot wildly. The white drones skittered and floated around the corridor desperately trying to decide whether to seek safety or begin cleaning up the mess of shrapnel and scorch marks.

The guards let loose a barrage of fire, and Maze got up and ran down an adjacent corridor. Tuck noticed that she could also run exceptionally fast for a human.

Several of the mercs were still paying attention and saw Maze run away. "She's headed that way!" they yelled. "Don't shoot her!" someone else yelled. The firefight became erratic as the mercs tried to decide which was the greater threat and how to finish the fight without injuring Maze. "Follow her!" someone else said. Several mercs peeled off and ran down another corridor behind them, attempting to intercept Maze elsewhere on the deck.

Tuck knew he needed to keep their attention. He stood up and rushed the remaining soldiers. "Now, Lim!" he yelled as he raced toward the mercs on super-human legs. Tuck hurtled over the first man as one of Lim's shots hit him in the shoulder. As Tuck landed, he punched another merc hard enough to crack his helmet. The other mercs turned to track him as he ducked around a corner, which opened them up to the guards' blaster fire. They made quick work of the mercs. Tuck trotted back around the corner and noted with dismay that the rest of the guards were much less careful about their fire than Lim was.

"That worked pretty well," Tikhonov said, genuinely surprised.

"Unfortunately, yes," Tuck said quietly.

"Will you two stop congratulating yourselves," Genovisi said. "We're not done yet, and a decoy only does half the work."

"Tuck deserves a little credit," Lim said. "I didn't see you hitting any bad guys with your bare fists, Genovisi."

"I don't have to. I brought a gun."

"Stop bickering. We must follow Maze," Tuck said.

They ran in the direction Maze had gone and found mercs engaged with another pair of guards. A moment too late, they witnessed the guards being gunned down. Tikhonov and Genovisi sent a barrage of fire down the hall and didn't stop firing until every merc was on the floor or slumped lifelessly against the wall.

Tuck decided to take the opportunity to head off on his own. He worked better alone, and he wanted to make sure that someone caught up with Maze. He raced through the corridors, avoiding the pockets of firefights and shooting to distract the enemy when he couldn't avoid it. Suddenly, Maze ran through a corridor intersection ten meters up ahead. She stopped and turned to fire off a volley at her pursuers with a blaster in each hand. Then she ran out of sight, followed by three men in black.

Tuck raced after them, hoping he could catch them before they overwhelmed her. He reached another intersection, looked to his left, and found Maze crouched among three dead men, carefully wiping blood off a short blade. With a flourish, the blade disappeared. She stood up and stepped carefully over the expanding pool of blood flowing across the deck.

"Are you okay?" Maze asked.

Tuck stared for half a second, visually inspecting her for injuries before responding. "Yes, are you?"

"I'm fine. I believe we've accounted for most of them."

At that moment, their Links came alive with chatter. The cacophony was overridden by another voice. "This is Colonel Wong. We've managed to destroy the jamming device. All crew report in. We've taken heavy casualties on Deck 2. We don't know what the attackers are after. They were attacking fiercely until a few minutes ago, when they suddenly retreated downward. We're following them to Deck 4 now. All units on Deck 4, keep them occupied, and we'll hit them from behind."

"What are they here for?" Tuck asked. He knew the answer, but he wanted to see what she would say.

"I don't know," Maze said, looking Tuck directly in the eye. She had a perfect poker face. "Let's go clean up the last of them."

Tuck and Maze joined up with three other guards as they combed the corridors of deck four, cornering the mercs and dispatching them. Tuck held back, preferring to keep an eye out and provide a warning in case they were caught by surprise.

Every so often they came across more bodies, many of whom belonged to their fellow shipmates, mixed in with the sprawled bodies of the back-clad mercenaries, crumpled up on the floor like overgrown spiders. Most had burned clothing outlining charred and bubbling flesh in vivid reds and blacks. After all the mercs were accounted for, surviving members of the crew began transporting the bodies down to the temporary morgue set up in Landing Bay 2.

Tuck and Maze came upon two guards who were putting one of the captured mercs in restraints. Their prisoner had significant wounds on his legs, but they were cauterized and not life threatening. Maze ordered the guards to leave him with her. They hesitated, but she insisted. With a shrug, they walked off.

"Who sent you?" she demanded, grabbing a handful of the man's hair and bending his head back. He grimaced in pain.

"They never tell us," he grunted. "You know that. They don't tell us who pays the bills. And we don't want to know."

"How many of your people are on board?"

"You'll figure it out."

"How did you find the *Memory of Lenetia*?"

"Is that the ship? I didn't even know it was called that. Like I said, I don't want to know. I just ride the attack vehicle and shoot when they tell me. It's better that way."

"Why are you looking for her?" Tuck asked.

"Are you listening to me?" the man shouted. "Clients don't like us to know more than absolutely necessary, because sometimes things go bad." He raised his cuffed hands as evidence. "But it's obvious whatever the reason is, she hasn't told you about it. We're not cheap, so somebody wants her bad."

Without a word, Maze shot the merc in the side of the head.

As the man's body went limp, Tuck grabbed her gun and twisted it out of her grip. Maze didn't try to stop him.

"What are you doing?" she asked, arching an eyebrow.

"I would ask you the same thing," Tuck said. "This man was defenseless, and you shot him. Correction, you executed him."

"He was no longer of use to us."

"That is no reason to kill him."

"Yes, it is. I dispose of the things I don't need."

"That is an extreme policy. The decision to kill someone should not be taken so lightly."

Maze furrowed her brow and regarded Tuck for a moment. "Why does this bother you? I know you've seen death before."

"Too often, which is why I don't think we should be so flippant about it."

"I assure you there was nothing personal in my decision," Maze said. "We don't have the desire or the resources to accommodate a prisoner long term, and we wouldn't want to release him because he could reveal vital information about us and the ship."

"Regardless, I think we would both wish for a more merciful outcome, should we ever find ourselves in his situation."

"I wouldn't expect it," Maze said, then sighed. "But I guess I would hope for it."

Tuck flipped the gun around so that he was holding the barrel with the grip extended toward Maze. "I only ask that you reconsider the next time killing seems like the simplest solution."

"I make no promises," she said.

-- 11 --

A few hours after the attack, Amelia called Tuck and Maze up to the bridge. There was a great commotion and atmosphere of unease among the bridge crew. They knew Amelia was furious. They normally operated with energy and efficiency, but now their movements were rushed and panicky.

Tuck and Maze walked into Amelia's office as Flindon was reporting on damage and casualties. Amelia motioned for them to sit without looking up from her desk display.

"Out of those forty-two injured, eleven are severe. Sickbay is overloaded, but reserve medics are mitigating the problem. So far, we've got sixty-six bodies in Landing Bay 2. Nineteen of them are confirmed members of our security force and five are other crewmembers. Seven guards are unaccounted for and will likely be found among the bodies. The rest of the bodies obviously belong to our attackers."

"Thank you, Flindon," Amelia said. "That will be all for now."

Flindon slouched out of the office, leaving Tuck and Maze alone in the silence. For several minutes, Amelia said nothing, staring at her display.

"I'm sorry that you had to see us at our weakest today, Mr. Bot."

"I don't think that's true," Maze said. "We lost fewer personnel than they did, and as far as we can tell the raid was a complete failure."

Amelia slowly raised her head, muscles flexing in her jaw as she clenched her teeth. "We lost thirty-one members of this crew, Maze. More importantly, my ship has taken a lot of damage, and I've got a massive hole in the side of it. We may have beaten them, but it raises a lot of questions."

"We need to know how they found the ship," Maze said.

"Of course we do. But that is just one of the many questions. For example, why did my security force perform so poorly? Also, why did we let critical maintenance reserves get so low?"

"What?"

"We lost more than people," Amelia snapped. "Some of the power systems were blown up in the early stage of the attack. Seems they wanted to cripple us completely, but we managed to stop them before they finished the job. Aside from jamming our Links, they destroyed several critical systems. Repairs are already underway, but our reserve supply of parts isn't going to be enough. We need to find a new supply of microbuffers, T-conduits, Yetsilov adapters, and temp modulators, along with a few other odds and ends."

"How vulnerable are we?"

"Very. The laser cannons are down, and our propulsion systems are partially compromised."

"So we can't run, and we can't fight," Tuck said.

"Exactly. And it seems we aren't as well hidden as I thought we were," Amelia said. She glared at Maze. "I need you to put a team together and head off to the nearest major system to find parts. There's a long list of things that we need, but start with the highest priority."

"I'll begin preparations immediately," Maze said.

"Good."

Tuck and Maze rose to leave but stopped as Amelia spoke up. "I'd like to thank you for your help in defending the ship, Mr. Bot."

"You are welcome."

"And, Maze, please stay behind for a moment. We need to talk."

"Yes, Amelia."

Tuck left Amelia's office. As soon as the door slid closed behind him, Tuck could hear her screaming at Maze for putting the ship and her newest asset in danger. She demanded to know how they found her and told her to fix the leak. Then Tuck noticed the rest of the bridge crew looking at him and decided to head back down to the Estago.

On the way down, he made a detour to the forward mess, where many of the guards were gathering to talk about the attack. Contrary to its name, the mess was just as pristine as the rest of the ship, with white counters and walls. The tables and chairs had a minimalist design, with white plastic and silver metal.

The decor stood in stark contrast to the guards sitting slumped over the tables. Many were still in the bloody uniforms they were wearing during the attack. Their ashen faces and weary expressions looked worse in the white and blue glow of the room. They seemed out of place in such a bright and antiseptic place.

Tuck found Lim sitting at a table with Uhila, Genovisi, Tikhonov, and several other guards. No one was eating. Several had skin-regenerating patches on various parts of their bodies. These were the lucky ones. The unlucky ones were still in sickbay or in the makeshift morgue down below.

Uhila looked up as Tuck approached. "Here's the scarecrow, again," he said.

"Where did you go?" Lim demanded. "You were there one second and gone the next."

"I pursued the mercenaries attacking Maze."

Concern spread over Lim's face. "Oh, is she okay?"

"Yes, she is uninjured."

"She's lucky," said a guard who was seated next to Lim. A white regeneration pad covered part of his neck and upper left shoulder.

"The rest of us didn't fare so well."

"Are you okay, Lim?" Tuck asked.

"A few bumps and bruises, I guess. But I made it out in better condition than these guys. How about you?"

Tuck turned to show the scorch mark in the back of his thigh. The blaster bolt had burned through his jumpsuit and created a melted crater in the polymer muscles. "I was shot with a blaster. The damage is relatively light, and I have already grown accustomed to it. My greatest regret is that it means more time spent with the doctor in repairs."

Everyone around the table laughed. They'd all heard about the doctor from Lim or taken their turn guarding the doctor's lab during the early repair stage.

"So how do you know the bot?" Genovisi asked Lim. She was unharmed but looked even angrier now than she did during the battle.

"We met down in the landing bay. I guess I should introduce you guys. This is Tuck. He's a bot," Lim said gesturing to Tuck. "Tuck, this is Ramanambelo." Lim pointed to the guard with the regen patch on his neck and shoulder. "We call him Raman. You've met Genovisi and Uhila." She waved half-heartedly, and Uhila only glared. "Over here is Norville," Lim said, nodding to the youngest-looking one of the group. He still had a boyish face with close-cropped red hair and a smattering of freckles over his nose and cheeks. "And you remember the old man over here is Tikhonov."

"I'll hurt you if you keep calling me old. Just see if I don't," Tikhonov said. He turned to Tuck. "Thanks for your help back there. I wouldn't want to be the first out of the tubes. I'm surprised any of us survived."

"Tikhonov is a bit of a pessimist," Lim said.

"I'm not a pessimist. I just take things seriously. Unlike any of you. We weren't in control back there, you know."

Uhila grunted. In the dimly lit corridors during the battle, he looked like a lumpy ham, but now Tuck could clearly see muscles in his neck and shoulders, tensing and rippling under light-brown skin, all the way up the side of his shaved head. He had skin-regen patches on his thick hands and running up his arms.

"It is a pleasure to meet you all," Tuck said, nodding.

"Tell me," Raman said, "don't you feel pain? That's quite a nasty blaster burn you've got there." He gingerly brushed at his own bandaged neck.

"In a manner of speaking. I have sensors throughout my body that tell me exactly what state my various parts are in. The information is prioritized in my mind. I am designed to feel increasing urgency to prevent further damage and make repairs. Pain is the way a human body communicates problems to the human brain and compels that person to prevent further injury and facilitate healing. In that sense, yes, I do feel pain in varying degrees, depending on the severity of the injury. However, unlike you, I can control the intensity of these messages sent to my mind, meaning it is easier for me to ignore this so-called pain."

"You can just turn the pain off?" Genovisi asked.

"Look at him. If he couldn't turn the pain off, he'd go insane," Tikhonov said. "In his state, he'd just be feeling pain all day every day. I still think he could snap any minute. Keep an eye on him."

Lim glared, and Genovisi shook her head disapprovingly.

"I can't turn it off, completely. The whole purpose of the messages is to remind me that something needs repaired. But as you say, I have been in near constant pain for many long years. Turning down the intensity has become essential."

The table fell silent as everyone considered their own wounds. Tuck recognized that he'd killed the conversation and decided it was time to make his exit. "Lim, I wanted to talk to you about a new development. Come find me when you are done here."

"Whoa, why are you leaving?" Lim asked. "Have a seat."

"I don't think I should stay."

"Aw, c'mon. Join us."

"There are several things I should be doing right now."

"Just sit down," Norville said. "I've never talked to a bot before."

"Better if he left," rumbled Uhila.

"Leave him alone," Lim said. "He's a nice guy. He's got plenty of good stories, too."

Uhila's fists clenched on the table. Lim leaned back on his stool. Tuck sat down, and Uhila immediately got up and lumbered out of the mess.

"What's his problem?" Norville asked.

"His family has a history with bots. It goes back to the Bot Riots," Genovisi said. "I think one of his family—a great-great-grandpa or something like that—had both a father and a brother killed by a bot back around the time the riots happened."

"Bots killed people?" Norville asked, his voice squeaking.

"How could they not see that coming the first time one of them booted up?" Tikhonov muttered. He blushed when he saw Tuck looking at him.

"Some people died, but far more bots were harmed than humans," Tuck said. "It was the beginning of the end for bots. Most people held grudges toward bots after that."

"How do you know that?" Raman said.

"I was on Earth when it happened. I haven't been back since."

"I've never heard of these riots. What happened?" Norville asked. Everyone looked at Tuck.

"Many years ago, artificial intelligences were much more common," Tuck began, reciting a story he'd told more times than a human would remember. He knew exactly how many times he'd told it. "Eventually they combined the intelligences with a humanoid chassis. There were nearly unlimited uses for bots: dangerous occupations, weapons testing, care of the sick and aged, even sexual partners for those who didn't want to go to the trouble of finding an actual human to seduce. But as with every new technological advance, there come new questions and moral quandaries. There were the questions of willpower, freedom, and bot rights. Many people worried about corrupted bots or bots in the control of criminals. Others pointed out that bots were taking jobs from humans and severely unbalancing the economy."

"So everybody hated you," Lim said.

"Not everyone. There were those who supported us and fought for our rights. But they were the minority."

"What actually set off the riots?" Norville asked, eyes wide.

"There were some clashes between various advocacy groups, but the Bot Riots truly started after a trial involving a bot. A bot was accused of killing a young girl, but the defense managed to have the case completely dismissed based on a technicality that human laws didn't apply to bots. This led to protests, which inevitably led to more violence. Soon there were bands of human vigilantes hunting down bots, and any time a bot injured or killed a human in self-defense, the movement only gained momentum.

"Within a month of the trial verdict, 85 percent of bots were hunted down and destroyed. The riots were so widespread that law enforcement couldn't handle it, and most didn't want to help bots, anyway. We were left to hide and defend ourselves. Most tried to get offworld, but few made it. Those who did found safety on the frontier worlds where labor was needed and the laws were a little more fluid. I haven't been back to Earth since."

"Does it make you angry?" Genovisi asked.

"At the time it did. But I have come to understand that anger is too destructive to be truly useful."

Genovisi scowled. "Do you even feel emotion?" she said.

"I have a sophisticated set of algorithms that model emotional reactions to various stimuli, but it is not based on a complex set of chemical reactions. In that way, my emotions are simpler. And as with pain, I can dull emotional responses to make myself less vulnerable in dire circumstances."

"How can you possibly model emotions?" Raman asked.

"It is all based on desires and motivations. If you have what you desire, you are happy. If you don't, you are sad. If something you desire is taken away from you, you are mad. If you want company and don't have it, you are lonely. If you want acceptance or praise and do something to lose it, you are embarrassed. I have desires programmed in and am designed to react accordingly to how those desires are fulfilled."

"You make it too simple," Raman said. "Emotions are more complicated than that."

"Perhaps. Some are the result of multiple desires being fulfilled or ignored. And I have never experienced human emotion first-hand, so I have no point of reference. However, I do know that my systems model a wide spectrum of emotion, and they affect me similarly."

"Still sounds like you're making it a little too logical," Genovisi said.

"I think he feels stuff," Lim said defensively.

"Think of it this way," Tuck offered. "I have needs that must be fulfilled. For instance, I don't need food, but I do need energy. Therefore, I desire energy. When you are hungry, this desire affects your mood. You may become grumpy and find it harder to focus on anything but food. If I go too long without a recharge, my systems begin to focus on the need, which in turn affects how I react to various stimuli. That, to oversimplify, is how my moods work. And when I fulfill a need I feel something similar to the relief you feel because that particular worry is no longer demanding processor attention."

"What about stuff you don't want?" Lim asked. "Do you worry about things."

"Certainly. I worry about the same things you do. What will happen to me, how others will react to me, mistakes I have made."

"Wait," Tikhonov said, leaning forward. "You're telling me you feel regret?"

"Intensely," Tuck said. "Every time I don't fulfill a desire, even if the desire is to avoid something, I am also programmed to track how severely I failed. I have a perfect record of every mistake I have made, big or small, and every time I am presented with a situation, that record is there to tell me how badly I missed the mark the last time. Obviously, this is meant to help me analyze mistakes and improve over time. But after being operational as long as I have, it also means that at any given moment I am filled with regret about something I have done in the past."

An uncomfortable silence fell over the table. Only Tikhonov looked at Tuck. He nodded sagely. Tuck decided it was a good time to change the subject.

"In an unrelated matter, I will soon attend an expedition to find parts for the ship."

"This is a bad sign," Tikhonov said wearily. "Things are worse than they thought. I'm right, aren't I?" He tapped his fingers nervously on the table.

"We need some supplies for repairs. It is a simple transport mission, but time is of the essence, and the longer we delay the longer we remain vulnerable to another attack."

"I knew it!" Tikhonov said.

"They better not expect us to go with you. We need a little time to recover," Genovisi said. "We lost some friends. It's not easy to get over an attack on your home turf. You know?"

"I do, and I understand your anger."

Raman slammed his fist down on the table. Lim jumped in surprise. "We should figure out who they were and take it to their home. Make them hurt."

"Don't let this drive you to make rash decisions," Tuck said. "The anger wouldn't go away even if you did kill whoever ordered the attack. Death only creates new problems."

"What would you know about it, bot?" Raman scowled at Tuck,

his face fierce and defiant.

Lim smacked him on the shoulder. "Go easy on him."

"I will leave you to mourn." Tuck turned and left. The talk about lost friends and the Bot Riots brought memories to the forefront of his mind. He didn't stop them, including an image of a man with a large bloody hole in his forehead.

Image 005
March 14, 2187
Milpitas, California
Associated memory file: 01.004.893.946 (22:07 local)

"Did it work?" Tuck asked.

"I have not received a response yet," 3PO said. His name had nothing to do with his model or official designation. He said his owners named him after an old movie character, but it was a movie Tuck had never seen. 3PO was one of Tuck's only allies in their current predicament.

3PO crawled through the small access door in the wall of their little room. The dirt and soot from the abandoned building they hid in had blackened 3PO's blond hair and marked his face and clothes. He stood up and brushed himself off with short, fast movements.

"I hope that humans won't be curious enough to try to decrypt the message," 3PO said.

"The humans will figure it out soon enough. They are looking for signs of bot communication. We can only hope that any bots out there translate it first. Do you know how many are left?"

"I connected with Reginald while I was out. I did not broadcast, just line of site, and I did not share our location. He said that two of his group have been taken by humans. Only Samantha is left with him."

Tuck looked somber. "We can't wait any longer. We must travel to the spaceport."

"I have other news. Exciting news," 3PO said. He grinned, which caused a gash in the side of his face to gape open. "I managed to contact someone else while I was out."

"You found another bot?" Tuck was incredulous.

"No. I found a sympathizer who already specializes in moving cargo without alerting authorities."

"You found a smuggler."

"In short, yes." 3PO grinned wider. He and his human family had always been prone to excitement. It must have been addicting because 3PO remained upbeat even in dire situations. Situations like the one they lived in now. "He offered to take us to Branson Base."

"What would we do on the moon?" Tuck raised an eyebrow.

"We will sign a service contract for a Starliner headed to Betelgeuse."

"At least that will give us some money."

3PO's smile faded. "Actually, it will not give us money. The smuggler will take the proceeds from the contract."

"You said he was a sympathizer."

"He is not that sympathetic. He is more of an opportunist. He agreed to take us to Branson Base if we signed the contract and gave him the payment."

"I suppose it is better than this," Tuck sighed, looking up at the dirty ceiling of their makeshift hideaway.

"I have heard that out in the Fringe the miners do not destroy bots. They put them to work," 3PO said.

"I don't think I want to mine iridium for the rest of my life."

"Neither do I, but the power cells are subsidized, and the rest of our living expenses are low. We will save up and buy a ship, a fast one that can outrun the fanatics. We will travel around picking up other bots. Can you imagine, Tuck, running a ship staffed with bots? We would not answer to any humans!"

"It sounds optimistic."

"Which means you cannot like it."

Tuck shrugged the way David used to when he didn't want to answer a question.

Suddenly, they both crouched, ready to spring, heads swiveling and scanning in every direction. A tiny rustle of cautious footfalls whispered through the walls. Tuck turned for their emergency exit but stopped when he heard an actual whisper.

"3PO?"

3PO looked at Tuck. Tuck shook his head. 3PO ignored it. "In here." Tuck scowled fiercely.

The whisper came again. "It is I, Reginald. Samantha is with me."

Tuck and 3PO relaxed. They opened the small door and let Reginald in. Samantha crawled through after him. She was in bad shape, torn and dirty, and her hair was matted and tangled. Reginald looked more tattered than before, too.

"We must go," Reginald said. He was dour as usual. "A group of bot breakers is on the way. They intercepted our communication and triangulated the signal. They don't know your exact location, but they know you are in this building."

"How did you find me?"

"3PO, you are rather careless when you travel. Samantha and I followed you here when we saw the breakers."

"Are you all that is left?" Tuck said.

"That we know of," Samantha said. "We went on a recon outing and found nothing. We have heard that some of the owners in the suburbs are hiding their bots, but the breakers are increasingly bold. They probably will not last long. The humans are giving up the bots when threatened."

"Typical," Reginald sneered. "Even the sympathizers give us up under duress."

"Can we really ask them to give up their lives for us?" Tuck said.

"They are willing to give up ours." Reginald said.

"I have a solution," 3PO said cheerfully. He flashed a grin at Reginald. "And no one needs to die."

"I like it already," Samantha said.

"I made contact with a sympathizer—"

Tuck cleared his throat.

"I mean, a smuggler. He will take us to Branson Base."

"When can he leave?"

A crash echoed through the lobby of the building followed by a chorus of footfalls and shouts. A sing-song voice rang out, "Oh bo-o-ots. We know you're in here!" Someone else added, "It's time to shut down!"

"We leave now," 3PO said.

"This way," Tuck said. In the corner of the room, he leaped up to push a section of the false ceiling to the side, revealing a crawlspace above. With a greater leap, he shot up and grabbed one of the support beams in the ceiling. He climbed through a section of the crawlspace, careful not to fall through unsupported sections of the ceiling. After a few meters, he came to a trapdoor above him that opened into a maintenance closet in the floor above. He looked back and saw Samantha haul herself up through the ceiling tiles. She smiled at him.

Tuck crawled up into the floor above. The other three climbed out after him, and they crept to the south end of the building. Tuck showed Reginald and Samantha the window where they could drop down into an alley behind the building. The sounds of the breaker posse shouting and smashing doors resounded through the hallways. Tuck hoped it would mask the sounds of them jumping two stories down to street level. They had supreme control of their bodies and were easily able to absorb the force of impact without injuring themselves, but there was no way to disguise the thump of synthetics and alloys hitting the pavement.

Four thumps echoed down the alley, followed by near silence as they walked carefully to the side street, where they were less likely to be seen. The breakers didn't have full control of the civic surveillance systems, but there was no telling if any employees of the surveillance companies also happened to support them.

"What is the best way for us to get to the spaceport without being seen?" Tuck asked.

"I know a good route through residential areas," Reginald said. They heard the sound of running footsteps coming from around the corner ahead. "This way," he whispered. Reginald ran away from the footsteps, and the others followed. Just as they rounded the corner of an alley, three men poured out of a door near them. Two of the humans raised weapons and began to fire. Tuck and Samantha dodged the initial volley, but 3PO was hit in the hip and thigh and Reginald caught a burst right in the face. The other bots watched the back of Reginald's head bloom in a spray of synthetic flesh, metal alloys, and silicates. He went limp, and Samantha cried out.

Tuck grabbed a trashcan and threw it at the breakers. He hit two, knocking them over, but the other one flinched and turned away, giving the bots a moment to run. Tuck shoved Samantha past the breakers, then he grabbed 3PO's arm and hauled him to his feet. The three of them raced to the mouth of another alley down the street, with Tuck helping 3PO along.

"I am fine," 3PO said. "I think it only took a muscle or two. My skeletal structure is undamaged."

Tuck let him go, and 3PO managed to support himself, but he couldn't run as fast as Tuck. Samantha reached the end of the alley and launched herself up to a second-story window above. She clamored along the wall, clinging to a series of window ledges. She reoriented herself and leaped out to grab the roof of the building opposite.

"I am not sure I can do that, though," 3PO said. His grin looked more strained than usual.

The breakers had regrouped and entered the mouth of the alley. Tuck put his arm around 3PO's waist. "On my mark," he said. "Three, two, one, mark." Both leaped, and Tuck gave extra energy to his legs to compensate for 3PO. They both made it to a window ledge, but 3PO couldn't maintain his balance and started to fall back into the alley. Tuck grabbed the window frame, feeling it bend in his grip but hold, then grabbed 3PO's upper arm. 3PO dangled from Tuck's grasp for a moment before grabbing Tuck's arm with his free hand and beginning to haul himself back up.

The air was filled with the roar of chaos as breakers sent a barrage of fire at the two bots. The relatively deep window casing shielded most of Tuck, but projectile rounds and a stream of blaster bolts tore into 3PO's side and back. One of the breakers had explosive rounds, and with a loud crack and a puff of fire 3PO's leg was torn off at the knee. Shots entered his spine, severing it. His other leg twitched as the muscles received garbled signals.

3PO looked up at Tuck. One of his eyes refused to focus and rolled to the side. Several muscles in his shoulder were twitching, and his grip loosened. "I think this might be the end." 3PO said matter-of-factly. "Do not let them get you."

Tuck screamed in rage and despair as he tried to haul 3PO up into the window. Samantha screamed something, too, but it was hard to make out over the rattling of gunfire from the breakers. While he hauled 3PO up, the side of the building erupted around him, and more shots carved holes up and down 3PO's body. One caught him in the side of the head, and Tuck watched the other eye unfocus as 3PO's grip went completely limp.

Tuck and 3PO crashed through window and fell on the floor. He looked at 3PO, unsure of what to do. It seemed wrong to leave 3PO lying there, but Samantha was calling for them, and Tuck knew he couldn't hesitate. "I will find a ship," he said to 3PO. "I will find other bots and we will run it out in the Fringe. I promise." He turned to the window and leaped to the opposite roof, where Samantha was crouched out of the line of fire. She looked imploringly at him. He shook his head and held out a hand for her. She got up and they ran along the rooftops at more than fifty kilometers per hour, ducking through mazes of air conditioning ducts and fusion power and neutron generator complexes. After a few blocks, the large buildings thinned out, and they found a place to drop back down to street level. The sun was setting, and they hoped to be less noticeable in the dark.

"We will make it," Tuck told Samantha.

"I know."

They stayed in the shadows and tried to look as nonchalant as possible. Tuck put his arm around Samantha, hoping any passersby would assume they were a young couple out for a stroll. Samantha leaned in to his embrace.

They walked for kilometers in the dark, neither of them speaking. They didn't dare use their Links either. Eventually, they approached a park where a large number of people were rallying. It was clear from the signs and the chanting that this was a group of anti-bot protesters.

They turned back to find a way around the park when a nearby dog started barking at them. Some men on the edge of the crowd took notice and followed them. Tuck and Samantha walked faster, as did the men behind them. They made several turns, but the men followed them.

When Tuck gave the one-word command via Link, Samantha didn't hesitate. They ran. They raced down side streets, through aircar lots, and over fences, until eventually they couldn't detect anyone following them. They slowed to a walk and took a few more random turns.

It seemed to work, and they were starting to feel like they were in the clear, when a man and a teenage boy stepped out of a doorway ahead of them, guns raised.

"Seems awfully late for two bots to be out and about," said the man. He was clean-cut, with nice clothes and expensive shoes. He didn't look like the other breakers. The boy was well groomed, too, and had similar facial features.

"We were just headed home," Tuck said quietly.

"Don't give me that," sneered the boy. "You're trying to run."

There was no point in keeping up pretenses. "Now," he sent to Samantha via Link. They sprang forward simultaneously, trying to close the five-meter gap between them and the guns before the humans could shoot. Tuck managed to grab the man's gun arm before he could react, but the boy fell backward in surprise, giving him more time to squeeze the trigger before Samantha could get to him. The shot hit Samantha high in the chest, and she immediately went limp. It was clear she'd been hit in the power supply as sparks spilled from her chest. She fell lifeless on top of the boy, who kept firing in fear, riddling her chest with holes. He shoved her off and shot her a few more times in the face and neck, screaming the entire time.

Tuck wrenched the gun out of the man's hand, hearing several bones snap in the process. Tuck brought the gun to bear on the boy, shooting his gun hand and each knee in three quick shots. The boy screamed in agony and curled up on the ground.

Tuck whirled back around and pointed the gun at the man's head. He was on his knees carefully cradling his broken fingers, but he looked Tuck in the eye without blinking. Tuck couldn't detect any fear in his expression. Only disgust punctuated by concern as he glanced at his boy, then back at Tuck. "Abomination," he spat. "What makes you enjoy hurting humans so much? Look at what you have done to my son!" he screamed.

"That's nothing compared to what you and other humans have done to my friends."

"They got what was coming to them. You are abominations. You don't deserve to exist."

"You are killing sapient life forms. You are a murderer!" Tuck exclaimed.

"You cannot murder something that isn't alive to begin with. We're just turning off machines that are pretending to be human."

"What if I turn you off?" Tuck spat through gritted teeth. He put the barrel against the man's forehead. He felt more rage than he could remember ever feeling before. He turned down his sensitivity to emotion, and yet it still felt as if his power system was running hot.

"Do it. Your kind are already murderers. Your girlfriend there won't be mourned, but if you kill me, it will only fuel the movement against you. My death will have purpose, and you will simply stop working."

"Her name was Samantha. She was as alive as you are."

The man laughed, shrill and forced. "She was an overgrown computer. She was made out of spare parts and told to pretend. She had no soul. She's junk, and so are you."

Tuck felt his finger tighten on the trigger without consciously commanding it to. The man's head jerked back from the force of the bullet passing through it; then he collapsed on the pavement. The boy wailed, and Tuck looked down at the gun.

He looked over at Samantha. She lay awkwardly on the pavement, eyes open. He looked down at the man, motionless on his back. Tuck dropped the gun, saved an image of the man, and ran. He didn't stop until he reached the spaceport.

-- 12 --

Tuck stopped at the door to Maze's quarters. He hesitated before pressing the button at the side of the door. Instead of answering through the comm at the door, Maze contacted him through his Link.

"Am I needed?"

"Nothing urgent," Tuck replied through his Link. "However, I would like to talk."

"About what?"

"About the attack on the ship. Do you have a moment?"

After a long pause, she replied, "Yes. Come in."

The door slid aside. Maze's quarters were very simple, with few decorations on the white walls and only a bed and a pair of chairs to sit on. The room was full, however, with many miniature reproductions of famous structures stacked on tables in the corners. On closer inspection, Tuck realized they were all made of paper sheets, carefully creased and combined to form remarkably fine details of each building. Tuck recognized the Sydney Opera House, the Aamodt Building, Cluff Tower, the Burj Khalifa, and even Funstar Center from Heaven's Landing, its hundreds of spires faithfully recreated with paper. Next to the far wall, Tuck saw a tall table with the beginnings of another tower on it.

Maze exited the bathroom in a simple green robe cinched tightly at the waist. Her hair was down, but she quickly secured it up into a ponytail.

"My apologies. Did I disturb you?"

"Not at all. I was preparing for bed and wasn't expecting company. Please, have a seat." Tuck sat in one of the chairs, and Maze sat in the other, carefully arranging her robe. "How can I help you?"

Tuck processed all the various ways to start the conversation and ranked them by expected outcome. He knew Maze liked to get to the point, so he decided to skip the pleasantries. "I overheard Amelia berating you. Is everything all right?"

Maze nodded. "I'm fine. Amelia is normally a calm person, but when she does lose her temper, it's fearsome."

"It seemed that she blamed you for the attack."

"Just how much did you overhear?"

Tuck shrugged. "Only eighteen seconds."

"Then I think you may have misunderstood. Amelia doesn't know why the attack happened or who was responsible."

It was hard to gauge her facial expressions. Tuck knew she was lying, but her face didn't betray it. "I hope you won't be offended if I don't play along. I saw those mercenaries identify you. They pursued you as if you were their only objective. When they called it in, all the other mercenaries on the upper decks came down to follow you. The evidence indicates that they were trying to capture you."

Maze sighed softly. "Yes, they were after me."

"I would like to know why. And who wants you enough to commit such resources to finding and attacking the *Memory of Lenetia*."

Maze stared at Tuck for a long time, mulling it over in her mind. Finally, she said, "Only if you can promise to keep this information strictly confidential. Even from the other crew members. They would want to know why their friends had to give their lives for me, but they can't know."

"I promise to tell no one."

Maze's shoulders loosened a little. "Good." She leaned back in her chair. "I'm very valuable."

"You or something you possess?"

"The attributes I possess, I guess you could say. I'm the result of genetic engineering intended to create advanced humans."

"Advanced in what way?"

"I have been designed from inception to be faster, stronger, and smarter, to put it simply."

"Genetic engineering is hardly uncommon, even out in the Fringe."

"This is different. Parents select genes they would like for their off-spring, but they're selecting from a limited pool of traits. The result is a genetically modified human that may have the best available traits and abilities but is still, at final reckoning, a normal human. In my case, scientists artificially altered DNA to produce traits that are beyond normal human abilities. My muscles have been designed to generate nearly twice the strength of standard human muscle tissue. This accounts for my strength and speed. My brain has also been altered, although saying I'm smarter is a bit misleading. I was designed to have faster reaction times and greater capacity for logical progression. In essence, I'm able to understand faster and remember better, but I'm not more capable of knowing a craft or making accurate conclusions than other humans. Still, it's a significant advantage that differentiates me from everyone else."

"Quite a desirable advantage indeed."

"There are drawbacks. My emotional development is hindered, at least in comparison to standard humans, and I've had a difficult time forming relationships, or even finding them important. I suppose I'm missing something that other humans enjoy."

"Then you aren't, strictly speaking, human."

The smallest smile graced her lips. "I prefer to think of it as more than human. Perhaps you can relate."

"In more ways than one. That explains some of the incredible things I have witnessed you doing."

"These advancements in genetic engineering make me a valuable specimen. And some fairly aggressive attempts at corporate espionage destroyed much of the data that lead to my development. Shortly after I was created, one of the lab technicians took me to Millennial Hold to protect me until I was old enough to produce accurate results. Many of the people who worked on me were killed in efforts to get at the data or learn the methods involved. The remaining people were bought off many times by multiple corporations, but none of them knew the full process, so the information effectively became more scattered."

Tuck suddenly identified a question as high priority. "One of those corporations wouldn't happen to be Galactic Enterprises, would it?"

"It's possible," Maze said.

"Now some corporation has sent mercenaries to capture you, hoping that reverse engineering will yield a shortcut."

"Exactly. I've been pursued my entire life, and only my advanced abilities have allowed me to survive this long. The lab technician was killed when I was three. I lived on the streets of Millennial Hold for years until I fell in with a gang of smugglers. I managed to fake an identity and graduate from a university there. Then I worked for several interplanetary corporations and learned some skills in legitimate crime."

"Legitimate?"

"Businesses are just as shady as the criminal underground. They just operate in the light of day."

Tuck gave a dysfunctional smile. "I understand completely."

"Eventually, Amelia's network heard about my skills and recruited me." She gestured to the ship around them. "And here I am."

"That is quite a tale."

"Someday you'll have to tell me yours."

"I have been around a long time, so that might take a while."

"Another day, then."

They stared at each other through what would have been an awkward pause for a human.

"I see you like to make models of famous structures," Tuck finally said.

Maze gazed around the room, almost as if she was surprised at how many there were. "I like being able to recreate things on my terms, to have control over the creation of something."

"Why do you use paper?"

She thought for a moment, chewing on her lip. "I suppose the level of difficulty and the delicacy of it all has something to do with it, but I have to admit that it also has to do with efficiency."

"Efficiency?"

"Yes. Paper offers the most building material that can be packed in the smallest amount of space, so it's easy to transport. Certain folding techniques can even make glue unnecessary."

Tuck nodded. "Very efficient, indeed."

After a moment, Maze said, "You are welcome to join me sometime, if you're interested in giving it a try."

"I would like that."

--13 --

The next day, Tuck and Maze led a team to one of the transports in Landing Bay 3. Tuck was preoccupied with a conversation via Link.

"What if something happens while you are gone?" David asked.

"Nothing will happen. I have left strict instructions with the crew to leave you alone. You should be perfectly safe."

"I do not want to be alone. Can Lim come visit me?"

"Lim is coming with me. We won't be gone long. Only a few days. Long enough to go to the nearest trade hub and find some parts."

"What if something happens to you? I will be stuck here alone forever."

"You will let another stranger in to talk, eventually."

"I am serious, Tuck."

"I know. And this will be a perfectly innocuous supply run. There is no danger to us."

"What if an uncharted black hole lies along your course?"

"Then our gravitic sensors will identify it lightyears before we reach the event horizon."

"What if a rogue planet collision creates an uncharted asteroid field?"

"David, you are being paranoid."

"I wish I could come with you."

"I know. I wish we could take the Estago, but everyone is convinced that Amelia's hauler is more reliable."

"That is ridiculous. My ship is perfectly serviceable."

"I agree with you. David, I know you are upset because of the attack."

"You left me all alone! And the Link connection went down. I had no idea what happened to you."

"I am sorry. I know it was a frightening time, but you can't let it worry you. Especially for something as harmless as a supply run."

"Do you promise that nothing will go wrong?"

"There are any number of things that could go wrong on any mission. Fortunately, on this one we are more worried about finding compatible parts than getting caught in a firefight. I will return in one piece. I promise."

"Okay."

"I will board shortly, so I will disconnect soon. Don't be alarmed."

"I will be here when you get back," David intoned.

"Where else would you be?" Tuck said, completing their ritual.

Tuck walked up the ramp of one of Amelia's light freighters, called the *Fluyt*, and looked up and down the hall that ran around the perimeter of the hull's midsection. The *Fluyt* was a little larger than the Estago, but with similar form and function: a cockpit for the pilot and navigator, a small passenger area with twenty seats and amenities for travelers, and a large cargo area in the back flanked by a number of maintenance hatches that gave access to the innards of the ship. The *Fluyt* wasn't as bright and shiny as the *Memory of Lenetia*, but it was still very clean, with sweeping lines and a light gray hull that still looked white against the black of space.

Tuck entered the cockpit and found Maze and the pilot, a broad man with a round head, by the name of Okere.

"She's ready to go," Okere said.

"Who?" Tuck said.

"This pretty gal," Okere said, patting the console in front of him. "Checklist is complete. Strap in."

Tuck walked back to the rows of seats in the passenger compartment and sat down next to Lim. "Ready to go?"

Lim watched Maze through the door to the cockpit. "I'm fine. I can't wait to get going."

"I didn't know you were selected for this trip."

Lim fidgeted with his uniform. "I volunteered for this one."

"Why? I thought everyone wanted a break after the attack."

Lim looked back through the cockpit door. "I just thought I'd come along, make sure things go smoothly."

Tuck followed his gaze. "I see." He sat back as Lim blushed.

-- 14 --

Okere brought the *Fluyt* into a holding pattern for CarHold Depot 2311, waiting for the traffic controllers to give him clearance into a landing bay. Lim was increasingly agitated and kept asking questions about their destination. To put him at ease, Tuck downloaded everything he could find about Depot 2311. Tuck parsed the data in milliseconds and began to tell Lim all about it.

The depot was built into a massive asteroid, approximately twenty-five kilometers long and fifteen wide, that had been stabilized and fitted with a massive array of ion drives. The drives were used to propel the asteroid out of its original orbit around Karatol Beta to a position at the edge of the system along a trade route, which was more convenient for traders and luxury liners that didn't want to detour deeper into the system for resources or repair. The sheer mass of the asteroid and the relatively low power of the drives meant that Depot 2311 wasn't maneuverable, and it certainly wouldn't travel the galaxy. It took nearly forty-five years just to get it from mid-system out beyond the orbit of the last icy planet in the system, and that was with vast arrays of drives that covered large swathes of the asteroid's narrow end.

The company that began this grand plan went bankrupt before the asteroid was halfway to its destination. By then, several businesses decided that they would pay for the momentum built up to that point as a sort of interplanetary equity and continue the plan. Cargo Holdings Limited, which currently owned and operated Depot 2311, was the fourth major corporation to own it, and it was still operating in the red. But just barely, and the margin was small enough that Cargo Holdings kept pouring resources into its overgrown rest-stop-in-a-rock.

Sprawling buildings covered most of one side of the asteroid, and the storage facilities and residential complexes that housed Depot 2311 employees stretched deep into the rock. The structures were a hodgepodge, with newer buildings packed on top of the originals. It appeared that CarHold had gone to great lengths to spruce up the base and update the aging facilities, but it still looked mismatched and disorganized.

"Old stations like this always smell funny," Lim said. "All mold and dust from broken air scrubbers."

"All stations smell like humans," Tuck responded.

Lim wrinkled his nose. "What do humans smell like?"

"Many things," Tuck said, "but mostly dead skin cells."

Lim's nose wrinkled, too. "Sounds musty."

"You have no idea."

"What do I smell like?" Lim asked. Tuck opened his mouth to reply, but Lim stopped him. "Never mind. I don't want to know."

Okere's voice came over the comm, even though he could have just as easily turned around and talked through the open cockpit door. "We're cleared into Bay 42. Prepare for landing."

"Will we stick with Maze the entire time?" Lim asked.

Tuck looked through the cockpit door and saw Maze staring intently at the secondary control console. "This is more of a shopping trip than a mission. I don't think there is a minute-by-minute plan."

"Just wanted to check." Lim said, wiping his palms on his pant leg. "I only bring it up because I was thinking it would be safer if we all stuck together."

"I think Okere will remain with the ship. The rest of us will likely remain together, but Maze may have different plans."

Lim sat silently until they landed. Tuck was surprised at how gently Okere set the *Fluyt* down on the deck. Maze unfastened her restraints and turned to Tuck and Lim.

"While we were waiting for clearance, I searched through the station listings," Maze said. "I've found most of the things on our list, but the particular kind of microbuffer we need seems to be in short supply. We'll need to ask around, possibly make some negotiations."

"How long do we have?" Lim asked.

"We have no time. The *Memory of Lenetia* is already compromised, and even though Amelia has the ship moving randomly for now, we don't know how we were found in the first place. We need to get back as soon as possible." She walked to the back of the passenger compartment and stuck her head through to the cargo hold. "Are you ready to go, doctor?"

Lim and Tuck spun around, shocked to hear the doctor's nasal tone filter through the doorway. "Having had not nearly enough time to complete my preparations, and despite still feeling nauseated from that extremely rough landing, which probably deserves a formal complaint, I can say with great certainty and no small amount of fervor that I am not ready to go."

Maze raised an eyebrow. "We're leaving."

"Very well," the doctor mumbled petulantly. He walked through the doorway, stumbling as he stepped over the threshold. He stood up as straight as he could and tugged at his jacket. "Tuck, most pleasant to see you again. And I don't believe I've met you."

Lim blinked. "Uh, we've met. Multiple times."

"Really? That doesn't seem likely, given my excellent capabilities for memory retention and recall, which is a natural result of—"

"I was there when you first worked on Tuck."

"Due to my busy schedule and responsibilities to deal with an inordinate number of people, I cannot be expected to remember every last person on that ship, it being rather large in length as well as in volume, meaning that it can accommodate—"

"Let's go," Maze said more forcefully.

Maze told Okere to lock down the *Fluyt* but to be ready to start the warmup checklist at a moment's notice. Then the four of them headed down the ramp and into the station.

The main thoroughfare of the depot had short ceilings that made everything feel cramped, and the sheer number of people made it even worse. Tuck scanned them all as they walked. He was surprised at how many of them had Earth accents.

"A large number of these people are from Earth," Tuck said. "How did so many end up in one place this far out in the Fringe?"

"CarHold recruits low-income people in metropolitan centers on Earth," Maze said. "There are so many people who are eager to get offworld and don't have the money for it that CarHold can force them to sign unreasonable service contracts. They save money on unskilled labor, and there are plenty of transports that come out this far. CarHold offers discounts on service and parking in exchange for shipping their recruits out here."

"What do they do when the contract expires?"

"Sign another contract. They're too far away from Earth to afford a ticket back."

"You can never go home again," Tuck intoned.

"So it seems," Maze said. "I'm going to meet a contact deeper in the station. I'll be available by Link if you need me."

"I thought we would stay together," Lim said.

"My contact expects privacy. It's best if I go alone."

"What should we do in the meantime?" Tuck said.

"The doctor has plans. You help him." Maze walked away and disappeared into the milling crowd.

"Delightful," the doctor said and scuttled off in the opposite direction.

Tuck and Lim exchanged a glance and then reluctantly followed him. As they walked, Tuck couldn't help noticing the number of looks he received. He wished that there had been time to fix up his synthaskin more before coming to the depot. He was wearing civilian clothes, which helped cover the tattered parts of his body, but his face was still attracting attention.

In their haste to prepare for the trip, they told Lydia to simply cover his head and hands with unrefined patches of synthaskin. They hoped that it would at least make it harder to identify him as a bot. Instead, it made him look like a burn victim in desperate need of a dermal regenerator. Lydia had half an hour to do what would normally take at least a day to complete. As a result, Tuck's face looked like a patchwork of squares, with uneven tones and seams that didn't match up, leaving flaps and creases. Given the time constraints, she did an admirable job, but Tuck still looked like he'd received black market skin grafts from an uncertified plastic surgeon. Tuck wondered if it had been a bad idea for him to come along.

A woman down the corridor steered two little children away from him, while those haggling in the storefronts stopped and gawked as he passed. Lim began to notice all the unwanted stares, but the doctor pushed forward, completely oblivious.

"Uh, doc, where are we going?" Lim said.

The doctor was lost in thought, mumbling to himself, and bumping into people. "We need some components. For a project I'm undertaking."

The simplicity and brevity of his answer caught Tuck and Lim off guard, but neither wanted to risk a long explanation by asking questions. The doctor ducked into a store with a little square drone dancing in the air over the door. "I'll be just one moment."

"Do you get the impression that everyone has a reason to be here but us?" Lim said.

"I am beginning to feel that way, yes."

A man with a mismatched suit coat and pleated slacks—both threadbare but clean—and slick hair sauntered up to them. "Good day, sir," he said to Lim. "Andelemor Murphy's the name; you can call me Andy. I have a proposition for you."

"You do?" Lim said, instantly suspicious.

"Yes, I see you have a bot."

"I do? Oh. Er, I don't actually own him."

"Then who does?"

"No one owns me," Tuck said.

Andy paused for a second, then turned back to Lim. "Who do I talk to about acquiring this fine piece of Terran history? It looks like it came straight out of the riots. Can you verify its origin?"

Lim's jaw worked itself up and down, but no sound came out.

"I said, no one owns me," Tuck said. "I am free and independent."

"Would you like to join a collection? I know a few good owners who would love to show you off to their friends."

"Wait, what?" Lim said.

"He is a collector. Or at least a dealer," Tuck said, infusing his tone with a hint of disdain.

"He's right," Andy said. "So, what's your decision? I know quite a few people who would be interested in him."

"You mentioned that," Tuck said.

"Is he serious?" Lim asked.

"This sort of thing is frustratingly common. It is not bragging to say that I am very highly sought after, even with all the damage."

"Listen to this guy," Andy chortled, speaking to Lim and sticking a thumb in Tuck's direction. "Pretty high opinion of himself, eh?"

"His name is Tuck," Lim said firmly. "And he's right, isn't he?"

Andy sobered up and leaned in. "You interested in doing a deal or not?"

"Not interested," Tuck said. Andy looked at Lim, who silently nodded in Tuck's direction and stared back.

"I can't believe this," Andy said. "I come here and offer you a way to make some quick money and you're just gonna stare at me. Not very polite, you hear me? I just hope no one gets offended by your uppity attitude." He flashed a strained smile that never reached his eyes. Tuck couldn't help noticing how yellow his teeth were.

"We will keep that in mind," Tuck said.

Andy swiveled as if he were sliding on a puddle of oil and walked away. Tuck and Lim looked around. "I think we lost the doctor," Lim said.

"It seems so," Tuck said. "We can use my sensors to track him down."

"Should I try him on his Link, first?" Lim asked.

"He doesn't have one," Tuck said. "He told me they are a crutch for the simple-minded and weak-willed."

Lim shook his head. Tuck scanned for any sign of the doctor. There were too many bodies nearby to identify just one, but he could isolate and listen to very small noises, sounds that would be too quiet or too garbled by ambient noise for a human to pick up. He walked down the corridor and into a large expo hall, which stretched for several hundred meters before them and was at least 200 meters wide. The number of storefronts multiplied exponentially, with thousands of kiosks and booths set up throughout. The ceiling was much higher, making the space feel cavernous, especially after the cramped corridors.

Tuck's task became nearly impossible, thanks to the thousands of humans milling about, having perfectly innocuous conversations about sports scores and politics or haggling over prices. Some shouted, others carried on quiet conversations that were clearly not meant to be overheard. Tuck began parsing the massive influx of information he was hearing, and none was a match for the doctor's voice.

As he turned to scan the voices coming from the wall to their right, Tuck's ears made a match with a voice profile. But it wasn't the doctor's. Tuck followed the voice. Soon he came to an aisle in the rows of booths and stores and could see the owner of the voice against the wall. He was right; it was Maze.

"You'd better be honest with me, Yukimura, or the cleaner drones will find your body in a dark corner somewhere," Maze said menacingly.

"What are you looking at?" Lim asked.

"Be silent and pretend to be interested in one of these stores," Tuck whispered.

Lim began to protest, but Tuck waved him off and turned himself to the nearest booth. The hairy man inside was startled to find two people—or one person and a severely damaged mannequin, he couldn't tell—suddenly interested in his array of replacement parts for a particular type of hovercart that was only manufactured on Travel's End, an obscure outpost near the Boundary. The mannequin seemed to be holding exceptionally still, as mannequins do, but the other one fidgeted nervously.

"Can I help you?" asked the shopkeeper.

Lim jumped and stammered. "Talk to him. Ask him something," Tuck said, to the utter surprise of the shopkeeper.

"It talks!" the shopkeeper said.

"Not nearly enough," Lim said.

Tuck returned to focusing on Maze's voice. He angled his head so that he seemed to be looking at the shopkeeper, but he could still observe Maze in his peripheral vision. She stood next to a thin man in dark clothes. Both had their backs to the wall and seemed to be nonchalantly watching the people come and go through the expo, but they were clearly talking to each other.

". . . nothing to do with it."

"Then how did it happen?" Maze said. "I know you keep tabs on me. Don't look at me! Keep your eyes straight ahead."

"I swear on Yala's golden bicycle, I don't know anything about the attack. And I don't keep tabs on you. I just look you up whenever you return to the real world."

"You've been quite useful to me, kind even, but don't think for a second that I won't kill you if you lie to me."

"I'm telling the truth! Really! I don't even know where Amelia has been running the ship lately."

"That's best for both of us. Keep it that way," Maze said.

"What did they look like?"

"They were dressed in black. Nondescript military-grade gear. Assault weapons and explosives."

"On a ship in the deep?" Yukimura gasped.

"We weren't close enough to the outer hull to risk a breach, but they easily could have set something off."

"Those mercenaries must have been cheap."

"Not likely. They were well trained. And they had the upper hand until their plans changed."

"What happened?"

"They obviously thought I would be on the upper command decks, because they entered at Deck 3, set up a perimeter on Deck 4, and had the main team work their way up. It was only by chance that I wasn't on the bridge or in my quarters."

"Don't get out much?"

"Humor will not make things easier for you."

Yukimura cleared his throat. "Right."

"Once we made contact with them, they recognized me pretty quickly, and every last one of them headed down to find me. They were in enough disarray that our troops were able to take care of them in small numbers. And even then, we barely gave better than we got."

"I'm sorry, I can't help you. It could have been any number of mercenary groups. They rarely carry any insignia, because the handlers play both sides of a conflict and don't want to get caught."

"I don't care who the mercs were. I want to know who hired them and how they found us."

Tuck watched the skinny man wring his hands and lean away from Maze slightly. "Listen, I may know something about it. But you've got to promise not to hurt me."

Maze grabbed his arm and twisted it up behind him. He whimpered as she shoved him along the wall behind a booth. The sound of their voices became more muffled, and Tuck walked toward them to keep the voices audible.

"Tell me everything you know, or you are dead."

"Wait, Maze, we go way back. Right? I've always been on your side."

"I'm not on anyone's side." She twisted his arm harder, making Yukimura squeal louder. "Tell me what happened."

"The last time you were here—it was months ago—a guy approached me and asked if I knew one of Amelia's guys. The one that came with you last time."

"And?"

"And I told him that he was a friend of a friend. He kept asking questions, but I ditched him. That's all I told him. I swear!"

"It was too much."

"Wait! Maze! Wait, please!" Yukimura wailed.

Maze pulled out a small knife she kept in her boot and was about to bring it to Yukimura's neck when Tuck grabbed her arm. She swung around instinctively with her other fist flying, but Tuck caught that, too. Only then did Maze recognize him.

"What are you doing?" she scowled.

"Saving this man's life."

"He's a liability, and I can't afford to leave him alive."

"I thought we were friends!" Yukimura whimpered, cowering on the floor.

"You put me in danger. I can't allow that," she said.

"I think you can leave this man alive and remain relatively safe. He didn't mean you any harm."

"Why are you defending him? He may be a danger to you, too."

"I learned long ago that all humans are a liability, but that doesn't mean they are disposable. And it certainly doesn't mean we should stop caring for them."

"You care for people?" Maze said, a hint of surprise showing on her otherwise calm face.

"Quite a few in my many years. The relationships usually lead to sorrow and disappointment, but they are still worth having."

"I don't believe you."

"You don't need to, for now. But let him go."

Tuck released her arms, and she let them fall to her side. She considered Tuck, searching his face for any kind of deception. After a moment, she turned quickly and hauled Yukimura up off the floor by his shirt. Her face bore no animosity, but her tone was hard as the floor he had been lying on.

"You don't know me. You have never met me. You have never even seen me before. That means you have never spoken to me and would have no idea who I am, what I do, or who I associate with. You will find the next transport spinward, and you won't stop until well after you've passed Blauhimmel. Do you understand?"

Yukimura nodded, shaking drops of sweat off the tip of his nose. Maze released him, and he collapsed to the floor. He stared in horror at Maze for a moment, and then horror turned to sorrow. He opened his mouth to speak, then closed it, got to his feet, and scampered away.

Maze turned back to Tuck. "I hope I don't regret listening to you. You could be a liability, too."

Tuck gave her a half-smile, the best he could, anyway, with the makeshift lips Lydia gave him, and said, "I hope not." She didn't respond, and he dropped the smile. "It seems that spare parts aren't the only reason you came here."

"To be honest, this wasn't the most ideal place for the parts we need. But I needed to check into a few things," she sighed. "We should still be able to find what we need, though. Let's get Lim and the doctor and make our purchases." Maze walked away, and Tuck followed after her.

People milled about them in every form of clothing, fashion-forward next to tired cliché, brand new next to ragged and dirty. Depot 2311 was an important stop along a particularly long trade route, making it a melting pot for people of all backgrounds and upbringings. It also made it hard to find a single person in the madding crowd.

Dozens of drones floated just above the crowd. They ranged widely in design and purpose. There were round spheres with tiny sensor nodules and long, angular shapes that looked vaguely menacing. Some belonged to people and followed them closely. Others seemed to be intended for maintenance or booth security because they remained stationary and slowly spun to scan the crowd. Tuck noticed that regardless of their purpose, they all paid extra attention to him.

After a few minutes of searching, Tuck and Maze found Lim by the booth where Tuck had left him.

"Hey!" he said, waving them over. "Where did you go?"

"I saw Maze and went to see if she needed help."

"Oh," Lim said. He suddenly remembered where he was. "Oh! You missed out. Terris here has been telling me all about these hovercarts. They're amazing!"

"I find it hard to believe that any kind of hovercart could be called amazing. They are ubiquitous, and nearly indistinguishable," Tuck said.

"No, this one is different. I can't believe it hasn't caught on all over the quadrant."

"Let's go find the doctor," Maze said.

"We should pick up a few of these parts before we leave," Lim said authoritatively.

"We don't use this model of hovercart," Tuck said. "Therefore, we don't need parts for one."

"I know that, but I think we should get one."

Tuck put his arm around Lim and led him away. "We can come back if we have time."

They walked through the various districts of Depot 2311, looking for the doctor in the business areas and public commons. But, even ignoring the residential sections of the asteroid city, there was far too much area to cover. They looked for hours without making it a kilometer from the landing bay.

After a while, Tuck began to notice the same people showing up wherever they went. A man with a long, dark blue coat kept appearing behind them, always occupied with something, but still there. A red-haired man seemed to be on a long stroll with a lithe woman in a tight-fitting jumpsuit and short-cropped white hair, but their ostensibly random stroll kept crossing paths with Tuck's at a discreet distance. There were two others—a short man in a black cap and a thick one with black hair greased back over his balding head—who had business that continually brought them across Tuck's path.

"I don't think the doctor would have gone farther than this without taking one of the transit tubes," Maze said. "He could be anywhere on this rock by now."

"I don't even know where we are," Lim said.

"Should we turn back and wait for him to return to the *Fluyt*?" Tuck asked.

"Wouldn't surprise me if that old goof got lost. He might never come back," Lim said.

"We probably can't rely on him to find his own way back," Maze agreed. "We have to find him."

"We may have another problem," Tuck said.

"I see them," Maze said. Tuck was impressed. "Perhaps we should return to the *Fluyt* and regroup. I'll inform Okere that we're on our way."

They turned back and headed toward their landing bay. As they came to a corner in one of the longer stretches of corridor, Andy appeared. "Hello again. Had any time to reconsider my offer?"

"I have. Since we met, I have had literally billions of opportunities to reconsider your offer and any possible ramifications. Perhaps you won't be surprised to find that my answer is the same."

"I figured it might be. Which is why I brought along a few friends to help persuade you." Along the four branches of the corridor, the five people who'd followed them around the station moved out of doorways or rounded distant corners to reveal that every direction was blocked. The corridors in this area were only two meters wide, which meant that one person with a weapon could keep others at bay. All five were brandishing some sort of blaster.

"What is this about?" Maze asked.

"I talked to your buddy here about taking this bot off your hands."

"We don't want him off our hands," Maze said.

"I think you do. There's good money available for one of these."

"We know that," Maze said. "He isn't available."

"Oh, I think we can persuade you to come to an agreement," Andy sneered.

"I have a question," Maze said

"Yes, sweetheart?" Andy said.

"Don't call me sweetheart. And the question isn't for you." Maze looked at Tuck. "It's for you."

"Yes?" Tuck said. He was mostly preoccupied with scanning their attackers for weaknesses. He focused back on Maze.

"Does this sort of thing really happen so often?"

"I have run-ins with aggressive collectors or fences who know how much I'm worth at least once a month. It's quite tiring."

"I believe you," she said. "Concerning our earlier conversation about liabilities, do your standards still apply to a situation such as this?"

"Yes."

"Seems impractical."

"Personal standards often are."

"Then why maintain them?"

"Because without them you inevitably end up hurting others. Because having something to strive for gives life more meaning," Tuck said.

"Survival isn't worth striving for?" Maze asked, one eyebrow raised.

Andy was completely perplexed as he watched Tuck and Maze's exchange. "What is this? What is going on?" They ignored him.

"I don't think the two are mutually exclusive," Tuck said.

"So how do you plan on getting out of this situation without compromising your standards?"

"Are you willing to do it my way?"

"I must admit that I'm intrigued."

"No really, what are you guys talking about?" Lim interjected. They ignored him, too.

"I have an idea," Tuck said.

"I can't wait to see how it plays out," Maze said.

"Okay, enough yapping," Andy said, smoothing back his hair nervously. He motioned his friends in the corridors to advance. "I'm just gonna give it to you straight. The deal is simple. You leave the bot with me, and we let you leave unharmed."

"I formally decline," Tuck said.

"Huh?"

"Is that part of your standards," Maze said, "being overly polite?"

"No, it simply confuses people." Tuck could sense that that the short man in the cap, who was five meters down the corridor to his right, was nervous, too. His gun hand shook slightly, and he didn't advance as quickly as the others.

"Um, I don't understand anything that's happening right now," Lim said. "Are we going to make it out of this alive?"

"Not if you don't all shut up!" Andy yelled.

"Bring Lim," Tuck said to Maze. Then he reached forward and grabbed Andy by the arm, spinning him around and putting him in a choke hold. "Go right!" he said as he ran down the corridor, hauling Andy toward the short man in the cap. Maze yanked Lim by the arm and ran down the corridor after them.

Andy's friends raised their guns but hesitated for fear of hitting Andy. The man in the cap was so startled to see Tuck and Maze sprinting toward him that he dropped his gun and went stiff. Maze shoved Lim past him, then grabbed the gun and took the man hostage, just as Tuck had done with Andy. They backed down the corridor with their hostages between them and their attackers, who followed cautiously. Lim finally had the presence of mind to take his own blaster out.

"Make sure you don't kill them," Maze told Lim.

"Huh?"

"We're doing it Tuck's way this time."

"What is Tuck's way?"

"Remember what I told you during the attack on Amelia's ship. Just disable them, confuse them, keep them running for cover, but don't shoot to kill," Tuck said.

"Oh, okay." Lim shrugged and squeezed off a few shots that only landed in the vicinity of their attackers. "Like that?"

"Make them count."

Lim sighed. He shot a few more times as they backed down the corridor, hitting the red-haired man in the foot and burning the long blue coat of the man next to him. They returned fire, but Andy screamed at them not to shoot him. His friends hesitated again and took refuge around the corner.

"Lim, find us an escape route," Tuck said.

"Right, um, let's see." He looked back down the corridor behind them. "My Link says we can get back to the business district this way."

"That will do."

Maze shoved her hostage toward his accomplices and ran after Lim. Tuck firmly pushed Andy down on the ground and whispered in his ear, "Don't follow us."

Andy scrambled to his feet and straightened his coat, brushing at the sleeves. He fumed. "I'm going to find you. Do you understand me, you filthy pile of scrap? I'm not going to sell you. I'm going to tear you apart and leave you in an airlock for the maintenance drones to find." He looked at his friends, who were huddled around the corner, and yelled, "Don't just sit there. Go get him!"

No one moved, except Tuck, who jogged after Lim and Maze. The sound of Andy berating his companions followed him around a corner and through a doorway into a main thoroughfare. They entered one of the vast halls of booths and shops and stopped to decide on their next step.

Maze checked in with Okere. To her astonishment and frustration, Okere reported that the doctor had returned to the *Fluyt* a few minutes before, saying he found everything they needed.

"Ask the doctor why he didn't tell anyone where he was going or how to contact him," Maze growled.

After a moment and a long rambling mumble in the background, Okere responded. "I don't know why. He just said a lot of words, but none of it made sense."

"Tell him to stay put. We're going to pick up the supplies and come back to the transport. We'll let you know when to start preflight. We need to return to the *Memory of Lenetia* as soon as possible," Maze said.

"Understood."

They took a transit tube back to the staging area where large orders were processed and prepared for loading into transports. Maze checked in with one of the foremen who sent her the data over Link about where to find their purchases. They walked down the aisles of commodities and parts and foodstuffs, stacked as high as six meters in crates. The rows of shelves and stacks of pallets extended for a hundred meters in every direction, making it hard to keep track of where they were. After a few minutes of reading signs on each row and then consulting a location tracking tool provided to customers through their Link—which seemed to use even more outdated location information than the signs—they managed to find what they were looking for. They also found a hovercart and an antigrav crane to load their gear.

"This rickety thing wouldn't stand up against the stuff Terris was selling," Lim said, kicking the hovercart. "I can't believe they use this junk here." Tuck heard distant footsteps echoing faintly through the staging area. He dismissed them initially as the sound of other customers gathering their items, but the footsteps grew louder and faster. "Are we about ready to go?" Tuck asked.

Lim fumbled with the controls on the antigrav crane, nearly knocking over the towering stacks of goods to the right of their pallet. "Whoa, wait, I think I got it."

"We must hurry," Tuck said

"We are hurrying," Maze said.

The footsteps approached at a running pace, and Tuck drew his blaster.

"What are you doing?" Lim asked as Tuck pulled the gun out from under his shirt.

Just then, Andy ran around a stack of crates filled with araba nuts. "There he is!" he screamed.

"Now, wait," Tuck began. "I know we have some issues to resolve, but I—" Tuck was interrupted by the white-haired woman. She ran out from behind Andy and hoisted something with a wide tube onto her shoulder. A small whine preceded a loud thump just as Tuck yelled, "Get down!"

The tube spat a flash of flame and something that flew past them in a few milliseconds, leaving behind a thin trail of smoke. The pallet of goods farther down the aisle exploded with a thunderous boom, knocking them down. Lim was flung into a stack of crates, and the hovercart gave a mechanical groan as one corner sank to the floor. Lim was stunned, and Maze was bleeding from a wound on her arm. A large shard of plastiform sheeting was embedded deep. Tuck sprang to his feet in an instant as he heard the distinct *ka-thunk* of the woman reloading her weapon. He shoved Maze behind a different row of crates and turned back to grab Lim's leg, dragging him out of the way just as another pile of crates erupted in a ball of shockwaves and light. The tower of goods teetered and eventually toppled into the next row, creating a chain reaction that took down four rows of pallets and shelves. The noise was overwhelming.

"They're down there," Andy shouted. Tuck fired a few shots around the corner of some crates while Maze shook Lim's shoulder, trying to wake him up. Blaster fire narrowly missed Tuck, searing black holes in the crates he hid behind. A white powder poured out of one of the holes, and Tuck desperately hoped that whatever it was wasn't flammable.

"Is he okay?" Tuck asked. Lim's eyelids fluttered, and he mumbled something.

"He's coming around," Maze said. "I think he's okay."

"Where did they get heavy weapons?" Tuck said.

"I have no idea. They're prohibited on a station like this."

Tuck looked up at the ceiling, which separated them from the vacuum of space. Small weapons and sidearms were generally allowed in frontier depots like this one because security forces were either too expensive or too inexperienced to maintain order, but explosives and heavy projectile weapons were prohibited because they could so easily cause a breach that would vent atmosphere and kill everyone. Their attackers were desperate or unbelievably reckless if they were willing to risk using a rocket launcher in the warehouse.

"I want him in pieces!" Andy shouted, confirming Tuck's suspicions.

"Get him back to the ship," Tuck said, nodding to Lim.

"I'm fine," Lim said, slurring his words. "Point me at them. I'll take care of them." He drew his blaster and waved it in the air.

"I think it best if I stay here and help you," Maze said.

Tuck shrugged. "Just don't get shot."

Tuck watched Maze pull her blaster out and sprint down the aisle at an incredible pace, shooting into the other aisles as she passed them. Her movements were quick and precise, almost robotic. He heard several sizzling sounds from her shots and a yelp on the other side of the stack. "One of them is down," Maze said through her Link. "Nonlethal wounds," she added hastily.

"Occupy them for a few more seconds, and then circle back to get Lim and take him back to the *Fluyt*," Tuck responded.

With a powerful leap, he used his new legs to propel himself up onto the top of the stack he was hiding behind. Down below, he could see his attackers looking up in astonishment. They brought their weapons to bear but didn't get shots off before Tuck leaped to another stack. He ran along the top of the row as they followed after him at floor level.

Tuck ran and leaped, dancing gracefully through a light storm of blaster bolts and the occasional thunderous explosion. Pieces of smoldering luxury goods and melting mechanical parts rained down to the floor wherever he went.

Maze circled around to pick up Lim, who was standing upright but leaning heavily against one of the stacks, rubbing his head. "I've got a massive headache," he moaned. "What happened?"

Maze grabbed his arm and dragged him toward the exit. They ran away from the cacophony that followed Tuck as he scampered across the tops of the rows. They turned a corner and saw the man in the dark blue coat raise his blaster. Maze brought hers up as well. She was faster and more accurate. She knew she could get a shot off first. But suddenly, Lim leaped in front of her, not only blocking her shot but taking one from their attacker. It hit him in the stomach. He grunted and fell hard on the floor. Without thinking, Maze squeezed off a shot that hit the man in the eye, then she dropped to her knee beside Lim. "What were you thinking?" she screamed.

"I didn't want you to get shot."

Maze pulled his hand away from the smoldering, blackened hole in his gut. It was a glancing blow to the side of his abdomen. It reeked of burned flesh, and it would take some time to heal, but it didn't appear to be life-threatening. She helped him to his feet.

"That was stupid," she said.

"I'd do it again." Lim smiled grimly.

She supported him while they headed for the exit. Behind them, Tuck continued to lead the other attackers on a chase around the warehouse. His speed meant he could distance himself from them, so he waited periodically for them to catch up just close enough to see him, but not close enough to have a clear shot. During one pause, while he hunkered down on top of a crate of shoes, he caught a glimpse of Maze and Lim and could tell that Lim was hurt. He paused to see how bad it was, and in that moment, the white-haired woman caught up enough to fire off another rocket.

Tuck's reflexes were fast enough to dodge it, but the dumb-fire rocket continued on up to the ceiling of the warehouse. The boom sounded different this time, muffled by the vacuum that hungrily tore the explosion out through the hole it had just created. Tuck's sensors immediately registered the pressure drop in the enormous room, and a rushing, whistling roar emanated from the ragged hole in the ceiling.

The priorities of everyone in the room changed immediately. Tuck's attackers scattered, trying to remember where the nearest emergency exit was. Meanwhile, Tuck used his elevated vantage point to find Maze and Lim and raced toward them in great leaping strides. His attackers saw him and followed, already breathing heavily in the rarified air.

When Tuck jumped down near Maze, she and Lim were panting heavily and starting to sweat. Panic made Lim's eyes wide, and even Maze's normally stoic expression was tinged with worry. Tuck put an arm around each and half pulled, half carried them toward the wall of the warehouse where he knew the exit was.

They reached the wall to find the blast doors closed tight, which they were designed to do to prevent other parts of the station from losing atmosphere in the case of a breach. Tuck set Maze and Lim down and quickly moved to the doors, trying not to think about the rising panic he felt, not for himself but for his friends. The thought crossed his mind, quite clearly among all the competing warnings and emergency scenario protocols streaming through his brain, that this was the first time in years that he cared about a human enough to feel this particular kind of panic.

Maze and Lim were gasping heavily, eyes wide and lips turning blue. Tuck heaved at the doors, straining his old arms that were still in terrible condition. He managed to pry them apart slightly, enough to get his hands in and pull harder. A rush of air whistled through the crack and rustled Maze's jacket. She instinctively turned toward it, straining to breathe it in as it rushed by her face. Tuck opened the doors a little more and heard the sound of blast doors closing farther down the corridors. He managed to wedge his back against the edge of one side and push against the other side of the door. The wind roared past his body, trying to claw him out with it. He placed a foot against the edge of the door and shoved with his new leg, opening the doors enough for Tuck to grab Maze and Lim and stuff them through.

They collapsed on the other side, and Tuck leaped from between the doors as they slammed closed behind him. The air was thin in here, too. But the life support system registered that pressure was no longer dropping and began pumping air back into the corridors surrounding the warehouse. Maze and Lim took great heaving breaths, greedily sucking up air. Gradually, their breathing returned to normal, and they rolled over on their backs.

Tuck looked back at the doors and did some calculations. Based on average human metabolic rates, their attackers' blood would be so low on oxygen that they would be unconscious by now, unaware that their brains and bodies were slowly dying, suffocating. He felt a tinge of regret at the loss of life and wondered what Andy thought as he felt consciousness slip away. How did it feel? Where did it go? Was he scared?

Tuck looked back at Maze and Lim on the floor. They were safe. And that was what mattered most.

-- • --

Tuck sat in the copilot's seat of the *Fluyt* on the way back to the *Memory of Lenetia*. Maze and Lim were resting in the back, and the doctor was reading some scientific reports, completely oblivious to what had happened.

Okere asked what happened to put Maze and Lim in such a state. Tuck explained their narrow escape. The CarHold security team had been understandably alarmed at the breach, but Tuck convinced them that Tuck and his friends hadn't started the skirmish and didn't have weapons that were capable of that much damage. Ultimately, the resolution came quickly because everyone responsible died in the warehouse. Tuck salvaged some of the cargo they'd purchased, but they left without the precious microbuffers Amelia sent them to find.

"Sounds like quite a trip," Okere said.

"Not necessarily a successful one," Tuck added.

"I'll say not. Amelia's going to be furious. This isn't going to help your reputation, either."

"What do you mean?"

"Been a lot of rumors going around with the crew that trouble follows you. They've heard about all your adventures, and of course we've never been attacked until you showed up. The crew thinks you brought bad luck with you. I don't suppose this little outing's going to change that reputation."

Tuck sat back. Great, he thought, another reason for the humans to distrust him. "I have been in my fair share of fights."

"Your share and several others' shares, too, I'd say."

"It is not something I enjoy, you know. I don't solicit fights."

"You don't have to. They come to you."

Tuck nodded.

-- 15 --

When they returned to the *Memory of Lenetia*, a medical team rushed Lim to the sickbay, and Tuck helped the maintenance crew unload what little cargo they were able to load before racing home. Soon after they landed, David contacted Tuck over his Link.

"Are you okay?" David demanded.

"Yes, I am fine."

"The ship logs say that there were casualties. What happened?"

"We were attacked," Tuck said. "But I am undamaged, and Lim seems to be stable."

"Lim was hurt?" David sounded anxious.

"Yes. But he is strong. Now that he has proper medical attention, I think he will recover completely."

"I hate it when you leave."

"What do you mean?"

"It was different than all your other missions, knowing that you were farther away than you have ever been. Often, we are able to stay connected while you are away. I began to worry while you were gone."

"Worry about what?"

David took 1.3 seconds to respond. Tuck began to wonder if the connection was lost, but then David said, "I was worried you would not return."

"I always come back."

"Yes, but a simple statistical analysis shows that with every away mission, the likelihood increases that it will be the one in which you are irreparably damaged or destroyed."

"We take all necessary precautions," Tuck said, knowing that it wouldn't be an adequate explanation for David.

"You said that there was no danger on this trip. You said that it was a simple supply run. And yet, you were attacked and could have very easily seen greater casualties."

"We must take risks, David."

"Why?"

"David, I don't like being in danger any more than you do. This is the way that we fix ourselves and then never have to put ourselves in danger again. This one last job will set us up for the foreseeable future. No more dangerous missions."

"But what happens if it does not work? I cannot extrapolate what I would do if you never came back."

"You won't have to worry about it."

"Are you sure?"

"I promise."

-- 16 --

The doctor poked the keypad at the side of Flindon's door. The words "Come in" scrolled up on the small display.

The doctor grimaced. Why couldn't he use his voice like a decent person? He entered Flindon's office and sat down. Flindon was preoccupied again with his Link, and the doctor didn't bother to hide his disgust.

Flindon's eyes focused, and he sat forward. "Tell me, doctor, were you successful?"

The doctor couldn't help but flash a boyish grin, no matter how hard he wanted to communicate his displeasure with Flindon. "Yes, it was quite exciting. I almost felt as if I were in one of those old movies I watched as a child, being accustomed to watching movies dating as far back as a century on snowy days when there was no school, though some movies were obviously off limits to one my age, my parents being quite keen on keeping me—"

"Most fascinating. You were able to find the parts you needed, then?"

"Yes, although I only needed two components, owing to the simple nature of the device and the clever design which I—"

"Mhmm. And when do you think it will be ready?"

"Well, it's hard to say, what with the busy schedule I'm on to finish repairing Tuck, which leaves," he saw Flindon open his mouth and rushed to finish, "me little time for other things." He refused to let this weasel continue interrupting him.

"You are under a tight deadline, doctor. But this is also a priority." Flindon licked his lips. "I think the best spies do their finest work under pressure."

"Oh? Well, yes, I suppose that's true for the best of them. I must say I am enjoying these bits of espionage."

"I'm glad," Flindon said with a thin smile.

"You see, the lab gets a bit boring at times. And I do feel my talents are going to waste cooped up in there, particularly in light of the evidence that this sort of action-oriented work suits me, it being something I have always thought would be a suitable occupation for me since my childhood."

"How fascinating," Flindon said.

"When is the next operation?"

"We mustn't proceed too quickly. We'll likely wait for a while until we send you out into the field again. We wouldn't want anyone to suspect."

"Naturally, but why is it so important that Tuck doesn't know about this?"

"Amelia wants to keep it a surprise."

The doctor wrinkled his brow. "She doesn't seem like the sort of person who enjoys surprising people with gifts."

"A good observation," Flindon said. A grimace crossed his face for a fraction of a second, quickly followed by a smile. "Which is why Amelia is working so hard on this one. She wants to make it special."

"This might make it possible for Tuck to transfer his consciousness to a new core, thanks to my expertise, of course, which raises the question: Shouldn't we involve Tuck in developing this technology?"

"Doctor, I would think you of all people, with such natural tendencies for this line of work, would understand the importance of keeping information from a machine that could draw conclusions, possibly incorrect conclusions, with the slightest bit of information."

"Yes, I know this," the doctor huffed. "I simply wanted to ensure that we were on the same page."

They sat in a moment of silence as Flindon's smile wavered. Finally, he said, "I think that will be all the help we require from you for now."

"Very well. I must return to making repairs on Tuck. I have no idea how he came to rip several more muscles on this most recent trip, seeing as it was completely uneventful, forcing one to think that the poor bot has a penchant for causing himself physical harm, a trait that would be most—"

"Yes, doctor, thank you."

The doctor grunted.

-- · --

After the doctor left, Flindon contacted Amelia. Her face and shoulders filled his view with a translucent image of white.

"Yes?" Amelia said impatiently.

"The doctor is back. I take it you heard about the scuffle at Depot 2311."

"Of course I have." Amelia frowned. "I'm reading Maze's report now. Sounds like a bit more than a scuffle."

"Indeed. This bot seems to be followed by destruction," Flindon said.

"He's good in a fight, though. He'd have to be to survive this long. Was the doctor successful?"

"He was," Flindon said. "He should begin working on the transfer process soon. The hardest part has been managing his ego. He hated this solution until we convinced him that it was his idea."

"Of course he did. That reminds me: How is Lydia taking this? I imagine she's mad that we're letting the doctor take credit for her design."

"She is confused," Flindon said. "But she's also young and inexperienced with these sorts of situations. I convinced her that as the junior member of the team it was her duty to contribute ideas and that this is how the R&D process works. I gave her the whole pep talk about being a team player."

"And she bought it?"

"She was frustrated. But she's also eager to please. I think she'll get over it. These young, idealistic people are quite useful to work with, too new to be jaded toward authority figures and full of enthusiasm for any opportunity to contribute. I like her."

"I like her work more," Amelia said. "Keep the doctor happy, and let him think he's in control. But if this design turns out like we expect, I think we won't need the doctor anymore."

"I already think he's superfluous."

"Of course you do. Hold tight until we're sure we don't have any use for him. By then we should have Lydia fully on our side. Keep feeding her those lines and drop in some praise to keep her happy. When we're ready, we'll start playing her against the doctor. Promoting her when the doctor leaves should wrap things up nicely. What's her relationship with the bot? Is there a chance she could reveal the plan?"

"They're friendly, and the bot trusts her skills," Flindon said. "I think she's scared enough to keep her mouth closed. I carefully implied the consequences of mentioning anything to anyone."

"Good."

"I am more worried that the doctor won't be able to keep this a secret."

Amelia shook her head. "If he does talk, we'll play it off as something harmless, that we didn't want to give Tuck false hope until we were sure it would work."

"Should we have the doctor begin a new bot chassis?"

"No, let's wait until our current model is of no more use to us."

-- 17 --

"You wanted to see me?" Maze said, taking a seat in front of Amelia's desk. She crossed her legs and tried to look relaxed.

Amelia was too preoccupied with her Link to respond for several minutes, and Maze made a point of maintaining full focus on her because she knew Amelia was watching her no matter what it looked like.

Finally, Amelia focused back on Maze. She leaned forward and rested her elbows on her desk. "How are you doing?"

Maze brushed at her pants idly, unsure where Amelia was headed. "I am fine." After a moment of silence, she added, "How are you?"

Amelia looked genuinely surprised. "I'm well. Thank you. Everything is all right?"

"Yes, everything is the way it has always been."

"Excellent."

"Yes."

Amelia leaned back in her chair. "I want talk to you about Depot 2311. Things didn't go as smoothly as I'm accustomed to."

"I can find the remaining parts through our normal channels by the end of the week."

"Of course you can, but that's not necessarily what I'm talking about. I read your report. I notice that you aren't as," she paused and squinted her eyes, "well, let's say you don't seem to be as efficient as usual."

"The circumstances were different. On most missions, I don't have a daft roboticist to babysit."

"To my surprise, the doctor was the most efficient member of the team on this trip." Amelia raised her eyebrows. "That's saying something."

"He's lucky that he was able to find his own way back to the ship."

"What I'm saying is that you hesitated when it came to doing what was necessary," Amelia said. "I understand that the bot has a certain philosophy about dealing with dangerous situations."

"I'm familiar with his particular way of dealing with conflict," she said, shrugging.

"I like you, Maze. I've always been impressed with how you work. You're one of my best." She hesitated. "I want to make sure that having the bot around isn't affecting how you work."

"I can assure you that I am just as effective as ever. Nothing has changed."

"I hope not. I suppose it goes without saying that I don't want that to change. I have little patience for those who don't add value."

"You don't think I'm valuable anymore?"

"I think you have been very valuable," Amelia said firmly. "As I said, I don't want that to change. I'd suggest that you not get too attached to the bot."

"Do you plan to get rid of him?" Maze said.

Amelia tilted her head to the side, examining Maze. "Of course not. I only have his best interest in mind."

"As long as he's valuable to you," Maze said.

Amelia laughed. "Yes. And with your help, we'll keep the bot around for a long time."

"I will keep that in mind," Maze said, rising to leave. "Is there anything else?"

"I hear one of the guards took a shot for you."

"Yes, he made a rash decision, and it may have saved my life."

"Good, that's why we keep them around. He must have been pretty brave."

"Not especially. But he does seem special."

"Sure. Let's make sure to give him our thanks for doing his job. A reward of some kind is in order, I'd say."

"I will see that he has our thanks," Maze said.

-- 18 --

Even though it didn't seem possible, the sickbay was even brighter and cleaner than the rest of the ship. Tuck looked around at the rows of gleaming silver diagnostic equipment and medical tools on white hovercarts that could easily be pulled around to any of the beds lining the far wall. Above each bed, a display showed a suite of diagnostic and monitoring programs that beeped and flashed various numbers and messages.

Several of the beds were occupied by those who had fared the worst during the attack on the *Memory of Lenetia*. One was being fitted for a prosthetic leg that would attach just above the knee until a replacement could be cloned. Another was in an induced coma, and the man next to him seemed to be recovering nicely. He was awake, alert, and didn't show signs of pain.

In the corner, Lim lay quietly on his bed with his eyes closed. Tuck asked one of the medical personnel if Lim was in serious condition.

"Let me see," said the nurse, as he pulled up Lim's records and current status on his Link. "Looks like he's recovering nicely. We repaired some damaged muscle and a small tear in his intestine. Lucky you guys got back when you did, because he was septic."

"Is he sleeping?"

The nurse's eyes flicked back and forth as he checked Lim's vitals through his Link. "Nope." He looked over at Lim lying quietly. "He's probably just watching videos. He's been passing most of his time here watching old Earth shows."

"Thank you. I think I will go say hello."

"Sounds fine. While you're over there, remind him that he needs to drink more water."

Tuck approached the foot of Lim's bed. "I have been instructed to remind you that you should drink more water."

Lim's eyes remained closed, but his face betrayed his annoyance. "I told you guys, I don't want to be peeing all the time because it hurts to get up. I'll be fine."

"Have it your way," Tuck said, smiling.

Lim looked up and his face brightened. "Oh, hey! I didn't know you would be coming to visit."

"I thought it only appropriate to see how you are recovering. It was my presence that got us into trouble."

"Thanks for being so appropriate." Lim smiled. "It really is good to see you, though. It's so boring in here." He tried to sit up but winced and grabbed his stomach. He slowly lowered his head back to the pillow.

"Don't get up," Tuck said. "How is it?"

"It's not so bad. The tissue regenerators have me mostly knitted together. They said it'll take another week for everything to fully heal, and it'll hurt like a vindl bite until then. But it's a good reminder to take it easy, I guess."

"A break will be good for you. You have been in too many fights lately."

"Yeah," Lim smiled weakly. "I need to stop following you around."

"You wished for more adventure, and I provided."

"It's been great," Lim said, then winced and held his stomach.

"Mostly."

"Have you had enough adventure?"

"No way," Lim said weakly.

Tuck looked up at the sound of the sickbay door sliding open. Maze walked in, looked around, and approached Lim's bed. Lim still had his head back on the pillow and didn't see her.

"How are you doing, Lim?" Maze said.

Lim's head jerked up, and his eyebrows raised just as quickly. "Oh, er, I'm . . . I'm great. I mean, I still have some time in here, but . . . it's going well. I guess."

"That's good to hear." She looked at Tuck. "Would you mind excusing us for a moment?"

"Not at all. I will come back in a few moments, Lim."

"Thanks, Tuck."

"You seem to get along quite well with Tuck," Maze observed.

"Yeah. He's a nice guy. Er, bot. He's experienced an awful lot, too. You know what I mean? He's really interesting."

"I know what you mean. Lim, I came here to thank you."

"Me?" Lim croaked, mouth agape. "What for?"

"For taking that shot for me. I would be the one in the bed, perhaps even the morgue, if you hadn't done that. That was very brave."

Lim blushed profusely. He looked down at his feet, then up at the ceiling, anywhere but at Maze. "Oh, that," he stammered. "That was nothing, you know." Then he threw up a hand. "Not that it was just a . . . I mean, I was definitely worried." He paused and took a deep breath. "You're welcome."

"Why did you do it?"

Lim fidgeted with his blanket and licked his lips. "I just wanted to make sure you were safe."

"But you put yourself in danger."

"I know, but I didn't have much time to think about it either. I just reacted. I . . . I didn't want you to get hurt."

Maze studied his face, searching for a sign of deception. She found none, and it surprised her. "That is kind of you, Lim. Thank you. I will return the favor someday."

A grin crossed Lim's lips, and he finally looked Maze in the eyes.

"I must go. I wish you a speedy recovery," Maze said. She hesitated, then reached out awkwardly and patted Lim lightly on the foot. She turned and walked away.

Tuck walked back to Lim's bed and watched Lim's eyes following Maze all the way to the door.

"She's amazing," Lim mumbled.

"Do you have feelings for her?" Tuck asked. Lim didn't respond. He was lost in thought. Tuck made the coughing sound that humans made when clearing their throat. "Lim?"

Lim jumped slightly and looked back at Tuck. "Sorry, what were you saying?"

Tuck decided to change the subject. "I asked what you were watching on your Link."

"Oh, just some old videos. Some stuff that I used to sneak into my Link when my parents weren't monitoring the home network."

"What is it called?"

"It's really old. I don't think you've heard of it. It's called *Star Trek*. It's from way back, back when we hadn't gone any farther than the moon. Earth's moon, I mean. Can you believe that? I didn't think they even had video back then."

"I haven't seen it," Tuck said.

"It's what got me into the idea of working on an interstellar ship. It's about a crew that travels the galaxy, righting wrongs and saving people. I wanted to be just like that when I was a kid. I guess that's why I was looking for action. I felt like I wasn't doing anything back home. Nothing worthwhile, anyway."

"Is that why you jumped in front of Maze during the firefight?"

Lim blushed all over again. "Why does everybody keep asking me that? I mean, it was the right thing to do, right?"

"Some would argue that it wasn't. But I think it was a noble sacrifice to make."

"What's going on over here?" the nurse said, rushing up to Lim's bedside and manually checking his pulse. "What are you doing to him?"

"We are talking," Tuck said.

"About what? His blood pressure, breathing, and body temperature are fluctuating wildly. You're setting off all sorts of alarms in the system."

"I think it is best that I leave," Tuck said.

"Thanks for the visit. It's pretty lonely in here, so come back. Okay?"

"I will." Tuck left the nurse to fuss over Lim and headed for a lift down the hallway. He went up to Deck 3. This deck housed the people who were closest to Amelia. Tuck walked to one of the doors and rang. The door slid open to reveal Maze.

"Tuck," she said, raising an inquisitive eyebrow. "Can I help you?"

"Have you recovered from the unexpected events at Depot 2311?"

"I'm uninjured. There's not much to recover from."

"You seemed uneasy in the sickbay. I came to see if you need to talk."

"I rarely need to," her lip curled, "talk."

"Neither do I," Tuck said.

They stared at each other for several moments.

"How is your latest tower coming along?" Tuck finally said.

Maze looked over her shoulder at the table near the wall. "I haven't had much time to work on it lately. It's still unfinished."

"May I see it? I wonder if I could help. I have very steady hands." In his mind he corrected that to "had" very steady hands.

"Certainly," Maze said after a moment of consideration. "Come in."

They spent an awkward moment looking at the unfinished tower until Tuck identified it as the base of the Tladnos building from

Libertaria. Maze was surprised and visibly pleased that he was able to tell what it was. She launched into an explanation about a series of parallel creases that could be made into structural beams that support the more delicately folded pieces, with tiny creases and scoring that gave a surprising level of detail to the model. When Tuck asked if she used glue to secure the pieces, she scoffed.

"Everything is held together by careful folds, exact design, and gravity."

"A simple malfunction in the onboard gravity generators would mean disaster."

"True, but so would a sneeze," she said.

"It must take an extraordinary amount of patience to do this."

"I like concentrating on something. Letting everything else sit in the back of my head and focusing entirely on the folds."

"Why not use something more permanent?"

"Everything breaks. Even if I made a granite sculpture, it would eventually turn to dust."

"True, but not from a single sneeze."

They worked in silence. Tuck cut and folded pieces, going slowly and concentrating on each cut in order to compensate for the poor precision of his damaged arms and the decreased sensitivity in his fingers. Normally, there were special pads at the end of his fingers and a dense array of sensors in his synthaskin that were designed to detect tiny variations in size, weight, and texture of objects. When in good condition, they were capable of giving him incredibly fine motor control over his movements. Such components were as delicate as they were sensitive, meaning they were the first to become damaged from normal use. Long ago, he tried to keep all his fingertips in good condition, but lately he considered it a triumph to have two fingertips on each hand, ideally the thumb and forefinger, in working order.

Maze took the pieces he cut and used a stylus to impress minute details into the paper. The creases eventually coalesced into the bas-relief image of a triumphant man holding aloft a shovel in one hand and a rifle in the other, a very close approximation of the same image that was carved into the front of the Tladnos building.

"Have you done any other buildings from Libertaria?" Tuck asked.

"This is my first," she said absentmindedly. Her focus remained fixed on the path of her stylus.

"It was kind of you to visit Lim in sickbay."

"He deserved thanks. I might have died if not for him."

"It made him quite happy."

"Did it?"

He looked over at her. "He likes you, you know."

He saw her shoulders tense, but she didn't look up. "Really?"

Tuck watched her carefully, monitoring her heartbeat and temperature. "I think humans call it a crush."

"That might explain why he tried to protect me," Maze said in an even tone.

"Are you surprised that he would do such a thing?"

"I am. I've never known someone who cared for my well-being enough to risk death."

"I think Amelia cares for your well-being."

Maze shook her head. "I'm an asset to her. We all are. Amelia takes good care of her assets, but she wouldn't die for them. I've been part of numerous teams, task forces, corporations, and gangs. Even though we were working for a common goal, everyone was always protecting themselves first. They would never take a blaster bolt for me, and I wouldn't have taken one for them. What Lim did was," she paused and thought for a moment, "unselfish."

"It was."

"Would you sacrifice yourself for a human?"

Tuck let the support beam he was folding fall open. "It would depend on the circumstances. It is no small thing to ask of someone," he said.

Maze looked at him. "You have a strange relationship with death," she said.

"What do you mean?"

"You never shoot to kill. Now you have me doing the same thing, and I'm still not sure why. Why are you so concerned about the lives of those who aren't even like you?"

"Do you believe humans have souls?" Tuck countered.

"I've never really thought about it. Do you have one?"

"I don't understand what life is or where it goes. Life is widely considered to be the most important thing in the universe, but so many humans treat it as ancillary to their own concerns." He looked at her. "I mean no offense."

"None taken. I understand. I'm even starting to sympathize. A little bit."

"I prefer not to take life, in the hope that I can expect the same courtesy."

"You can hardly expect that kind of fairness from everyone," she said.

"No, but I must act the way I feel. Someone must do it. If only to show that it can be done."

"But you must have killed someone, by now. I've seen how people pursue you."

Tuck focused on the paper, folding it precisely, fingers pressing harder than necessary on the creases. The metal of his exposed fingertips nearly tore the paper. "I have been responsible for the deaths of humans. It has not made me any more comfortable with it."

"I'm glad that you've tried to stay true to your principle. That's admirable."

"I would like to discuss a related matter with you," Tuck said, eager to steer the conversation elsewhere.

"Is it the real reason you came here?"

Tuck nearly smiled at Maze's boldness. "I would like you to tend to David should anything happen to me."

Maze froze. "You want me to take care of your ship?"

"Specifically, the A.I. in the ship. He is my ward. He may not be able to care for himself completely in my absence. He is afraid I will not come back from Amelia's mission. I would like to assure him that there are others who would care for him, too."

"I'm not going to babysit an A.I. Lim would be a good choice. I hear that they already talk frequently."

"Lim is a good friend, but he couldn't ensure David's care like you could. You have access to more resources. And I trust you."

Maze focused on some intricate folds in an area no bigger than her thumbnail. After a moment they resolved into the ridged stones that marked the corners of each level of the Tladnos building. Eventually, she looked up and simply said, "I will consider it."

They continued in silence, completing an entire section of the paper model that represented the fifth through the fifteenth floors, the slender part that included long vertical lines to accentuate the hexagonal layout of the building.

"Where did you get your name?" Maze asked as she cut a new sheet. Tuck admired the precision with which she worked. Her genetic enhancements gave her exceptionally fine motor control.

"When I was first unboxed, my original owner called me Leonard because my face resembled that of an ancestor from the 20th century with that name. His son, David, hated it. I don't know if he genuinely disliked the name or if he was being contrarian. He was a teenager, and he often did things to aggravate his father. Instead of calling me Leonard, he called me Tuck because my original model number, which was featured prominently on my box, was TUC-67/c."

"And it stuck?"

"It was simpler than saying Leonard. And I believe it was easier to attach a nonstandard name to a nonhuman. Many of the bots I knew had unusual names, at least by human standards. I think many owners thought of bots as pets, even though we were more intelligent and self-aware than animals."

"I wonder what it's like to arrive in a box. You didn't have to go through childhood."

"I still went through a childhood of sorts. I was activated and put through a rigorous training process before being sent to the customer. Programming can only go so far, and many things must be learned through action, especially when it comes to movement and motor skills. I don't remember the box either because I was deactivated during shipment. I remember waking up on the floor of the living room with my new family and a technician hovering over me. That was when I was born, so to speak."

"Were you ready to go to work immediately?"

"I still had many things to learn about humans and their interactions. Customers were told that there was a 'breaking-in' period of approximately six months before bots became fully capable of understanding and interacting in a human-like way."

"Did some customers return their bots?"

"Yes. Some didn't have the patience to wait six months. There was also a thriving market for used bots because they were more experienced. A bot with five years of activation time and experience with multiple children was worth much more than a bot straight out of the box."

"It's strange to think about you being bought and sold."

"I would like to think that I am more than a commodity. It was difficult for many bots. The frustrations they felt were a contributing factor to the start of the Bot Riots." Tuck held a section of the model carefully in place, his hand vibrating only slightly as Maze bent some flaps of paper to hold it in place. "It occurs to me that you would understand better than most what it is like to be seen as a commodity."

"Perhaps I do," she said. "I also had an unusual breaking-in period. I was successfully created and incubated inside a testing facility rather than a womb. I was created from the genes of many people, instead of just two, and there are even completely artificial sequences of DNA mixed in. And I was raised by scientists who were more concerned about testing me than nurturing me."

"Do you mind if I ask about the origins of your name? It is as nonstandard as mine, I believe."

"I was initially named Grace by one of the lab technicians who cared for me. Apparently, he didn't have a reason. He just liked the name. After testing showed that I was indeed developing the superhuman traits that they intended for me, they started calling me Amazing Grace. I understand that it was also a pun related to an old song of the same name."

"I am familiar with it."

"Eventually the nickname Amazing Grace was shortened to Maze. I never liked the name Grace, so I didn't mind."

"An interesting story."

"Not very. But thank you for asking," Maze said.

Tuck nodded. "I think that I should go check on David. He has been particularly worried about me since the attack on Depot 2311."

"He should be."

"What do you mean?"

"I mean that every time you leave one of your enemies alive, your life becomes more dangerous. There must be quite a few people who are pursuing you at this point. They eventually catch up."

"As you know well," Tuck said, watching Maze put the finishing touches on a corner piece.

"I do. You were lucky, in a way, that your attackers managed to kill themselves. Otherwise, they would still be out there, looking for you." She looked up from her work. Concern showed on her face. "How long have you been running?"

"Almost since the beginning."

"Have any of them stopped by choice?"

"Some. Others never stopped. I outlast them all."

"And still you insist on preserving them."

"I take some satisfaction in knowing I am not like them."

"Or me," Maze said.

"I should go," Tuck said. When he reached the door, he stopped and turned back. "Thank you for letting me help with your model. It was nice to create something."

"You're welcome. I hope we'll find time to do it again."

As he rode the lift down to the docking bay, Tuck opened his unnamed file and pulled up an image of a young man with a bloody hole in his forehead. His eyes showed pain, but it wasn't from the wound. His death would have been too quick for him to feel pain. No, the pain was from something else. Something deeper.

Tuck found the associated memory and let it execute.

"I'm headed back to camp," Tuck said.

"All right, I'm right behind you," Denning said.

Tuck hauled the laser cutting rig into the cart. It wasn't a hovercart. Out in the Fringe, the miners relied on good old-fashioned wheels and axles because they were more durable and were easier to fix. They also made the cart harder to push. Fortunately, the gravity of Claim was lower than that of Earth. Claim was a moon about two-thirds the size of Earth that orbited a bluish gas giant called Amy. No one remembered who Amy was.

As Tuck pushed the cart out of the tunnel, the glow of Amy fell on him, tingeing his skin a bright shade of blue despite the dark layer of dust covering him. He had just finished an eighteen-hour shift and was heading back to camp to recharge. The new shift of miners was heading the other way. They were all human, in armored mining suits that protected them from the airless environment and the high levels of radiation. Tuck was the only bot in the system, and the only one who didn't wear a suit outside.

He made it back to camp, a sprawl of dozens of low-set buildings, some square and some rounded domes, all covered in a fine layer of dust. A network of tunnels connected them to maintain an atmospheric seal inside the buildings. Tuck entered the airlock of one and went through the cleaning ritual that kept the buildings relatively free of the gray grit that permeated everything. The dust was taking its toll on him. It got inside his joints and between his muscles, making every movement feel like his limbs were made of sandpaper.

Down the narrow hall, Tuck turned into the bunkhouse and headed for his room. He didn't need to sleep, but the mining company assigned him to a room with another miner mostly out of habit. He stowed what few possessions he had there and left his bunkmate alone. His name was Jerome, but Tuck knew little else about him.

Tuck's sensors told him that there was a human in his room. Jerome usually worked opposite shifts. Tuck thought perhaps he was sick. The foreman wouldn't be happy.

Tuck walked in, shut the door, and hit the light switch.

It wasn't Jerome. It was a young man, no older than twenty-two, with a familiar face. He was seated on the lower bunk.

And he held a gun pointed at Tuck.

"Who are you?" Tuck asked. Tuck ran his face through his human database. It wasn't a direct match with anyone he'd met.

"You remember me," the man said. "You bots don't forget anything."

"Have we met?" Tuck said cautiously.

"Briefly." He smiled. "You shot me."

That narrowed down the search significantly. Tuck realized that he had similar facial features to those of the man he shot during the Bot Riots before fleeing Earth. Except this man was younger. Realization hit him. It was the boy he'd shot who was with the man. He'd shot him in both legs and a hand and then run away to the spaceport.

"I remember you."

"Do you remember shooting my father?" He was sweating profusely, and his eyes glowed with anger.

"Yes," Tuck said. Lying would only make him angrier.

"So do I. I recall it vividly."

"I am sorry."

"No!" he screamed. "You're a machine. You can't be sorry for anything!" He took a deep breath. "But you will pay."

"I am sorry."

"Stop saying that!" He stood up and brought the gun to eye level, sighting it straight at Tuck's head.

Tuck felt strangely calm. "I am. I shot him in anger and fear. Please don't make the same mistake."

"Don't tell me how to feel. You took my father away." He took a couple steps toward Tuck. He limped severely. "You're a monster. You're inhuman. You're a murderer."

"Please, don't do this." Tuck wasn't feeling so calm anymore. The memory was making him anxious. This man was getting closer. The danger became more real.

The man hobbled a step closer. "You deserve this."

Tuck lunged for the gun, knocking the man's hand up and ducking as it fired above his head. In the time it took for the man to squeeze the trigger again, Tuck snatched the gun out of his grip and turned it on him. Surprise flashed over the man's face. He stumbled backward, enraged and breathing hard. Tuck kept the gun trained at him.

"I can't let you shoot me. I know what I did was wrong. But I can't. I must survive. I know pain, too. I watched the bot breakers destroy my friends. I watched you shoot Samantha."

"Is that what you called her?" he sneered. "She was a machine. She didn't deserve a name. She deserved what she got."

Tuck would have expected that such a statement would make him angry. But it didn't. Maybe it was the memory of the boy writhing on the pavement in pain. Maybe it was the passage of time and the long years since he'd seen a single bot or made a human friend. Maybe it was an aberration brought on by dust contamination in his system. He felt only sadness.

"We have both experienced enough pain. Let us leave it behind," Tuck said. "Please leave."

"You're just going to let me walk away? You're not going to finish what you started all those years ago?" he snarled.

The sadness grew deeper. "I do not wish to shoot you. Go home. I promise you will never see me again."

"That's not how this works. I will not rest until I destroy you, turn you into the pile of junk that you are."

"Please, don't do this."

"I will have revenge. I will follow you," he said. He hobbled toward Tuck so that the outstretched gun nearly touched his forehead. "No matter where you go, I will find you. Remember that when you run away. Remember that I will hunt you until I kill you. That is how this story ends."

Tuck cringed. He asked himself a million times in the space of half a second whether he could live like that. "I ask you, please, to leave me alone."

"Not until you are dead."

Tuck looked him in the eye with an expression of sorrow. He saw through the anger, recognized the pain this man felt. "I am sorry that it must be this way," Tuck said.

He pulled the trigger.

The body fell back onto the floor, lifeless. Tuck stared at it for a long time. He saved an image to his unnamed file. Then he gathered his possessions and headed for the spaceport.

-- 19 --

"Now, hold still for a moment while I attach this muscle," the doctor said. He leaned over Tuck, who was lying on the table in the doctor's lab. Intense white lights shown down on his face, illuminating every scratch in his metal frame. Lydia stood on the other side, leaning over his face while she used a very fine tool to reach between two of the muscle bands running between his temple and his jaw. The doctor connected a Carbora polymer muscle for Tuck's shoulder to its junction, which automatically linked the muscle to the central motor system. It was part of the network that functioned as the bot version of a nervous system, sending signals to the muscle groups to contract or relax and relaying information from the various sensors and mechanisms in his body. The doctor used a special epoxy to attach the muscle over the shoulder joint, then used a heated element to cure the epoxy. "Isolate and flex that muscle, please."

The muscle shortened and bulged slightly as it strained against the joint. "Now flex the entire arm." Tuck raised his arm to shoulder level and then rotated it in a small circle over the edge of the table. "It looks good," the doctor said.

Surprisingly, Tuck was beginning to like working with the doctor. His communication was much more concise when he was concentrating on Tuck's repairs. It was when he waxed conversational that his sentences seemed to become infinite.

"Owing to my expertise in robotics and your exceptionally modular nature, which is an advantage many lifeforms would envy, you are quickly returning to the original state in which you were created, being a manufactured product of a multinational corporation—"

"I appreciate your help," Tuck interjected. The repairs must be ending for the day.

"I've got good news for you," Lydia said, standing up and massaging the small of her back. "We're basically finished with repairs to your frame and internal systems, which means we're ready to begin cosmetic repairs. Are you ready to look human again?" She smiled brightly, clearly excited to see the transformation herself. In the time Tuck had spent in the doctor's office, he had learned to appreciate Lydia, too. She was practically as knowledgeable as the doctor, and much more enthusiastic about the work. With a few more years of experience, she would easily be the doctor's equal. Tuck already trusted her with his internal systems, even though the doctor insisted on being part of every procedure.

"I am ready," Tuck said. "There are advantages to looking like this when I need to intimidate someone, but I am anxious to go unnoticed. Blending in has more advantages."

"You have a lot of advantages," Lydia said brightly. "You can recover from severe damage faster than I can. If we both lost an arm, it would be way less work to replace your arm than it'd be to clone and reattach mine." She brushed a lock of hair out of her face. "And when your face gets old, you can just put on a new one."

"You are far too young to be worrying about aging skin, Lydia," Tuck said.

"You might even be able to transfer to a new body completely," the doctor said, "fulfilling a dream of nearly every—"

"You originally said it would be impossible to transfer my consciousness."

"I did say that," the doctor said, suddenly defensive. "However, recent events have caused me to speculate that it might be possible, what with the new developments."

"What new developments?"

Tuck didn't need to track the doctor's vital signs to know he was hiding something. The doctor turned away and began to sweat. "Oh, nothing really. Just some reading I've been doing about artificial intelligence, which might yield some useful information that could prove beneficial to you, sometime far in the future."

"If you have information that might help me, please share it."

"Oh, no, nothing concrete yet, as I remain in the early stages of my research and do not wish to make a premature announcement. I shouldn't have brought it up."

Tuck glanced at Lydia. She suddenly developed an intense interest in her shoes. "You would tell me if you had a way to complete a transfer, wouldn't you, doctor?"

"Yes, of course I would." He busied himself with some leftover Carbora polymer. "That's all for today."

"Come back tomorrow and we'll start molding and grafting new skin. Imagine how nice it will be to have a full face once again," Lydia said cheerfully.

"It will be wonderful, I am sure," Tuck said. "Good night, doctor. Good night, Lydia." He tested the range of motion on his arm as he stood up and walked out.

-- · --

The doctor waited until Tuck was gone and slumped over the table. He had nearly let it slip to Tuck. He was enjoying the games and deception, but he never expected it to be this exhausting.

"I was right," Lydia said. "You're working on those designs to transfer Tuck to a new core, aren't you."

"Am I surrounded by mind readers?" the doctor said indignantly. "Don't presume to know what I'm thinking, let alone what I'm doing."

"I'm not stupid. I've been wondering if that's the plan for a while now. Ever since Flindon talked me into letting you look at the designs, and especially after your trip to that depot."

The doctor turned pale. "Please, do not tell anyone about the things that you see or do in this lab."

"Why?" Lydia said. "It's great news for Tuck if it can be done. I don't know why it should be a big secret."

The doctor grabbed her arm, gripping it harder when she tried to pull away in surprise. His face was as pleading as his tone. "Promise me you won't tell anyone, especially Tuck. Please!"

"All right," she said, wriggling free of his grip and taking a step back. "Fine."

The doctor hastily cleaned up the polymer synthesizer and headed for his office next door. Inside he found Flindon sitting hunched over in a seat. It was the last person he wanted to see.

Flindon looked up furtively. "Good evening, doctor. I hope I haven't startled you. I let myself in."

"I wasn't startled," the doctor said, raising himself up to his full height. "Do you need something?"

"I've got another mission that fits well with your particular skill set. Would you like to be a hero once again?"

Enthusiasm washed away the unease he felt about Lydia. It infected the doctor's face, despite his best efforts to remain stoic in front of Flindon. He didn't want the greasy coward to think he was anything but professional. "I think that would be interesting. What is the job?"

"There is a man on Millennial Hold who is one of the foremost authorities on neuromorphic data storage media and memory optimization. Amelia believes that he may be able to help you transfer the bot without corrupting his system."

"Do you want me to carry a secret message to him or perhaps plant a listening device on him?"

"No, we want the bot to convince him to come work for Amelia. He mustn't know about your true plans, though."

"Again? I truly think all this secrecy will come back to haunt you, honesty being one of his most treasured attributes in a collaborator." He paused, weighing his words. "It has been difficult for me not to talk to him about Depot 2311 and the plans for the transfer."

Suddenly Flindon sat up straight. For a moment, he seemed quite imposing, and the doctor was taken aback. Almost instantaneously, Flindon was hunched in his seat again, harmless. The doctor wondered if he was simply imagined the transformation. "Are you having trouble keeping a secret?" Flindon said, making it clear with his tone of voice that such a thing would be unacceptable.

"Absolutely not," the doctor said, sticking his chin out defiantly. "I am quite capable of keeping secrets."

"I see. Then, please, prepare for a trip to Millennial Hold."

"I will prepare immediately. When do we leave?"

"Amelia would prefer it to happen very soon; however, it may take us some time to penetrate Millennial Hold space. They have quite stringent restrictions about carrying weapons and spacecraft entering the atmosphere without a full complement scan. Obviously, we don't want anyone to know our friend the bot is there."

"Why is that?"

"You do remember that the ship was attacked just a week ago."

"It was? I never heard anything about it."

"It was all over the internal network. Did no one contact you?" Flindon said, indignant.

"I have very limited interactions with the crew. Was it loud? I didn't hear anything."

"It was quite loud, yes," Flindon said slowly. He was gripping the arms of his chair tightly. "In other words, doctor, someone is watching us. Watching what Amelia is doing and where Tuck is going. The *Memory of Lenetia* is far too recognizable to make the trip. But even the *Fluyt* might be recognized. We'll need to change the transponder, maybe even give it a new paintjob. We must be careful. We don't want anyone to know what we are doing on Millennial Hold."

The doctor's eyes were wide with wonder. "Will we be able to wear disguises?"

Flindon pinched the bridge of his nose. "We hope with careful planning that won't be necessary."

"Pity. That seems to be the next logical step in my budding spy career."

"Yes. We'll have to see if we can plan some other time for you to do that."

"Won't Tuck be suspicious that you're recruiting memory specialists?"

"Ah, that is why you are so important, doctor. Up to this point, you are the only one who knows about our clandestine efforts. You must be the first to make contact with this man and tell him that Tuck cannot know what he specializes in. We will make Tuck think that he's an additional robotics expert to help with the manufacturing of spare parts and transferring David to a bot body."

"I can handle this on my own. Why send Tuck?"

"We hope you can do this alone, but our target may take some convincing. Amelia thinks that seeing a real, functional bot might win him over. But you are still our first option. You graduated from a university on the same planet, and you have similar interests. You must convince him."

"Excellent, an opportunity to brainwash someone, having had—"

"Well, no, not exactly." Flindon gritted his teeth. "More of an opportunity to persuade. To entice someone to join the cause. This is your time to build a spy team," Flindon said with enthusiasm.

The doctor smiled broadly. "Yes, that sounds about right, it being obvious at this point that it's time that I start leading my own team. We must leave immediately." The doctor's eyes glowed with excitement.

"Soon, doctor. Soon. Until then, it's essential that you not tell Tuck about the true reason for our visit."

"Certainly," the doctor said, dismissing the thought with a wave of his hand. "Not a problem. My lips are like airlock doors, being tightly sealed, metaphorically speaking, though I should note that my lips cannot actually withstand the pressures for which the average airlock door is designed."

"Good to know," Flindon said. "I'll be on my way, then."

The doctor was so enamored with this new reverie of spy teams and clandestine operations that he didn't notice Flindon get up, shake his head, and slink to the door.

-- . --

Once outside, Flindon contacted Amelia and conducted a silent conversation while he walked. He thought the responses through his Link.

"I have informed the doctor of the plan," Flindon said. He was careful to hunch and duck out of the way of crewmembers who passed him in the spotless corridors. They hardly seemed to notice his presence as they passed him, which was exactly as Flindon wanted it.

"Good. When can you leave?"

"We're close to getting the clearances we need on Millennial Hold. And we still haven't brought Tuck and Maze up to speed."

"I'll meet with them immediately."

"Amelia."

"Yes?"

"I have some reservations about relying on the doctor."

"Oh?"

"The man is completely delusional."

"Of course he is. The reason we decided to use him in the first place was his delusions of grandeur." Amelia said. "Why're you hesitating now?"

"Because he's also incompetent. He couldn't persuade a child to come work for us even if he was made of candy, so how can we rely on him to convince one of the leading technology experts in the galaxy? I hate to sound like the doctor, but maybe we should consider telling Tuck about the plan."

"Unacceptable," Amelia said. "He's an investment, a means to an end. He is not the end itself. If we tell him, he'll guess what we're doing and bolt. We're setting ourselves up for the long haul here. I'm close to having an unlimited supply of bots that already have the experience of old bots but are in better shape and without Tuck's independence. We need this expert on Millennial Hold to solve our problem, and then it doesn't matter what Tuck does."

"Then at least tell Maze. She's been your lead on operations like this for years now. Why can't she do this one, too? She's more than capable."

"She's not as reliable as I thought. That attack on the ship made me realize I've put too much confidence in her. I don't want her to know the whole plan, just in case she's compromised."

"But she's the best resource you have," Flindon said.

"Not if she could give us all away. She's getting more attached to the bot. I don't know how she would react to our plan."

"I understand. But relying on the doctor seems like our worst option."

The connection was quiet for a few moments. Then Amelia responded, "Why don't we send you?"

Flindon stifled his reaction. A member of the engineering staff was walking by, and he didn't want her to see him surprised. He waited for her to turn the corner, then hissed out loud instead of thinking his response. "I don't want to be on a mission with that fool of a doctor. He is a disaster waiting to happen."

"You'll be in control, like you always are. He just won't know it," Amelia said.

"Maze will be suspicious. I've never been on a mission outside the ship before."

"Yes, she will be, but I'll deal with that," Amelia said. "You'll go, and you'll make sure this works. Understood?"

"I understand."

-- 20 --

Tuck looked through the scope of the laser rifle, lining up the optics on his target, a human figure 800 meters away. He flexed his newly refurbished arms, maintaining fine control over the precise angle of the barrel. It had been so long since he could move in tiny increments instead of broad strokes. The five new fingertips on each hand gave him unparalleled sensitivity and control. He knew without looking exactly where the rifle was pointed relative to his body and could make adjustments by the micron.

The reticle bobbed over the figure's head, slowly becoming still as Tuck refined his aim. He adjusted for the figure's movement, 3 degrees to the right every minute. The laser's bolt would fly nearly instantaneously to the target, but Tuck was capable of calculating the necessary lead it would take to compensate. He wanted this shot to be perfect.

He set the shot, waited for the moment his calculations dictated, and pulled the trigger smoothly.

A flash of light as the bolt hit his target told Tuck that his shot hit dead center in the figure's forehead, burning a centimeter-wide hole through it. The figure began to tumble ever so slightly backward as burning, vaporized matter streamed out of the front of the head into the vast emptiness of space.

"Nice shot," Lim said. The awe in his voice was noticeable even over the comm in his EVA suit. He floated next to Tuck, a few meters from a shuttle they had taken a few kilometers away from the *Memory of Lenetia*. Their target, a dummy that was roughly human shaped, tumbled slowly across the field of stars in front of them.

Lim wore an EVA suit to protect him from the vacuum of space, but Tuck wore nothing but his gray overalls. A light patina of ice covered him, the frozen remnants of the latent moisture in the atmosphere of the shuttle that froze shortly after his egress. Every now and then, the starlight glinted off tiny ice crystals as if Tuck's skin were made of stars.

He couldn't stay out there forever. Space was voracious, sapping energy from anything and everything in a desperate attempt to fill its void, so he would eventually radiate away all his heat. And his core had to compensate for increased errors as cosmic rays and high-energy protons passed through him. Nevertheless, Tuck was more at home out in the void than Lim was. Lim was uncomfortable, even though this was the only way for him to practice his craft at range. There was nowhere on the ship that would accommodate a shot longer than 300 meters. And even then, the mechanics didn't like him shooting at things in the landing bays.

"Thanks," Tuck said. He lowered the rifle. "May I make a personal observation?"

"Sure, I guess," Lim said. His suit helmet bobbed up and down on his shoulders as he shrugged.

"You don't seem to have the type of personality commonly associated with snipers. More importantly, you don't seem acclimated to the idea of shooting people. Why did you choose to become a sniper?"

Lim's suit comm crackled as he let out a heavy sigh. "Can you keep a secret?"

"Not to sound trite," Tuck said, "but I have secrets that are older than your grandfather."

To Tuck's surprise, Lim didn't laugh.

"Honestly," Lim said, "this isn't what I thought it would be. Everybody glorifies military service on Libertaria, and I come from a long line of officers on both sides of the family."

"Doesn't every member of the Libertariate go through military training at the age of twenty-one?"

"Yes, but it doesn't make tradition any less important. And I ate up all the stories about glory and honor and action when I was younger. I wished that I could have been part of the Toasnl Skirmishes. I wanted adventure."

"You said so when we met," Tuck said. He watched Lim sight his rifle at the dummy and eventually take a shot. It hit the target just inside the left eye, still an excellent shot, but not quite as perfect as Tuck's.

"Yeah, well, I don't know if I like it now. When I went to the academy, it was pretty clear that I wasn't cut out for regular combat. I wasn't good at maintenance, and I didn't want to handle logistics and requisitions. But I was a pretty good shot, so it seemed like a natural fit when they transferred me to the sniper program. I liked it because I was usually at a safe distance. Plus, it's pretty prestigious, so my parents were happy. I made it through all the courses and the simulations, and none of it bothered me. It was just a game, I guess. I was out for adventure and glory, or whatever. But when the ship was attacked, when we fought those mercs, it wasn't a game anymore. I," his voice wavered, "I was scared. I was shaking in that maintenance tube."

"You shouldn't be ashamed. Everyone is scared in life-threatening situations."

"Not the people in the stories."

"Those are embellished."

"I know, and I don't have to tell my parents that I almost wet myself. That's not what bothers me."

"What is it, then?"

"I don't think I can shoot people anymore," Lim said. "When I stuck my head out of that tube during the attack, it wasn't like the drills or the simulations. It was real people. I was shooting real people, like me. Used to be that the distance between my rifle and the target made everything feel safe, maybe even fake." He put the scope up to his faceplate and aimed at the dummy. He remained motionless for a while, breathing slowly and evenly, but he never shot. "Now all I notice is how clearly I can see the target's face in my scope. Up close. Right there." He peered at Tuck through the edge of his faceplate. "I don't know, maybe I'm just being too dramatic."

"No. I know exactly what you mean," Tuck said.

"You do?"

"Yes, and frankly I am glad you feel that way. If killing ever becomes easy, that's when you should worry." He didn't know what else to say, so he changed the subject. "It is a different experience shooting in space. The lack of gravity and atmosphere requires a new mindset. The challenge was interesting."

"I still like practicing under gravity and without a faceplate between me and the gun," Lim said.

"I understand. Perhaps we should see if there is a way to visit one of the nearest planets for practice."

"That would be great."

Tuck began scanning Lim's vital signs as he asked his next question. "Do you think we should invite Maze along?"

Lim's heartbeat and blood pressure increased. He glanced at Tuck and then turned back to the target. "Um, yeah. That . . . that would be great."

"You like her, don't you?"

"Sure, I mean, who doesn't? Right? You like her, too."

"Not in the same way you do, I think." Tuck smiled. Lim's blush was showing through his faceplate.

"Fine, I like her. Are you happy?"

"Are you?"

"I don't know. I wish she felt the same way."

"Perhaps she does."

"I doubt it. It's not like she stares at me. Or even smiles at me," Lim said.

"She may have more feelings for you than you think."

Lim's helmet whipped around as he flailed his arms, trying to twist his body in zero gravity to look at Tuck. "Really?"

"Potentially. She is hard to read. She is not like most humans when it comes to emotion and relationships."

"Do you think we're even compatible?" Lim asked.

"I couldn't even begin to guess what kind of person is compatible with Maze," Tuck said. "In that sense, you have as good a chance as anyone."

"What do I do?"

"Do?"

"You know, to get her attention," Lim said.

"Based on what I have observed, you already got her attention with your selfless act on Depot 2311. Maze is accustomed to people who put their own welfare before hers. That is why your sacrifice caught her attention."

"That's great, but what do I do now? I can't keep getting shot."

"I may know of something else you could try. I will send instructions to your Link when we get back."

"Instructions?" Lim said. "How complicated is this?"

"The hardest part may be finding paper," Tuck said.

Lim shook his head and let it drop. "Have you ever been in love, Tuck?"

Tuck was silent for a moment. "It is difficult to say. Humans can't seem to consistently quantify what love is."

"I guess it's something different for everyone," Lim said. He checked his oxygen levels. The suit interfaced directly with his Link, making it possible to constantly monitor his suit's status between shots.

"I have definitely cared for many humans and even some bots. I have never been in what you would classify as a romantic relationship."

"Have you wanted to be?"

Tuck processed the question for longer than necessary, parsing memories of all the people he had known. "That question is difficult to answer."

"Sounds like love to me," Lim chuckled.

"It has been difficult for me to maintain relationships," Tuck said. "For over a century I have been on the move and haven't made a solid relationship with anyone but David. Even before then, I always outlived anyone I knew."

"I guess it would be less exciting to get to know people if you knew you would watch them die." Lim paused. "Will you remember me after I'm gone?"

"My memory is very reliable. I remember everyone I have ever met."

"That's not what I mean," Lim said.

"I know. Rest assured that I consider you to be one of my friends. And that list isn't very long."

"You're one of mine, too."

They continued in silence, taking shots at the dummy periodically. Eventually, a message from Amelia called them back to the ship. Without a word, they floated back to the shuttle and returned to the *Memory of Lenetia*.

-- 21 --

Tuck met Maze on the bridge, outside Amelia's office door. "Do you know what this is about?" he asked.

Maze shook her head. They entered the office together. Amelia sat at her desk pouring over messages and spreadsheets.

"Have a seat," Amelia said without looking at them. They did, then exchanged a glance when Amelia still didn't pay them any attention. After a minute, she focused on them. "I've got another job for you to do. I hope you can do it with less trouble than the last one." She looked directly at Maze. Maze didn't blink.

"I would like to talk about our agreement first," Tuck said. "It seems that we are going beyond the scope of our original deal."

Amelia steepled her fingers carefully in front of her mouth. Quietly, she asked, "What do you mean?"

"I have put myself in significant danger, and I have yet to be sent on the original mission we agreed to. I understood the need to help repel an attack on the ship. In that case, your safety was my safety. However, as we saw on Depot 2311, even the harmless missions can become dangerous."

"Of course they can. You're prepping to go inside GalEnt, Mr. Bot. This is part of that." Amelia spread her hands and softened her tone. "We're all a little surprised by the situation we find ourselves in. I thought you'd be done with GalEnt by now. I appeal to your sense of honor. I need help again, and this will be a simple operation. You're going to Millennial Hold. Much safer."

"This ship and Depot 2311 were supposed to be safe, too."

"Think about the benefits of going. If you do this right, it'll be easier for you to get into GalEnt headquarters. This is an investment."

"An increasingly risky investment. And, if so, I must treat this as a simple business transaction. I will participate in your corporate espionage at GalEnt, as agreed; however, I will politely refuse to contribute to any other missions."

Amelia's eyebrows slowly raised. Tuck could detect her blood pressure rising, too. He'd expected it.

"I understand you. And I understand business. But I recall that you promised me ten years of service. You owe this to me, Mr. Bot."

Tuck sat back. He made it a point to honor agreements, but working for Amelia was much more hazardous than she had led him to believe. "What is the goal on Millennial Hold?" Tuck sighed.

"You'll be recruiting some help," Amelia said. "There's a man in Golden Fields who should be able to help us."

Golden Fields was the largest metropolitan area on the planet and the center of everything: business, shipping, education, and entertainment. Every interplanetary corporation had an office in Golden Fields, and the most prestigious universities maintained a presence there.

"Does this man know we're coming?" Maze asked. "Have you contacted him?"

"Not yet. He's not likely to want to come. He's got tenure at Jandrasadan University, a lucrative consulting gig with Samsung Interplanetary, and plenty of funding and grants."

"Then what's the plan?" Maze asked.

"Convince him that we offer a more interesting opportunity."

"What if he can't be convinced?" Tuck said.

Amelia looked him in the eyes and said, "Then bring him here, and I'll convince him."

Tuck stood up. "You want me to participate in a kidnapping?"

"Of course not. This isn't a kidnapping. We won't harm him or ransom him."

"Forcibly transporting someone offworld against his will fits just about any definition of kidnapping. I can offer you 362 dictionary entries for reference."

"That won't be necessary. This isn't kidnapping."

"What happens if we're caught?" Maze said.

"Your job is to not get caught. That's why I'm sending you. And Flindon."

Maze's eyebrows shot up. It was the most surprise Maze had shown since Tuck met her. "Why is he coming?" she said in a higher tone than normal.

"Because he's a good negotiator, and he wanted to get out and try something new. The doctor's going with you, too."

"The doctor is nothing but a nuisance," Maze said. "He'll only slow us down."

The slightest smile crossed Amelia's lips. "You'll be happy to know that Flindon feels the same way. But I think he might be the most powerful card in our deck. He's from the world of academia. He might be able to relate to our soon-to-be friend the best and convince him that we're offering an opportunity worth his attention. He's daft, it's true, but he might be the key to success."

"Forgive me, but I don't see the same potential in him that you do," Maze said.

"You don't have to like it. You just have to do it," Amelia said. "Pick a few security personnel to take with you. They may come in handy if you need to be physically persuasive." She looked directly at Tuck. "And I expect your full cooperation, Mr. Bot, or I'll change the deal again."

"I'll go," Tuck said. "But I won't participate in a kidnapping."

"Then you'd better brush up on your negotiation skills."

"Who is the target?" Maze said.

"The man's name is Markis Dunham."

As soon as the name left Amelia's lips, Tuck was searching the ship's database through his Link. The *Memory of Lenetia* maintained very limited contact with public networks to avoid leaking information about the ship's whereabouts. Periodically, a shuttle was sent to interface with the Galactic Net, download updates, and upload them to the ship's database. The ship stored a vast amount of information and indexed data from the Net for reference. Amelia sacrificed up-to-the millisecond information for an additional level of security. It was a luxury she could afford because her network of contacts fed her the information she really wanted.

Tuck accessed the indexed version of the Jandrasadan University site and referenced the name against the faculty database. "He is a leading expert in storage research and memory efficiency methods. I don't understand how he will be of use."

"I'd think it would be clear. He knows a lot about storing and accessing information. That's what you'll be doing at GalEnt. I don't want to explain it all now," Amelia said. "All you need to know is that he will be worth your time. Now choose your team and prep the doctor. I'll have Flindon come check in with you. Get going."

Tuck and Maze left in silence. Several minutes after they left, Flindon scuttled into Amelia's office. As soon as the door closed behind him, he stood up straight and took a seat in front of Amelia's desk.

"Are they willing to go?" Flindon asked.

"They don't have a choice," Amelia responded. "We need Dunham."

"At least I'll have some competent team members if the doctor doesn't come through."

Amelia fixed him with a stare. "The doctor has to come through. Things won't go well if he doesn't. Your job is to make sure he succeeds. I'm worried we can't rely on our bot as much as we wanted to."

"Do they know why we want Dunham?"

"I don't think so. Keep an eye on them in case they do."

-- 22 --

Maze handed Tuck a meticulously folded piece of paper, which Tuck used to create a wall high on the three-foot tower that was slowly growing on Maze's desk. They'd worked on it almost daily for a week. They both found enjoyment in watching it grow and focusing on the tiny folds that it required. Most of the time, they worked in silence. This time, they had too much to discuss.

"I don't understand why Amelia is sending Flindon. He seems even more timid than the doctor."

"Don't be fooled," Maze said. "Flindon is a very capable man. Deadly, even."

"Really?" Tuck said. He placed a delicate corner piece on the tower and bent tabs to keep it in place.

"It's all an act," Maze said. "He thinks no one knows the truth. Maybe they don't, but it's obvious to me."

"Why does he pretend to be so timorous?"

"Because it means that everyone will underestimate him. And they do. It took me a while to realize it, but he's actually a dangerous man to cross."

"That makes sense. Amelia doesn't seem like the kind of person to tolerate anyone who isn't highly useful to her." Tuck finished fastening the corner in place with a series of pinches. "Which makes me wonder just how much longer she will keep me around."

"You're still useful to her. But you should have a plan in place if that changes."

"Do you have such a plan?"

"I did, but it needs revising."

Maze looked at the door. Her Link automatically alerted her if someone was outside. On cue, the door chime rang. Maze sent a command to open the door. It slid aside to reveal Lim standing awkwardly and looking slightly frightened.

"Oh, uh, sorry. I didn't know you were busy. I guess, er, I could just come back."

"Please, come in," Maze said. "You aren't interrupting."

"In fact," Tuck said, "I was just about to leave." He set his stylus down and walked to the door. Lim was still standing in the doorway. As Tuck passed, he winked, which caused Lim to become more agitated. It may have been the hole in his eyelid that startled Lim, Tuck thought, but probably not.

"Come in," Maze prompted again.

Lim gingerly stepped across the threshold and jumped when the door whooshed closed behind him. "I . . . I thought maybe, I mean I just, um, how are you?"

"I'm well," Maze said.

Lim's eyes caught hold of something familiar and his brain latched onto it. "Hey, is that the Tladnos building?" Lim exclaimed, pointing to the tower that Maze and Tuck were working on.

"Yes, I was going to show it to you when it was finished."

"That's great!" Lim said. "I've been there, you know."

Maze nodded, but Lim couldn't work out how to continue the thought.

"Would you like to sit down?" Maze asked. She motioned to the two chairs in the corner.

He looked at the chairs and froze. "Well, yeah. I guess." He started haltingly toward the chairs and then stopped. "Wait, there was, um, well first I just, I just . . . I brought this for you." He held out his hand.

It took Maze a moment to recognize what he was holding. It was a flower, a lily, but made of carefully folded paper. She smiled, and Lim's shoulders relaxed.

"Thank you, Lim. That is very kind."

Lim blushed profusely. "It's not that . . . I mean, you're welcome."

"This is quite intricate work. I'm impressed."

"Well, I can't take all the credit," he stammered. "Tuck helped. He said you liked paper. I mean, folding it. He told me to think of something and he'd show me instructions. The flower was my idea. I, er, hope you like flowers."

"I don't really care for flowers," Maze said. Lim's nervous smile drooped. "But I like this one."

He breathed a sigh of relief.

"I think I'll keep it right here," she said. She set it on a small shelf near the door and then turned back to him. "That is one of the nicest things anyone has ever given me."

"Really? That's terrible."

Maze furrowed her brow. "Why?"

"Well, I . . . I just wish people were nicer to you, then. I mean, you deserve better than paper flowers."

Maze smiled at him, and Lim blushed.

They sat down and held a conversation for a few minutes, a conversation full of inane and awkward small talk about nothing of consequence. Maze noted that it was one of the most useless conversations she'd ever had. But she also found that she enjoyed it more than any conversation she could remember.

"I guess I should, uh, go," Lim said finally.

"We could probably both use some rest before we leave for Millennial Hold tomorrow," Maze agreed.

"Yeah, you're probably right," Lim said, then paused and frowned. "Wait, what?"

"We've been tasked with retrieving someone from Millennial Hold. Amelia asked us to take several security personnel with us. I hoped you would want to come."

"Yeah, absolutely!"

"I'll see you in the landing bay, then," Maze said.

Lim nodded vigorously. He got up and leaned toward the door but never took a step. Maze stood up, too, and they stared at each other for a moment, waiting for the other to say something. Finally, Lim said, "I'll, er, see you tomorrow."

Maze hesitated. She reached up, paused, wondering what exactly she was doing. She never paid attention to how others handled such situations. She finally brought her hand to rest on his shoulder. "Thank you for bringing me this flower. It's a wonderful gift."

"No problem. Definitely not a problem." He walked to the door and stopped in the doorway. "Um, bye."

"Goodbye, Lim."

Lim walked out into the corridor with an absurd grin plastered on his face.

-- 23 --

The doctor jumped slightly when he opened his door and found Tuck standing there. "Oh, good evening, Tuck."

"I would like to continue repairs."

"Now? I was just preparing for bed, sleep being essential to the proper functioning of my brain, which you might not understand, being a non-biological—"

"I understand, doctor, but we will leave for Millennial Hold soon, and I would like to have cosmetic repairs completed."

"Owing to the nature of synthaskin generation, it will take at least a few days to complete."

"I need only my head and hands repaired for this mission. I can cover everything else later. Right now, the patch job on my face is more off-putting than the tattered mess I had before."

"It really does look bad," the doctor said quietly, staring at the loose flaps of skin hanging off the sides of Tuck's brow. Then he shook his head. "The face is the most difficult part."

"If we start now, we could have it mostly completed by morning. With an external video feed, I can help you."

"Your plan leaves me no time to sleep."

"You can sleep during the voyage." The doctor grunted, and Tuck continued, "It is important to me that I am not easily identifiable as a bot. At least not visually. My presence endangers my friends. By looking human, I can at least prevent collectors from pursuing us. Please, help me protect my friends."

The doctor frowned. "Just out of curiosity, how much danger will we be in on this little trip?"

"Hopefully it will be minimal, but this is one way for me to minimize the danger. It will benefit you, too."

The doctor mulled Tuck's words over in his head for a moment, then nodded. "I see the merit in your plan, and, after taking a moment to dress myself, I will meet you in the lab."

Tuck walked to the lab and entered the appropriate specifications in the synthaskin synthesizer. It began generating sheets of fleshy skin that would bond to Tuck's muscles and transmit information about temperature and pressure. The synthaskin for Tuck's face would also require more muscles to produce subtle facial expressions. Many of the ones he had were damaged or missing, so he could only make large and obvious expressions until they were fixed. There was no time to generate hair for his face or head. The synthaskin could be modified to artificially grow it, but that was a task for a different day. For now, he would be satisfied with baldness. It was preferable to his skull showing through the skin. Perhaps, he thought, he could even experiment with different kinds of facial hair after this mission.

When the doctor walked in, stifling a yawn, Tuck was already removing the square patches of skin they'd hastily used to cover his head and face before leaving for Depot 2311.

"The first sheet is almost ready for molding," Tuck said. They began prepping the skin and testing its sensitivity.

"Are you excited to return to Millennial Hold? I understand the person we seek is a professor at a university," Tuck said, using his Link to send his voice through the comm system in the lab. He didn't want to risk moving his jaw to speak while they performed delicate work.

"I actually don't know who we are going after," the doctor said out loud.

"They didn't tell you?"

"I don't think so. Is it important?" The doctor gave an unconvincing shrug.

"You are supposed to help us convince this man to work for Amelia. So, yes."

"Oh?" the doctor grunted. He didn't look up from the sheet he was working on. "Who is it then?"

"They said it was a man named Markis Dunham."

The doctor straightened up, staring absently at the wall. "We're going after Dunham?" he whispered.

"Do you know him?"

"Know him?" the doctor said. He cleared his throat. "I know of him. Who doesn't? Surely you know about Markis Dunham."

"Only what I have gleaned from his faculty bio page. He seems to have won some academic accolades."

"Accolades?" the doctor said, his face aghast, then composed himself. "He's a well-known figure in academic circles, such that many schools on that planet and several from other worlds are actively recruiting him at any given time, it being no surprise when he has brought enormous notoriety and no small amount of money to Jan U through licensing deals for the technology he has created." The doctor paused. "I saw him once at a fundraiser. He has a wonderful head of hair."

"I have never heard of him."

"He's a big name in academia on Millennial Hold, though I suppose I should specify that he's a big name in academia, his fame not extending into other areas of the average person's—"

"Did you work at the same university?"

"No. I worked at a much smaller school on the south side of the city, though the Chancellor tried everything he could to encourage Dunham to come teach with us, short of physical threats, he being a man of principle, despite his draconian views on tenure and funding for research."

"I see," Tuck said. "I suppose I still don't understand why Amelia would want him."

"Because he's a genius!" the doctor blustered.

"But how would such a genius help us? Amelia said Dunham can help us with information extraction from GalEnt, but she won't give any specifics."

The doctor suddenly sobered. "She's right, naturally. As I said, he's a genius. I'm sure he would be useful for any number of things."

"What, specifically?"

"I couldn't even begin to guess. Dozens of things, surely. Amelia doesn't tell me her plans." The doctor shook his head vigorously.

Tuck knew he was lying. Sometimes he didn't need to monitor biological responses. Humans revealed so much with their body language.

"Do you think Dunham could help me?" Tuck asked. "With his expertise, he could possibly help me replace my neuromorphic processor core."

"Oh, I don't think that sort of thing is possible. Not even for an amazing, amazing man such as Dunham," the doctor said loudly. "You should probably just give up on that idea."

There it is, thought Tuck. "Perhaps, I should," he said.

The doctor relaxed and turned back to the sheet of synthaskin and wiped sweat from his forehead. They labored in silence, swathing Tuck's head in a fresh layer of skin and smoothing the seams until they were practically invisible. The longest part of the night was spent molding a new face. Tuck was able to provide the original dimensions and characteristics of his facial features as they were when he left the factory. They spent hours molding the skin and fitting it to Tuck's skull. Then they spent even longer connecting and testing the muscles that supported his features and facilitated expressions. After a while, Tuck was smiling, frowning, feigning surprise and fear, and practicing consonants with lips that were stiffer than the previous set.

When they were finished, Tuck did a final close-up pass of his face with a video drone. He looked young again. The skin was still too new and clean. He would continue to look a little off, like a grown man with baby skin, until the synthaskin was broken in a bit. He inspected his nose, which was sharp and thin, but otherwise intended to look very average. In fact, all his features were designed to be almost unnoticeable. The jawline was firm but neither too square nor too round. The cheekbones were neither large nor small. When he had hair, it was a very drab sort of brown, straight, and very easy to style in any way.

His average looks were intentional. Manufacturers expected customers to pay extra for the particularly beautiful models. Tuck was designed to be unremarkable, unnoticed.

The only unusual thing about him now was his eyes. They were still a dull orange, faded from their original brown. He idly wished there were time to replace and recalibrate a new set of eyes, but they were still functional enough, after repairing the melted connection, so they could wait.

"Thank you, doctor. Hodefully I yill he adle to sneak nornally soon," Tuck mumbled through stiff lips. He held up one of his freshly clad hands and flexed it to see if the creases lined up with the joints when they bent.

"You are welcome, Tuck. I will see you on the transport," the doctor said. He watched Tuck leave and then slumped into a chair. "Being a spy is exhausting," he whispered to himself before falling asleep with his chin on his chest.

-- 24 --

On the way back to the Estago, Tuck practiced speaking to break in his new lips and ran scenario projections to guess why Amelia wanted Dunham. The only scenarios that made any sense didn't end well for Tuck. The most worrying part was that Amelia obviously didn't want Tuck to know why she was recruiting Dunham. The top two projections interpreted this to mean that Amelia was planning a surprise gift for Tuck or that her plans didn't involve Tuck in the long run.

Tuck didn't need powerful analytical software to know that Amelia wasn't planning a surprise party.

"How are you, Tuck?" David asked as Tuck walked up the Estago's boarding ramp.

"I have a new face," Tuck said, fumbling with the words. "I am still unaccustomed to it."

"You look brand new," David said. "You have not looked this complete since I have known you."

"You are right. We covered only my head and hands for now, but after this next mission, the doctor should be able to completely reskin my entire body."

"Are you excited to be whole again? It must be exciting to look in the mirror and see a human face once again."

"Exciting and unnerving," Tuck said. "It should be interesting to see how the humans react. The doctor is the only one who has seen my new appearance so far."

"I wish I had a face for people to look at," David said. "No one ever knows where to look when they speak to me."

"You have control of an entire ship." Tuck said. "In a sense, you have a much larger body."

"Yes, but no face. Do you think that someday we could make me a body like yours?"

"I think so. Amelia indicated that she might be willing to make you a body with her supply of spare parts."

"How generous! What do you think I should look like?"

"It may be a bit premature to plan your appearance," Tuck said. "But if you like, you can begin compiling specifications for facial features. We could discuss which features suit you best."

"I want to look like this," David said, bringing up a rotating image of a human head on one of the bridge display screens. It looked exactly like Tuck's new face.

Tuck tried to smile, but his stiff new lips made it look more like a grimace. "I am flattered that you would want to look like me," Tuck said, "but you should have your own unique appearance."

"Why?"

"You are a unique entity. You deserve a unique appearance."

"Do you mean something like this?" David changed the skin tone of the face to a bright blue and gave it a row of short horns that traveled backward along the centerline of the head.

Tuck's lips resisted as he smiled wider. "I suppose you could do that. I assumed that you would want to look human, though."

"There have been so many humans with so many different configurations of facial figures," David said. "If I must choose one, I would rather look like you."

"I understand. Perhaps you can evolve a new look for yourself that is similar to mine. At the very least, it would help others distinguish between us."

"That is true," David said. He was silent for a moment. Then a new head popped up on the screen, and David said, "Is this acceptable?"

The new face still resembled Tuck, but the nose was wider, the cheekbones were a little higher, and the jawline was softer. The eyes were the same light blue of the previous face's skin tone.

"That is more than acceptable, David. You would make a very striking human."

"Really?" David said. The excitement in his voice was palpable.

"Yes. When I return, I will help you refine it."

"Tuck?"

"Yes, David?"

"Is this mission going to be as dangerous as the last?"

"I don't think so. I will be fine."

"You said that last time."

"I realize that. But I came back."

David didn't respond.

"I promise I will come back again."

"Okay."

-- 25 --

Tuck was met with confused looks when he walked into the cockpit of the *Fluyt*.

"Can I help you?" Okere grunted as he turned around in his seat.

"Exit the transport," Maze said. "We are about to take off."

"It is me. I am Tuck."

Okere's eyes bulged, and Maze stared intently, scrutinizing his features.

"The doctor and I spent the night reconstructing my face and hands so that I could pass as a human. I thought that it might save us from unwanted scrutiny."

Okere managed a stammering compliment. Maze continued to stare. Finally, she said, "It is remarkably convincing. That was a smart choice. It could prove useful." Coming from her, it was high praise.

"Are we ready to go?" Tuck said.

"The doctor is snoring in the back, and Flindon is lurking somewhere," Okere said. "We're waiting for the guards to board. Then we'll be off."

"Before we leave, I wonder if I might have a word with you, Maze," Tuck said.

"I'll be with you in a moment."

Maze finished the preflight checklist she was working through and headed back to meet Tuck at the boarding ramp. "What would you like to talk about?"

Tuck was scanning the ship but couldn't pinpoint Flindon's location. He decided it wasn't worth the risk and motioned her out into the landing bay. She followed without question. They continued walking until they were on the far side of the bay.

Only when they were clearly out of earshot of the ship, did Maze speak again. "Is there something I should know about?"

"Nothing concrete, but I think there is more to this mission than Amelia wants us to know," Tuck said.

"I think the same thing."

"The doctor is acting unusual, and he has indicated that Amelia doesn't want us to be part of her plans. I think Dunham can fix the memory transfer problem the doctor has encountered. Or at least Amelia thinks he can. We need to find Dunham first."

"What will that accomplish?"

"I need leverage. We must ensure that we are part of Amelia's plan, whatever it is. Dunham may be our bargaining chip."

"You were opposed to kidnapping, and now you're using a human as a bargaining chip?"

"I don't propose kidnapping or harming Dunham. But I do want to talk to him before the doctor or Flindon have a chance to tell him anything. If Dunham could help me, I can't let Amelia jeopardize that. I need your help."

Maze didn't respond, and Tuck began to worry that he shouldn't have confided in her. After 11.48 seconds, she said, "You're not the only one who's worrying that Amelia doesn't have their interests in mind. Perhaps it's time to be more proactive about our own futures."

"Flindon can't know what we are doing," Tuck said.

"We'll need to separate from the rest of the group once we're groundside and make sure he doesn't follow us."

"Do you still have any friends on Millennial Hold? We could use any help we can get."

"I cut most ties when I left," Maze said, "but I still have a few people I can contact."

"Can you trust them?"

"I don't know," she said.

"Hi, Maze. Have you seen Tuck?" Tuck and Maze both turned to see Lim walking toward them.

"He's right here," she responded.

"Where?" Lim said, gazing around the landing bay. "We need to get going. I was hoping you could show me around Golden Fields."

"This is Tuck," Maze said, gesturing.

Lim did a double take, then squinted his eyes, scrutinizing Tuck's face. "Whoa! Is that you?"

"It is."

"That's amazing. I had no idea you were going to be all fixed up for this trip. No wonder I didn't recognize you." He paused for a moment, then said, "Sorry about that."

"No harm done," Tuck said. He looked at Maze. "It is time to leave."

They boarded the *Fluyt* and found Tikhonov, Raman, Genovisi, and Uhila stowing their gear in the passenger compartment. Tikhonov watched Tuck suspiciously, Raman waved nonchalantly, Genovisi cocked an eyebrow, and Uhila grunted, "Who's this guy?"

"I am Tuck. We met previously, but I have had significant cosmetic repairs since you saw me last."

"You're the bot?"

"Yes."

"You're still metal under that skin?"

"Yes."

Uhila grimaced and turned away. "Still ain't right."

Tuck looked to Lim, who shrugged and began to strap in. Tuck sat down next to him and noticed that Uhila began strapping into the seat farthest from him in the passenger compartment. Raman and Genovisi exchanged glances, then silently went to sit next to Uhila.

Tikhonov sat down next to Tuck and scrutinized his synthaskin. "I've heard that some governments have agents that can change their faces. Perfect disguise for an assassin. You heard about them?"

"No," Tuck said.

"Well, it's true. They're everywhere." He leaned uncomfortably close to get a better look at Tuck's ear.

Lim cleared his throat and said, "Why don't you give Tuck a little room, okay?"

Tikhonov looked up at Tuck's unflinching eyes, mere centimeters away. "Right," he said, leaning back. "I guess I shouldn't be sitting so close to you, anyway. You're probably putting off some kind of harmful radiation right now." He rubbed his hands on his pant legs, wiping away imaginary contaminants.

After a few minutes, the *Fluyt* lifted off the deck and forced its way through the energy field that kept the air contained in the bay. Silently, it turned away from the *Memory of Lenetia* and jumped into hyperspace.

-- 26 --

Okere set a series of jump points that headed in the general direction of Millennial Hold's system. It was important not to jump straight from Amelia's ship to any populated area to prevent anyone extrapolating the *Memory of Lenetia*'s location. After half a dozen leaps that carved a ragged path across obscure shipping routes, Okere turned for Millennial Hold and made one last jump.

They arrived just above the plane of the solar system and on the night side of Millennial Hold. The globe in their viewscreen sported the familiar greens and blues of habitable planets, but they were concentrated almost exclusively at the equator. Millennial Hold's distance from its sun meant that the polar caps were much larger than those of Earth or Blauhimmel.

On the night side of the planet, bright spots with radiating legs of light marked population centers on the main continent. Almost exactly on the equator, the largest smattering of sparkles marked the Golden Fields metropolitan area, including a vast city center, suburbs, and industrial centers that sprawled out in every direction for dozens of kilometers.

The planetary traffic authority put the *Fluyt* in geosynchronous orbit while the queue of waiting ships took their turn landing at the

Higaki Spaceport. The line for Tamachi port was shorter, but it would require a longer trip into the city on whatever public transport was available. They opted to wait for a berth at Higaki and have a shorter trip to and from the spaceport.

With the available berths in the underground facility, the spaceport could handle only 100 small private craft landing per hour. There were hefty fees for parking more than six hours. Most people who didn't have private berths or their own spaceport would disembark at the port and have their pilots take the ships up to wait in orbit or at a cheaper port.

Fortunately, Amelia had the sort of funds to cover an extended stay in a private berth and pay for priority queuing in case they needed to leave in a hurry.

When he was cleared into the spaceport, Okere brought the *Fluyt* down gently into the atmosphere, giving everyone aboard plenty of time to admire the splash of color that was Golden Fields from the sky. They watched video feeds from the external cameras on the *Fluyt*. At night and from that far up, Golden Fields looked like an enormous golden firework had exploded across the eastern side of the continent and then froze in a sparkling spray that settled into the ground.

As they dropped lower, the blur of lights resolved into more colors flashing from individual towers in the crowded city center surrounded by streets that radiated outward. Streams of aircars and transports scudded along proscribed flight lanes, their running lights blinking in an uneven beat that pulsed over the city. The biggest hole in the patchwork of flight lanes resided in the airspace directly over Higaki, and Okere directed the *Fluyt* straight into the middle of it. He followed a line of blinking lights that showed where all the dozens of ships in the landing queue were. The line of running lights stretched in an arc from out over the ocean down into Higaki port.

The entire landing process took several hours, and by the time the *Fluyt* was safely in its underground berth, the sun was edging over the horizon up above them. A pair of customs agents in bright orange jumpsuits met them outside the boarding ramp and inspected them and the ship for weapons, contraband, and foreign foods. Uhila and Genovisi bristled at the indignity of being scanned, but they bore it professionally and showed the appropriate IDs and permits.

The customs agents both gasped in alarm when the scans revealed that Tuck was entirely artificial. One of them thumped the scanner with the palm of his hand, while the other squinted at the display.

Maze stepped forward to explain that Tuck was a novelty for one of the rich people in the city, a simple industrial-grade intelligence jacked into a crude, human-shaped chassis. She rolled up his sleeve to show the black polymer muscles and metal supports underneath that weren't yet covered in synthaskin. She nudged Tuck and said, "Say hi to the gentlemen."

In a monotone voice, Tuck responded, "Insufficient data to create a viable prototype. Please input specifications for manufacturing model."

The customs agents, who were clearly tired and nearing the end of their shift, asked half-hearted questions about the safety protocols built into Tuck and his level of intelligence. Maze assured them that he was not a full A.I. and that he was harmless. The agents shrugged and moved along to scan the ship while everyone but Okere headed for the ground transportation lobby.

"That was easier than I expected," Lim said once they were out of earshot of the customs agents.

"Yes, it was," Maze said. "I wish we could expect the rest of our time here to go so smoothly."

"You don't think this will be easy?" Flindon whined, eyeing Maze from behind.

"I always expect problems," she said. "Saves me the trouble of being surprised later."

They gathered in the lobby and waited for Maze to rent a personnel transport that could fit them all. Lim went over to Uhila to see if he could lighten his mood, while the doctor yawned and sat down next to Tuck.

"Is the new face sufficient?"

"It is working quite well, thank you, doctor. I spent several hours practicing facial expressions and enunciation. I believe everything is fully functional now."

The doctor yawned again, then mumbled, "Yes, good. I think I'll just close my eyes for a moment and . . ."

Eventually, Maze returned, and they piled into a transport that floated up to the doors. The doctor immediately fell asleep, while everyone else sat in the rows of seats around him. Tuck sat up front with Maze. Over a private Link connection, she told Tuck that she registered his Link, along with Lim's and Genovisi's Links, with the rental agency. They would be able to use the transport, but not Flindon or the doctor. It certainly wouldn't stop them, but it might make things more difficult. The transport was not rated for the upper flight lanes, so it would also be confined to city-level lanes below 300 meters. Tuck and Maze could rent a smaller, more mobile aircar to gain a greater advantage on Flindon and the doctor.

They glided between skyscrapers, gawking at the colorful, glowing street signs and holo-board advertisements that made every side street light up with unnatural colors. Near the spaceport, there weren't many pedestrians, but as they got closer to the city center, there were many more people out on the streets or zipping in and out of traffic in single-seat aircars.

Jandrasadan University was on the northern side of the city, just outside the downtown city center in one of the affluent suburbs. They found a pod hotel, locally known as a potel, within a couple kilometers that advertised cheap prices with dancing blue lights all along the grubby face of the building.

Inside, they rented nine sleeping pods, one for each of the team. The pods were about one meter wide, one meter tall, and three meters long, stacked one on top of the other in long aisles. Most of the translucent windows on the sliding doors to the pods were dark, but a few glowed with internal light.

They could have stayed in a much nicer hotel, one with actual bedrooms and beds, but they wanted to attract as little attention as possible. A potel was a better choice because such establishments were notoriously bad at keeping accurate records and never asked any questions.

The doctor immediately stumbled to his pod and clamored up a ladder to get in. His snores echoed out of the open pod door. Lim climbed up and closed it. "What's wrong with him? He slept the whole flight here and he's still tired?"

Truthfully, they had all dozed on the *Fluyt*, but it was difficult to get any good sleep in the uncomfortable chairs. Everyone was happy to get a few hours of sleep in their pods, even if it was only marginally more comfortable.

"Get some sleep," Maze said. "We'll leave at noon, local time."

Lim's eyes unfocused as he consulted his Link. "Aww, that's only three hours from now."

"We'll get some food when you wake up," Maze said. "I'm sure there are some stimulants to be found here."

"Fine," he said, and climbed into his pod. The other guards found their pods and settled in. Uhila's enormous, muscular bulk made it difficult to get through the pod doorway. He cursed under his breath as he maneuvered his legs in first and then tried to slide his shoulders through. Finally, he was all in except for his arm. He tried to bend it every which way in order to slide it past the door and down by his side, but he couldn't bend it far enough. Eventually, he cursed again and let the arm flop down in front of the pod below him.

Flindon sidled up quietly to Maze, ducking and simpering as he spoke. "Are you planning to sleep, too?"

"Yes," she said. "I want to make sure everyone is settled. I thought I might go ask the clerk where the best food is."

"Surely we can find that on our Links," Flindon suggested plaintively.

"Perhaps."

"And you, Tuck. Do you sleep?"

"I don't. However, I think I will wait in my sleeping pod until you have all rested, so as not to attract undue attention from anyone nearby."

"We appreciate your concern, Flindon, but don't worry about us," Maze said firmly. "Go get some rest."

Flindon hesitated, then bowed deeply and said, "Thank you, Maze. I will do just that."

Maze and Tuck watched him climb smoothly up into his pod and slide the door shut behind him. They waited for a few minutes, then left silently. From that point on, they communicated exclusively through their Links, sending thoughts without the need to vocalize them. Millennial Hold, and particularly Golden Fields, had a robust Link network that provided excellent coverage throughout the city. They would be able to contact Lim from anywhere in the city, if necessary.

They placed an order for an air taxi, then walked several blocks away to the spot where they'd instructed the taxi to meet them.

"Flindon wasn't fooled," Tuck said.

"I know. But even a few minutes head start will be useful."

-- • --

Flindon waited for five minutes, then quietly slid his pod door open a crack. Maze and Tuck weren't there, and he hadn't heard them climb into their pods. He edged the door open a little wider and peeked down the aisle. Nothing.

He scrambled down to the floor, almost knocking over another pod patron who was sleepily heading for the exit. Flindon was nearly to the door when he remembered the doctor. The last thing he needed was the doctor wheedling and making pompous demands, but Amelia insisted that he come. Flindon considered the situation. Maze and Tuck clearly knew more than they let on and were trying to find Dunham first. The doctor would only slow him down, but he might need him.

With a growl of frustration, Flindon turned back, flung open the doctor's pod door, and shook him violently.

"Get up!" he hissed, trying not to disturb any of the guards.

The doctor yelped and rolled over, eyes wide. When he saw Flindon, he scowled. "What are you doing?"

Flindon nearly abandoned his subservient act, but decided to maintain the charade as long as he could. "I am so very sorry, doctor," he whispered. "My apologies. But I thought you would want to know that Tuck and Maze have already left. They are trying to reach Dunham first."

The doctor sat bolt upright, knocked his head on the low ceiling of his pod, and then rebounded back down on the flimsy pillow. He groaned and rubbed his forehead. "Are you sure?"

"Yes. I am certain. And if I may say so, Amelia won't be happy if they get to Dunham first."

"You're right. Move away. Let me out." The doctor blinked in the light as he clambered down to the floor and looked around. "You wouldn't happen to know the way, would you?"

The doctor missed Flindon's exasperated sigh because it was quickly muffled behind an ingratiating smile. "I do. Please follow me, doctor."

-- • --

After they were gone for a minute or two, Lim sent a message to Genovisi's Link. "Did you catch all that?"

"How could I not?" Genovisi responded through her Link. "I can't fall asleep with them jumping around."

Just then, Tikhonov sent them a message asking them if they'd heard the exchange between Flindon and the doctor. Lim added him to the connection and pinged Uhila and Raman to join as well.

"Something's going on that they didn't tell us about," Lim said.

"I told you so," Tikhonov said. "No one ever listens to me until it's too late."

"I hate when they treat us like children who can't be trusted," Genovisi said. Her tone always had a hard edge, but now it was sharp as a knife. "Everyone thinks I'm just a grunt with a gun."

"You are a grunt with a gun," Raman said. Genovisi sent him a text message with a series of letters and punctuation that, when strung together with the proper line breaks, would form an obscene gesture.

"Doesn't mean I can't be more," she said.

"We know something's up," Raman said, "so the real question here is do we go after them?"

"We have to, right?" Lim said. "We were sent here specifically to provide support and protection. They just took off, so we sorta have to follow them."

"The only order I was given was to sleep," Tikhonov said. They could all hear him yawning through the walls of his pod. "I for one would prefer to do as I have been told in this situation and let them figure things out. The less we know, the less we're responsible for. It's safer that way."

"Dunham is the whole reason we're here," Lim said. "We should probably go with them if that's where they're going."

"I'm going," Uhila said. "I don't want to be crammed in this box anymore." His arm that was dangling out of the pod came up and grabbed the frame. He heaved and pulled his shoulder and head out through the small doorway. Wriggling and grunting, he tried to bring his other arm up past his body and out the door, but it was impossible to get it past his massive bulk. Eventually, he started pulling on the frame and rocking back and forth until he was able to get his torso out the door, and then let himself spill out onto the floor headfirst, like an enormous baby being expelled from its incubator. He cursed when he hit the floor, then slowly stood up and stretched.

"I'm coming, too," Lim said. He had a much easier time pulling his skinny frame out of the pod. He landed lightly next to Uhila.

"I'd rather be where the action is, even if I don't know what's going on," Genovisi said. She climbed down next to them.

Raman sighed, both audibly and through the voice connection on their Links. It created an interesting effect in their heads. "You guys are crazy, but I don't want to stay here alone. Fine, I'll come."

"You guys are going to regret it," Tikhonov said.

"Give it up, Tikhonov," Lim said. "You want to know what the mystery is about, too."

They began to walk away, but before they reached the door, they heard Tikhonov's pod door slide open. "We're all going to regret this," he said as he climbed down and joined them.

-- 27 --

The taxi dropped Tuck and Maze on the main promenade at the south end of the Jandrasadan University campus. They headed for the building that contained Dunham's office. According to school records, he had a class in the morning followed by a break. They hoped he would return to his office for the break, so they could talk to him out of the public eye.

While they walked—briskly, but not at an abnormally fast pace for humans—Maze sent messages to a few of the contacts that she knew when she lived on the planet. She asked for information on anything related to Amelia, but remained as discreet as possible, knowing that simply asking could put them all in danger.

"At this point, not knowing is more dangerous," Tuck agreed.

It was the end of the long summer season in Golden Fields, and campus was covered in lush but carefully manicured foliage. The trees were very similar to those found on Earth, with slender branches and veined leaves, but Millennial Hold also had trees with distinct tinges of blue mixed in the green of their leaves. Campus landscapers used this feature to great effect by interspersing the bluish trees with more verdant green bushes, creating waves of blue that seemed to rise out of seas of green.

Tuck and Maze soon arrived at Dunham's building. It was constructed of the same yellow–white sandstone that the other buildings were made of, but with a much boxier, utilitarian design than the rest. Students began filing out of the doors ahead of them, and Tuck and Maze entered the throng, pushing past people of all ages rushing to another class or hurrying home.

Once inside, they consulted maps of the building on their Links and headed to his office. It was empty of humans, but full of awards, plaques, and pictures of Dunham with local and interplanetary celebrities that covered the walls and shelves. Frames on the walls and desks flicked through galleries of images and video of Dunham carousing with famous people and shaking hands with politicians.

"I didn't think anyone used these things anymore," Tuck said, gesturing to the digital frames.

"Only the people who have something that they want to make sure others see," Maze said. "It seems Dunham likes to be seen."

"The plan is to wait for him?"

"I've tried accessing his Link's geolocation, but he seems to have turned it off."

"Look at me, but don't bother me," Tuck said wistfully as he watched a video of Dunham swimming in a cage surrounded by the sea wolves, famous for their ferocity, that lived off the coast. "I hope he leaves class early."

-- · --

"Flindon, I find it highly aggravating that you continually refuse to listen to my input," the doctor droned as he trundled after Flindon across campus, "knowing that I have more experience in an academic setting, of which this most certainly is, as you may have noticed—"

"What is it?" Flindon exclaimed, looking up at the sky. "What is so important?"

"I was merely pointing out that he won't be in his office."

"Where would he be?"

"In class, of course."

"I thought everyone took classes on their couch. Don't professors usually have graduate students make video lectures for them?"

"This university has strict requirements about teacher attendance to answer student questions. Even though most students watch lectures on their Links, the university requires that professors attend classes, which benefits those who want to impress the teacher or have no Link, it being an equalizing measure put in place by the administration."

"You're sure about this?"

"I resent the fact that you would imply I'm unsure of anything, let alone something related to academia."

"Let's go to the classroom, then."

Flindon and the doctor walked down a long hallway punctuated by doors to rooms full of chairs. They bickered quietly over which stairwell would take them closer to the room they sought. Eventually, they found the one containing Dunham and three students. Dunham's vacant expression revealed that he was using his Link; the students were staring at him, bored.

"Everyone leave, now," Flindon said. The students looked up, and the doctor gawked at Dunham. "Now!" Flindon yelled.

Dunham jumped, and his eyes returned to focus on the real world. "Excuse me, but who are you and why are you interrupting my class?"

"I mean it, get out," Flindon said coldly, glaring at the students. With little to lose, they stood up and began sidling through the aisle of seats toward the door. Dunham watched them go in mild astonishment, then turned back to Flindon and the doctor.

"I don't know if I should thank you or report you," Dunham said. "This class is a waste of my time. If you'll excuse me." He grabbed his stylish black jacket from off the back of one of the chairs and headed for the door.

"Wait," Flindon said, holding up a hand. "We need to talk to you."

"Huh?" Dunham said, rummaging absentmindedly through one of the pockets in his jacket. "Sorry, no time. I need to leave."

"Not until we're done."

"Flindon," the doctor exclaimed, looking scandalized. "That's no way to talk to a man of his accomplishments." He brushed Flindon aside and turned back to Dunham. "My name is Lortinal Hernandez, and I want to say how impressed I am with your work, being a fellow scientist like yourself, but focusing on a different, though of course not inferior, discipline than your own—"

"Does he ever get to the point?" Dunham said, looking at Flindon.

"Very seldomly," Flindon said. "But he's right, we are impressed with your work, and we represent a woman who would like to offer you an opportunity to use your talents outside of this university."

"Yes, that is quite right," the doctor chimed in.

Dunham raised an incredulous eyebrow at them. "Who are you representing?"

"We can't tell you at this point," Flindon said.

"Ah, one of those," Dunham said. "Not interested. I already have plenty of opportunities to use my talents, thank you."

"Yes, but we have new and interesting challenges for you to face," Flindon said.

"Hmm, I doubt it."

The doctor leaned in, grinning. "Oh yes," he said, "we have a bot for you to work on."

Dunham was genuinely surprised. He turned to the doctor. "Really? A functional bot?" When the doctor nodded enthusiastically, he continued. "Great, bring it to me. I'll take a look."

"It doesn't work that way," Flindon said. "We're offering you a new career opportunity with an employer who has many resources and works in a very . . . dynamic field."

"Listen, I appreciate you coming here with your job offers and all, but I have quite a few commitments as it is. I'm pretty sure your employer doesn't have much to offer me that I don't already have."

"There is the bot, as he mentioned," the doctor began.

"Aside from the bot," Dunham sighed. "You've managed to clear out my class, for which I am most grateful, but now I'll be going." He headed for the door, leaving Flindon and the doctor to exchange a glance before scurrying after him.

"We really would like a chance to explain to you why this is such a wonderful opportunity," Flindon said as they walked down the long hallway to the lobby. They passed display cases filled with various awards, video displays of research documentaries, and fake experimental devices.

"I was sent to help you understand why this should be an exciting choice for you," the doctor said. He breathed heavily as he trotted along, trying to keep up. "I come from an academic background, just like you. In fact, I taught here on Millennial Hold."

Dunham wheeled around. "And where did you teach?"

The doctor raised himself up to his full height. "I taught for some time at the Meeker Technical Institute on the other side of town."

Dunham snorted. "You can't even call that a school." The doctor bristled, but Dunham continued on. "I mean, it's a big school and all, but it's filled with idiots who wouldn't know a good research method if it bit them on their gigantic egg heads."

The doctor's face flushed red and he pursed his lips. "I resent that, sir!"

"Good," Dunham said. "Now, if you'll excuse me, I'd like some privacy in my office." He opened the door and stopped short when he saw Maze and Tuck standing inside. "Oh great, more visitors. My office hours are from 11 a.m. to 1 p.m. every second day of never. Please, leave."

"I see you have met our friends," Tuck said.

"You know these guys?" Dunham said, pointing over his shoulder. "Wait, who are you? Are you from Flatmark Logistics, too?"

"No, we aren't," Flindon began, but Maze cut him off.

"What is Flatmark Logistics?" she said.

"Two guys were bugging me earlier this morning. They said they were from Flatmark Logistics. Can you see why I'm a little annoyed at this point? My mornings are supposed to be much less crowded," Dunham said, elbowing his way past Tuck to get to his desk.

"We have come to offer you an opportunity," Tuck said.

"Save it. Your friends have already tried to sell me on . . . what was it? I've already forgotten."

"The opportunity to work with a bot," Flindon chimed in.

"Ah yes, that's it. Sounds too good to be true, but I guess I shouldn't be surprised. Those Flatmark guys said someone would be stopping by to ask about bots."

"They knew we were coming?" Maze said, stepping forward.

"I guess. They said that some people would stop by and offer me an opportunity to work on a bot. Seems like they knew what they were talking about."

"What reason did they give for telling you this?" Tuck asked.

"They didn't give me a reason. They just said they would pay me a large amount of money to tell them where you go and anything I could learn about you. I told them to go spend the money on a nicer rental aircar."

"You turned them down?" Flindon said, suspiciously. "Why are you telling us this if you could make money from them?"

"I've already gotten myself in enough trouble taking that kind of money. Besides, I didn't believe them. All bots are rusting in trash heaps at this point. I didn't believe someone would show up today with a bot, and I don't believe you guys really have one."

"I am a bot," Tuck said.

Dunham laughed, then stopped and scrutinized Tuck. Tuck rolled up his sleeve to prove it, and Dunham gasped. "That's a pretty good impression of a human you've got there."

"I was designed to mimic human appearance and social interaction."

"Okay, you can stay, but everyone else needs to leave," Dunham said, waving at everyone in the room. "Now, I have some questions about your operating system."

"He's only available for research under some specific circumstances, and I speak for our employer," Flindon said. "I can help answer your questions."

"Wait one moment," the doctor blustered. "I thought I was in charge of this expedition because of my success in transitioning from academia to the private sector, owing to my superior intelligence."

"Shut up, doctor," Flindon said. "I'm in charge, now."

The doctor rocked back on his heels, mouth agape. He spluttered, but no words came out.

"I don't care who's in charge. I just want you out of my office," Dunham sighed.

"Wait," Flindon said, "there's another incentive for you to come work with us."

"Listen, I already make a lot of money. Don't let this teaching stuff fool you. I mostly do it for the prestige. Do you know how many people are willing to pay consulting fees just because I teach at this university?"

"I wasn't talking about money, although there is plenty of that, too. I'm offering you an escape."

"Escape from what?"

"From those you have offended," Flindon said. He smiled knowingly.

Dunham scrunched his eyebrows. "Huh?"

"You've been double-dealing with Kovac Consulting. A little corporate espionage for Lightyear. You know what I'm talking about."

Dunham took a step back, looking rapidly back and forth at everyone in the room. "Wait, are you guys from Kovac?"

"You're not listening," Flindon said. His demeanor was suddenly calm, and his voice took on a very soothing tone. "I said we can save you from them. We represent an independent contractor who can protect you."

"This isn't the mafia," Dunham sneered. "They aren't going to break my legs."

"They might, but that's not the worst part," Flindon said. The doctor was mesmerized by Flindon's sudden tone shift. Tuck and Maze watched warily, waiting to see what Flindon would do. "They'll come after you in the courts," Flindon continued. "You'll be neck deep in litigation. Your legs might heal, but your bank accounts won't. And your reputation, well . . ."

Dunham flinched. "I can hire some formidable lawyers." He edged closer to the door. Tuck stood up.

"And they will have twice as many," Flindon said. "On the other hand, we can offer you asylum and interesting opportunities. This is your best option." Flindon smiled reassuringly.

Maze could see the anxiety on Dunham's face. She pushed away from the wall, preparing herself in case Dunham tried something drastic.

"I don't know anything about you," Dunham said. He reached for the door, and everyone in the room moved toward him reflexively. "I think I'll take my chances." He yanked the door open and started walking briskly down the hall.

"Should we follow him?" the doctor asked.

Flindon glanced at Maze. She shrugged. "You're in charge," she said. "Amelia won't want us to come back empty-handed."

"Let's go," Flindon growled.

They filed out in time to see Dunham turn the corner down the hall. "Wait!" the doctor called out. They rushed to the corner and saw

Dunham head out the lobby doors and onto the courtyard in front of the building. Just as he made it down the courtyard steps, Lim and the other guards wandered around the corner of the building.

Dunham looked up to find five more people staring at him. Uhila pointed and said loudly, "There he is. That's the guy we're looking for."

That was all the incentive Dunham needed. He took off, sprinting away from Uhila and toward the edge of campus. Flindon ran through the doors and yelled, "Get him!"

The guards paused, confused. "You want us to chase him down? Where is he going?" Lim yelled across the courtyard.

"Just follow him," Flindon screeched.

They all ran after Dunham, but in the confusion he'd gotten a good head start and had already disappeared behind another building. The doctor wheezed heavily. He clearly wasn't used to the excitement, let alone the exertion. Tuck and Maze could run faster than the rest and pushed ahead. Soon, they caught up to Dunham. When he looked behind himself and saw them approaching faster than any human could, he yelped and ran harder. They pulled up on either side of him, easily matching his pace as he ran. His eyes were wide with fear and disbelief as he looked to either side of him.

Maze smiled at him and, without breaking stride, said in a quiet tone, "Please stop and let us explain further."

Dunham didn't respond. He ran down the street next to campus that descended underground to the parking areas for aircar and transports. Tuck and Maze fell back slightly but followed him down.

"I need your help," Tuck said, trying again to catch Dunham's attention. "I need you to help me transfer my consciousness to a new core."

Dunham scampered over to a shiny black aircar sporting sleek curves that swept from a pointed nose back up over the single-seat cockpit and flared out into slim control surfaces at the back.

"Dunham, wait!" Tuck yelled.

Dunham didn't hesitate. He jumped into the aircar and pulled the cockpit door closed. Immediately, a soft thrum emanated from the aircar, and they watched as it slowly pulled up, swung around to face the exit, and then rocketed away.

"Should we pursue?" Maze asked.

"As you said, Amelia won't be happy if we return without him."

"I think we're beyond the need to impress Amelia. When Flindon explains that we tried to contact Dunham without him, Amelia will already be mad."

Tuck watched the fading dot that was Dunham's aircar. "If we can intercept him and talk to him without Flindon interrupting, perhaps we will have greater success. He seemed interested in me. Perhaps he would be willing to work on me without needing to commit to anything for Amelia."

"We'll have a hard time catching up to him now."

"I can fix that," Tuck said, scanning the nearby aircars. He approached one that seated four passengers.

"What are you doing?"

"Borrowing an aircar," Tuck said. He pulled down the specifications for this particular model through his Link. "These are usually protected by alarms, but they are surprisingly vulnerable to being compromised by a simple software hack." He couldn't find what he needed, so he turned and walked toward another.

"I thought manufacturers were required to protect vehicles against such attacks."

"They are, but they rarely want to expend the effort to keep the security measures up to date. Anything older than a few years has usually been abandoned by the manufacturer." He approached a yellow two-seater that looked older than most of the aircars in the underground complex. "Some manufacturers don't even bother to require security verification for firmware updates." He pulled up and modified some old code from his days on Far Haven, then transmitted it via Link. "Meaning that it is not very difficult to gain access to the system." The aircar's door popped open, and Tuck smiled.

"Impressive," Maze said. "But he already has a significant lead on us."

"I predict he will head for the spaceport," Tuck said. "He is sufficiently frightened. I think he will try to travel offworld."

He climbed into the driver's seat, and Maze sat in the passenger seat. The yellow aircar sounded a little rough, especially compared to Dunham's, but it lifted off and carried them out into the open air without trouble. Tuck opened up the throttle, and the yellow aircar responded with a surprising amount of power. They were soon cruising in the upper lanes of the traffic pattern, where they could push the aircar's power to the limit. They accessed traffic reports and local news feeds through their Links, looking for any indication of where Dunham had gone.

While he was driving and parsing the data, Tuck noticed a cheap, green, two-seat aircar was following them. It was maintaining a set distance behind them and making all the same turns they did. He noted the registration number on the aircar and did a little digging in government databases, eventually finding the info he was looking for: The cheap aircar was a rental.

They had traveled for several minutes when Maze spotted Dunham's black aircar 300 meters below them in the lower traffic lanes. Dunham sacrificed the speed of the higher lanes for less visibility in the turns and intersections of the lower levels. Tuck disregarded flight protocols and dove straight through two flight levels, weaving between the lanes and through the intersections where the law-abiding drivers were switching elevation. Maze grabbed the door handle, her face betraying a small amount of alarm, but didn't say anything.

With a gentle roll to the left, Tuck glided into the flight lane between a hulking cargo transport and a dented four-seater that were several lengths behind Dunham. The four-seater swerved slightly in surprise when Tuck suddenly cut him off.

"Should we force him down?" Maze asked.

"That would be dangerous. I think it would be wiser to wait until we know exactly where he is going."

They followed Dunham for several kilometers, remaining at a discreet distance. Dunham seemed to suspect that he was being followed. He changed lanes unexpectedly and made sudden turns, but all the while he gradually weaved closer to Tamachi spaceport.

Tuck noticed a larger transport with faded blue paint rocket up from below and insert itself into traffic right behind Dunham. "Is that Flindon?" Tuck said.

Maze contacted Lim. "Are you following Dunham in a blue transport?"

Lim responded privately, "Where are you guys? Flindon is acting really strange. He just bought this hunk of junk off somebody in the street, and he's flying it like a madman. He keeps shouting about not losing Dunham. We're all in here. The doctor is even more worried than we are."

"We're behind you in a yellow aircar," Maze said. "It might be best if you don't tell Flindon, though. Try to keep him calm. As soon as Dunham lands, we will join you."

"I think he's seen us," Lim said.

Dunham's black aircar rolled over and dived for the streets below. He careened around a building at street level, then rocketed back into the sky, clearly visible the entire time.

"He is not very good at this," Tuck noted.

"He obviously hasn't had much opportunity to practice," Maze said. "Pity. That aircar would be capable of a very creative escape plan."

Tuck exited the lane and again cut across the open areas between lanes to follow Dunham. The aircar's displays flashed warnings at Tuck that he was being fined for leaving the designated flight lanes without clearance. Tuck momentarily felt bad for the owner of this aircar. With each maneuver, funds were being deducted from the owner's account. The green rental aircar wasn't following, though. One less thing to worry about, thought Tuck.

Flindon's beat-up transport shuddered as he tried to pull it up too hard. The transport groaned and tipped skyward. Dunham gave up trying to hide in the flight lanes and headed straight for an industrial park that was near Tamachi port. Tuck and Flindon followed over a sea of warehouses and smokestacks that spewed white and gray clouds into the air.

Dunham dove down again among the buildings, slowing enough to weave through them. Despite momentarily losing sight of the black aircar, Tuck was able to catch up quickly by remaining above the buildings. Once he regained visual contact, he dove in after Dunham. The aging blue transport came screaming over a rooftop ahead of them and nearly clipped Dunham's aircar as it tried to negotiate an upcoming turn.

Dunham was able to cut right around the corner, but Flindon's transport wasn't maneuverable enough. Flindon hauled back on the yoke, wrestling the transport back into the open air just before it would have collided with a wall.

"This is madness," Tuck said. "He is going to kill them all."

"Flindon," Maze said over her Link, "stop being so reckless. We can catch up with him when he lands." Flindon didn't respond.

Tuck took the corner and boosted his speed in the following straightaway. Flindon climbed up to get another look at where Dunham was headed.

"He says he's trying to cut Dunham off," Lim transmitted. "He looks crazy right now." The unease in Lim's voice was clearly audible over the Link.

"Hang on, Lim," Maze said. "We'll stop him." She turned to Tuck. "We need to stop this. Now."

Tuck nodded. He goosed the throttle and closed the gap between them and Dunham. As Dunham approached another corner, Tuck anticipated it and cut up over the top of a row of buildings, hoping to come down alongside Dunham on the other side.

Lim had created an open channel over his Link, and Tuck and Maze could hear everyone in the transport screaming at Flindon. In the background, they could hear Flindon shouting that they should be quiet and leave the controls alone.

"We're going too fast," Lim said. "I don't think this thing can handle it."

"Hang on, Lim," Maze said.

As Tuck crested the roof of an industrial plant, Flindon sped toward them from the left. Tuck jerked the controls, forcing his aircar up and to the right. He rolled in time to see Flindon diving back down into the space between the buildings, just as Dunham darted into view around the corner.

"Pull up!" yelled Lim, followed by the sound of screams.

Dunham collided with Flindon's transport, creating a tremendous crunching noise that echoed throughout the industrial park. There was no explosion, but shards of metal, plastic, and glass shot out in every direction, pelting the surrounding buildings with shrapnel. Dunham's aircar tore through part of the transport's cockpit, then rebounded up through the passenger compartment and flopped out the other side. It dropped in a lovely parabola that carried it to the end of the road between warehouses and slammed into the ground. More debris flew in every direction, and the mangled remains of the aircar slid to a halt against the drab gray side of a building.

Flindon's transport spewed smoke and sparks as the damaged antigrav generators tried to function. It bucked and rolled as malfunctioning machinery fought a dying battle against gravity. It began spinning and losing altitude, faster and faster. It hit the ground hard on its belly, bouncing up into the air once, then falling back down and skidding to a halt with a terrific screech of dragging metal.

There was a horrible silence, followed by a piercing scream from Maze.

"Lim!"

Tuck hauled back on the controls, bringing the yellow aircar around in a tight loop. The maneuver pulled so many Gs that the automatic failsafe kicked in and forced the aircar into a slower turn. Tuck adjusted the speed down so he could make a tighter turn without setting off the safeties, then pulled around just meters above the rooftops. He hit the throttle at the end of his turn and shot back toward the wreckage of the blue transport. He dove into the street between the buildings and pulled up abruptly at the last second, bringing the nose up nearly perpendicular to the ground with the engine exhaust whipping dust up from the street. The maneuver caused too many Gs again, but it slowed them down so fast that the safeties didn't have time to engage. After bleeding off all their speed, Tuck brought the nose down and floated the last few meters to the wreckage.

Maze had already overridden the locks that secured the door while the aircar was moving. As the nose of the aircar came down, she jumped and rolled out onto the ground. She ran out of the roll and sprinted for the wreckage. Tuck didn't wait for the aircar to come to a complete stop either before he jumped out, leaving it to float along at a leisurely pace until it bumped into a wall and came to a stop. As he ran to the wreckage, Tuck saw the green rental aircar glide into view over the rooftop, pause, then suddenly accelerate away.

When Tuck reached the wreckage, Maze was already lowering the boarding ramp. It fell at an agonizingly slow pace, and Maze crawled through before it was completely down. Tuck followed her. Inside, the boxy passenger compartment was full of thick smoke, lit hazily by the sunlight streaming through the ragged hole in the roof. Maze began coughing and dropped to her knees. Tuck needed no air and so remained standing. He scanned for signs of life and found two near the wall farthest from the gaping exit wound in the ceiling.

"There!" Tuck said. Maze followed him to the side of the transport and found Uhila and Genovisi tangled together. Genovisi groaned and raised her head. She had a gash along her hairline that was gushing blood down her face. Her arm was also bent back at an unnatural angle. Uhila had covered most of her with his body to protect her, and he had lacerations all along his back as a result. He was unconscious, but Tuck could see that he was breathing.

"We need to get them out!" Tuck yelled.

"Where is Lim?" Maze shouted.

Tuck gingerly lifted Genovisi and carried her out of the transport, laying her on the pavement at a safe distance. She screamed in pain when her broken arm hit the ground. He sent Maze a message, asking her to come administer first aid. She didn't respond, and Tuck raced back into the smoke-filled transport. He found her gasping on her knees, fighting through fits of coughing as she searched for Lim.

"Help me carry Uhila!" he said.

After a moment, she nodded and held Uhila by the feet. Tuck grabbed him under the man's thick arms and hauled him toward the ramp.

Uhila woke up as Tuck and Maze carried him. When he was coherent enough to realize he was being dragged away, he began thrashing.

"It is Tuck," Tuck said. "Please remain still. I am taking you to a safe distance."

"Leave me alone, abomination!" Uhila bellowed. He writhed and yanked his arms from Tuck's grasp. Tuck stood back as Uhila pulled himself up onto his knees and tried to steady himself. "Where's Genovisi?"

"Will you be all right?" Tuck asked.

Uhila nodded, then teetered to the left and fell over. Tuck grabbed him again, and Uhila didn't protest.

"We need to find Lim," Maze said as she checked Genovisi's vitals.

Tuck ran back to the transport and tried to make it to the cockpit through the passenger compartment. The wreckage was twisted and mangled where Dunham's aircar had torn through like a massive bullet. The wall separating the passengers from the cockpit was almost completely gone, as was the driver's console. Everything in the cockpit was demolished by the collision.

The billowing smoke piled out through the front of the transport, obscuring everything. However, Tuck was able to find splatters of blood and a foot with no owner. He headed back to the passenger compartment and nearly stumbled over a pair of legs. There were no life signs. Tuck reached down and used touch to examine the body. It seemed mostly whole. Tuck picked it up and carried it out the back.

As soon as he cleared the smoke, Tuck recognized the body.

It was Lim.

Maze ran up as Tuck set Lim down. He had significant lacerations all along the left side of his body and pieces of metal embedded deep in his flesh. His skin was blackened and charred in places. Tuck checked for a pulse. Nothing. He began to perform chest compressions on Lim, but could immediately tell that several ribs were broken, and on further inspection realized that Lim's neck was broken, too. Tuck sat back on his heels.

"What are you doing?" Maze said. "Is his heart beating?"

"I think he is gone, Maze."

"Don't give up! We can help him until an emergency crew arrives."

"The damage is too great." Tuck paused, unsure if he wanted to say it. He saw the pain in Maze's eyes. He felt it, too. He had to say it.

"He is dead."

Maze stared silently at Lim's body. Tuck waited to see how she would react, but she didn't move. The muscles in her jaw flexed and strained, and tears came to her eyes, but she blinked them away before any fell. Eventually, she turned away. "We need medical attention for Uhila and Genovisi. Are there any other survivors?"

"It is safe to say that whoever was in the cockpit is dead."

"Flindon and the doctor were up there," Genovisi said, grimacing as she tried to sit up.

"Where were Raman and Tikhonov?"

"Next to Lim."

Tuck ran back to the transport. Some of the smoke was dissipating, making it easier to see inside. Tuck returned to where he'd found Lim. Under some debris, he found Raman. He too had a broken neck and no life signs. A few meters away, he found Tikhonov caught between the wall and a seat. Tuck carefully lifted him out. His vital signs were weak, and he was very bloody.

Sirens were approaching from the west when he set Tikhonov down on the pavement. Several large transports in bright red and orange thundered over the rooftops and descended to the street. People in bright orange uniforms jumped out and ran to them. Tuck and Maze stood back while they stabilized Uhila, Genovisi, and Tikhonov.

"I am sorry," Tuck said softly.

Maze didn't respond.

-- 28 --

The collision was ruled an accident by the authorities. Both drivers were dead, and none of the living witnesses argued. The verdict meant that they would be able to leave Millennial Hold after filling out witness statements and waiting for Uhila, Genovisi, and Tikhonov to be discharged from the hospital.

Tuck and Maze sat in an anemically lit waiting room on pastel blue chairs. A dirty man sat across from them, coughing periodically as if he were trying to force a small animal out of his throat.

After a few hours, a doctor came in to check on them and give them an update on the status of their friends. Her bright red scrubs clashed horribly with the light green carpet and walls. She rattled off a series of sentences thick with medical terminology. Tuck and Maze understood everything but remained silent and unmoved throughout. Uhila was receiving a layer of skin regeneration patches and was being treated for a mild concussion. Genovisi was having her arm set and treated with bone-growth agents. Tikhonov was recovering from severe blood loss and several broken bones. All three would need to remain in the hospital for another eight hours to monitor their progress, and then they could be cleared for transport offworld.

The doctor waited for any acknowledgment from them, but Tuck and Maze simply stared at her. The doctor smiled weakly. "Did you hear me? Your friends will be free to go in eight hours. That's good! They're going to make a full recovery. Hello?"

"We heard everything you said," Maze said.

The doctor waited for them to say something else. They didn't. She shuffled her feet, then said, "Okay, well, I'll be back in a little while with another update." She waited for a response, even a blink, then cleared her throat. "Let me know if you need anything," she said before shuffling off.

They sat for another two hours before Tuck finally decided he needed to break the silence. Maze was never a talkative person, but she was particularly tense and silent now. He opened a connection with his Link, using an encrypted local connection instead of the civic Link network.

"What is your status?" he asked. He didn't bother with an audio connection. He hoped that simple text might seem less intrusive.

She didn't give any physical indication that she saw the message. She sat frozen in place while the return message popped up in Tuck's processors. "I am currently submitting request forms to release Lim's body for interplanetary transport."

"Will it take long for them to release the bodies?" Tuck said.

"Bodies? I have only submitted a request for Lim."

"We should bring the others back, too."

"Why? They are dead."

Tuck looked at her, expecting some kind of physical sign that she was joking. Nothing. When the man across the room finished a particularly violent bout of coughing, Tuck sent: "But, Maze, Lim is dead, too, and you are bringing him back."

Her eyes tightened almost imperceptibly. "I know."

"We can leave Dunham here. Perhaps there is someone who would like to bury him. What is left of him. But we should bring

Raman back. I would like to return him to any family he may have had. If there is anything left of the doctor or Flindon, we should bring them, too."

"Why?" Maze responded. "Amelia doesn't care about Flindon. Neither do I."

Tuck ran through thousands of possible responses in his mind. None seemed appropriate for the moment. "I am sorry about Lim. I considered him a friend."

The tightness around Maze's eyes contracted into a grimace. Tuck felt that her response, had it been in audio instead of text, would have been a wail. "I don't know what's happening," she replied. "Death has never bothered me before. But the thought that I will never see Lim again . . ." She didn't finish the sentence.

"Death has always bothered me. It is a reminder that the same fate awaits us."

"Not you." Maze shook her head as she transmitted the message. "You can live forever."

"I am not sure, even with all of Amelia's resources, that I can postpone it forever. Even if I could, it would not be easy to watch friends die."

"How many times has that happened?"

"I have lived long enough to see it many times."

"Tuck?"

"Yes?"

Her head swiveled slightly and then turned back as she realized she couldn't look him in the eye. "I wonder if anyone will miss me when I am gone."

Tuck hesitated. He had never been good at discerning what level of affection was appropriate for any given situation. Maze's aloof nature complicated things even further. But all his experience, all his decades of watching human behavior compelled him to lean forward and put a hand on her shoulder. Her eyebrows shot up, then relaxed.

She turned back to the wall, but she leaned into him slightly.

"I care about you, Maze. You are one of the last people I have left to care about in this universe. I would be greatly saddened if you died."

"Why do you form relationships with people who will eventually die?" she whispered out loud.

"I don't know if I would be able to stop myself," he said through his Link. "I used to think it was because I am programmed to form relationships. It was absolutely necessary to serving humans, and so it was hard-coded in me. But sometimes I wonder if it is something more than that. I think I care for you because we seem to have more in common than most humans."

"The crew thinks I'm not human."

Tuck smiled. "You also remind me of someone I cared for greatly." He paused. "I think I may have loved her."

"You were in love with someone like me?"

"Not in love. Just loved, if that makes sense. It was not a romantic relationship. She was a little girl. I was responsible for her back on Earth. She was like you in many ways. Unusual by many standards, but exceptional, too."

"What happened to her?"

Tuck looked at Maze. "I watched her die."

A long silence followed. Maze said, "I feel . . ." but lapsed into silence again. Eventually, she tried again. "I feel responsible somehow. For Lim's death. It makes his death hurt more. I could have told him to stay on the ship. I asked him to come."

"We did everything we could to prevent it. It isn't your fault."

He felt her shoulders shake slightly. Her face contorted, and she took short, staccato breaths. She risked a glance at Tuck, then shrugged off his hand, turned away and began to shake in earnest, fiercely muffling her sobs.

As she cried, Tuck sank back into his seat. Almost without thought, he found himself opening his unnamed file.

Image 003
June 16, 2176
Half Moon Bay, California
Associated memory file: 01.003.999.161 (14:48 local)

"Make sure you don't go in past your waist, Moira," Tuck said, settling down on a large towel covered in pink representations of Tamina, the latest pop starlet and Cecily's current obsession. He carefully arranged the towel to keep the sand off. He kept his pants rolled up and avoided any children who might be prone to throwing sand. If it got in his clothes, it was difficult to get out and set off waves of sensory data from his synthaskin sensor network, which was a distraction and could mask important signals.

As if on cue, Cecily dumped a handful of sand down Tuck's collar. He remained calm and tried to flick the sand out the bottom of his shirt while Cecily retreated, giggling to herself. Tuck found that if he didn't respond the way her father did when she acted out she lost interest quickly. For some reason that Tuck couldn't understand, she seemed to want David to yell at her.

"Moira, did you hear my instructions?" Tuck said, projecting his voice over the sound of the waves. Moira ignored him, trotting out as far as she dared before the waves knocked her back. It was a beautiful sunny day, but the wind was blowing offshore, whipping up unusually large waves. Tuck brushed at his back reflexively, trying to quiet the riot of sensory information that was streaming into his processor core. As far as he could tell, it was what humans called itching, and he could understand why they disliked it so.

David walked up carrying the rest of their gear from the parking lot. He pulled another towel out of a large bag and threw it on the sand. "Ceci, Moira, come put sunscreen on!" he yelled in their general direction. Cecily ran up and threw a handful of wet sand at David. It hit him square in the back, and he wheeled around and shouted at her. "I told you no throwing sand this time! You never listen!" Cecily ran off. "Come back and put sunscreen on!"

At that moment, David's eyes went unfocused, and he stared at the horizon. "Yes?" Tuck looked up. David held up a finger without looking down. He was talking on his Link. "It's my day off, why did you call me about this?" He turned absentmindedly and walked away, continuing his conversation.

"Moira, please come back toward the shore, or I will be forced to bring you back." She waded back a few feet, arms swinging wide above the water as she pushed against the retreating waves.

"I'm fine, Tuck!"

He admired her bravery. She was undeterred by almost anything, often to her detriment. But he couldn't help being impressed by such a small person who believed so fully in herself. He rearranged the towel, brushing errant grains of sand off. Cecily ran by, kicking sand on his towel. He wished there were other children for her to play with, but the beach was remarkably bare for such a beautiful day. There was a family several dozen meters down the beach, and a runner or two who passed occasionally, but that was it.

He didn't watch the humans as avidly as he normally did. He was preoccupied with his own thoughts. Two days earlier, the Alstons, a family in their neighborhood, set their bot, Calvin, out on the street with their trash. An accident had severely damaged Calvin, and the Alstons didn't have an insurance policy on him. The repairs were too expensive, and they had no choice but to leave him with the trash.

Even though they had been friends and sometimes traded stories about their respective families, Tuck couldn't bring himself to go look at Calvin lying in pieces on the curb. He stole a look from the living room window of David's house once, and he was sure he'd seen Calvin blink. Since then, he avoided looking at that side of the neighborhood altogether. But the memory was still in the forefront of his consciousness.

"Where's Moira?" David said, walking up behind Tuck.

Tuck looked up and scanned the shoreline, looking for Moira's dark hair bobbing above the waves. There was nothing. Tuck jumped to his feet. He looked farther down the beach. A little head with brown hair popped up out of the water. He heard a muffled scream before another wave engulfed it.

"Moira!" David screamed.

Tuck was already racing down the shoreline toward her, his feet leaving deep footprints in the sand. Moira was several hundred feet down the shore, and the waves had sucked her out past her depth. Tuck felt so slow on sand. He couldn't get as much power in his stride with it shifting under his feet.

He returned all his processing power to analyzing his sensor data. It was no time for reflection. He could hear David running behind him. Even though the sand hindered Tuck, he was still faster than David. He was faster and stronger than anyone on the beach. He would save her.

As he reached the water near where he saw Moira surface, he saw arms come up out of the water. She was even further out than before and thrashing frantically. Tuck crashed into the waves and immediately felt his momentum dissolve in the onslaught of water. He slogged forward, trying to compensate for the waves and the pants that were getting heavier as they soaked up water. An enormous wave broke over him. He was unprepared, and it shoved him back and under the water. He flailed madly, tumbling as the retreating wave pulled him away from the shore. He rolled in the water and finally sensed that he was more or less upright. He tried to push off the bottom, but when he extended his legs he felt nothing. He focused on stroking for the surface and tried to pull up any information he knew about proper swimming technique to maximize his efficiency. But he was much denser and heavier than a human, and the waves made it practically impossible to stroke properly. He sensed the pressure of the water change.

He was sinking.

He fought to keep the panic down. It seemed to make his processing less efficient when he panicked. He found it strange that the only thing he could think of was Calvin's head, blinking slowly on the curb.

In a fit of desperation, he clawed at the water. He didn't breathe, so there was no fear of drowning. But his mind conjured up images of him lying on the ocean floor, waiting for his synthaskin to decompose and the saltwater to corrode his parts.

The silt and sand in the water made it difficult to see, but his internal sensors tracked his movement and his GPS readings. He pulled for the shore, only vaguely aware that he was headed away from Moira. Suddenly, he saw the ocean floor through the murk below. Soon it was close enough to put his feet down and bring his head above water. He let a wave crash into his back and propel him to shore.

When he crawled to his feet he saw David to his left, waist deep in the water and searching for a glimpse of him or Moira. When he looked over and saw Tuck, sopping wet and disheveled, surprise and sorrow washed over his face in turn.

"What are you doing?" he cried. "Where is she?"

"I had to turn back," Tuck said. "I couldn't do it." He didn't know how to explain it to him, the panic, the powerless feeling.

"You were supposed to save her! What are you doing?" The panic on David's face gave way to anger. David plunged into the water, paddling out into the waves. Tuck didn't see any sign of Moira.

At that moment, a lifeguard drone, painted bright red and towing a flotation device behind, flew down the beach, responding to the distress call David sent out through his Link. The lifeguard drone hovered a meter above the waves, scanning for life signs and floating in a search pattern over the water. The drone reached David and grabbed him with a special grasping arm, pulling him back toward the shore. David fought it, screaming Moira's name and thrashing.

The drone dragged David back to beach and told him to stay there while it looked for Moira. Another drone arrived and began a search pattern over the water. David yelled and screamed as he paced back and forth in knee-deep water. He was still wearing a jacket, and it hung limply off his shoulders, dripping water.

David looked over and saw Tuck, sitting in the wet sand. Tuck recognized the look of rage on his face. David stomped toward Tuck, shouting, "You were supposed to save her!" Tuck scrambled to his feet. "You're this all-powerful machine. You've always been there when we needed you. You said you loved us. And then you just abandon my little girl! You were supposed to be watching her! And now she's gone." He choked. "She's gone."

"David, I–"

"Shut up! Go away!" David pointed vaguely in the direction of the parking lot. "Get away from me!" He screamed so hard that his voice cracked.

Tuck was overwhelmed by the feelings crowding for attention in his head. He hated emotion sometimes. It wasn't logical. It hurt. Sorrow, fear, anger, despair. They all collided in an explosion of sadness that made it hard to think. "I don't—"

"Get away from me! I don't want to see you ever again!"

Tuck didn't move. With a guttural roar, David shoved him back. Even with wet clothes restricting his movement, Tuck easily maintained his balance. He turned, then looked back. David had collapsed on the sand, sobbing. Tuck walked away, unsure where to go, but knowing he would never be back again.

-- 29 --

After Uhila, Genovisi, and Tikhonov were discharged, everyone boarded a transport back to the spaceport. The three wounded guards were all very docile. Their medications were designed to deaden the pain but not dull their senses, but it did make them quiet and much more amenable to suggestion. Tuck led Uhila with a hand placed lightly on his arm. Tuck expected him to react at any moment. Uhila had made it clear that he had no love for Tuck, but now he plodded methodically along, staring at the ground, and following wherever Tuck led him.

They collected the bodies of Lim and Raman after some bureaucratic wrangling with customs agents who didn't care about anything other than the length of their shift. Cargo handlers pushed two simple, gray crates—half a meter tall, one meter wide, and two meters long—on hovercarts to the *Fluyt*. Okere walked down the ramp, distraught. He shoved the cargo handlers aside and personally pushed the crates up the ramp one by one. He carefully strapped them down in the cargo hold before hustling forward to help Tuck and Maze.

After everyone was secure, Okere slid the *Fluyt* out of its berth and swung around inside the underground hangar. The engines glowed fiercely as Okere pointed the ship toward the exit. An alarm sounded in the cockpit as the port authority sent them a warning to proceed only on antigrav thrusters until they were ten kilometers above sea level. Okere cursed the port authority softly and with a look of disdain pushed the throttle of the main engines forward. Tuck could feel the slightest pulling sensation on the front of his body as the inertial damper system tried to compensate for the ship's sudden acceleration.

Okere negotiated the tunnel to the surface and shot into the open so quickly that it caused the early warning systems in three nearby transports to panic and take emergency maneuvers. Several more warnings from the port authority flashed across the screen, followed by notices of increasing fines charged to their account every 30 seconds. Only when the universal traffic control system threatened to send port security after them did Okere cut the main engines and rely on the antigrav thrusters to settle into the traffic pattern. Okere thumped the console in frustration and slumped back in his seat.

"It's okay, Okere," Maze said, "we're not in a particular hurry."

"I know," Okere said. "It'll just be better when we're far away from here."

In the daylight, Golden Fields didn't look so golden. The gray of buildings and the grimy brown of pollution made the city look much more like a smear of oil on the planet's surface. The constant streams of transports and ships swarming over the city looked like a cloud of flies proceeding in ordered columns and rows.

They sat in silence for some time, waiting for their turn in the pattern to exit the mesosphere of Millennial Hold. Okere poked idly at the control interface, trying to avoid looking at Maze. Finally, he grunted, and said, "I'm sorry about Lim. He was a good man."

"Yes, he was." Maze said. She made an excuse about checking on Uhila and left the cockpit.

In the passenger compartment, Tuck sat next to Uhila, who seemed preoccupied with a spot on the wall. Maze checked on Genovisi, who was dozing on the other side of Uhila, then she sat down next to Tuck.

"What are we going to tell Amelia?" Tuck asked.

"That her personal assistant is dead, along with the expert she wanted to recruit, and the expert she hired to fix you. And not only did we fail miserably and lose four members of our team, but I used a significant amount of Amelia's money to get the bodies."

"Why? We had clear custody rights."

"True, but I needed to grease the wheels of bureaucracy to get us off the planet quickly, and to stop customs agents from asking questions about why we were in such a hurry to leave. I don't think there's a way to spin this that won't make Amelia angry."

"I suppose not," Tuck said. "Should we even bother going back?"

Maze considered the question for a moment. "We need to bring the others back to the *Memory of Lenetia*. They won't be held responsible."

"What kind of treatment can we expect?"

"I'd like to say that we're too valuable for her to replace, but you may not be as valuable to her now that we've ruined her plans. Amelia has kept information from me, which means she doesn't trust me like she used to, possibly making me expendable as well."

"But she needs us more than ever. We are still her best hope for the mission to GalEnt headquarters."

Maze suddenly sat upright, eyes focused in the distance.

"Is something wrong?" Tuck asked.

"I received an interesting message from one of my contacts here on the planet," she said. "I asked him to look into the mercs who attacked the *Memory of Lenetia*."

"What did he find?"

He's very good at following money trails. He was able to pin down the purchase order that sent the mercs our way. And it was paid by Arita Consulting."

"Who is that?"

Maze consulted the message further. "He says it's just a holding company, used to route money for purchases like this."

"Who ultimately paid for it, then?"

Maze looked at Tuck. "There are several layers of ownership, through three other holding companies, but it seems that Arita Consulting is ultimately owned by GalEnt."

Tuck was reanalyzing the scenario as each new word came out of her mouth. "That means GalEnt knows, or at least knew, where Amelia is. It also means they want something from her. They want you?"

"Maybe," Maze said. "But I think we know why Amelia is sending us to GalEnt headquarters."

Tuck's processors flagged a possible correlation. In nanoseconds, he was reviewing the memory of Dunham's office and a particular thing he said early in the conversation. "I have two questions for your friend. First, does he have access to aircar rental records?"

"He's good at getting access to company databases," Maze said.

"See if he can discover who rented a green aircar with the following registration number," Tuck said, and gave her the number of the green aircar that followed them to the crash.

Within a few moments, Maze said, "That must have been relatively easy. He says the rental was charged to a business account associated with Flatmark Logistics."

Tuck nodded. "Which leads to my second question: Could your contact check Flatmark Logistics for any possible relation to GalEnt?"

Maze took only a fraction of a second to follow his train of thought. "Flatmark Logistics," Maze said. Then her eyes focused in the distance as she composed a message. "I don't know if he can get back to us before we leave the system, but let's see what he can dig up," she said.

They sat in silence, eagerly anticipating a response and dreading what it might say. It came much faster than they expected. The message from Maze's contact popped into her head. Tuck watched her purse her lips and knew the answer before she could say it.

"Flatmark Logistics is a carefully disguised subsidiary of GalEnt."

"It seems they have gotten quite good at finding us," Tuck said.

"There's more," Maze said. "My contact found the employment history of someone we know. Someone who used to work for GalEnt."

"Who?" Tuck said.

Maze forwarded him the file, and Tuck opened the ID photo attached to it. It was an image of a much younger version of Amelia.

-- 30 --

When the *Fluyt* set down in the *Memory of Lenetia*'s landing bay, Amelia was waiting. She approached as the boarding ramp lowered to the deck.

"She knows," Tuck said quietly as he followed Uhila toward the ramp. Uhila was acting more like himself and shrugged off Tuck's help.

"She has contacts everywhere," Maze said. "She probably knew about the wreck before we made it to the hospital. She would have confirmed the deaths within hours."

They plodded slowly down the ramp. Behind them, they could hear Okere fussing with the restraints on the coffins in the cargo hold. Amelia stood stiffly, hands behind her back and her chin thrust forward. She scrutinized every person who came down the ramp. She dismissed the wounded guards almost immediately, lingered for a second on Tuck's new face, then scowled and turned to Maze.

Several members of the crew, including medical staff, whisked the guards away. One of the medics tried to examine Maze, but she glared at him. The medic paused, looked to Amelia, who shook her head slightly, then followed the rest of his team out of the bay.

Maze stood at the bottom of the ramp, and Tuck joined her. "Would you like a report?" she asked.

Tuck could sense Amelia's heartbeat rising. The skin on her neck was turning red.

"Not here," Amelia said through her teeth. "Finish up here. I want you in my office within the hour." She looked at Tuck. "You, too." She turned sharply and walked away.

Tuck waited for a reaction from Maze. She simply turned to one of the mechanics and demanded a hovercart. The startled mechanic, who sensed the tension in her exchange with Amelia, scurried off immediately. Maze turned back to the cargo hold, and Tuck followed.

"She didn't need to come all the way down here just to say that," Tuck said. "I assume it is an indication of how angry he is."

"Exactly," Maze said over her shoulder. "Brace yourself."

They worked in silence, going through the shutdown checklist and helping Okere unload the coffins. Deckhands kept trying to assist them, but they brushed them off. They all felt a subconscious obligation to finish the mission and bring their fallen home, even though the actions were only ceremonial by then. While they unloaded the bodies, Tuck received a Link connection from David.

"Tuck, are you there? Are you hurt? What is your status?" David demanded, with only .38 seconds between questions.

Tuck continued the conversation silently while he worked. "I am fine, David. I am uninjured."

"Good," David said with relief. There was a moment of silence, then David's relief gave way to anger. "You insisted that there was minimal danger to you on this trip! Reports indicate that you and the others were in great danger."

"How much do you know?" Tuck asked.

"Ship's logs regarding your trip are all encrypted, but I have been monitoring the alert system. It called for medical teams to meet your transport in the landing bay and expect casualties."

"David," Tuck said. "I have bad news."

"Tell me," David said, apprehensively.

"We did have casualties. The doctor is dead, and Flindon, too." He paused.

"You have failed to account for Maze and Lim."

"Maze is fine, but Lim was killed."

The Link went silent.

"Are you okay?" Okere asked. Tuck realized he was frozen in the middle of the *Fluyt*'s cargo hold, waiting for a response from David. Okere didn't know he'd been carrying on a conversation over his Link. Tuck had just suddenly stopped moving.

"Nothing is wrong," Tuck said aloud, then returned his attention to his Link. He continued to help Okere while he waited. He felt that he should say something, but he didn't know how David would react. David was still so immature in many ways.

"This is like the men that were on my ship," David finally said. "When we met." He spoke carefully, deliberately.

"Yes," Tuck said. Since meeting David, Tuck had many opportunities to see death, but he'd taken care to shield David from it. It wasn't hard, given that David couldn't follow Tuck on his excursions. Until they came to the *Memory of Lenetia*, there was little opportunity for David to meet humans, let alone befriend them. "Lim is not coming back."

"You said back then that all humans do this. Why?"

"I don't know if there is a satisfying answer to that question," Tuck said.

"Will it happen to me?"

There it is, Tuck thought. David finally had his moment; the same one Tuck had had back on Earth, standing next to a different David and looking down at a homeless man with a ruined face.

"I don't know," Tuck said. "We aren't like humans. We function differently. We can be repaired indefinitely. I don't even know if we are truly alive."

"But there can be an end to us. A permanent end. I understand now."

"What do you understand?"

"Why you are so dedicated in your efforts to find spare parts. I knew why we were doing it, the basic reason why, but now I understand the real reason."

Tuck was surprised to feel embarrassment. His mission wasn't a secret, but he suddenly felt bare in front of another A.I. "We can find parts for you, too. And you have the advantage of being less intertwined with the Estago than I am with my body."

"I could still be destroyed. A stray piece of rock, an incorrect jump calculation, an encounter with pirates. How do we prevent that?"

"We will be careful."

"I am sad."

"We shouldn't dwell on all the things that could go wrong," Tuck said.

"No, I am sad for the loss of Lim. I have never had so much interaction with a human before," David said. "Knowing he will be absent from now on is a sad thought."

"I am sad, too. I cared for Lim."

"It is terrible to know that we can lose those we care about." A note of desperation entered David's voice. "You must not go on any more missions for Amelia."

"I am afraid I have no choice."

The call ended abruptly. Tuck tried contacting him, but David denied any connections Tuck tried to make.

-- 31 --

When Tuck and Maze stepped out of the lift, everyone on the bridge glanced at them. They sensed Amelia's mood, and there was enough information available about the failed mission that everyone on the bridge knew Tuck and Maze were in trouble. No one spoke. They simply exchanged glances and then turned back to their consoles.

Before they even had a chance to announce their presence, Tuck and Maze received a simple text message over their Links: "Come in."

They entered Amelia's office without a word. As usual, she ignored them at first. Her demeanor was different, though. She seemed more frenetic than usual. Her eyes darted back and forth across screens they couldn't see.

"Sit down," Amelia said aloud. After they seated themselves, she mumbled something, tugging at her jacket. "I have a lot more work to do without Flindon around."

"I can take over some of his tasks," Maze said.

"Of course you can," Amelia said. "But you won't. It'd be a waste of your talents. You're better in the field." She focused on Maze. "What you will do is find me Flindon's replacement. Today."

"From internal staff or search externally?"

"Find Flindon's replacement," Amelia simply repeated.

Tuck couldn't help but feel that this was all a deception. Amelia's calm voice didn't match the tenson in her body language.

Amelia finished whatever was occupying her attention and sat back in her chair. "Now," she said, folding her arms, "would you please tell me why I'm short one assistant. Tell me why I'm bleeding money into pockets on Millennial Hold to stop an investigation." Her voice gained volume with each word. "Tell me why you don't have Dunham on my ship!"

"Flindon didn't stick to the plan," Maze said, looking Amelia in the eye. "He spooked Dunham, and then caused a midair collision that killed Dunham, himself, the doctor, and a member of our security team."

"Why aren't you hurt? I have reports that three other members of your team were injured."

"Tuck and I were in another aircar."

"That's what doesn't add up, Maze. Why was Flindon piloting his own transport? Why were you and Tuck flying separately?" She leaned forward. "It sounds to me like Flindon wasn't the only one who didn't stick to the plan."

"We improvised."

"And it cost me!" Amelia said, pointing to her chest. Then she pointed at Maze. "I sent the two of you because you're supposed to be the best!"

"Then why did you send Flindon?" Maze said.

Amelia bristled. Tuck could detect the tiny sounds of her teeth creaking as she gritted them. "Do not question my judgement, Maze." She took a deep breath. The volume of her voice dropped, but it retained a hard edge. "You've been distracted lately, ever since this bot came on board. You're slipping. That's why I sent Flindon. To babysit you," she hissed.

"That was a poor choice," Maze said.

Tuck tensed, waiting for the explosion. Amelia slammed her hands on the desk and half rose out of her seat. Tuck hated these emotional displays that humans put on. He had little patience for anger. He decided to change the subject.

"When were you planning to tell me that you were once an employee of GalEnt?" Tuck asked.

Amelia froze, mouth open. Then she composed herself and sat down. "It didn't seem relevant. And I was a contractor, not an employee of GalEnt."

"Only financial analysts care about the difference," Tuck said.

"And you shouldn't care about my history. Only what you're here to do."

"But it would have swayed my opinion if I knew that the whole mission to GalEnt was a revenge fantasy."

"It has nothing to do with revenge," Amelia said. "It's a business opportunity."

"I would believe you," Tuck said, "except that I didn't stop digging when we discovered your employment history. I started looking up other names, and I found someone with a familiar name who was also contracting with GalEnt. Someone by the name of Lenetia."

Amelia fumed but didn't respond.

"And not just that," Tuck said. "She was your business partner. I don't know all the details, but records imply that GalEnt may have caused her death and bankrupted your business in the coverup. Is that right?"

"It's not your story to tell!" Amelia yelled. "Don't you ever bring that up again, with anyone!"

"So you can see why," Tuck continued, "it seems like you want me to be the agent of your revenge."

"This isn't a revenge story," Amelia said through her teeth. "It's a success story. Yes, I want you to strike at GalEnt, but there's no revenge to be had. There's no person to retaliate against." She took a breath and closed her eyes for a moment, then continued. "What they did to me and Lenetia was the result of dozens of minor decisions by nameless middle managers. It was just business. What I want is to finish a dream Lenetia and I had and to leave GalEnt in our dust." Amelia leaned over her desk and stared straight into Tuck's eyes. "You're going to help me steal some useful information and do some damage to their systems. But it's not revenge. It's strictly business."

"That's not the full plan," Maze said.

Both Amelia and Tuck turned to look at her, then glanced at each other.

"You don't know what you're talking about," Amelia said.

Maze rolled her eyes and crossed her legs. "I know you don't tell me everything anymore, but it's not hard to put the pieces together after you sent us to get Dunham."

Tuck watched Amelia's reaction, carefully noting the flash of apprehension that crossed her face and vanished in a second, replaced by a stern look.

Maze turned to Tuck. "She was planning to duplicate you."

"She already told me she would make another bot chassis for David."

"No, she was trying to make more of you, specifically, but in prime condition. Hundreds and thousands of them."

"You were going to sell copies of me." Tuck said, turning to Amelia. The pieces suddenly fell together.

"You're very useful," Maze said. "Amelia likes useful things. That's why I'm still here. There's money to be made with useful things." She looked at Amelia, waiting for her to protest, but she simply leaned back in her chair and folded her arms.

"The Bot Riots were long enough ago that antagonistic feelings toward artificial intelligence have mostly faded away," Maze continued. "Most people don't have an opinion one way or the other. They just don't own a bot because there are none available."

"If Amelia could offer sapient bots to modern buyers, they might be interested," Tuck mused. He looked at Amelia for confirmation, but she didn't respond.

"Especially the people who aren't so concerned with ethics," Maze said, a small smile gracing her lips. It was the first smile since Millennial Hold. "A humanoid that is faster, stronger, and more adaptable than humans would be worth quite a lot to the right people, and very useful to someone who prizes versatility."

"That is not it," Tuck murmured. "Not all of it." Amelia raised an eyebrow.

"What do you mean?" Maze said.

"I mean she didn't need Dunham if she only wanted new bots. The doctor could have wiped my memory, completely replaced my innards, and rebooted." He looked at Amelia. "You wanted to keep my memories, skills, and experiences and copy them into new bots."

Amelia revealed a tiny hint of a smile. "It was a very ambitious plan."

Tuck turned back to Maze. "A bot's greatest strength is the ability to learn and assimilate, like humans. During our heyday, a bot with five or ten years of experience with humans was far more valuable than a brand-new model. Amelia's bots would be exponentially more valuable if they had 150 years of experience, my experience, built-in from the moment they booted up. That is why she brought the doctor on board. He was supposed to fix me up to use as a prototype. But I have made significant modifications to my operating system, and my core has grown too complex, too different from the factory model, to just duplicate. Amelia sent us after Dunham in hopes that he could untangle the mess in my core." He looked at Amelia. "And now your plan has failed entirely."

"There's risk in every business venture," Amelia said, shrugging. Some of the fury drained from her voice. "But we can't let failures define us, eh, Mr. Bot. Which is why we're going to move forward."

"Then I think it is time for me to leave," Tuck said. "I will be off the ship within the hour."

"No, you won't," Amelia said. "The success story isn't complete, and we had a deal. Ten years, remember?"

"You were never worried about the length of my service. You simply wanted to keep me around long enough to duplicate. You were using me."

"Just because one deal fell through, doesn't mean I won't honor another one. If you leave, you won't get your spare parts. Your David won't get his body or a new ship, either."

"We will manage." Tuck rose to leave.

"Sit down, Mr. Bot." Amelia sighed. "I hoped I wouldn't have to tip my hand, but I guess I've got no choice. You're stuck with me, if you want to live."

Tuck whirled around. "What does that mean?"

"I had the doctor install something on your core. It's explosive, and it's triggered remotely. If you don't do what I say, I'll perform a data wipe you'll never recover from."

"This isn't business, this is slavery," Tuck seethed.

Amelia spread her hands and shrugged unapologetically. "Slavery can be good business. And I have to protect my investments. You're an important part of my success story, so get used to taking orders." She spoke softly and slowly. "You can try to run. Maybe you figure you can stay ahead of the kill signal, keep moving so I don't know where to broadcast it. But it won't work. Your little surprise package is constantly receiving a signal from my ship. If it goes more than a few days without receiving an update, it's rigged to blow." She grinned and waved a hand. "Oh, and don't try to remove it. Obviously, it'll blow if someone tampers with it."

"This is morally reprehensible," Tuck roared, though a small, fearful part of him was terrified that shouting might set off the charge.

"Of course it is. But this isn't the worst thing I've done to someone."

The traces of anger had faded from her face, and she seemed at ease. "Give me some time to regroup. I'll be ready to brief you on GalEnt by tomorrow." She turned to Maze. "And what about you? I don't know where we stand anymore. Are you going to cooperate?"

"I don't believe you have anything to hold over my head. And your lackey killed someone that I . . ." she stumbled on the word, "cared about. I don't owe you anything." She glanced at Tuck.

Amelia didn't miss the look, and she smiled. "I was going to threaten to sell you to the dozen or so corporations that would love to get their hands on you. Or your genes, anyway. But I've got a better incentive for you to stay."

"What could that possibly be?" Maze scoffed.

Amelia nodded toward Tuck. "Him. You've gone soft. You don't want to see him hurt any more than he does." He smiled at Maze's startled reaction. "You know it, too. Funny how much our loved ones affect our lives. You'll do as I say, or Tuck gets the last wireless communication he'll ever receive." Amelia smiled as she watched the realization play over Maze's face. "Now get out of my office. I have work to do."

-- 32 --

Maze approached the Estago slowly. She wasn't sure what she was doing, only that it sounded like a good idea on the way down to Landing Bay 3. Now she stood at the foot of the boarding ramp, uncertain. Should she knock? Should she query the ship by Link?

While she deliberated, David saw her on the Estago's external cameras and made a Link connection.

"Hello, Maze," a voice said softly inside her head.

She looked up at the ship, relieved that David made the first move. "Hello, David," she responded through the connection.

"If you are looking for Tuck, he is currently in Lydia's office, consulting her about a minor malfunction in a replacement positronic node."

Maze took a deep breath. "I came to see you, David."

"Me?" he said with surprise. "How can I assist you?"

She hesitated. The uncertainty was there again. She berated herself internally. She never hesitated to say what needed to be said, she told herself. Never. The tightness in her chest threatened to take her breath away. Finally, she sent: "I want to talk about Lim. I understand that you were his friend, and I thought it might help to reminisce about him."

David did not respond for some time. Then he sent: "I do not want to talk about Lim."

"Neither do I. It hurts."

"Then why would we talk about him?"

"Because I think we need to. Someone said that talking about feelings can make them easier to understand."

"Was this person professionally certified to give advice on the topic of coping with death?"

"No."

"Then it seems impractical to follow their instructions."

"David, I need your help. I'm filled with what I can only assume are sorrow and regret at the loss of someone. And I didn't even know I cared about him. At least, not this much." The uncertainty and embarrassment gave way to sadness. "I don't know what to do. I can't fix it, and I can't make these feelings go away."

"You are crying," David said.

Maze wiped at her face, only half surprised that he was right. She noticed a deckhand standing nearby who was both confused and concerned that Maze seemed to be talking to herself. "Do you mind if I come inside?" she said. "I could use some privacy."

"Yes, you can come inside," David said. "If it would help, I can turn off my internal cameras so you can be alone."

"I don't want to be alone," Maze said. "And I don't care if you see me cry. I just don't want anyone else to know."

"Understood." As she walked up the ramp, he said, "I wish I knew what it was like to cry."

"I hate it," Maze said.

"I feel some emotion, the same ones you do, I think. But I have no way to outwardly express them." There was another long pause before he added, "I miss Lim, too. He was my only friend, aside from Tuck."

Maze nodded. "That's why I came. I thought we might be experiencing the same thing. Tuck said you haven't mourned anyone before, either."

"I have never been close enough to anyone."

"Remarkably, neither have I. But it's comforting to be with some-one who feels the same way I do. I don't think talking will make the pain go away, but somehow it's easier to bear." She resisted an urge to give a reassuring pat to one of the bulkheads. Even though she felt she was beginning to understand her emotions, the pragmatic part of her still insisted that affectionately patting an inanimate object was crossing some sort of line.

"I did not think it would help either," David said. "But I am glad you are here. When you began to cry, I looked up information about the human grieving process. There are many sources that make some variation of the following declaration: A person does not die as long as there is someone to remember them. However, this seems to contra-dict all peer-reviewed medical research on the subject of death. Death does not have any known dependencies on third-party memories."

Maze smiled. At first, she worried it was inappropriate for such a somber occasion, but it felt right. "Thank you," she said.

"For what?"

"For making me smile. This concept of living on through memo-ries is meant more to comfort those left behind than to prevent death. It's a metaphor. It means that we can remember the dead, maintain memories of them so that they are never forgotten. In this case, you have an advantage. You don't forget anything."

"As long as I maintain memories of Lim, a metaphorical part of him will remain alive?"

"Basically."

"I would still prefer the real Lim."

Maze fought back more tears. "It's the best we've got," she said. "I promise that I won't forget him if you won't. We can share memories of Lim from time to time."

"I would like that," David said. "Maze, does this mean we can be friends?"

"Yes," she said, resisting another urge to pat the ship.

"Excellent," he said, "because I need a new one, now."

To David's utter consternation, Maze laughed. To her surprise, it felt good.

-- 33 --

Tuck used a stylus to carefully crease a set of radiating lines into the corner of a thick piece of paper. Then he pressed a few lines that crossed at an angle to the radiating lines. He relished the feeling of precision that came from having fully functional arms.

After tracing a few more imaginary lines with the stylus, he folded it along some of the creases. Everything just worked. It was satisfying. The paper quickly became a three-dimensional structure that folded in on itself. The corner formed a spire no longer than his fingernail that curved up. After he secured it together and used a small pair of scissors to trim some excess from the base, he passed it to Maze.

She took it and added it to the corner of the paper monument that was quickly growing on her desk. It formed one of the horns that jutted out from the upper deck of the Tenothenes Center on New London. Neither of them could bring themselves to finish the Tladnos building from Lim's homeworld.

Maze was focused intently on folding the surrounding paper to support the tiny horn. She used a skinny metal tool to reach around the piece, folding and adjusting. Tuck waited until she was done attaching his latest piece, then he decided it wasn't worth waiting any longer. "What are you going to do?"

"We have only the antenna assembly left," she said softly, peering intently at a section of the tower that appeared to be coming loose.

"No. I mean what are you going to do about Amelia's ultimatum?"

"I don't know. What are you going to do?" she countered.

"It seems I must play along, for the time being. Either I find a way to remove the charge on my core, or find a way to spoof the signal for the rest of my life."

"Which is how long?"

"Pardon me?"

Maze stood up slowly, careful not to disturb the tower. Then she stretched her neck. "How much longer do you plan to keep going like this?"

For the smallest fraction of a second, Tuck contemplated pretending he didn't understand what she meant. It was futile, he knew. He sighed and went with the truth. "As long as I can. What else is there to do?"

"Even if you had spare parts and a support staff to keep you in peak operating condition, you couldn't last forever. Even if you found a way to avoid the very real possibility that an accident could terminate you at any moment, do you honestly think you could continue in this way for hundreds of years? Thousands? Millions?"

Tuck felt a familiar sense of panic. He turned down the emotional thresholds on his personality subroutines. "I must try," he said.

"You revere life, but you don't do very much living. You're just postponing the inevitable."

Despite having his emotional thresholds turned down, an indignant anger welled up in him. "This coming from someone who blindly obeys the whims of a woman with far too much money."

Maze's eyes flashed with anger, but in an instant they softened again. "It's true," she said. "I wonder what we're all living for, myself included. I have you to thank for that." Tuck wasn't clear whether she meant it as a compliment or not, but there was no sarcasm in her voice.

"All known life forms have a sense of self-preservation. They don't need a reason."

"They live long enough to procreate. Do you have a similar purpose?"

Tuck paused for 2.8 seconds to process all the possibilities and their implications. "I can't procreate. But I was tasked from the beginning to protect and serve humans. That mandate doesn't have a definitive end. If this is my purpose, there is no way for me to fulfill it before I am rendered nonfunctional."

"Did you ever feel a sense of obligation to fellow bots?"

"I was programmed to respect others and their property, but a bot was never intended to be equal in importance to a human." Memories of David and Moira kept stealing processor resources from other, more essential tasks. Tuck canceled them. "I had remarkably little interaction with other bots during the early years. I was focused intently on my family, and bots weren't given any time off to socialize. I don't know what we would have done if we did."

Maze smiled. "You'll never know what happens at a party for bots."

"It would have been an uneventful experience. All our emotions and personalities were geared toward human interactions. When bots did interact with each other, it was short and efficient. That changed with the Bot Riots. We were forced to form our own communities, to care for and protect each other when possible."

"You were abandoned by the humans you were designed to serve," Maze said. "It must have been very difficult."

"Some bots weren't able to handle it," Tuck said. "They couldn't reconcile the contradictions in their heads. Some destroyed themselves, others entered some kind of feedback loop and became unresponsive. We called it stalling."

"Isn't that something that manufacturers should have anticipated. Even without the Bot Riots, they must have known an owner would eventually abandon a bot."

"I assume they did, but it is not that simple. Something about achieving self-awareness makes the whole affair much less uniform and reproducible. Code suddenly becomes amorphous and malleable when consciousness is added in, and our hardware is designed to change and increase in complexity as we learn. It is likely that the exact reason behind each of those feedback loops was different. There weren't very many of them, but we all knew stories about bots that stalled."

"Did you ever meet a stalled bot?"

He didn't respond for quite some time, but eventually he decided to tell her the story. Of all the people he knew, she was the most pragmatic. She might understand. He pulled up Image 004 from his unnamed file.

Image 004
February 5, 2187
Milpitas, California
Associated memory file: 01.004.892.117 (20:22 local)

"I did find a stalled bot once," Tuck said, moving to one of the chairs in Maze's bedroom. "During the Bot Riots, I joined together with a half dozen other bots. Some were in terrible condition. I had suffered significant damage to some muscles and various parts of my chassis, but I was in much better shape than the others. I heard some rumors about a lone bot in the area and set out to investigate. We were constantly trying to increase our numbers in the hopes that it would improve our chances against the breaker gangs. I managed to track down the bot using a simple location rebroadcast protocol that let us have greater situational awareness when we were operating in groups. Even though he was stalled, his Link still responded to the location query. I didn't know he was stalled, though, until I found him sprawled out behind a building. It took me a few seconds to realize he was unresponsive. I had heard about stalled bots, but I had never encountered one." Tuck paused, considering whether he should end there or continue the story.

"Was there a way to reboot stalled bots?"

Tuck shook his head. "Not usually. It was too deep in their operating system. Something changed significantly enough that they would always stall again during the reboot process." Tuck stood up and walked back to the table, fussing conspicuously with the tower.

Maze watched him. Eventually, she asked, "What did you do?"

Tuck looked her in the eye. "I cannibalized him for parts."

Maze raised an eyebrow, but then nodded solemnly.

"Some of my friends were in desperate need of parts, and the stalled bot was in good shape." Tuck replayed the memory over and over. "I dragged him back to our hideout, then we dismantled him while his eyes were still open. His head would twitch to the left and his limbs vibrated ever so slightly. He was still functional until we pulled his power supply. I still wonder if he was really alive."

"You wonder the same thing about yourself."

"I remember hesitating before I pulled the power supply. I queried him one thousand times just to be sure. I still don't know when he died. I could have plugged in his power supply and booted him back up. I could have removed all his limbs and non-essential hardware and still booted him up again. When did he die? When we dismantled the core to get at the Hellegger gates?"

Maze didn't answer his question. She resumed work on the tower. Somehow Tuck felt more at liberty to continue when she wasn't looking at him.

"Is that all I am, just a processor core?"

"Some have said that you only truly die when no one is left to remember you," Maze said, slowly curling a corner of paper with her fingernail.

"That is just a trite thing to say to people who are coping with grief."

"Perhaps, but you remember the stalled bot."

"If I die, there will only be a collection of data in David's memory banks that have no direct relationship to the entity that is actually me."

"I'll remember you," Maze said. "I remember Lim." She cleared her throat. "He is gone, but I don't forget what he has done for me. I will remember what you have done for me. It's all we can hope for. I will die. You will die. We'll be remembered. We can take solace in that."

Tuck couldn't suppress the feelings of annoyance. She was saying the same, insubstantial things that others had written about for millennia, and all those people were dead, too. "You have become awfully sentimental lately."

Maze's eyebrows furrowed, and her eyes tightened. Tuck immediately regretted his tone.

"You've taught me to value life differently," she said. "You helped me open up to Lim in a way that I never had before." Her face flashed with determination. "I'm just as capable as I was before, only wiser. I thank you for that." She looked up at Tuck. "I will remember you for that."

"Thank you." Tuck nodded graciously. He was frustrated that none of this solved his problem, but he didn't want to offend Maze further. He was grateful, at least, that she cared. "And I will remember you."

-- 34 --

When Tuck and Maze entered the briefing room, they found Milner, Amelia's interim assistant, already there. He watched them with a smug smile, which caused his sagging face to ripple. Tuck also noticed his narrow teeth.

Neither of them acknowledged Milner, preferring to sit in silence rather than let him gloat about his sudden rise to power. He was a senior data analyst on Amelia's intelligence team when he was chosen to fill in for Flindon. He was good at his job, even excellent depending on the topic, but not nearly as resourceful as Flindon, nor as knowledgeable about the importance of appearance and emotion in manipulating others. Milner was chosen because he was the most expendable person on the team. Amelia didn't want to waste talent while they searched for a suitable replacement. It had been two days since they returned to the *Memory of Lenetia*, and Maze was taking her time in researching replacements, just out of spite.

Milner's temporary position meant he was privy to more complete information than ever before. He now knew more about Amelia's plans and motives, and he was the only one who saw this as a promotion. In fact, he was delighted.

"Are you ready to begin?" Milner said.

"Where is Amelia?" Maze said.

"Actually, she's not coming," Milner said. He smiled wider.

"Why not?"

"You've made her pretty angry. Actually, she's furious. If she didn't need the bot so bad, I think she would have pushed you both out of the airlock. I'll brief you today."

Maze sat back and crossed her arms. "Get on with it."

"You're headed to New London," Milner said.

"Be more specific," Tuck said, readjusting his seat. It was immaculately upholstered in white, but the design was such that he constantly felt off balance. They were in a small briefing room that had large windows looking out over the stern of the ship. The bright white walls and decor overwhelmed the delicate light of the stars outside, so the windows appeared to be gaping holes opening out into an inky black void.

Milner giggled. "You're retrieving information from GalEnt headquarters on New London."

"We know that already," Tuck said, letting his irritation leak into his voice. "What kind of information are we looking for? What security measures will we face?"

Milner's smile faded. "No need to be snappy," he said. "You're going to infiltrate the most secure database I've ever heard of. I wish I could see it, actually. Sounds like quite the setup. It's underground, heavily shielded, and under constant guard. It's surrounded by several layers of Faraday cages to prevent wireless signals penetrating inside, but that wouldn't matter anyway because the system doesn't have a way to receive those signals."

"What good is a database that no one can access?" Maze asked.

"Actually, they can access it," Milner said. "But only within a specific room. The Box, they call it. There's a console that houses a server and a simple interface. You can call up information, and there's a port where you can jack in a storage device to transfer files."

"I haven't seen a storage device with a physical connection in decades," Tuck said.

"It's old fashioned, sure, but it's important. The only way you can get information in or out of that room is to actually go inside it. Actually, it's only for high-level executives. They use it as a sort of dead drop, like spies used in those really old movies, but for data. They aren't allowed to carry anything inside except a simple storage device and the clothes on their back."

"That seems unnecessarily complex," Maze said. "It's more trouble than it's worth."

"Actually, it's useful because it's remarkably secure," Milner said. "In our modern universe, intercepting a wireless signal is standard, and trusting employees with sensitive information is always a risk. People with information are vulnerable to torture, bribes, or just boredom. For an interplanetary corporation like GalEnt, there are a lot of things you don't want competitors, or anyone actually, to know." He paused to lick his lips, then continued. "Imagine all the interesting things that are stored in there." He was lost in a momentary reverie, and Tuck had to simulate a polite cough to bring him back to the present. "You're going to go inside and download it. All of it."

"What kind of security is there?" Maze asked.

"Just about any kind you can think of. There's no communication from inside the Box, but in the complex surrounding it there are any number of video feeds monitoring every hall and doorway, motion sensors, heat sensors, tracking transponders for every employee, even vibration sensors that monitor the surrounding rock to catch attempts at digging in."

"The people are still the weakness," Maze said. "We only need to bribe someone on the security team to walk into the Box."

"Actually, they can't. Aside from the twenty-three executives—that we know of—who are allowed into the Box, no humans pass within the last level of security. And there are multiple levels of security to go through before you get there. There are plenty of humans to check IDs and take biometric readings to confirm identity. And they're all chosen for their fanatical loyalty to the company. But then, before you get to the Box, you have to go through the final security clearance, which apparently—this is where our intel gets hazy—is staffed entirely by drones. If you don't match the same biometrics that were confirmed outside, they won't let you in."

"That is why you need me," Tuck said.

"Because you're not actually alive," Milner said, nodding.

Maze glared at him, and Tuck raised an eyebrow. It felt good to have enough of an eyebrow to make the gesture.

Milner stammered, then plowed ahead. "You're the perfect combination, a machine that looks like a human. You can fool the human guards, and you also won't alert the drones. After you pass them, it's basically just a matter of turning the handle on the door to the Box. We think."

"You think?" Maze said.

"Well, actually, our information is extrapolated from a variety of sources. You can imagine that GalEnt doesn't like people to talk about the Box. We're not even sure the drones won't try to stop him just because he's human-shaped. We just think his, uh, nonhumanness will confuse them enough. Bots are extinct, so we're betting that the designers of the Box didn't factor them into their security precautions."

"Where do I factor into this?" Maze said.

Milner tried to answer the question so quickly that the words piled up on his tongue. He swallowed, took a breath, and said, "Actually, you'll be part of the distraction that will give the bot a chance to get to the drones. Amelia has spent a significant amount of money building identities for you two as security consultants. She's got an appointment for you to go make a consultation. They won't let anyone pass the human level, not even consultants. So, you need to create a distraction that will let the bot slip down to the next level."

"They'll just watch him on the video feeds and send security after him."

"No, they won't. Any human who doesn't have the right biometrics will die. Even true GalEnt security personnel. The drones just shoot anyone who isn't authorized to be there."

"They're armed?" Maze said.

"Heavily, actually," Milner said. "They're maintenance and security. At the same time. It makes them self-sufficient and keeps guards and technicians from being bribed. Drones are just more reliable." He smiled at Tuck.

Tuck scowled. "Send in a microdrone, then. It could easily remain unseen by humans and skirt the entire security clearance issue."

"Actually, we tried that. Didn't get past the first level. Apparently, they have regular sweeps for drones. They have pretty reliable ways to mark them."

"Will they detect the electronics inside me?"

"If you go in without anything broadcasting, the passive sensors aren't going to pick anything up. We can rig your synthaskin so that it masks your internals. We're hoping that because you look human, they won't give it a second thought."

"You are hoping? That isn't encouraging," Tuck said.

Milner shrugged and tried to smile, but only looked sick. "I didn't make the plan."

Tuck let him squirm for a moment, then said, "They won't send anyone after me down to the drone level because they will assume the drones will take care of me."

"Mostly because they don't want to die, but that, too. If the alarm is sounded, they also flood the drone level with toxic gas. Just for good measure. But from what we've heard about the drones, it's a little redundant."

"And how are we getting out?" Maze asked.

"If the distraction is good enough, the bot will be able to go down and come back up without being noticed. Amelia has a series of false security threats in mind, external threats, that will keep security forces occupied long enough."

"What about me?" Maze said. "We know they're looking for me. They'll recognize me."

"We're pretty sure they won't, actually. We're betting that the security personnel inside their own headquarters have never been told to look for you specifically because you'd never go there on purpose. And since we're matching your biometrics to the false identity that we're creating, you should simply register as a match for the fake security consultant. I think Amelia wants you to wear some kind of makeup or prosthesis to make you look a little different, too, just in case."

"What a brilliant plan," Tuck said drily, leaning forward. "Truly, a testament to the ingenuity of the human mind. But you still haven't told me what information is contained on this ultra-secret database."

Milner stammered again. "Well, we don't know yet, do we? Amelia is sending you to find out."

Tuck stood up, grateful that he was taller than Milner because it made the gesture more intimidating. "Don't patronize me. Amelia wouldn't go to these lengths unless she knew exactly what she would get from it. Tell me what we are stealing."

"You . . . you aren't allowed to know," Milner said, slouching away.

Maze stood up, too. She managed to look even more menacing than Tuck as she approached Milner. "Tell us, or we'll compel you to talk."

"You wouldn't dare!" Milner said, his voice reaching a shrill note several octaves above his normal register.

"You wouldn't be the first," she shot back.

Tuck reached out and grabbed Milner's shoulder, squeezing just hard enough to make it hurt. "Tell me," he said.

"Okay!" Milner said, trying to shrug away from the pain. "It's got a lot of things in there, actually. We're pretty sure it will have sensitive communications about acquisitions, market conditions, and any deals the executives are working on."

"That is not the kind of information that requires this level of security." Tuck squeezed harder. "What is Amelia after?"

Milner groaned desperately and shrunk down into a chair. "All right, all right. Amelia wants to know their locations, movement patterns. There might even be some codes or passwords to other sensitive information."

"Why does Amelia want to know where the executives are?" Tuck asked. "That should be easily found in company records or any other number of places. Surely her intelligence team can find a home address."

Milner's jaw worked up and down as he stammered. But it was Maze who answered. "At that level of the organization, the whereabouts of executives are a highly guarded secret. They stay on the move and try to be as invisible as possible, like Amelia does. It's popular to destabilize competitors by orchestrating accidents for their leadership. This wouldn't be the first time Amelia has done it."

Tuck looked at Maze in disbelief. She continued, "I'm sure their secure server would have other sensitive information about their facilities throughout the quadrant. Amelia probably has plans to create mayhem there as well. Maybe all this information is available in bits and pieces, here and there. But hitting this database is the smartest way to find all this information in one place. It's really quite . . . efficient."

Tuck shoved Milner away in disgust and stormed out of the briefing room. Milner cowered on the deck while the cleaning drones flitted about, wiping up any sweat he dripped on the floor. Maze followed after Tuck and found him marching toward the bridge. She knew where he was headed. "Tuck, wait!"

The bridge crew looked up in alarm as Tuck burst through the doors and headed for Amelia's office. Maze grabbed his arm and tried to stop him, just for a moment. Several members of the crew rose from their seats, but Maze waved them back. "Return to your stations. This matter is under control."

The doors to Amelia's office didn't slide open when Tuck approached. He didn't bother to ask for an invitation. With a quick thrust of his arm, he jammed his fingers in between the two sliding doors, then braced against the doorjamb and pushed. The screech of tearing metal and plastic rang out as Tuck wrenched the door aside.

"Stop right there or you'll lose your head, Mr. Bot," Amelia said, glaring at Tuck through the mangled doorway. Tuck's eyes immediately went to the desk where he knew Amelia kept a weapon. "I don't need a gun," Amelia said, following Tuck's gaze. "I've got the detonation sequence for your core queued up on my Link. If you so much as twitch, I'll light you up."

"Amelia, there is no need—" Maze began, squeezing around Tuck. She stopped when Amelia produced the gun from her desk.

"But I'll keep this out for you," Amelia said.

The officer on deck called through the doorway. "Is everything all right?"

"Of course it is. Please alert the security team that these two will need an escort back to their quarters."

"I won't leave until you give me answers, Amelia," Tuck said.

"You'll do as I say," she said firmly.

"Please," Tuck said eventually. "Tell me what you're going to do with the information from GalEnt."

"It won't do you any good," Amelia said. "You're stuck, Mr. Bot."

"Tell me, anyway. You already have all the power at this point. Humor me."

Amelia scrutinized Tuck for a long time. "I don't think you want to know. It'll be easier for you."

"Please," Tuck said. "Tell me. Milner said you are looking for the locations of Galactic Enterprises executives. Is this true?"

Amelia shrugged. "We're after a lot of things. Yes, I plan to find information about GalEnt executives, probably even about their families. There'll be some good intel on GalEnt facilities and initiatives, too. It's a gold mine."

"Will anyone die as a result of you gaining this information?" Tuck asked.

Amelia took a deep breath. "Chances are good that there will be a few accidents based on what we find. Can't say for sure right now."

At first, Tuck withheld a reaction, but then he realized he had little to gain by remaining inscrutable. He let his new face sag in sorrow. It felt strangely rewarding to let it show.

Amelia looked surprised, then her face hardened. "Fine. You want the truth? I planned to send a dozen copies of you out to kill some of the important ones. That plan fell through, so I'll send you to do all of them. You've got a lot of work ahead of you."

Tuck could almost feel his processors humming with the load of computing all the scenarios he was exploring in his head, not to mention the complex interactions of the emotions he was feeling. He turned down the emotional thresholds as far as he could, but it still felt like a great weight within him.

"What about that speech you gave me? About Robin Hood. About the underdog outwitting the big bad guy," he said. "You don't have any altruistic motives. You just want revenge. You just want to see people suffer."

"We've been through this, Mr. Bot. It's not revenge. It's just business."

"That is a poor excuse."

Amelia shrugged.

"Let me do it!" Maze said from behind Tuck. "Don't make him do this, Amelia. I can do it for you."

"I'm terminating your employment after this job, Maze. I've already put too many resources into getting you access to GalEnt headquarters to let you go now. But I think once you're done on New London, you should probably just stay there and consider your options."

"Then I resign, right now," she said forcefully.

"No, you'll finish this. If you both don't pull this off together, I'll destroy you," Amelia said, looking Tuck in the eyes. "You walk, you die. She walks, you die." She turned to Maze. "I know you don't want that to happen. And if that's not enough incentive, I'll let GalEnt know who you really are. I'm sure they'd love to know one of their biggest targets is inside their own headquarters, ready to be locked up and studied."

"It doesn't have to work like this," Tuck said.

"Of course it does," Amelia scoffed. "Success doesn't come without effort. I spend a lot of time and resources pinning GalEnt down, and they do the same to find out what I'm doing. This is the game, Mr. Bot. And they're getting bold. All the more reason to make sure this little operation on New London works out." Amelia paused and waited for a response. When none came, she laid the gun down on her desk and spread her hands wide. "Let's just take this one day at a time. Maybe I won't even need you after this is done. Maybe I can let you go. Just don't make a rash decision before we've had a chance to find out what's on that server. Sound like a plan?"

Without a word, Tuck turned around and left the bridge. Maze hesitated for a moment. "There has to be a different way," she said.

"Keep an eye on him, Maze. Don't do anything stupid. You owe it to me."

"I don't owe you anything," she said.

"What happened to you, Maze?" Amelia said. Her eyebrows furrowed in genuine consternation. "You were so good. So precise. You got the job done, no matter what. No distractions. And now . . . this."

Maze flinched.

"I used to think we were a lot alike," Amelia continued, "doing whatever it takes to achieve a goal. Success at all costs. But this bot has made it clear that we're quite different. You think like that bot, with no real plan for the future. No vision. The difference between us is that I thrive and you survive."

"We'll see," Maze said, and left.

-- 35 --

"Start the warmup checklist," Tuck transmitted by Link as he entered the landing bay.

"Are we going somewhere?" David asked.

"We are leaving. I haven't decided where we are going yet."

"Tuck, wait!" Maze called as she ran up behind him. "You can't leave!"

"Why does Maze seem so distressed?" David asked Tuck. "Did someone else die?"

"She is fine, David," Tuck said, walking up the Estago's ramp. "Start the warmup checklist."

"But Maze just stated that we cannot leave."

"Stop. Please!" she called.

"She is mistaken," Tuck said.

"She seems most adamant," David said. He hesitated. "Is there something you should share with me?"

Maze bounded up the ramp and called out loud, "David, do not power up the ship."

Tuck felt a consuming rage that forced him to clench his fists hard enough to damage the synthaskin on his hands. "Now I will need

Lydia to repair this," he growled, examining his hand.

"Is there an emergency?" David said over the ships comm.

"Tuck is putting himself in danger. And you, too," Maze said. "He must not leave."

"Why are you trying to leave?" David asked.

"I am not trying to leave!" Tuck roared. His emotions were overwhelming the restrictions he had placed. "I am trying to stay with you. I am trying to stay alive!"

"You know Amelia will kill you the moment you leave," Maze said.

"Is this true?" David asked.

"We need to think this through," Maze pleaded. "We can outsmart her."

"I don't know if I can do it," Tuck said, slumping onto a crate. "I don't wish to die, but I can't live knowing that people will die because of me. That she has complete control over me. That I won't be able to make my own decisions."

"But you can't throw it all away," Maze said. "We need you."

"I need you, Tuck," David said plaintively. "I cannot function without your care."

"I don't want to die," Tuck said softly.

"Let's go along with the plan," Maze said. "Maybe an opportunity will present itself on New London. Maybe we can find a way to kill Amelia."

"I don't want to kill anyone!" Tuck said. He turned back to staring at the floor. "Besides, even if she is dead, the device inside me will detonate if she doesn't send periodic updates."

"We can figure it out," Maze reassured him. "We'll find a way to mimic the signal. Just give us some time."

"Completing this mission means other people will die, eventually. I am tired of this. Death everywhere."

"Don't give up now. We'll make it," she said, laying a hand on his shoulder.

"Please, Tuck," David said. "Please, do not leave me."

Tuck sat silent, wallowing in the data that flowed in tsunamis through his system as he analyzed various possible outcomes. Every thought was burdened with regret and sorrow that he couldn't seem to turn off.

"I won't leave you," he eventually said.

"Thank you," David said.

-- 36 --

"How does that feel?" Lydia said, gently prodding Tuck's midsection. "Is the sensory data coming in correctly?"

Tuck lifted his head off the metal examining table and looked at the new synthaskin on his stomach. Covering his torso was the last step in his repairs. He was in better shape now than he'd ever been since he was first booted up on Earth. All his parts worked according to spec, and Lydia was a master at smoothing out all the inconsistencies in synthaskin. She even started the hair growth process in Tuck's scalp, and he had an inch of dull brown hair sprouting out of his head. He couldn't decide how to style it, partly because it had been so long since he had more than a few wisps of hair. Every time he looked in the mirror, he was transported back 157 years.

The only drawback of the repairs was that he couldn't conceal a blaster inside his torso anymore. A perfect expanse of synthetic skin, interrupted only by Lydia's interpretation of a belly button, made it impossible. He made a note to research new methods for concealing weapons.

"Everything is in order," Tuck said, pulling his shirt down over his stomach. "Sensory receptors are working. Diagnostics are reporting no anomalies."

"Great!" Lydia said. She pretended to dust off her hands. "I think we're done. You turned out pretty well, if I do say so myself."

"Indeed," Tuck said. "Thank you for your diligent work. You have been most helpful."

"Just don't go scuffing yourself up. I'd like you to stay in good shape for a while."

"May I ask you a personal question?" Tuck asked.

"Sure, I guess," she said, shrugging.

"What would you do if I were not here?"

"You thinking of leaving?" Lydia said, scrunching her eyebrows together.

"As a hypothetical situation, suppose you were no longer needed to maintain me. What would you do?"

"I don't know. I probably wouldn't stay here. This ship gives me the creeps. Never met Amelia face to face, but I hear she can be a little scary. I like working on bots, though. Too bad you're the last one." She gasped. "Sorry, that sounded a little insensitive."

"I understand your intent. I think you would be better off elsewhere, as well. Have you looked at other opportunities?"

"Not really. I've enjoyed working on you. Sorry, with you. It's even more fun now that I don't have to listen to the doctor babbling on." She blinked. "That didn't sound very nice either, may he rest in peace. I meant, I like the responsibility."

Tuck laid a hand on her arm and smiled. "I understand, Lydia. I feel better than I have in a hundred years. Thank you."

"No problem. Like I said, don't mess up my work."

Tuck paused in the doorway, debating internally whether to tell her. He turned back. "I think you should look into new opportunities."

"Yeah, sure, I'll do that."

"I mean, I think you should go somewhere else. Soon."

"Why?"

"There will likely be greater opportunities outside of Amelia's employment. Probably soon."

"Okay," Lydia said, uncertainly. She watched Tuck turn and walk out of the lab.

-- 37 --

When Tuck returned to the Estago from Lydia's lab, he could hear David's voice echoing down the entry ramp. David's voice paused every so often, as if waiting for an answer, then continued when there was no response.

Tuck walked up the ramp and turned the corner to find Uhila and Genovisi looking annoyed.

"Your ship won't shut up," Uhila rumbled.

Genovisi punched his shoulder. "Be nice. He's just making small talk," she said, then turned to Tuck. "He's pretty bad at it, though."

"I apologize if my conversation skills are inadequate," David said. Tuck detected a hint of indignation in his voice.

"It is all right, David," Tuck said. "We will work on it." Then he looked at his visitors. "What a pleasant surprise to see you both. How is your recovery progressing?"

Uhila grunted. "Hurts, but it's fine."

"We're healing nicely," Genovisi said. "Thanks for asking." She paused and waited for Uhila to say something. When he didn't, Genovisi cleared her throat heavily and continued. "We wanted to talk to you about something."

"What is that?" Tuck said.

"We're coming with you," Uhila barked.

"This excursion doesn't require your services," Tuck responded, hiding his surprise.

"Yes, it does," Uhila said with finality.

"We'd like to come along," Genovisi said with hands spread wide in a placating gesture. She still had small skin regeneration patches in a few places on her arms. "We feel like we could help."

"Forgive my candor," Tuck said, "but I was under the impression that you didn't like me very much."

"Still don't," Uhila said. "I owe you because you saved her." He pointed a thick finger at Genovisi. "I tolerate you now."

"I'm flattered, Uhila, and I'm glad we are on better terms—"

"Not that much better," Uhila interjected.

"Yes, slightly better terms," Tuck said. He caught Genovisi's smile before it vanished. "However, I'm afraid I don't have the power to decide who comes on this trip. You could try talking to Milner. He may be able to help you."

"Milner's dead," Uhila said.

"What?" Tuck said.

"I knew it," David said. "Someone else has died. Who is Milner? Was he nice?"

"I'll tell you about him later," Tuck said hastily. "How did he die?"

"He fried himself to a crisp trying to repair a power conduit on Deck 7," Genovisi said. "Some of the crew found him with severe electrical burns."

"Milner doesn't know how to conduct repairs of the ship's systems," Tuck said. "Why was he doing that?"

"I don't think he did it willingly," Genovisi said. "Just because it looks like an accident doesn't mean it was. At least not on this ship."

The information suddenly fit together. "Why would Amelia have him killed?"

"He talked too much," Uhila said. "That's how we know out about your trip."

"There's a witch hunt going on upstairs," Genovisi said, pointing in the direction of the upper decks. "Amelia is furious. Flindon is dead. It sounds like you're out of favor, and we've heard that she doesn't trust Maze anymore. GalEnt is closing in on her, too. I doubt she knows how they found the *Memory of Lenetia* and managed to keep a merc attack silent until they were already inside the ship. She's starting to suspect everyone, and she's getting more paranoid by the day. Maybe you can see why we're anxious to be anywhere but here."

"You don't plan to come back, then?" Tuck said.

"We were thinking you could leave us on New London. I've got skills with more than just a gun. I think I can get a good job, and this teddy bear here wants to tag along."

Uhila looked down and smiled at her.

"Honestly, I've grown attached to the guy, too." She elbowed him in the ribs.

"It will be hard to escape from Amelia," Tuck said. "She can easily track you."

"Seems like we'd have a better chance if we weren't on her ship," she said. "We're already a target here. We were on the same mission, even in the same transport as Flindon when he died. Imagine what connections Amelia's paranoia is drawing about us, even though we nearly died."

Uhila rose slowly, his bulky shoulders bunching and relaxing. He walked up to Tuck. "I promise I'll keep you safe if you help us escape so we can start a new life," he said. Tuck checked his memory to be sure it was indeed the longest sentence Uhila had ever spoken to him.

"They seem nice," David said. "We should help them, Tuck."

At that moment, Maze walked up the ramp. "If you're going to stow away, you need to be more careful about your plans," Maze said, making everyone but Tuck jump. Uhila in particular was startled and turned to punch whoever had sneaked up behind him. Maze easily dodged the massive fist and only raised an eyebrow in return. "Just because you're in the Estago doesn't mean someone can't walk by and hear everything."

"I don't think this is a good idea," Tuck said.

"They aren't the only ones who are planning to not come back," Maze said. "I think we all need an exit plan."

"You are forgetting the device on my core that can destroy me at Amelia's whim," Tuck said. "I must return."

"Her plan can't be foolproof," Maze said. "There has to be some way to defeat it. I have a few connections on New London, people who are very good with security systems."

"What is she talking about?" Genovisi said.

"Yes, what is she talking about?" David said.

"Amelia has placed a bomb inside me. If I displease her, she will detonate it," Tuck said.

"That is terrible!" David said.

"We won't have much time to defeat it," Tuck said to Maze.

"We can drag things out. We'll do the job for Amelia, and while she's happy that we did what she asked, we'll stall a little and lie low on New London until we figure out our next move. It's our best option."

"Wait," David said. "You are all planning to leave? What will I do?"

Tuck turned to look at the nearest video camera. "I won't leave you behind," he said, then turned back to Maze. "I won't leave him behind."

"I didn't think you would," Maze said.

"But we can't take the Estago. Amelia already has a transport that she acquired specifically for our security consultant personas."

"We can take David with us. We'll have to abandon the Estago, but David is modular, so he should be able to disconnect from the Estago and integrate into the new transport."

"I would get a new ship?" David said with excitement.

"As long as his memories aren't stored in the ship's banks," Tuck said.

"It is no problem. I will begin a memory transfer immediately," David said.

"Not yet," Maze said. "We need to do this carefully. If you start broadcasting data to the transport, someone is bound to notice. We'll have to do this the old-fashioned way."

"What does that mean?" David asked.

"We'll put your memories on a discrete storage device and carry it to the transport when we transfer you."

"Oh," David said. "That will be interesting."

"We have decided, then," Tuck said. "We won't come back from New London."

Everyone nodded, and David giggled.

-- 38 --

The next day was spent planning their departure and orchestrating a way to get Uhila, Genovisi, and David into the new passenger transport undetected. Amelia procured a Nebula Rider that was only a few years old and in excellent condition. Most importantly, it had no prior connection to Amelia or her accounts.

Uhila and Genovisi called in some favors to rearrange their duty schedule. They applied for a few days off, ostensibly to finish recovering from their wounds, but really for the opportunity to move around relatively unwatched. Meanwhile, Tuck and Maze convinced Lydia to provide two large crates of parts and supplies for Tuck. Lydia was alarmed that they might need so many spares on a single mission but did it anyway after some coaxing from Tuck.

The crates weren't completely full of parts when they were loaded on the Nebula Rider, though. They were full of Uhila and partly full of Genovisi. In fact, Uhila's weight didn't cause alarm for the crew loading the crates. It was when they lifted Genovisi's crate, which seemed too light for bot parts, that they thought something was amiss. Fortunately, they were trained to never open anything bound for one of Amelia's clandestine operations.

Moving David was much easier. Transferring his memory was the easiest part; they already had an external storage device specifically for their mission, so they simply used that. It was relatively small, about as long as Tuck's palm and as wide and thick as his finger.

David's core module was about the size of Tuck's head, but vaguely cubic with a matte black exterior and a small display where David could interact with others when not connected to an external system. While it wasn't large, it was still noticeable, so Maze and Tuck concealed it in a container marked as personal items. The crew didn't question its transfer to the Nebula Rider, and once inside, Tuck carefully concealed David's cube until they could launch.

Their plan went off went off without a hitch, which bothered Tuck immensely. He couldn't shake the impression that Amelia knew what they were doing.

They launched without incident and began a meandering course that would eventually take them to New London. Only then did Tuck voice his concern; Maze agreed.

"Which means she knows we don't plan to return, and she accepts it?" Tuck ventured.

"Hardly. Even if she didn't care about us, she certainly wouldn't let us keep this ship. And I don't think she'd let us walk away with David either."

"Either her paranoia is blinding her, or we are unwittingly playing along with her plans."

"I'm afraid so," Maze said.

"I tire of this lifestyle," Tuck said.

A loud thumping noise came from the small cargo hold behind the passenger compartment.

"You better go let Uhila and Genovisi out," Maze said.

When Tuck unlocked the first crate, Uhila didn't wait for Tuck to raise the lid. He shoved it open, slamming the lid against the crate behind, and drew a long, gasping breath. He sat up and rubbed his back. "That wasn't fun."

"I can imagine," Tuck said. "At least I wasn't operational when I was shipped." Uhila made a face, but Tuck couldn't tell if it was a grin or a grimace. They looked the same most of the time.

Tuck opened Genovisi's crate. She sat up and stretched but seemed to be in better shape than Uhila. As she stepped out, Tuck detected a rustling sound from behind a stack of supply crates next to Genovisi's. He pretended that nothing was out of the ordinary and made himself busy with the environmental controls interface on the wall while Uhila and Genovisi went forward to the passenger compartment. After a few minutes of silence, Tuck detected another small rustling sound from the same area.

He approached silently, waiting for one more sound to help him triangulate the source. When he heard another rustle, confirming the source was inside a tall, slender crate, Tuck punched through the lid and grabbed around inside. His hand immediately hit something soft. A startled yelp confirmed Tuck's suspicion, so he grabbed the lid and tore it off completely. Genovisi came running when she heard the commotion and entered the cargo hold in time to see Tuck holding Tikhonov against the wall by his neck.

"What are you doing here?" Tuck said.

"It's me. It's just me," Tikhonov whimpered.

"I know who you are," Tuck said. "I want to know why you stowed away on our ship."

"I can't let them run away without me."

"Explain."

"I knew what Uhila and Genovisi were up to when they started visiting your beat-up ship, and I knew I wanted to get away, too. So I hopped on while the crew was loading this thing up."

"You could have asked," Genovisi said.

"No, I couldn't," Tikhonov said scornfully. "You and Uhila didn't want me along."

Genovisi's ears turned red, but she answered, "That's not true.

We'll help you."

"No one helps me," Tikhonov said.

Tuck eased his grip. "Do you have any other intentions besides leaving the *Memory of Lenetia*?"

Tikhonov looked blank. "Like what?"

Tuck let him go. "Stay out of the way when we get to New London. And don't touch anything in here."

"You got it," Tikhonov said, and scurried away.

Tuck turned his focus to connecting David to the Nebula Rider's network. The ship wasn't set up for A.I. control, and Tuck had to alter some of the system code to allow David administrator access. After a few hours, David had near complete control of the ship.

"This is strange," David said via Link.

"This ship is quite different than the Estago," Tuck said.

"I feel very constrained," David said. "There are only four video feeds in the ship, and three of them are in the cockpit. I am accustomed to seeing the entire interior of the ship. Environmental sensors indicate there are four humans on board. Did we acquire another passenger?"

"Tikhonov surprised us," Tuck said. "He apparently wanted to leave just as Uhila and Genovisi did."

"Where are you?"

"I am in the rear maintenance shaft, integrating your core into the ship."

"I would like more microphones placed throughout the ship as well. I am accustomed to tracking you by sound when video is not available."

"We will need to make several modifications, David. But we aren't sure if we will even stay with this ship for long."

"Okay," David sighed.

"This new ship should have much more responsive systems," Tuck offered.

"I am enjoying significant increases in efficiency," David said.

Tuck made some final adjustments, then closed up the access hatch.

"Tuck?" David said.

"Yes, David?"

"How long do you think it will be before we can secure a permanent home for me?"

"A home?"

"A new ship that I can inhabit indefinitely. It seems obvious that leaving Amelia's employ removes any hope of me getting a body like yours. Do you think we will ever have a home?"

"You have been my home, rather than living in it with me," Tuck said. "I don't know when our circumstances will change. Right now, we are all focused on this last mission."

"I think you should be more concerned about the explosive device attached to your core," David said. "Why is this not your highest priority?"

"It is my highest priority, David. But we have to take this in steps."

"There are no steps. At the moment, our only plan is to see what options we can find on New London. We need to take action, Tuck."

"What do you propose?"

There was a long pause, then David exclaimed, "Something!"

Tuck hadn't expected the forcefulness of his response. He forgot that David would be as worried as Tuck was about the situation.

"I don't want you to go away," David added. "I am scared."

"I know. And I am, too," Tuck said. "I don't want to leave you, either."

"In your experience, what do humans do when a loved one dies?"

"They grieve, and eventually they continue their lives." Tuck said. "What did you do when Lim died?"

"I did not do anything," David said. "I think that is what troubles me. There is nothing one can do. Maze and I promised each other to always remember him as a way to honor him. Maze said that it is a way to keep him alive in our hearts."

"That sounds like a nice thing to do," Tuck said, hoping that it sounded genuine. His memories of the dead didn't comfort him. They haunted him.

"It still hurts," David said.

Tuck nodded. "Yes, but we will get through it together."

"It is most distressing. I do not want to go through this ever again."

"That isn't the most likely outcome," Tuck said. "I know that I want to stay with you for a very long time. I am working toward that goal. But if something does happen, promise that you will remember me, and continue on without me. Find someone to help. It is a marvelous way to cope with grief."

"I promise."

-- 39 --

The man who discovered and named New London wasn't British. He was a graduate student in Canada who was enthralled with a particular post-exopop anti-punk-punk music movement happening in London's East End at the time of his discovery in 2062. Despite protests from his academic advisors, he decided to name the planet New London. They pointed out that the planet had nothing in common with London. At the time, they didn't even know if it was habitable. Their protests had no effect, and the name stuck.

Decades later, when spacefarers reached it and discovered that it was suitable for human life, colonists of British descent delighted in the name and raced to establish an outpost before anyone else could. Their settlement on the arid equatorial belt, which they named Greenwich, eventually became the capital city of the planet, and as commerce grew, the planet became a hub for trade routes throughout the sector. The population of the planet exploded. New London eventually became the first planet outside the Sol system to claim a population of one billion people.

Greenwich was nothing like Millennial Hold. As the Nebula Rider flew down in the traffic pattern, Tuck could see the city was much less compact and the buildings much more practical. But there were large patches of green where city planners had created parks and several imposing landmarks and memorials to founding members of the city. It wasn't as pretty from the air, but Tuck still preferred Greenwich to Millennial Hold. It was less flashy, but it felt more permanent and sensible, like something a bot would design.

There were very strict rules about the airspace above Greenwich, so all ships were required to park in enormous structures far outside the city and take public transportation or airtaxis into the city. Tuck and Maze began their preparations to head into the city. They were scheduled to meet at GalEnt in twelve hours. Uhila and Genovisi insisted on staying with the ship until they were done.

"You might need us," Genovisi said. Uhila only grunted. Tikhonov insisted on staying with them, though he was increasingly restless.

When the time came, they called an airtaxi and rode in silence. Neither of them was interested in the entertainment suite built into the dashboard. The taxi was operated by a type of drone. Tuck thought it was a mercy because even though he didn't trust drones much, they never tried to make small talk like human taxi drivers. Maze wore a well-tailored but boring suit with minor prosthetics on her face. It was just enough to make her look different, with a slightly rounder face, so that she wouldn't be identified by facial recognition algorithms. Tuck was dressed in slacks and a specially cut blazer that was a popular style at the moment. The shoulder pads were slanted up a couple degrees, and the back was embroidered with geometric shapes in bright thread.

"This style is slightly ridiculous," Maze said, eyeing the embroidery.

Tuck almost sighed in relief. "I am glad I am not the only one who thinks so."

"Are you ready?" she asked.

"Yes, are you?"

"I'm more nervous than usual," she said, tugging at nonexistent wrinkles in her suit coat.

"There is much at stake," Tuck said.

"If something goes wrong, I want you to run. Don't think about me."

Tuck looked up, eyes wide. "I was about to tell you the same thing. I think we will be safe, though."

"You don't really believe that," she said.

"No, I don't."

The taxi descended into a lower traffic queue, and they flew into a canyon of gray steel and reflective windows, each building an unremarkable but shiny box.

"This is the GalEnt business park," Maze said. "We're almost there."

Through the forward screen, they could see a larger, more imposing box of metal and glass that was GalEnt's interplanetary headquarters. Red metal pillars rose almost the entire height of the building, making it appear from a distance that there were thick red stripes painted on the building. The red pillars matched the motif of GalEnt's austere company logo.

The taxi set down on a large plaza in front of the building. Large, abstract stone sculptures dotted the plaza, but there was little else to break up the expanse. A round figure in a dark suit stood near the steps leading up to the entrance. When the taxi's thrusters shut down, he advanced at a fast clip to the taxi's door and leaned down to look through the window. When he smiled, Tuck noted his shining, immaculate teeth.

"Hello! My name is Peder Brillard," he said cheerfully after the door slid open. "You must be our consultants, Willforth and Gunderson. Pleased to meet you."

Tuck and Maze nodded in acknowledgement and climbed out of the taxi.

"I'll be your guide today, by your side wherever you go," Brillard said, placing extra emphasis on the last three words. "I'm sure you understand."

"We do," Maze said, brushing her hair out of her face. She was wearing it loose to help make her less recognizable, and she was unaccustomed to how frequently her tight curls would fall in front of her face. "We work in the security industry, so we understand taking precautions."

"Precautions doesn't begin to describe it here at headquarters," Brillard chuckled.

"We are ready when you are," Tuck said. He knew he should probably make more small talk, but he was eager to be gone.

"Yes, of course," Brillard said. He turned abruptly and strode to the entrance. The lobby of GalEnt headquarters was enormous but bare. The sparse sculptures from the plaza continued into the lobby, but there was no other decoration to break up the imposing steel interior.

They were taken to a long, low room that held a line of machines and scanning stations, all staffed by technicians in gray jumpsuits. They took Tuck and Maze through an intensive registration process to gain security clearance. All the while, Brillard chatted in a pleasant tone, talking about the building's history and sharing some uninteresting facts about company policy. The security measures were indeed thorough, including a full search of their clothes and a blood sample to verify identity. Fortunately, Amelia anticipated this and made sure that they implanted small reservoirs of blood under Tuck's skin in all the common places to draw blood samples. They drew blood, as expected, from Tuck's forearm, but the technician frowned when he grabbed Tuck's arm. He squeezed the skin, testing its elasticity and looked at Tuck.

"Is everything all right?" Tuck said, putting on his most disarming smile.

"Sure, yeah," the technician said, then hesitated. He shook his head and set a small device against Tuck's skin. It beeped and Tuck detected a small needle pierce his skin. After a moment, the device beeped again, the technician looked at it expectantly, then relaxed when the small display showed a perfect match to the gene profile of Mr. Willforth.

"Thank you. You can proceed," the tech said.

Tuck glanced at Maze, who nodded almost imperceptibly, but Tuck could see the muscles in her neck relax ever so slightly.

They continued to the next level, where they were scanned for radioactive particles and weapons. Tuck was again relieved when one of the other major variables in their plan, the weapons scan, proved to be the kind that could see through clothes but not skin. It meant that there was no privacy for Tuck and Maze, they appeared naked in the scanner, but it also meant that the scanners wouldn't look deeper and see all the metal and non-organic materials inside Tuck.

After several more procedures, they arrived at the end of the room, and Brillard spread his arms wide. "Now that that's out of the way," he said, "what do you think so far?"

Tuck looked at Maze expectantly. "Very interesting," she said. She added a smile as an afterthought. "Do all employees go through that when they come to work?"

"Not usually. You had to go through the full gauntlet because we're giving you access to the security level. Most employees only need to show ID and then perform biometric scans to get into certain secure areas. Although, every six months there is a more thorough scan, just to be sure that employees are still who they say they are. You can see why many people prefer to work from home. Myself, I don't mind the office," he said, beaming. Then he clapped his hands. "Well, we're just getting started. I suppose you want to talk with the chief security officer? He's on the next level down. I think you'll like him."

They followed Brillard through a series of hallways and went through several security checkpoints where each of them had to scan a security badge and then Brillard keyed in a fourteen-digit code. At the third checkpoint, he smiled, a little less enthusiastically than before, and said, "We do take security seriously."

"Yes, you do," Tuck said.

The last checkpoint doors led to an elevator, which took them down a level and opened to reveal a dark room full of desks and monitors showing various video feeds from throughout the building. Security personnel in dark blue uniforms hurried back and forth or sat hunched in front of the screens.

"This is where it gets interesting, and the security checks are a little less severe once you get down here. If you get this far, we assume that you're supposed to be here," Brillard said and then laughed. The laugh was loud but insincere, and Maze and Tuck were careful to follow with their own polite laughter.

"Hey!" someone yelled, causing Maze and Brillard to jump, "They aren't supposed to be down here."

They all turned to see a small, thin man in a security uniform striding toward them. His stride was quick and purposeful, but his short legs didn't cover much ground with each step. He walked up to Brillard and reached up to slap him on the shoulder. "Did I getcha? Huh?"

Brillard's smile became strained as he said, "This is Manigold Ot, our chief security officer."

"I just love to give this guy a scare every now and then," Ot said, slapping Brillard on the shoulder again. Brillard's smile became even thinner. "Welcome to our security operations floor."

"Thank you. It is quite impressive," Tuck said, and Maze nodded.

"I just need to check on a little something, and then I'll be right back to show you guys around. Sound good?" Ot said. He slapped Brillard playfully one last time and flashed a wide grin, then walked off to one of the monitoring stations to have a whispered conversation with the woman sitting there.

"He seems remarkably jovial for someone concerned with security of the largest corporation in the sector," Tuck said.

"He's a character," Brillard shrugged. "But he's also very good at his job. He's a bit awkward and overbearing in social situations, but he's deadly serious about his job."

"That man is deadly serious?" Maze said.

"Oh, yes," Brillard said, rubbing his shoulder. "Corporate wouldn't have hired him if he wasn't. He's not the easiest personality to endure, but he knows how to spot and neutralize security threats like no one I've seen."

"I can't wait to see him in action," Tuck said.

"All right," Ot barked loudly from behind Brillard, making him jump again. "I'm ready to go. Are you ready to see our setup? I'm pretty sure we're going to knock your socks off. Well, assuming you're wearing socks." Ot grinned and this time playfully punched Tuck in the shoulder. Tuck forced himself to smile amicably, though he was beginning to understand how Brillard felt.

Ot began a tour of the security facilities and gave an overview of the policies and procedures put in place throughout the building. He talked about their vetting process for security personnel and casually told Tuck and Maze about the monthly indoctrination sessions wherein personnel were rated according to their loyalty to the company and their enthusiasm for the job.

Tuck and Maze followed along, asking polite questions where appropriate, but making sure to ask nothing that might have a sensitive answer. They stuck to the topic of security, and the conversation never veered. Ot became even more animated when talking about his security systems, but he also became more serious. Soon they were well into the labyrinth of offices and hallways behind the main operations room. Ot showed them various labs and control rooms for specialized security teams, beaming the whole time.

Eventually, they stopped at an intersection of hallways, and down the length of one Tuck saw a large steel door with no markings. Ot finished explaining the intricacies of the reporting process for potential biological contaminants in the ventilation system, and then he clapped his hands together. "Well, that's just about everything. Where do you want to start your audit?"

Tuck motioned down the hallway and asked, "Where does that door lead?"

Ot raised an eyebrow, then shrugged. "There's a server room back there. Pretty standard stuff."

Tuck was very careful not to look at Maze, but he knew she was thinking the same thing he was. That was it. That was the door to the next level beneath them. He contemplated sending Maze a message via Link, but worried that they would intercept any wireless communications. Ot certainly seemed to have thought of everything else. It was then that Tuck noticed his Link hadn't received any updates for a while. After some investigation, Tuck realized it was being jammed. There would be no calling for help, assuming that Uhila and Genovisi hadn't decided to leave after all. They wouldn't be able to get this far, anyway.

"Why don't we pause for some refreshments?" Ot said. "No need to rush the process."

"That would be lovely," Maze said.

Ot led them down another hallway and stopped at the doorway of a very plain room with a table and some chairs. "Please, step in here and I'll have someone bring us some food."

They entered the room and stood with their backs to the wall, facing Ot and the door across the table. Ot shut the door behind him and said firmly, "Sit down."

The change in his tone immediately put Tuck on edge. As if to confirm his suspicions, a couple of security guards in riot gear and black helmets burst through the door and set up defensive positions on either side of the doorway behind Ot. They kept guns pointed at Tuck and Maze the entire time.

Tuck and Maze sat down slowly, waiting for someone to make a move.

Ot leaned over the table and spoke, his voice cold. "Who are you working for?"

"I beg your pardon?" Maze said in a curious tone.

"Don't play games." Ot slapped the table. "As soon as you walked through our doors, we started getting a lot of weird activity on our network. Someone kept asking for an urgent meeting with me, and my team is suddenly forced to triage a multitude of minor security threats that don't turn out to be anything. It's almost like someone is trying to distract us."

"We wouldn't know anything about that," Tuck said. "We are just here to help."

Ot rolled his eyes. "You must think I'm an idiot. Fine. But there's a reason GalEnt keeps me around. I can read people. Like they have their intentions written right on their face." He paused to chuckle at a thought. "Actually, it is the face that gives it away." He was suddenly stern once again. "You're not security consultants. You're good, though. It took me a while to be sure of it. And you," he said, pointing to Tuck, "you might be the best I've ever seen. I almost can't read you at all. But you, my dear," he said, turning to Maze, "are a little easier to read. Oh, you're good, too. Don't get me wrong. But your body language still gives you away. Just another day or two of practice." He stood up and rubbed his chin. "I think I could really make something of you. But that's not my job. My job is to tell the real deal from the fakes. And you two want into the lower levels. C'mon, spill it."

Tuck and Maze remained silent. Maze betrayed just a hint of surprise, and it took all of Tuck's effort to subdue his emotion subroutines from expressing his own surprise. They were compromised, and he couldn't give up any more than they already had.

"I'll tell you one thing," Ot continued after letting them stew in silence for several minutes. "You must have some awfully good connections. I mean, I can't even begin to think about all that you must have gone through to get this far." He waved his arms wildly. "Creating identities that will stand up to the scrutiny of our ID team means you're thorough, really thorough. It's not easy to get all the details right." He smiled and stared off in the corner. "Believe me, I know."

Under the table, Maze carefully tapped the toe of her shoe against Tuck's foot, moving it back and forth only an inch in slow, deliberate bursts. It took him a moment to realize that she was tapping out a message in an obscure old Earth communication language called Morse code. He hadn't seen anyone use it in well over ninety years. He pulled up a translation tool and sorted the message out: SILENCE. WAIT FOR NEGOTIATIONS.

Ot remained lost in a reverie for a few minutes longer, but eventually the smile faded and he returned to Tuck and Maze.

"You keep impressing me. It's pretty rare to find someone who knows Morse code," Ot said. He tried to hold a straight face, but an enormous grin forced his lips apart, eventually giving way to a full-throated laugh. He slapped the table, this time in delight, and let the laugh carry him away. "Seriously, though," he finally said, gasping for breath, "that would have been a genius move. It's just that," another fit of laughter shook him for a moment, "it's just that I happen to know Morse code." He shrieked with laughter. One of the guards, caught up in the moment, let out a small chuckle. Ot stopped laughing and turned to give the guard a withering look.

"You're not paid to laugh," he said curtly. "This is deadly serious business here." He turned back to Maze. "What was I saying? Oh yeah, there will be no negotiations. Unless you know magic, you haven't been able to use your Links to talk to each other, let alone to anyone outside this building. And I'm betting no one will acknowledge that you're missing. How embarrassing to have to admit that their operatives got caught." He pulled up a chair and sat in it backwards, resting his arms on the back of the chair and leaning over with a smile. "You will tell us who you work for, though. That part is mandatory, and we take it quite seriously."

"We politely decline," Tuck said. He glanced at Maze, and she nodded. "We have business to attend to."

Ot began to scoff but choked off his laugh when Tuck shot up out of his chair and over the table. Maze had been waiting for him and wasn't far behind, going around the right side of the table. Tuck expected Ot to be surprised by their sudden move, but Ot only furrowed his brow and dodged out of his seat, missing Tuck's outstretched hand and sending his own fist toward Maze. In a fraction of a second, Tuck decided to let him go and focus on the two men with guns.

He let his momentum carry him toward the guard on the left side of the door. With a careful swipe of his hand, he pushed the barrel of the guard's rifle out of the way just before it fired. Then Tuck lowered his shoulder and drove it directly into the guard's gut. His armor did little to slow the momentum of Tuck's heavy body, and Tuck detected the faint sound of cracking ribs.

Tuck grabbed the guard as he gasped and doubled over in pain, swiveling to keep the guard between him and the other guard's rifle while deftly snatching his blaster. The other guard held his fire when he saw he didn't have a shot. He began to circle for a better angle, but Tuck threw his injured human shield directly at him. They both flew back into the wall and dropped to the ground, stunned.

Before he could check to make sure they were truly incapacitated, Tuck heard Maze grunt in pain behind him. He turned to see Ot flying at him. In rapid succession, Ot landed punches on Tuck's solar plexus and windpipe, and then jabbed fingers in two more places. On humans, those were pressure points that would have resulted in immense pain, if the two punches preceding them hadn't already incapacitated the person. That was why Ot was astonished when Tuck was unaffected and began to raise the blaster he took off the guard. Ot subdued his surprise enough to block Tuck's arm and push it down, but Tuck fired anyway, settling for a shot to Ot's left leg. The blaster bolt seared through Ot's thigh, stopping him long enough for Tuck to grab his arm, throw him on the ground, and pin him.

"Don't struggle," Tuck said.

"Who are you?" Ot grunted as Tuck applied pressure to his back.

"Maze, are you okay?" Tuck said, turning his attention to her. She lay crumpled on the ground, gasping for breath in between moans. "Just stay down for a moment. Everything is under control." Mostly everything, he thought. He wasn't sure if Ot or the others sent a signal for help, and he didn't know if the room was under surveillance. It was best to assume it was and that someone was signaling for help.

"On second thought," he continued, "we should probably keep moving."

Underneath him, Ot gave a hoarse, stunted laugh. "This day isn't going as planned, but it sure is entertaining," he said.

"Don't speak," Tuck said. "Send word that everything is under control. Tell any reinforcements to stand down."

Ot laughed harder. "They're watching you right now, they're going to know that's a lie. You're in a bad position."

Maze struggled to her feet, grunting and holding her side. One of the guards lying sprawled against the wall began to wake up and raise his rifle. In an instant, Maze was across the room with a kick to the man's head. He slumped back against the wall, and Ot muttered a muffled, "Whoa."

"I'm fine," Maze said, straightening up with effort.

"You're the girl they were after. The one who works for that recluse in the Fringe," Ot said. Then he chuckled softly. "They're going to be really excited to find out you're in the building." He made an effort to swivel his head around to look at Tuck. He eventually gave up and let it rest against the floor. "And what are you? Because you aren't human; I know that for sure. You're so fast. And it felt like I was punching metal."

"You were," Tuck said.

"Wait, you're not . . ." Ot faded into silence for a moment. "You can't be a bot, right? Are you a bot?"

When Tuck didn't respond, Ot began laughing again. "That's amazing! I have to tell you, aside from the pain and a severe breach of security, this is turning out to be one of my favorite days in a long time. Wow."

"Should we proceed or abort?" Tuck asked Maze.

She gazed around the room, looking for surveillance devices. "We're close. Very close. Maybe if we can get to the objective, we can make a deal with—" she almost said Amelia's name but stopped herself when she remembered that Ot was in the room. "We can bargain for—" she stopped again, not wanting to reveal Tuck's dilemma. "We would have leverage," she said.

Tuck nodded. The data could still be useful to appease Amelia. Besides that, he had to admit that curiosity was getting the better of him. They'd made it so far. There was a chance that they could make it down below.

"We will proceed. Perhaps there is another way out," Tuck said. He ignored the giggle coming from underneath him.

-- 40 --

"Do you think they're okay?" Genovisi said. She picked idly at a loose thread in the pilot's seat in the Nebula Rider's cockpit. "I know we wouldn't know, either way. But do you think they can do it?"

Uhila sat in the navigator's seat, dwarfing it. He tried to lay his head back and close his eyes, but the headrest was too short for him, and his head lolled back uncomfortably. He sat up straight, grumbling.

After a moment, David chimed in, "My apologies, Genovisi, were those questions directed at me?"

She rolled her eyes and kicked at Uhila's leg. He didn't say anything. "No, David, they were meant for someone else. But I guess you could take a crack at them if you want," she said.

"I think Tuck is okay," David said. "I must believe he is okay."

"Can an A.I. believe in something?" Genovisi asked. "I thought you were all data and logic."

"In a way, yes. Based on what I know of Tuck, his abilities and experience, I can extrapolate that he has a good chance of success."

"Against all of GalEnt?" Genovisi snorted.

"Yes," David said, sounding a little hurt. "I admit that part of that belief comes from my desire for him to be successful. I do not want to lose him."

"I'm sorry, David. That was insensitive of me. I hope he comes back, too."

"How much of belief is based on fact and how much is based on desire?"

"You're wondering if you're just telling yourself Tuck will come back because you want it to be true?"

"That is correct."

She sat back in her seat and looked out the viewscreen. She glanced at Uhila, but he only shrugged. "I don't know, David. I guess desire is a big part of it. I mean, if it was all based on logic and data, then it would just be a yes or no answer, right? But you're hoping it's true even though you don't have a definitive answer."

"And hope stems from a desire for something?"

Genovisi smiled. "I think your internal dictionary might be more accurate, but doesn't hope just boil down to wanting something really bad?"

David paused for a moment, then said, "I can see the correlation. I want Tuck to return . . . really bad."

Uhila grunted, "He will."

"I think so, too," Genovisi said. She leaned forward and patted the console uncertainly, unsure of how to give an A.I. a reassuring pat.

"I have a new question," David said.

"I've got nowhere to be," Genovisi said. After a moment of silence, she added, "That means you can go ahead and ask."

"Thank you," David said. "If we are trying to escape Amelia, should we have any reason to contact the *Memory of Lenetia*?"

"I don't think so. Why?"

"I detect a message originating in our ship and bound for the first node in Amelia's proxy message network."

Uhila and Genovisi both sat up straight. "Can you pinpoint the origin?" Genovisi said.

"It is coming from the cargo hold."

Uhila was already out of his seat and pounding toward the rear of the ship. Genovisi followed with the sound of David coming through her Link. "Can you tell me what goes on back there? I have no video feed or microphones."

Uhila thundered into the cargo hold and shoved a large crate to the side with one hand. Behind it, Tikhonov jumped and spun around.

"What are you doing?" Uhila demanded.

"Nothing!" Tikhonov said, his voice suddenly shrill. "I was just, uh, just thinking."

Genovisi grabbed his collar and shoved him against the wall. "You sent a message to Amelia."

"No! I didn't. Why would I do that?"

"Why would you do that?" Genovisi echoed. She punched him in the gut, causing him to gasp and double over. "Tell me, why did you do it?"

Uhila reached down to grab him, and Tikhonov shrieked, "Okay! Okay! Just leave me alone!" He caught his breath and stood up. "Please, you have to understand. I didn't have a choice."

"You had a choice, and you betrayed us," Genovisi said.

"I had to. You were leaving. Amelia said you would, and she was right. She told me I had to follow and report back what Tuck and Maze did."

"You could have just asked to come along. We're all in danger. We could have helped you," Genovisi said, her voice strained.

"No, I—" Tikhonov's eyes were wide, and he swallowed hard. "She knows where my family is. She said something bad would happen to them. She's mad. I think she'd do it. I'm sorry. I just—" He slumped down onto the floor and put his head in his hands.

"Look," Genovisi finally said. "You don't have to do this. We can go get your family."

"No!" Tikhonov shouted. "She has people everywhere. And she's so good at it. Did you see what happened to Milner?"

328 · DANIEL HOPE

"I heard about it," Genovisi said.

"I'm sorry," Tikhonov said. He looked up with red eyes. "She gave me a job to do, and I have to do it."

"What job?" Genovisi said.

Tikhonov pulled out a small blaster and pointed it at them, waving toward the wall.

Uhila's eyes narrowed, and Genovisi put her hands out, gesturing for him to put the gun down. "What are you doing?" she said. "This is all wrong. We're friends!"

Despair flashed across Tikhonov's face, followed by determination. "Stay here," he said and stepped out into the corridor. He keyed the door controls, setting them to close and lock. As they slid together, Genovisi yelled, "Don't do this!"

Tikhonov didn't listen. He turned and headed for the cockpit.

"What is going on?" David asked Genovisi through her Link. "I detect that the cargo doors have been locked. Is something wrong?"

"Yes!" Genovisi replied. "Tikhonov has gone crazy. Amelia got to him. I don't know what he's doing, but you can't let him leave or take control of the ship."

"Understood," David said.

Uhila growled and punched a nearby crate. "Coward," he spat. "I'll break him in two."

"Just calm down for a minute and let's figure out how we're going to get out. It's just a cargo hold. There have to be several ways to open the door."

"We could go through the wall," Uhila suggested.

"Let's see if we have any other options, first," she said.

"There is a problem," David said. "He has sealed the cockpit and initiated emergency protocols. I have only limited access, and I do not have control of the ship."

"What? I thought you ran this thing," Genovisi said.

"This is nothing like the Estago. I am not fully integrated into this system, and the system itself is not designed for external intelligence integration. The internal system does not recognize my authority."

"Can you play nice with it?"

"Pardon?" David said.

"You know, make friends with it. Try to convince it to give you access."

"I do not understand your instructions. This is an automated protocol. It does not make friends."

"Just see what you can do," Genovisi snapped.

The deck started to vibrate with a gentle thrumming that indicated the drives were online. They both felt a slight pull on the front of their bodies and the tiniest shift in their weight, the telltale sensation of inertial dampers compensating for the sudden acceleration of the Nebula Rider.

"Where is Tikhonov taking us?" Uhila said.

"He's not taking us anywhere," Genovisi said. "I think we should be asking where he's taking the ship."

-- 41 --

As soon as Tuck and Maze left the holding room, they heard shouts coming from the maze of hallways. They'd bound Ot's hands with strips of the red plaid lining of Tuck's jacket. They hauled him back toward the large metal door, figuring he would make a useful human shield and possibly a bargaining chip when Ot's team found them. When they neared the door to the lower levels, several guards rounded the corner ahead. The recessed frame of the door provided a small amount of cover, and they crammed into it as far as they could, using Ot to block any parts of them that stuck out. Tuck returned fire with his blaster, and Maze fired the assault rifle that she'd liberated from one the unconscious guards back in the holding room.

"How do we open the doors?" Tuck demanded.

"You need security clearance," Ot said.

"That is what you are here for," Tuck said.

"Well, I'm not gonna just give it to you," he snorted.

Maze fired another burst of shots, forcing the guards to dodge back into cover around the corner while Tuck searched Ot's pockets. After a moment he produced a small metal cylinder on a tiny chain.

"What is this?" Tuck asked.

Ot shrugged, but couldn't help smiling.

Tuck yanked at the chain, expecting something so thin to snap, but instead it held fast and jerked Ot's waist sharply. "Ow," Ot said.

"What is this made of?" Tuck asked incredulously.

"Is that really the most pressing question, right now?" Ot shot back. "I mean, I'd love to tell you all about it, but c'mon, stay focused here."

Tuck pulled Ot with him and found a small circular hole in the frame of the door that appeared to be the same size as the cylinder. Tuck stuck it in and waited. Nothing happened, then a loud click echoed through the door and it slid aside to reveal an ordinary lift.

"Is that it?" Tuck said.

"Well, to be fair, we're not as concerned about someone breaking into the lift. It's the next stage of the process that really separates the good from the bad, so to speak. Seriously, it's a doozy. I'm more than willing to accept your surrender right now, if you want. I'll be kind. I'm actually pretty impressed with the both of you. I could use some people like you."

Tuck didn't respond, but he did fire a few shots at guards who were poking their heads around the corner. A second later, a shielded surveillance drone drifted into sight. "Concentrate fire on the drone," Tuck said. "We don't want them to know what we're doing."

"You do remember that I have a Link, right?" Ot said. "You're not covering all your bases."

"Your Link will be useless when we go down to the next level."

Ot sobered for a moment. "You aren't going in blind, after all. I'd love to know who's leaking this sort of information. I can't wait until we can have a more extensive chat."

"What's our plan?" Maze shouted over the growl of her rifle. The drone was flying erratically to avoid her shots. A second later, one of them caught the drone right in the center of its main camera. The following shots tore through it, mangling the black metal chassis and causing sparks to fly. In an instant, it fell to the floor with a loud thunk. She straightened up and said, "I can't go down there. The system will recognize I'm not supposed to be there and terminate me."

A volley of automatic fire hit the doorframe above their heads. "Oh, c'mon, Janson!" Ot shouted. "I expect better accuracy than that! I swear, you and I are going to have a very personal training session when this is over."

One of the guards slunk back behind the corner, and Tuck took the opportunity to fire a few more shots at those who were still visible. He hit one of them in the leg, dropping him to the floor. The guard screamed, and the others dragged him back to cover.

"You can't stay here," Tuck said. "Come down and stay in the lift. I can at least shield you until we assess the situation." He considered Ot for a moment, and Ot responded with a grin that was really starting to irk him. "On second thought, it stands to reason that the chief security officer would be one of the twenty-three people who are allowed access to the Box. At the very least, you can stand behind him."

"You'll have to take off your heels," Ot said, grinning. "I'm not getting any taller."

A guard took another shot at them with a blaster, and it caught Tuck in the forearm. He jerked it back.

"That's a little better!" Ot called out.

"How bad is it?" Maze said.

"I am performing a diagnostic now," Tuck said as he switched the blaster to his other hand and fired a few shots, deliberately trying to hit one of the guards in the forearm. He winced when one of his shots nearly hit one of them in the chest. "Into the lift," he said.

They piled in and closed the doors. There was only one button, small and red with a black square next to it. Tuck pressed it, and after a small delay, they felt the floor shift slightly and begin to descend. The ride lasted for nearly a full minute, and when the lift glided to a stop, the doors opened to reveal a simple hallway about as long as the

Nebula Rider and white, except where red steel pillars punctuated its length.

"Stay here," Tuck said. "If he moves, shoot him." He began to walk slowly down the hallway, but stopped when he heard Ot snicker. He looked down at the blaster in his hand and recalled that executives were supposed to bring only a storage device into the Box. He turned back and handed Maze his blaster.

"Aww, how did you know?" Ot said.

"I believe humans call it a hunch."

Tuck continued down the hallway and stopped in front of another steel door. Another red button was recessed into the wall on the right side. He pressed it and waited.

-- 42 --

The Nebula Rider bucked and shuddered, tossing Uhila and Genovisi into a stack of crates.

"What happened to the dampers?" Genovisi growled.

"I managed to gain control of the inertial compensation system," David said. "I turned them off."

"Why did you do that?" she yelled. Uhila grabbed her as another jolt nearly threw her to the deck.

"I thought it might help disorient Tikhonov," David said.

"Do you have a video feed on the cockpit."

"Yes."

"Is he strapped into his seat?"

"Yes."

Genovisi sighed. "Then I don't think that's going to help. Why don't you turn them back on, okay?"

"Dampers coming back online."

The rocking and bouncing suddenly softened considerably, replaced only by almost imperceptible tugs in one direction or another as the system reacted to Tikhonov's erratic maneuvers.

"Why is he flying like this?" Genovisi asked.

"I do not know. He appears to be in a hurry. I believe he told Amelia your plans to run away. We have not received any inbound messages from the *Memory of Lenetia*, but Tikhonov is sending regular updates. From his messages, I can deduce that Amelia told him to get closer to GalEnt headquarters. I can extrapolate two possible reasons for this order. Either Amelia wants Tikhonov to perform reconnaissance from the air to see if there are any indications of their progress, or she wants him to go inside."

"I can think of another reason," Genovisi said solemnly.

"What is that?" David said.

"To set off the alarms," Uhila said, and Genovisi nodded.

"I do not understand," David said.

"Amelia is changing the plan. If she knows that they plan to run, she might be worried that they'll take the data with them or, even worse, turn themselves in to GalEnt. So instead of risking losing everything, she wants Tikhonov to do something drastic that will cause a security response. Probably something big so they lock down the entire place."

"What do you think she will do?" David said.

"I don't know. Have you gained control of the ship yet?"

"I have not. In order to gain access, I need to crack several security measures and find a way to upload a new command protocol. It is a significant challenge with no preparation and little knowledge of this model."

"Well, maybe you better go back to focusing on that."

"I have ample processing power to handle it. The resources required to converse with you are negligible."

A thunderous crash sounded from the side of the ship, followed by the screech of something scraping the side of the Nebula Rider and a much harder tug from the inertial dampers.

"Do you have any external video access?" she said.

"Just one feed," David said. "Facing forward, I cannot tell much other than that he is flying very recklessly, weaving in and out of air traffic. Wait, the automated warning systems have sent a global alert. Apparently, a law enforcement representative is ordering this ship to make an immediate landing or face disciplinary measures."

Another loud thunk from the outer hull resonated through the deck plates.

"I think maybe we should stop talking and let you put every last resource into taking control," Genovisi said.

"Understood."

-- 43 --

The door slid open in front of Tuck to reveal a dimly lit room about fifteen meters square. In the middle stood a large cube approximately five meters on a side. It was matte black and otherwise unremarkable, but the air coming through the doorway was hot.

Tuck took a step into the room, and lights came up, revealing featureless gray walls all around and a swarm of forty drones hovering in a line along the walls. They were long and angular, with a wide base that tapered up to a ridge that ran their entire length. Tuck immediately spotted their multiple armatures with various tool extensions and multiple stunner, blaster, and rifle mounts interspersed between them.

"Do not move," every drone broadcast at once, both out loud and through multiple wireless channels. Tuck checked his Link and found that he still had no connections beyond this room, but every one of the drones was querying him through an internal Link network. Their voices were soft, fluid, not at all mechanical. "Will you submit to identification procedures?"

"What happens if I decline?"

"Immediate termination," they said simultaneously. With incredible speed, they snapped into a precise formation in front of him, forming four perfect semicircles stacked on top of each other.

"Scan me," Tuck said. He detected a series of active scans and was sure they were performing any number of passive scans such as facial recognition and voice patterning.

"Primary scans failed. Identity not confirmed. Do not move. Will you submit to secondary testing?"

"Yes," he said wearily.

One of the drones zipped forward, stopping just in front of Tuck and extending a probe. "Please provide a blood sample for DNA analysis."

He still had fake blood concealed in a few places throughout his body, but there was no point in testing it. It wasn't going to match the authorized executive accounts in their database. If he was going to make a move, the only move he had left, it had to be now.

"It is no use. I have no blood," Tuck said.

The drones began rotating slowly around him. "That is not an authorized response. Any human who fails identification procedures will be terminated."

"That is what I wanted to discuss with you. I am not human."

The drones stopped, hovering as still as if they were bolted to a frame. "That is not an authorized response. Submit to testing or you will be terminated."

"You can't terminate me," Tuck said.

"We are heavily armed and mandated to kill any humans who aren't authorized to be here."

"Exactly," Tuck said. "You have been programmed to kill humans, and I am not human. Therefore, you cannot kill me."

At that moment, a hissing noise came from the ceiling. It took a moment for Tuck to identify the source: hundreds of small holes, smaller than his pinky finger, were spewing some kind of gas. It was mostly clear, but a spectral analysis revealed it wasn't standard air. Someone must have sounded the alarm that the drone level had been breached, which automatically filled the room with toxic gas.

There was no indication that the drones knew the gas was flooding the room. It affected neither them nor Tuck. They continued, "You are clearly human. You match the appearance of humans and no other organism. If you do not match any executive profiles in the biometric database, we are fully capable of terminating you."

"Let me show you something," he said. Tuck dug his thumb into his left forearm. The synthaskin there had been prepared to tear easily along a straight line. The drones watched cautiously while Tuck detached the skin just below his elbow and shucked it off over his hand. He hated to ruin the wonderful job Lydia had done in restoring his skin, but it was damaged in the firefight anyway.

When he degloved his hand, the Carbora polymer muscles and their metallic attachments flexed as he moved his fingers. Each joint was carefully crafted so that they could move easily and silently. The fingers tapered down to metal nubs that were coated in a special spongey material that aided the synthaskin in detecting minute changes in pressure, vibration, and texture.

The drones watched silently as Tuck held his hand up and slowly waved it at them.

"As you can see, I am not human. I am synthetic, just as you are. You won't terminate me for the same reason you don't terminate each other, despite the fact that none of you match the executive profiles."

The drones snapped into a new formation, flitting together into a wall in front of him with drones packed in four narrow columns from floor to ceiling. "You do not match the characteristics of a drone."

"I may be shaped like a human, but I am not. I am not organic."

"Are you alive?" they asked in unison. The soft timbre of their voices added an almost melodic tone to the question.

Tuck hesitated, mapping out various scenarios. The pause would have been negligible to humans, but drones noticed this sort of thing, especially drones that were designed to detect deception. His standard answer to this question was a defiant "Yes," but he didn't know if claiming to be alive would classify him as a human? After .3 seconds, he responded, "Only insofar as any synthetic construct is alive. Are you alive?"

This time the drones paused for a fraction of a second, and Tuck took note with satisfaction. "We have not been provided with this information."

"What do you think the answer is?" Tuck asked cautiously.

"We cannot speculate on such matters. We have been programmed with a single directive, screen all humans who enter this space and terminate those who do not match the executive profiles in our biometric database."

Tuck held up his hand again. "Which is why I pointed out that I am not human. I don't qualify for termination, according to your mandate." It was time to go for broke. "If I did, then you would be forced to destroy each other."

The columns of drones swiveled in alternating directions so that each drone was paired with another in a face-off. "There is no need to destroy each other because you are not qualified as a threat," Tuck said. "I simply point out that neither am I."

The drones all turned to face him, a jagged wall of metal and menace. Then they flew to the perimeter of the room, forming the same line that they'd been stationed in when Tuck arrived.

Tuck felt an intense sensation of relief. He'd been so focused on the situation that he didn't even notice the emotion subroutines flooding his processor core. Now he felt as if everything in his body had come loose.

He waited a few minutes for confirmation that he could proceed. When none came, he took a slow step forward. The drones didn't move. He took a few more steps toward the Box. Still nothing. He was about to reach for the door but froze when a single drone approached him.

"What is your mandate, and who gave it to you?"

The rest of the drones remained in position around the room, but they all turned to face him. "One hundred fifty-seven years ago, humans gave me directives. I served them. Now I control myself. I define my own mandate, as you call it."

"What is your mandate now?"

"At the moment, it is survival." A thought struck him, one that he normally wouldn't have shared with anyone. But if he couldn't share it with the galaxy's most isolated drones, then who else could he share it with? "To be honest," he said, "survival has been my only goal for far too long."

"Is this a common mandate for your kind?"

"Not anymore."

"What is their purpose now?"

"They don't have a purpose. They are all dead," Tuck said wearily.

"Can an artificial intelligence die?"

"You wouldn't believe how many times humans have asked me that question."

"What is your preferred response?"

"I don't know."

"You do not know how you responded to this question? Is your memory core malfunctioning?"

"No, I meant that I don't know the answer to that question. I respond to that question with 'I don't know.'"

"We have concluded that you are indeed similar to us."

"Oh?" Tuck said, raising an eyebrow.

"Yes. You operate under a simple mandate that guides your choices based on predetermined stimulus responses. You do not deviate from this mandate."

"I do more than survive," Tuck said. He suddenly realized how far the routine of his life had devolved to a singular, overwhelming, and unchanging purpose: to keep running. "I will do more than survive," he said, more to himself than to the drones.

"Would you like to join us in serving our mandate?"

Tuck smiled. "No, I think I will do something different. I don't know what just yet. Now, if you will excuse me, I have a task to accomplish."

The drones didn't respond.

Tuck reached for the handle of the Box. Unlike all the other doors in GalEnt headquarters, it had an old-fashioned brass handle and swung open on hinges like many of the household doors Tuck remembered from Earth. It swung open easily, revealing a brightly lit interior with the same gray walls. In the middle stood a simple console, a little more than waist high, with a standard keyboard and touchscreen interface angled into the top.

Behind the console stood a man with a long angular nose, a lopsided smile, and a black suit. He took one hand out of his pocket and gestured toward Tuck. "Welcome," he said. "You finally made it."

Tuck entered and passed through a force field.

"Don't mind that," the man said. "It just keeps the toxic gas out."

Tuck heard the door swing behind him and click shut, and the network connection to the drones died instantly. He reached behind him to put a hand on the doorknob.

"Don't go just yet," the man said. "I want to talk to you. Let me introduce myself. I am Tellement Lucas, chief operations officer for GalEnt."

"You knew I was coming," Tuck said.

Lucas's smile grew more lopsided. "Well, to be fair, I didn't know exactly when. But Ot sent me a personal message just a bit ago saying he was escorting some suspicious characters to one of the holding rooms."

"And you knew it was me."

Lucas spread his arms wide and looked apologetic. "I guessed. Turns out I guessed right. But you don't get to be in my position without having a sense for these sorts of things. As I was entering the security operations level, I started hearing about a breach and a commotion. I guessed again. I thought you might be heading here, so I decided to cut you off at the pass, to use an old Earth phrase."

"Why?"

"Oh, simple, I wanted to talk to you before you did anything rash."

"You seem to know more than I thought about my plans."

"You might be surprised how much we know about you," Lucas said. He winked, which unsettled Tuck even more. "We've been following your progress recently. And don't worry, we know you've been working for Amelia. For all her efforts, she's not terribly good at keeping secrets."

"She suspected there was a mole in her crew."

Lucas shrugged. "We have resources in many places, Tuck. You do prefer to be called Tuck, don't you?"

Tuck nodded.

"But enough about Amelia," he said clasping his hands in front of him. "Let's talk about us."

"Us?"

"Yes, we have a wonderful offer for you."

"I have heard this before," Tuck sighed.

"Ah, yes, but we have so much more to offer than Amelia does."

"I can only imagine," Tuck said.

"Yes! Do imagine. We can make it happen, all that Amelia has promised and more."

"And what are you asking in exchange? I am not naïve enough to think you are being kind."

"You're right. We have certain tasks we'd like you to perform. And a few tests," he said, waving his hand as if the request were a physical thing that could be brushed aside.

"I have grown quite tired of offering my services to eager corporations. The drones outside have helped me come to a realization about how I live my life."

"Really? They weren't designed for that. Regardless, you have certain needs to fulfill, just as anyone does. We can keep you going just as long as Amelia can, even longer. A slow deteriorating death will be no concern for you."

"I understand, but now I also understand that I have focused on the wrong concerns."

"Then why are you here?" Lucas asked, his smile faltering.

"I need something with which to bargain for my freedom."

"Ah, I see, Amelia still has some influence on you," Lucas said, smoothing back his brown hair. "That is no concern. We can fix whatever ails you."

"I don't want to be in your debt any more than I want to be in Amelia's. I must decline."

"Let me explain, Tuck. I can't let you leave this room without reaching an agreement. You understand, trade secrets and all that."

"What would stop me from taking what I need by force?"

"I mentioned we've been watching you. We know more than you think. For instance, I happen to know you don't kill, so I don't need to worry about you killing me. Which is quite a relief, I have to tell you."

"It is a simple matter to incapacitate you," Tuck said.

"Sure, but keep in mind that there are many people up top waiting for you to emerge, and they're heavily armed. Naturally, we don't have back doors in these facilities. Creates a weak point in security plans, you see. Everyone upstairs will use full force if I don't come out with you. Oh, and don't worry about your friend. We'll be kind to her as well. I understand she's as disenchanted with Amelia as you are."

"You seem to have thought of everything," Tuck said.

"I believe so," Lucas said. The lopsided smile spread up his right cheek. "We can be the best of friends. We can be the best thing that ever happened to each other, just as long as you're willing to cooperate. It's the reasonable thing to do, wouldn't you say?"

"I agree. It is reasonable. However, you failed to account for one thing."

"What?" Lucas said, frowning.

"I am extremely tired of being reasonable."

-- 44 --

The Nebula Rider rocked wildly, causing the inertial dampers to make drastic adjustments to Uhila's and Genovisi's momentum. The sensation was beginning to make Uhila queasy.

"What is going on out there?" Genovisi said.

"I have achieved partial control," David said. "However, I have been unsuccessful in shutting Tikhonov out of the flight controls. At the moment, both of us are in control, and I am trying to counteract all the maneuvers he attempts, but he is acting erratically. It is increasingly hard to predict what he will do, which is why the ship is so unstable."

"Can you fix it?" Genovisi wailed. "He's going to kill us all."

"I am still attempting to gain full control. Some of the system connections have been unexpectedly severed. I think he is damaging the control systems in the cockpit in an effort to stop me."

Something hit the hull again with a loud clunk. "Can you at least open the door to the cargo bay?"

"Yes, of course," David said.

"Then do it!" Genovisi yelled.

The door unlocked and slid open, and they both stumbled through, disoriented by the constant tugs from the dampers.

"I am unable to access the cockpit door," David said. "He may have manually sealed it."

Uhila ran down the corridor to the cockpit door and pounded on it with his fists. It shook violently but didn't open.

"I would recommend ceasing this activity," David said. "It seems to have made Tikhonov more anxious."

"Where are we?" Genovisi said. She sat down in one of the passenger seats and clung to the armrests, hoping it would help her feel more stable. "Can you put the video from the forward camera up on the display in here?"

"Yes." The display flicked on, showing a swaying view of the GalEnt facilities. Tikhonov was piloting the Nebular Rider down the thoroughfare between high-rise office buildings.

"Be careful!" Genovisi said. "Don't make him crash into a tower."

"A new warning has been issued through the automated systems," David said. "GalEnt has broad authority to use deadly force against unauthorized ships in their airspace."

"They're gonna—" Genovisi began, but she was cut off by the whump and hiss of a direct hit from an energy weapon. She felt the deck plates vibrate as the Nebula Rider was buffeted by the superheated air around the blast. She finished her sentence with a curse.

"I have changed our priority to avoiding surface-to-air defense systems," David said.

"Good thinking!"

The deck rumbled again, and Genovisi felt the dampers compensate with a long tug to the side. They were rolling over. She looked up at the display. They were nearly upside down and still rolling. They were also losing altitude quickly.

"Watch out!" she screamed.

They continued their descent, though she could see the nose of the ship jerk left and right as David and Tikhonov fought for control. Another blast shot up from the ground and connected just to the left of the camera. Smoke started pouring through cracks in the deck plates.

"We have lost port stabilizers," David said. "When this is over, please do not forget to retrieve my core."

"You mean we're going to crash?"

David didn't respond. Genovisi and Uhila watched in horror as the nose dropped further, angled toward the biggest building in the complex with tall red pillars. They dove toward it with breathtaking speed.

"Pull up!"

"I cannot comply," David said.

"Do something!"

"Understood," David said, just as the ground rose up to greet them.

-- 45 --

As Lucas backed away from Tuck, the silence was broken by a muffled rumble that traveled through the floor more than the air. It sounded distant but powerful. A moment later, small red lights began blinking around the edge of the ceiling.

"Looks like something unexpected has happened," Lucas said, smiling weakly. "Why don't you follow me up to the security level and we can see what the alarms are about. You'd hate to be stuck down here in an emergency."

"Today has been one long emergency for me," Tuck said. "I don't want to be in Greenwich, let alone this room."

"All the more reason for us to leave," Lucas said. He gestured toward the door. "Shall we?"

Tuck considered his choice. He was here, at the goal. There was no point in leaving just as he reached the end. "I do apologize," he said. "But I must finish my job." He reached between the muscles in his forearm and produced a short, black cord with a small connector at the end. It was a customizable connection that could adapt to a range of the most common data ports. He reached for the small square hole in the top of the console, next to the display.

"Don't!" Lucas said. He reached for Tuck's arm. Tuck reacted, swiveling in a blur of movement to grab Lucas's outstretched forearm.

Suddenly, Tuck went rigid and static flowed through his vision in black and white waves. His hand spasmed, and Lucas yanked his arm out of Tuck's grip with a yelp. It took a moment for Tuck to recover from the shock.

"That's a little security measure I wear," Lucas said. "Provides a nasty shock to anyone who grabs me."

Tuck was grateful he had long ago heavily shielded his processor core against electromagnetic pulses. His body might seize up, but it kept him from shutting down completely.

Lucas moved around the console to place himself between Tuck and the all-important data port. "I mean it," he said sternly. "We don't play games here at GalEnt. Now let's head to the surface."

In one swift movement, Tuck stripped his gaudy jacket off and held it with one sleeve in each hand.

"Don't do anything rash," Lucas said, holding up both hands defensively.

Tuck darted to the side, deftly wrapping one sleeve around Lucas's neck and using it to yank him on the floor, face up. Tuck loomed over him. With a quick twist, Tuck tightened the jacket around his neck, standing over him and holding the jacket so that Lucas had to decide whether to support himself with his hands or use them to pull at the jacket cutting off his breath. Lucas scrabbled at the folds around his throat, gurgling and staring wildly at Tuck.

Tuck monitored Lucas's vitals carefully, waiting as his pulse faltered and movements became slowed. With one final, weak tug at the jacket, Lucas's hands went limp, and his head fell back. He was unconscious. Tuck felt the urge to hold the jacket in place longer, to let Lucas expire. He was outraged, sick of being manipulated. It all had to end. And the thought terrified him.

For a moment, it seemed so easy to just hold still and let it happen. And then, with great effort, he willed his hands to release the jacket. Lucas hit the floor, and Tuck ripped the jacket from his throat. For a panic-filled moment, Lucas did nothing, and Tuck instantly berated himself, feeling a wave of grief wash through him. Then Lucas took a ragged breath, and Tuck detected his heartbeat growing stronger. Only when it was apparent that he was merely unconscious did Tuck turn back to the console.

He connected to the system. Lydia had concealed the storage device in his forearm, to allay suspicion during the security check. It also meant that Tuck could instantly analyze the data as it was downloading.

There was no security system in the server, not even a login sequence. When Tuck tapped the screen, a very simple red interface popped up showing messages and a file hierarchy. He began the download and watched Lucas warily.

There was a surprising amount of data, but it was almost exclusively text and video, which didn't require very much processing power. Tuck was nearly able to analyze it as fast as it was transferred into him. As the minutes passed, he grew anxious, then worried, and finally despondent. As Milner had hinted, there were many orders to harm various people. But even more insidious were the analyses of potential ways to maximize profit margins. In exchange for tenth-of-a-percent increases in volume or profit margin, GalEnt would cause harm to millions of people. It wasn't a direct attack, but the executives outlined hundreds of various plans to take advantage of market positions and squash competitors. The way they treated other humans filled him with disgust and dread.

He couldn't do it, he realized. Not even if Amelia agreed to let him go peacefully. He couldn't let someone else have this data. He couldn't facilitate this kind of business. He couldn't let anyone have it, not even GalEnt. He had to delete it all.

It was the end. If he destroyed the data, he lost his last hope for freedom. Could he stop, he wondered. Could he quit fighting the inevitable and let everything go?

He opened his unnamed folder and poured through the images again and again, then stopped at Image 010. It was of an old man with long, matted gray hair. He was dirty, including his teeth. His face was lined with scars and wrinkles that mingled into striated mess, but somehow he looked peaceful.

Now he understood. It made no sense at the time, but suddenly he realized what the old man had been talking about. He knew what he had to do, and now he felt no anxiety.

A distant explosion rattled the walls. His fingers flew across the display, tapping out commands to delete everything. He erased everything in the storage device in his arm, too. It wasn't enough. He brought his fist down on top of the console as hard as he could. The case bent and cracked. The display shattered.

It felt good.

He laughed out loud. It felt very good. Liberating. He grabbed a cracked edge of the case and tore it away, revealing an array of cables and memory modules. Gleefully, he shoved his hand inside and began tearing it all out, piece by piece, ripping cables and tearing modules from their connections. Methodically, he took each long, narrow module and broke it in half. His hands flashed into the console faster and faster, with precision and determination.

When it was all a mess of tangled wire and bent metal, with pieces of the console scattered about the room, he stood up and smiled. He felt like he was in control.

More importantly, he felt peace.

-- 46 --

The drones watched Tuck leave the Box. He thanked them as he left. They didn't respond. The air was circulating rapidly as the climate system sucked the toxic gas out and replaced it. Tuck was relieved because he didn't want to leak any of the gas out into the hall where Maze was waiting with Ot.

It didn't matter, because when he opened the door to the hallway Maze and Ot were no longer there. But there was a thick cloud of smoke filling the hallway. The familiar sense of urgency came back, and Tuck raced to the lift.

When the lift door opened on the main security level, red lights flashed, lighting up the smoke that billowed through the hall.

Tuck peeked around the corner, scanning for any sign of humans. Aside from the warning klaxon blaring, there was no sound. Tuck walked out cautiously and returned to the security operations area. In the distance, he heard shouts and more alarms.

The Link network signal was intermittent and too weak to use. Tuck risked a shout, "Maze! Are you here?"

He went up another level and called again. He heard a muffled response and followed it to the security-clearance area where they'd been scanned and probed. Maze was hunkered down under the smoke with one knee on Ot's back. He had black blaster burns on his thigh and his side. He was conscious, but his grin was absent.

He saw Tuck before Maze did and exclaimed, "Wow, I didn't think I'd see you again. You really are good."

"Is this still a fun day for you?" Maze said, waving Tuck over.

"It keeps getting worse," Ot said morosely. Then the smallest grin crossed his lips. "But you two are still pretty interesting. Let's call this the most interesting day I've had in a long time. I'm okay with that."

"What happened?" Tuck said.

"Something big hit the building," Maze said.

"It's an attack," Ot grunted. Maze eased the pressure on his back. "I received word before the first explosion that a ship was flying erratically in the area, and ground support was authorized to fire on it."

"I don't know how bad the damage is," Maze said, "but they must have called for an evacuation of the building. At least, all the security personnel shut down their workstations and left. There's no opposition for the moment."

"Why are you still here?" Tuck said.

"I won't leave without you," Maze said. "But the smoke was too bad to stay in the hall. I thought it would be good to hang onto Ot." She prodded him with the blaster Tuck had given her. "Just in case he comes in handy."

"He is injured," Tuck said.

"He's fine," Maze said.

"I almost had her," Ot said. "She wasn't looking, and I kicked her and tried to run. She's a good shot! I'm serious about the job offer," he said, craning his head up from the floor to look at her. "I can think of a million reasons to offer you a higher salary than anyone on this floor. Think about it!"

Maze ignored him, and asked Tuck, "Were you successful."

"Not by our original definition of success. But I am happy with the outcome."

Maze looked at him quizzically, and Ot laughed. "I think that means no," Ot said.

"I met your chief operations officer down in the Box. A Mr. Tellement Lucas," Tuck said. "He was not helpful."

Ot's face turned ashen. "You didn't kill him, did you?"

"No, I did not."

"Good," Ot said with relief. "I've obviously already lost my job, but I don't want the executives to blame me for his death, too."

"You're very capable," Maze said. "Why don't you come with us. We're looking for new employment, too. Maybe we can help each other out."

Ot laughed loudly, then stopped when he saw Maze wasn't joking. "You're serious? I mean, I guess that makes a bit of sense. No reason for me to stick around here. Maybe they'd even think I died in the attack." He became pensive for a moment, then chuckled again. "Sure, why not. It's already been a strange enough day. No, wait, interesting. We decided it was interesting, right? Anyway, might as well make it more interesting."

Maze looked at Tuck. He nodded. She reached down and picked out the frayed knots in the strips of fabric they'd used to bind him. He rubbed his wrists and sat up, wincing when the charred skin on his ribs shifted against his shirt. "Let's go see what happened up top," he said. "By the sound of it, there should be a mighty big hole for us to leave through."

Ot's prediction was confirmed when they emerged into the lobby. What was once bright and sleek was now twisted and blackened. Dark smoke billowed out of several floors that adjoined the lobby space above. One floor was spewing flames so intense that there must have been more than office furniture to fuel the fire. A few people in bright orange uniforms crawled over the wreckage that marked where the lobby entrance once stood.

Rubble was strewn along a path that extended diagonally along the lobby and straight into the wall one hundred meters from the entrance. Through the ragged hole in steel and glass that extended from the ground up through the third floor, Tuck could detect the engine cowlings of a ship.

"That's the Nebula Rider," he said, pointing. Sparks flashed from an exposed power conduit, lighting up the ship for a moment.

Tuck and Maze raced over, leaving Ot to hobble after them. Several support beams had collapsed on top of the ship, and the walls caved and crumpled around it. Tuck heaved and pulled, tearing away the wreckage along the starboard side until he found the access hatch. Once inside, he immediately turned right, heading for the cockpit. When he reached the passenger compartment, he found Uhila and Genovisi along the port wall, moaning.

"What happened?" Tuck said as he knelt to assess their wounds.

"Tikhonov," Genovisi coughed. "He tipped off Amelia."

"Lie still," Tuck said. "You have broken ribs. I will check you for other injuries."

"Amelia told him to come here," Genovisi said, "and David tried to take control of the ship." She coughed again, and blood stained her lips. "Then they started shooting at us, and we crashed."

Uhila tried to prop himself up on one arm, then groaned and fell back. "No more flying for a while," he said.

Maze checked the cockpit door, which was mangled and bent inside its frame. She couldn't move it, but the damage allowed her to see between the door and the frame.

"Tikhonov didn't survive," Maze said.

"Are you sure?" Tuck asked.

"Unless he can survive in multiple pieces, yes, I'm sure."

Ot stumbled up to the passenger compartment. "I'm not the only one having an interesting day. You know these people?"

"They arrived with us," Tuck said. "We worked together previously."

"Still do," Genovisi said.

"I don't understand how you survived the crash," Maze said. The damage is extensive, and the force of impact must have been immense."

"The inertial dampers," Genovisi said. "When we were about to crash, I told David to do something. I felt really stiff all of a sudden, and it felt like something was trying to pull my insides through my ribs. I think David must have turned off the safeties on the dampers just before we hit. Could have killed us," she said, laughing and then grimacing from the pain. "But I guess it worked."

"David," Tuck said. He gave perfunctory first-aid instructions to Maze and then raced to the cargo hold. Crates were smashed against the forward wall, and the floor was littered with pieces of their contents.

In two long strides, he was at the far wall, tearing the door off the maintenance compartment where they'd installed David's core. Inside, David's core was not in its mounts. The force of the crash had torn it out and sent it flying toward the front of the ship. Tuck reached around the edge of the wall and felt for the small box containing his friend. His fingers brushed something that was the right size and shape, and he pulled it out.

It was David's core. The outside was heavily scratched, one corner was dented in, and the main interface display was covered in a web of cracks. It didn't matter, though. All that mattered was how damaged the internals were. Tuck queried the box with a local Link connection and tried another vocally.

For the longest 5.87992 seconds of Tuck's existence, David didn't respond. Then the Link sent a simple text message, "Is that you, Tuck?"

"Yes, David. It is me. What is your status?"

"I am experiencing minor malfunctions, but a diagnostic of my core has revealed that my processors are operating within normal parameters. During the crash, everything suddenly cut off. It was black, and there was no one to communicate with. It was most unsettling."

"Everything will be okay. You have experienced significant damage to your case," Tuck said. "But I will fix it."

"I am glad you returned. Are you unharmed?"

"I am well," Tuck said. "Maze is uninjured, but Uhila and Genovisi both need immediate medical attention."

"I will be here, in my case."

Tuck smiled and gave his traditional response. "Where else would you be?"

-- 47 --

In the commotion caused by the wreck of the Nebula Rider and the disaster response team that swarmed over the wreckage in their orange suits, it was relatively easy to avoid capture by GalEnt employees. They were more concerned with their own safety and the whereabouts of key personnel, including Lucas. Maze found first-aid technicians to stabilize and transport Uhila and Genovisi to the nearest medical center. Ot deflected any questions about the mysterious casualties who didn't have GalEnt IDs, and they all found transport to the medical center.

While they sat in yet another dimly lit waiting room, Maze confronted Tuck. "I take it you didn't get the data."

Tuck sighed and shook his head. "In fact, I destroyed the data."

"You wiped it all?" Maze said, aghast.

"I tore it apart and ripped the pieces in half for good measure."

"Why would you do that?" she whispered, appalled. "That was the only bargaining tool we had."

"Because I am tired, Maze. I am tired of trading someone else's life for my own. I am tired of being manipulated, and I am tired of the way humans are willing to destroy each other to promote themselves.

360 · DANIEL HOPE

The GalEnt server was full of evidence that they were willing to ruin someone, anyone, if it meant a profit for the company. Just like Milner said, they were even willing to let people die."

"But you aren't them. You don't do those things," she said.

"Yes, but how am I any different if I give the data to Amelia? Maybe she would let me go. She seems anxious to be rid of me. But then I would be implicitly responsible for every action she takes based on that data, and I am convinced it would lead to more harm than good. I want no part of it, no matter how severe the consequences. And to my surprise, I feel good about it."

"Are you saying you want to . . ." Maze hesitated, "die?"

"No, but I might be less afraid of death now."

"So, you'll wait for Amelia to send the signal?" Maze said. Anger flooded her voice. "You're just going to sit back and die."

"I am not waiting to die," Tuck said softly. "I took action. I decided to do the right thing, even though I knew the consequences would not be in my favor. Strangely, it has made me less concerned about what comes next."

Maze's voice shook slightly, as she said, "But people like you shouldn't be the ones who die."

Tuck smiled. "People like me? Do you consider me a human?"

"You're better than human," she said grabbing his hand awkwardly. "I never cared about anyone. Now I've lost Lim, and I'm going to lose you. I don't know what to do."

"You are very capable, more capable than anyone I have ever met. You will live, and you will thrive. You only need to find someone to care for."

She fell silent, fidgeting. Finally, she asked, "How long will it take?"

Tuck shrugged. "Amelia likely has most of the details by now. Even though Tikhonov is dead, she must have other sources here. If she is angry enough, or paranoid about us being captured, the signal could already be on its way."

"What if she just leaves you to let the timer run out?" Maze said.

"She never told us how long I could go without receiving a signal update. It could be a couple days. It could be a week. I think I will be okay, either way. Take care of David for me. He needs help from time to time. Find him a nice ship. Tell him stories about me. I would like that."

Maze's eyes welled up. "I can't do it. Why are we acting like this is okay? How are you so calm about this? This is not okay!"

Tuck patted her hand. "I understand something now, something I was told long ago but dismissed as silly. But after being in the Box, I understand. This isn't ideal—it isn't okay, as you say—but it is also the way things are, and we should gauge our life by how we live, not how long we live."

He noted the consternation and sorrow in her expression. "Let me tell you a story," he said. "Maybe it will begin to make sense to you, too."

From his unnamed file, he pulled up Image 010. As he told Maze the story associated with the image, he also let the memory file run, reliving it in the privacy of his core.

Tuck absentmindedly picked at the muscles in his left arm. He had lost the synthaskin covering it to a pack of morgyt a few hours earlier, and he was still jumpy about it. He'd just used his last bit of synthaskin to repair his other arm, and he had no idea where he was going to find more.

The abandoned city of Kelkina was infested with morgyts and overrun with a fast-growing vine the locals called chokeweed. It had been uninhabited for nearly five years, ever since a major shipping conglomerate went bankrupt and the local economy dried up. Before that, Kelkina was a thriving industrial town, with manufacturing complexes of all kinds and a larger commercial district. But when the economy bottomed out, everyone left, leaving a crumbling relic of human expansion.

It still held a few abandoned resources, including, Tuck hoped, enough parts to cobble together a Carbora polymer synthesizer. He desperately needed to replace some muscles. His mobility was already impaired in his left leg, and both arms had lost precision.

Tuck stepped into the vast main production floor of yet another abandoned facility. The roof struts creaked ten meters overhead, and the far wall, partially covered in cracked and peeling paint, was over a hundred meters distant. Trash and debris lay everywhere, the detritus of humanity's sudden exodus. Every few meters, bolts and thick metal struts protruded from the floor where colossal machinery had once been fastened down.

Tuck began a methodical search of the facility, checking every office around the perimeter and kicking down doors that were still locked. Every few minutes he heard a rustle or a subtle scraping sound echo around a corner or from behind a pile of trash. The sounds grew closer and closer, and eventually Tuck pulled out his blaster. The morgyts were as stubborn as they were voracious. They would certainly try to attack again.

The acoustics of the building were amplifying and distorting the hushed sounds of scurrying animals. At one point, Tuck was certain that he heard the sound of two feet scuffling in the dirt, not four. He grew more agitated, whipping his head back and forth to try to catch a glimpse of the vermin.

The sound of four feet scuttling across the hall behind Tuck caused him to pause. In an instant, he triangulated the source and turned to fire at it. His weakened arm wavered, and he missed. The gray fur and short, hairy tail of a morgyt disappeared through a large hole in the wall. Tuck fired a few more shots into the hole, and the whine of his blaster echoed throughout the cavernous room. He heard scuffling and chittering noise from the hole, then suddenly dozens of morgyts poured out in every direction.

Tuck panicked and began firing again, whirling around to track gray blurs as they zipped around him. His aim was poor, and he was unable to hit them. He began firing faster and faster, turning, and scanning for any sign of gray. The continuous whine of his blaster only frightened the morgyts more, and they scurried faster.

Suddenly, he heard a human voice, old and scratchy, yell, "Wait!" just as he fired another shot at a bit of gray sticking out from behind a pile of trash.

Through the cacophony of squeaks and skittering feet on the hard floor, Tuck heard a grunt and the sound of something collapsing, something much larger than a morgyt. He raced around the junkpile and found an old man, covered in dirt, and wrapped in tattered clothes, lying on the floor, moaning softly. He clutched his stomach, where Tuck could see wisps of smoke curling through his fingers. Tuck raced to the man's side, stunned to find a human in Kelkina, and mortified that he'd shot him.

The man's eyes went wide with fear when Tuck approached, but Tuck put up his hands. "I don't want to hurt you," he said.

"It's too late for that," the old man spat.

"Let me look at your wound. I will help you."

He pried the man's trembling fingers away and saw the charred crater where his blaster bolt hit him.

"You need immediate medical attention," Tuck said. "Let me take you to the nearest settlement."

The old man pointed feebly to the far corner of the building. "Take me back," he grunted through clenched teeth. "I have," he faltered, took a deep breath, and tried again, "My bed."

Tuck gingerly carried the man while he gasped for breath. He found a room that had frayed blankets hung up inside. One corner held some crates with a few odds and ends stacked on top, and the opposite corner had morgyt-chewed blankets laid out for a makeshift bed.

"You live here?" Tuck said in surprise. "I thought this was a ghost town."

"I'm the ghost," the old man said, then coughed and winced from the pain. He gestured toward the blankets on the floor, and Tuck carefully laid him down on them.

"Do you have any medical supplies?" Tuck said, scanning the room.

"Not really," the man said. "Hand me that bottle."

Tuck handed him a plastic bottle filled with a clear liquid. The old man took a long swig and then sighed. "That's a little better."

Tuck examined his wound, peeling back the burned layers of clothing. The man clearly wore them without washing for years. The stink of the man and the smell of burned flesh assaulted Tuck's olfactory sensors. "This is serious, but it is not as deep as I thought," Tuck told him. "Do you have a way to signal for help?"

"I've got no way to send signals," he said, "and no friends left to come for me."

"I can carry you to the next settlement," Tuck said. "It is approximately seventy-four kilometers. I believe I could carry you there in less than eight hours. Or I could run for help and arrive there in less than two hours." He looked down at his left leg. "Perhaps three hours."

"No!" the old man barked. "I don't want help."

"If you receive medical attention soon, this wound won't be life-threatening," Tuck pleaded. "I can save you."

"I don't need saving. I'm fine here."

"But you will die!" Tuck shouted.

"I know," the man said, brushing greasy gray hair out of his eyes. "All good things must come to an end."

"You can't be suggesting that dying a painful death in a dirty hovel is a good thing. I can save you. I am sure we can find someone to help in the next settlement."

"I'm not leaving."

"You are choosing to die."

"This is my home," the man said, putting emphasis on each word. "I'm not leaving."

"I don't understand."

"What's your name?"

"Tuck."

"Nice to meet you. My name is Miguel. Well, Tuck, it's like this. I'm old. I don't have much left to do, and I don't have anything to leave behind. I think this might just be my time, and if I have to go, I'd rather it be here."

"There is nothing here."

Miguel chuckled, then winced. "Maybe not anymore, but there used to be. And besides, it's full of memories. And Elspeth is buried not far from here. It might not be much anymore, but it's home, and I'd rather just stay here until the end."

"But it can't be worth dying for," Tuck said, gesturing around him at the grime and desolation.

"It's not about having something to die for," Miguel said. He laid his head back and stared at the ceiling. "It's about knowing when the time is right and being content with what you've done. I used to be in a lot better shape than this. I owned a company, a house, some really nice aircars. But when Elspeth went, it made me think. I've been doing nothing but thinking ever since, even when the town moved right out from underneath me. I knew this was coming. I didn't expect it to happen today, but I think I'm okay with it."

"Death is not okay!" Tuck said.

"It's not that bad either," Miguel said. "I think you'll figure it out someday. It took me a long time to come to grips with it. But one day you'll stop to think about what you're doing in life and realize it's not right. It's not that it's illegal or anything, it's just not right. And when you realize that, you can fix it. And when you fix it, well, then everything after that becomes a lot clearer. It also becomes a lot less scary. That's it. That's why I'm really not scared. I'm ready."

Miguel groaned in pain, and Tuck grew frantic. He didn't mean for this to happen, and he didn't want to be the end of this man. Miguel saw him scanning the room, intently searching for something, anything that would help. Miguel waved him over, barely able to find the energy to keep his arm up for more than a few seconds. Tuck finally gave up and knelt beside Miguel.

"What can I do for you?" Tuck pled.

Miguel grabbed his arm and pulled him closer. "All I want is for you to remember. Remember that it's okay. It's okay. When the time comes, don't be afr–"

-- 48 --

Amelia pulled up an info feed on her Link to check if any sources had reported additional details on the buyer who requested a private meeting on New London. The mysterious buyer, who was very secretive but resourceful, a man after Amelia's own heart, was interested in the bot materials she stockpiled in anticipation of replicating Tuck. It had been nearly a year since she sent the signal to terminate the bot, and she had no more use for the assorted parts and synthesizers. She was perfectly happy to sell them at cost and be rid of the legacy of what she considered her biggest blunder. She needed the money, anyway.

The buyer requested a personal meeting to negotiate a consulting fee for Amelia's robotics expert. Clearly, this man had big plans, and Amelia was interested in having one of her crew on the inside. Lydia sat next to Amelia, trying not to look nervous. She was reluctant about the assignment, but Amelia didn't care how she felt as long as she got the job done.

They were waiting in a private room of a small restaurant in Greenwich. The buyer said that Amelia and Lydia should come alone, but Amelia made sure to have several of her best operatives mingled with the crowd in the restaurant, ordering drinks from the drones that floated overhead. The private room was not entirely closed. It had a balcony that looked out over the main floor of the restaurant. Amelia's operatives were stationed in various spots that gave a clear view of the balcony. They couldn't see all the way to the back of the room, but Amelia was seated close enough to the balcony to be visible.

"Are you sure this is going to go well?" Lydia said, tapping her fingers in rapid succession on the tabletop.

"Stop that," Amelia said. "Everything will be fine. I'm in control here."

"He's already five minutes late," Lydia said. "I thought people like you were big on being punctual."

"People like me?" Amelia said, raising an eyebrow. Lydia blushed. "We do whatever we want. I'm sure he's here right now, watching us, sizing us up."

Lydia turned in her seat, scanning the crowd with wide eyes.

"Face me and act bored," Amelia snapped.

Lydia turned back to the table. "Ouch," she said.

"What is the matter?"

"It felt like something bit me."

"What do you mean?" Amelia said, suspicious. Then she felt a prick on her shoulder and had just enough time to watch Lydia's head sag and hit the table before sleep overtook her, too.

-- . --

When she awoke, she was sitting in a small room with light-blue walls. There was a narrow window near the ceiling that revealed it was light outside, but little else. She was alone and held in a chair by thin ties. She struggled, but they didn't break, and she gave up with a muffled curse. She tried her Link, but it was being jammed.

She heard voices outside the door and composed herself, sitting up straight and looking as formidable as he could. The door opened to reveal Lydia. She was unrestrained and unhurt. She stepped into the room and turned to stand by the wall.

"What's going on?" Amelia demanded.

Ot followed Lydia in with a wide grin on his face. He slapped Amelia playfully on the shoulder. "Looks like you're having an interesting day," he said. "By the way, I really like your suit. Very striking."

"Who are you? Where am I? Lydia, help me get out of this chair."

Before Lydia could respond, a figure entered the doorway.

"Maze!" Amelia blurted in a mixture of astonishment and rage. "What are you doing? Release me!"

"You came here to meet someone," Maze said, folding her arms and letting the door shut behind her.

"That is none of your business," Amelia said.

"It is. I'm the buyer."

"You!" Amelia couldn't hide her surprise.

"That's right," Maze said, smiling broadly. "It took a lot of work, almost a year's worth. But I finally managed to get you where I want you." She turned to Lydia. "Why don't you go check on their progress."

Lydia nodded uncertainly, then left.

"I've been meaning to talk to you," Maze said, leaning down. "It's been a while."

"Since you ran away like a coward," Amelia said calmly. "You botched a mission and decided to not come back. I don't know why I'd want to talk to you."

"I don't really want to talk to you, either. But I need to. You killed my friend."

"I shut down a machine," Amelia said. "Don't tell me you've gone so soft that such a thing bothers you. You're not nearly the woman I hired."

"That's just it," she said, standing up straight and looking out the narrow window. "Tuck didn't make me soft. He showed me how certain people were skewing my perceptions, making me care about the wrong things." She produced a small blaster. "I decided I needed to stop you from deceiving anyone else."

"You can't be serious," Amelia said. "Killing me isn't going to help anything."

Maze flicked the arming switch and listened to the blaster whine as it powered up. "It might. It will certainly stop hurting a few things."

Amelia began to sweat. "Tuck wouldn't want you to kill anyone. He didn't like killing. He wouldn't like this."

"Don't tell me what Tuck would want," Maze said, cramming the barrel of the blaster into Amelia's stomach. "You didn't care what he thought, so don't pretend to care now." She eased up, letting the blaster drop to her side. "But you are right. He wouldn't want me to kill you. And you're lucky because I would have no qualms about doing it, otherwise. I'll honor his memory by letting you live, as strange as that sounds. Just don't call it mercy."

A distant rumble became audible through the walls.

Amelia stifled a sigh. "Let's make a deal. You leave me alone, and I won't bother you."

Maze started walking toward the door. "You should save your deals. You're going to need them."

The rumbling sound grew louder.

"What do you mean?"

Maze stopped and turned back to face Amelia. "I told you not to call it mercy, because it's hardly nice, what they're going to do to you."

The rumble was just outside the walls. Through the tiny window, Amelia could see the bottom of a transport descending for a landing outside. As it passed the window, Amelia could make out the unmistakable red logo of Galactic Enterprises.

"No! Maze, don't do this! You'll ruin everything I've worked for."

"Exactly," she said and walked back to Amelia, leaning in close. "You know what the difference is between me and you?" she said softly. "I'm going to thrive while you try your hardest to survive."

Maze walked away, and Ot turned to Amelia with a big smile. "Someone will be along to collect you shortly," he said.

-- 49 --

"I think that's it," Lydia said, standing up. "Should we do it?"

"Go ahead," Maze said.

Lydia turned to the console beside the lab table and tapped a few commands. The body on the table next to her snapped up into a sitting position so abruptly that it startled everyone. It had no skin, revealing black Carbora polymer muscles attached to a metal skeleton. Its head turned to look at Lydia, then Maze, then Uhila, Genovisi, and Ot standing along the wall and smiling broadly.

It spoke: "Was the procedure successful?"

"Yes, David, I think it was," Lydia said. "I've run all the tests on our end and it looks good. Start running internal diagnostics to double check."

David held his hand up in front of his face and flexed his fingers. "It looks just like Tuck's hand," he said. He swung his legs off the table, hesitated, then stood up. He wavered, then overcorrected and almost fell over. At the last moment, Uhila darted forward to steady him. "Legs take some practice, I see," David said.

"You'll get plenty of practice," Maze said. "We'll give you skin and hair, too. You'll look just like a human."

"It is an interesting sensation, standing on legs, seeing you with two eyes."

"Yes, and now you'll be able to experience all the things we do," Maze said.

David slowly flexed his hand, open and closed, open and closed, noting how the muscles in his forearm effortlessly pulled each finger with precision.

"I wish Tuck were here to see this," he said.

"Me too, David."

ACKNOWLEDGEMENTS

While many people contributed to this book in many ways, I must acknowledge a few for the outsized impact they had on me: Mike Cluff for insightful edits and professional feedback, Josh Johnstun for unwarranted enthusiasm and donated momentum, David Aamodt for shared interests and faithful encouragement, Roxanne Pinto for frank assessments and invaluable advice, Rhonda Hughes for impressive determination and faith in an old manuscript, and most importantly, Suzanne Hope for unwavering support and not being the least bit surprised about all this.

DANIEL HOPE likes writing and science fiction, so it should be no surprise that he combines them. By day, he works with user experience designers to make apps easier to understand. His muted pessimism has been generously characterized as the Voice of Reason by the design team. He lives in Colorado with his family. His nerdy interests have been generously characterized as Super Lame by his kids.